Ruth had kept Jack's civilian clothes in the spare-room cupboard. There weren't many – he'd only needed them when he was home on leave – and she'd never been able to bring herself to throw or even give them away. But now, without hesitation, she went to the cupboard and looked among the clothes folded there. A few blue working shirts, soft from much washing – one of those would do for him in the morning, if she cut it down a bit. And a pair of pyjamas with blue stripes. She took out the jacket and held it against her cheek.

'I know you wouldn't mind, Jack,' she whispered. 'I know you'd want the poor little mite to have a bit of comfort.'

She stood for a moment with it in her hands, then took it downstairs to where Sammy was sitting, still wrapped in his towel, in front of the fire. Gently, she lifted the towel from his thin shoulders, gave him a few final dabs to make sure he was properly dry and hung the pyjama jacket round his shoulders.

It fitted him like a nightshirt, reaching to below his knees. She looked at him, as thin as a reed, his hair almost white and as soft as a rabbit's fur, his eyes even larger in a face that, cleansed of its grime, was as pale and smooth as ivory, and her heart seemed to move in her breast.

'You poor little soul,' she said, gathering him gently in her arms. 'You poor, dear little soul . . .'

Lilian Harry grew up close to Portsmouth Harbour, where her earliest memories are of nights spent in an air-raid shelter listening to the drone of enemy aircraft and the thunder of exploding bombs. But her memories are also those of a warm family life shared with two brothers and a sister in a tiny backstreet house where hard work, love and laughter went hand in hand. Lilian Harry now lives on the edge of Dartmoor where she has two ginger cats to love and laugh at. She has a son and daughter and two grandchildren and, as well as gardening, country dancing, amateur dramatics and church bellringing, she loves to walk on the moors and – whenever possible – to go skiing in the mountains of Europe. She has written a number of books under other names, including historical novels and comtemporary romances. Visit her website at *www.lilianharry.co.uk*.

By Lilian Harry

Goodbye Sweetheart
The Girls They Left Behind
Keep Smiling Through
Moonlight & Lovesongs
Love & Laughter
Wives & Sweethearts
Corner House Girls
Kiss the Girls Goodbye
PS I Love You
A Girl Called Thursday
Tuppence to Spend
A Promise to Keep

Tuppence to Spend

LILIAN HARRY

ORION

An Orion paperback

First published in Great Britain in 2003
by Orion
This paperback edition published in 2003
by Orion Books Ltd,
Orion House, 5 Upper St Martin's Lane
London WC2H 9EA

Second impression 2003

A CIP catalogue record for this book is available
from the British Library

ISBN 0 75284 264 1

Typeset by Deltatype Ltd, Birkenhead, Merseyside

Printed and bound in Great Britain by
Clays Ltd, St Ives plc

For my lovely granddaughter
Samantha Anne – our own Sammy

Chapter One

'They're sending you all away?' Nora Hodges said, staring at the letter in her hand. 'They're sending all you kiddies out of Portsmouth to the country – *this Friday*? But why? I thought they were still trying to make Hitler stop it – I thought they didn't want there to *be* a war.'

It was almost the end of August. Sammy had been given the letter at school and had almost forgotten about it, but his teacher had said that the letters must be given to the children's mothers the minute they got home, so he fished it out of his pocket and handed it over, grubby, crumpled and sticky from a half-sucked bull's-eye Tim Budd had given him in class. He pulled the sweet off the letter and started to pick off the fluff.

At first Nora had stared at the envelope, her heart sinking. Letters from school usually meant trouble – she'd had plenty of that sort from the school while Gordon was there. Or, more often, *not* there. Playing truant – being cheeky – tormenting little girls by sticking their pigtails into inkwells – and, worse, pinching things from the cloakroom. Gordon was always in trouble of some sort. Sammy hadn't ever got into that sort of trouble before, but then he was only seven – there was plenty of time for him to follow in his brother's footsteps.

'What is it?' she said. 'What've you done?'

Sammy had picked off most of the fluff and popped the bull's-eye into his mouth. He sat down on the floor and began to stroke the tabby cat curled up on the mat. 'I haven't done nothing. It's about the war. We all got one. We're being sent away.'

'The *war*?' Her heart sank further. She'd hoped, tried hard to believe, that it wasn't going to happen. Even with the Anderson shelters all delivered and standing like grey hillocks in all the back gardens, even with those horrible gas masks being handed out to everyone, even with the blackout and leaflets being dropped through the door almost every day, and men being trained for Air Raid Precautions, even after Sammy's recall to school for rehearsals for the evacuation – she'd hoped and hoped that it wouldn't really happen, that Hitler would back away and not invade Poland after all, that Mr Chamberlain would find some way of persuading him. He'd promised, hadn't he? Peace in our time – that's what he'd said when he came back from Munich, waving his 'piece of paper'. Peace in our time.

'When?' she asked Sammy now, staring at the piece of paper in her own hand. 'When are you going?'

Sammy took the bull's-eye out of his mouth to examine it. He'd sucked off the rest of the fluff and it had reached the red layer now. With another few hard sucks it would turn yellow and then green, before reaching the hard little bit in the middle. 'Friday,' he said. 'We've got to have our suitcases packed and go to school at seven o'clock. It says so in the letter. Have I got a suitcase, Mum?'

'No, of course you haven't! Where would *we* get the money to buy suitcases? Anyway, we never go anywhere to need them. I don't know what we're going to do.' She looked at the envelope again and began to open it. 'Oh, Sammy – I don't want you to go away.'

Sammy got up and came to lean against her. He was small for his age and very like her, with fair hair that curled all over his head and large blue eyes. Gordon was dark and solidly built, like his father. He'd always been a handful, even as a toddler, able to climb almost as soon as he could walk and into everything – you couldn't leave him alone for a minute. And as he'd grown up he'd followed his father everywhere, wanting nothing more than to do the things Dan did – going to football matches to see Pompey play at Fratton Park, working on the ships at Vosper's, or at Camber dock. He hated school from the very first day, and made everyone's life a misery until he finally reached his fourteenth birthday and left school to go to work at Camber.

But Sammy had been much more his mother's boy, content to be with her. Gordon sneered and called him a cissy, and Dan said the boy needed toughening up, but for once Nora took no notice of her husband. Sammy had come after three miscarriages, and it had been touch and go whether he'd survive, he'd been so tiny, but she'd tended him through those early weeks, keeping him literally wrapped in cottonwool, and now, even though he was still small he was strong enough and there was a bond between them that would never break. And just because he was close to her and had fair curls and big blue eyes didn't mean he was a cissy, she told Dan. Sammy was every bit as much a boy as Gordon was – he was just a different kind of boy, that's all.

'I don't want to go away either,' Sammy said to her. 'Couldn't you come too? Some of the mothers are going, I heard Tim Budd say so. His mum's going.'

'That's because she's got a little baby,' Nora said, putting her arm round him. 'Maureen can't go without her mother, can she? She's only a few weeks old.'

Sammy looked at her. 'So if we had a baby you could go as well and we could go together. Couldn't we have a baby, Mum?'

Nora gave a short laugh. 'A *baby*! No, Sammy, we couldn't. It takes nearly a year to get a baby, and—' Her voice broke suddenly and she rubbed the back of one wrist across her eyes. 'Well, anyway, we can't.' She opened the envelope at last and pulled out the sheet of paper. 'Seven o'clock Friday morning . . . But you don't *have* to go. It says here, it's just *advising* that you should.'

'So can I stop home with you, then?'

'I'll talk to your dad about it,' Nora said, folding up the sheet of paper again. 'Tonight, when he comes home from work.' She leant back in her chair, feeling a great wave of tiredness wash over her. The thought of finding Sammy a suitcase, collecting his clothes together and packing it, was almost too much for her.

I'm getting more and more tired these days, she thought. It's all this talk about the war. It's upsetting me, it's upsetting everyone. I just feel I'm crawling through the days, and can't hardly manage to do all my jobs. Getting the dinner ready's about all I can do and even that's a struggle.

Perhaps she would feel a bit better when they'd finally decided whether there was going to be a war or not. Perhaps everyone would feel better then, once they knew what they had to face. But then she thought of the bombing they'd been warned about, the possibility of the Germans invading Britain itself, and a sick fear gripped her body. Almost without realising it, she pulled Sammy against her. I can't let him go, she thought. I can't let him go without me, to strangers who wouldn't understand him and might not be kind to him. I can't.

'Lay the table for me, Sammy, there's a love,' she said, leaning back in her chair and closing her eyes. 'Your dad'll be in soon, wanting his tea, and so will our Gordon. And I'll have a talk with him later on. I don't see why you've got to go away if you don't want to, specially when we still don't know that there's going to be a war. It might not happen even now.'

Sammy spread the old tablecloth on the battered table in the middle of the room, and got knives and forks out of the sideboard drawer. They'd been brought from the pub

4

when the family had left it to come to number 2 April Grove, along with a few other bits of furniture. The brewery had claimed a lot of it was theirs, but Dan had had a row with the man who came to oversee the move and told him they had to let the family have beds and tables and chairs, it was the law, and anyway a lot of the stuff had belonged to Nora's parents and even her grandparents, and if the brewery tried to keep them it would be stealing and he'd go to law about it, see if he wouldn't ... And the man had looked at Dan, towering over him, big and dark and powerful, and backed away. They ought to send my Dan to talk to Hitler, Nora thought, remembering it. He'd soon sort the horrible man out!

But it didn't seem as if anyone could sort out Hitler. And now the war, that had been looming for so long, had come terrifyingly close. The children were being sent away ... She leant her head back again, feeling once more the wash of sickness and fatigue. I can't manage it, she thought. I just can't manage it. I'll have to talk to Dan.

'They're taking all the kiddies away. Sammy brought the letter home today. They've got to go to school early on Friday morning, with sandwiches, and we don't even know where they'll be going.' Her voice shook.

Dan pushed the tabby cat off his chair and sat down to unlace his boots. He was tired and frightened, though he could never admit that to Nora. He couldn't even admit it to himself. But when he thought of the war he had known – the trenches, the mud, the endless noise, the crying and the screams, the dead men at his feet – he felt sick. He felt furiously, helplessly angry. It was coming again and there was nothing he or anyone else, it seemed, could do to stop it.

He scowled, his eyebrows drawing together in a thick

black bar. 'They're bloody mad, the lot of 'em. Any tea on? I'm parched.'

Nora heaved herself up from her chair and moved slowly across the little back room to the scullery. I'm so tired, she thought, but if I feel like this now, what's it going to be like when the bombing starts? She caught a glimpse of herself in the bit of cracked and freckled mirror hung above the sink and wondered when her fair hair had started to go grey, and when its curls had turned into straggles.

She filled the tin kettle with water and set it on the gas stove. The tea packet stood on the cluttered cupboard top and she put three spoonfuls into the chipped brown teapot. While she waited for the kettle to boil, she took down two cups, adding milk from the meat safe outside the back door and sugar from the blue paper bag it had come in from the grocer's.

Tibby had followed her into the scullery and was mewing for milk, so she poured some into an old saucer and watched him crouch over it. She made the tea, gave it a couple of minutes to brew, then poured it into the cups and carried them back into the living room. The effort of it all left her exhausted.

'Dan, I don't want our boys to go,' she said, sinking back into her sagging armchair. 'I don't want them going out to the country, to strangers.'

'Well, our Gordon won't.' Dan slurped his tea. 'He's out at work, he won't be qualified to go.'

'I don't want Sammy to go either. He's too little.'

'He's getting on for eight. They're taking kids younger than that.'

'Yes, but he's so little for his age and he still needs me. And I need him, Dan. He helps me.'

'Well, it don't look much like it,' Dan said, glancing round the bleak little room. 'There's dust you could grow potatoes in on that sideboard and there was mouldy bread in the bin when I went there for me sandwiches this morning.'

'I know, it's the heat . . . But he does the shopping, and hangs out the washing and things. And I'll miss him so much. I don't want him to go, Dan, I don't really.' Tibby came back and jumped up on her lap. 'And there's the cat, too. He'd break his heart if he had to leave Tibby behind.'

Dan rubbed a hand across his forehead. He didn't want to think about it, didn't want to think about the war at all. He looked at his wife, lying back in her chair, weary and white-faced, and wondered if she was ill in some way. The thought brought fresh fear and that, in turn, a fresh surge of irritation.

'Well, what d'you want me to do about it? It's for you to decide, you're the boy's mother. If you don't want him to go, just tell 'em so. They can't force you. It'll save us some money anyway. They want five bob for each kid, you know. We can feed our Sam on less than that, he don't eat enough to keep a sparrow alive.'

Nora closed her eyes. 'It's just that all the other kiddies are going. The Budd boys and the Collinses, and those two from Atkinson's, the greengrocer's. I don't want people to think I don't care—'

'I don't give a toss what people think!' Dan broke in. 'Lot of snobs round here, think they're better than anyone else. I passed that Mrs Glaister coming down the street just now and she turned her head away as if I smelt! And that Mrs Chapman, she ain't no better.'

'They're all right when you get to know them. Jess Budd at number 14, she's a nice little body, and I thought you got on all right with her hubby. It was him told us this house was up for rent.'

'Yes, well, Frank Budd's all right; he went through the last lot with me. But he's so strait-laced he's not human! Won't go to the pub, won't have a drink – and he was just the same in the Army, the blokes used to go on at him to have a pint and he never would, no matter what they said or did.' He was silent for a moment, struggling with unwanted memories. 'Had to put his fists up more than once – good job he's a big bloke.'

There was a short silence. Then Nora said, 'It's all right, then, if I tell the teacher Sammy ain't going? Only there won't be no school here for him to go to, see, there'll be no teachers left. They want all the kiddies to go.'

Dan looked at her, unsure for a moment what she was talking about. He had retreated briefly into that dark place in his mind that he tried to avoid. The familiar anger gripped him and he stood up quickly, knocking over his tea. The cat leapt down from Nora's lap and fled from the room.

'Now look at that! Bloody tea wasted ... Well, if that boy's going to stop home he can make himself a bit more useful about the place. He can clear this up for a start. *Sammy*!' he roared, knowing that his younger son must be upstairs. 'Come down here! There's a job for you!'

Nora closed her eyes again. I don't know if I'm doing the right thing, she thought as she heard Sammy's timid footsteps on the stairs. Perhaps it would be better for him to go away after all. It couldn't be worse than being at home ...

But she knew that she could not let him go. Sammy was her companion. If he went away, she felt, she might never see him again. Whether there was bombing or not, he might be lost to her for ever. And Dan did think a lot of the kiddy really, she knew he did, it was just that he didn't know how to show it. It wasn't Dan's fault he was the way he was.

The door opened and Sammy came slowly into the room, small and pale, his blue eyes and fair, curly hair a mirror image of her own at that age. His thumb was stuck firmly in his mouth and his eyes, huge with anxiety, went straight to her face, and she gave him a tremulous smile.

'It's all right, Sammy. You ain't done nothing. Your dad's just spilt his tea, see, and wants you to wipe it up. Bring him another cup, there's a good boy, there's some in the pot.' She held out her hand to him. 'And guess what, he says you can stop at home with me, instead of being evacuated.'

Sammy stared at her and then at his father.

Dan gave him a reluctant nod. 'That's right,' he growled. 'Your mother don't want you to go, so that's it. But you got to be a proper help to her, mind. You're not going to be on your holidays. And take that everlasting thumb out of your mouth!'

Sammy nodded, then slipped across the room to his mother and buried his face against her thin chest. Nora held him for a moment before pushing him gently away.

'Get your dad his tea now,' she whispered, aware that Dan's irritation could break out again at any moment. 'Go and fill up his cup and don't forget the sugar.'

A wave of dizziness swept over her and she lay back again, waiting for it to pass. It always did, after a few minutes. It was just the worry of it all, she told herself, the worry of the war and whether she would lose Sammy. But at least she didn't have to think about that any more. Sammy was going to stay with her.

None of the children of April Grove had ever been at school by seven in the morning before. If they'd been told a few weeks ago that they would do it, they'd have laughed themselves silly. Go to school early? You must be crackers.

Yet here they were, up at dawn to collect their things together – their little cardboard suitcases of clothes, their gas-mask boxes, their paper bags of sandwiches to see them through the day. And where would they be when the day ended? They didn't know. Even their mums didn't know.

Even though he wasn't going, Sammy got up early and went along to the playground as well. He had an obscure feeling that he had to, and anyway it might be the last time he would see the other boys and girls for months. Years, even. Already feeling abandoned and lonely, he wandered among the milling throng and came face to face with Tim Budd, arguing fruitlessly with the teacher about having to wear a luggage label on his lapel. Tim stared at the smaller boy.

'Here, why haven't you got a label on? And you haven't got your gas mask neither, nor your sandwiches. Aren't you coming on the train with the rest of us?'

Sammy shook his head. Since the Hodges family had only come to live in April Grove a few months ago, he'd been ill with whooping cough and didn't know any of the children well. The Budd brothers, from the other end of April Grove, were friendly enough, though, and while he didn't see much of them at school, being a few years younger, they had sometimes let him join in a game of cowboys and Indians, or in kicking Tim's old football along the road. He wished they weren't going away. He would have liked to be real friends with them.

'My mum doesn't want me to go away. She's poorly.'

'Your mum's always poorly,' Tim observed dispassionately. 'My mum says she's—'

What Jess Budd said about Nora Hodges was lost in the shriek of Miss Langrish's whistle as she marshalled the children together in the playground. In the road outside a fleet of buses waited to take them to the railway station and as soon as the children could be got into their lines, class by class, they would climb aboard them. There was a flurry of last-minute kisses and admonitions to be good, and mind you send that postcard the minute you arrive so I know where you are. Suddenly panic-stricken, children began to cry and cling tightly to their mothers, so that their fingers had to be prised away, while mothers found the tears streaming down their faces as they watched their children climb aboard the buses, wondering when they would see them again, wondering who would put them to bed that night and whether they would be kind to them and make them wash properly and eat their greens.

'I've heard they don't even have proper lavvies out in the country,' a woman standing near Sammy said. 'Just buckets full of dirt, down the bottom of the garden. My Wendy won't never be able to bring herself to use something like that.'

Sammy Hodges knew most of the women standing there. There was Wendy and Alan Atkinson's mum from the greengrocer's shop, and Martin Baker's from October Street, nearly frantic over her Martin. And there were one or two dads as well – Brian Collins's dad, who worked shifts, and Mr Cullen, the milkman, who'd had to bring his Susan because Mrs Cullen had died a few days ago of TB and was being buried this very day. He looked as if he'd been crying and Susan's pigtails looked like rats' tails, as if he hadn't been able to do them properly.

Sammy wondered what it was like to have your mum die. His own was often poorly and had to stay in bed a lot, but she wasn't going to *die*. He hoped not, anyway. He didn't like thinking about what it would be like at home if she did. There'd be only Tibby to love him then.

'Aren't you and Gordon going, Sammy?' Mrs Budd asked him and he shook his head again.

'Mum doesn't want us to.'

She gazed at him with a funny look on her face, as if she was trying not to cry. That was because she was sending her own boys and her girl, Rose, off to the country. But Sammy had heard Martin Baker's mum say that Mrs Budd would be going herself next day, with the baby Maureen, so there wasn't really anything to cry about. She looked as if she was about to say something else, but Sammy didn't want to answer any more questions. He ducked away and slipped between two other mothers to stand at the back of the crowd.

The buses trundled away and some of the mothers followed them, hoping to catch another glimpse of the children before they got on the train at Portsmouth Town Station. Jess Budd turned in the opposite direction and began to push Maureen's pram, and Sammy followed at a little distance, shuffling his feet along the gutter in his broken shoes.

He didn't really understand why the others were going away. It had all been explained to them at school, but he felt they hadn't been told the whole story. There was something about a war which might start soon, and that was why they'd all been given the tin Anderson shelters to build in their gardens and the gas masks in their brown cardboard boxes. People said there would be bombs dropping on places like Portsmouth that had a harbour and a naval dockyard, so children and people who were blind or couldn't look after themselves were going to live in the country, where it was safe. But nobody had told them *why* there was going to be a war.

'There just *is*, once every twenty years,' Tim Budd had told him. 'The last one finished in 1918, see, so this one's a bit late, but that's because Mr Chamberlain went to Germany to see Hitler last year and got a piece of paper saying they wouldn't have one this time. Only Hitler's broken his promise, see, so we're going to kill all the Germans.'

'But why do *we* have to go away, then?' Sammy had asked. 'If we're going over there to kill them, how can they come and drop bombs on us?'

'Because it's a *war*,' Tim said. 'You can't have a proper war without fighting, can you?'

Sammy drifted home, still trying to work it out, then he gave up. Grown-ups did a lot of things you couldn't understand. Like his mum always being poorly and his dad always being in a bad temper, as if it was Sammy's fault.

It was only a few streets to April Grove. You went down October Street, or March Street, from September, and there it was, running along the bottom of them both. There were allotments at the back, almost like real country, and up at one end, where Sammy lived, they came right down to the road. Mrs Budd went down October Street, still with Sammy following at a safe distance, and stopped to talk to Granny Kinch, who was standing at her front door.

Sammy quite liked Granny Kinch, although he was half afraid she was a witch. She was old – *really* old, probably about a hundred years old, he thought – and she stood or sat on a chair at her front door all day, watching what went on up and down the street. She talked in a funny, mumbling voice as if her teeth might drop out at any minute, and she wore her hair in steel curlers under a faded scarf. But she always had a smile for the children and, better than that, she always had a few sweets too. Sometimes she would get all the boys and girls gathered round on the pavement and throw a handful of toffees over their heads for them to scramble for.

Granny Kinch lived with her daughter, Nancy Baxter, and Nancy's children – Micky, who was a few years older than Sammy, and her baby Vera. Micky hadn't been evacuated either. Sammy had seen him by the school, watching the buses depart. He'd looked half envious, half scornful, and when they'd gone he'd run off on his own, his face dark.

When the Hodges had first come to April Grove, Micky had quickly palled up with Sammy's brother Gordon. They'd gone off together, playing truant from school and pinching things from shops. They'd got bolder, and in the end they'd been caught pinching from Woolworths. Gordon, who had been in trouble when they lived at the pub in Old Portsmouth, had been put on probation, and Micky given a good telling-off. If they did anything else, the man at the court had told them, they'd be sent away to an approved school.

'Don't care,' Micky had boasted afterwards. 'Wish I *could* go away. Wish I could go to *London*.'

As Sammy hung around at the top of April Grove, watching Jess Budd go into Granny Kinch's house, Micky himself came round the corner. He stopped when he saw Sammy, then came on more slowly.

'What you doing here? Wouldn't they let you be 'vacuated?'

'Mum didn't want me to go,' Sammy said. 'She's poorly.'

Micky stared at him. 'So you got to stop and look after her, then?'

'Not all the time. I can play out as well.' Sammy glanced up and down the street. 'Only there's not many people left to play with now.'

'There's me. I didn't want to go. I wanted to stop here and see the bombs.'

'I'd like to have gone out to the country,' Sammy said wistfully. 'There's trees and things out there, and fields to play in. I bet they'll have a smashing time.'

'Bet they won't. Bet they'll be fed up after a couple of days and wanting to come back to Pompey. Bet they'll wish they hadn't gone.' Micky kicked at a stone. 'Where's your Gordon? S'pose he's at work, is he?'

Dan Hodges had got Gordon a job down at Camber dock. He'd had his fourteenth birthday, so could leave school, and Dan said he'd got to bring some wages into the house. He'd keep an eye on him, see he didn't get into any trouble.

Micky was disgruntled when he heard this. Gordon was

just that bit older and bolder, and Micky had looked forward to more lucrative mischief with him. But Gordon didn't want to be bothered with him now he was working. There were all sorts of dodges at the docks, and a twelve-year-old boy wasn't any good to him now.

Micky thought Sammy was a poor substitute for his brother, but he was all there was so he might as well make the best of it.

'What shall we do now, then? Go over the allotments, see if there's anything worth getting?'

'I can't. I've got to go in and see if Mum wants anything.'

Micky looked exasperated. 'Well, when you've done that, then? There's no school now, we can do what we like. Go down the harbour, do a bit of mudlarking. Go up the Lines and see if the soldiers'll let us look at the guns. They're putting up real big ones to shoot planes down. They might let us have a go.'

Sammy shook his head. He was nervous of Micky, who was much bigger than he was and not afraid to do things that could get him into trouble. The man at the court had told Micky that he and Gordon were lucky not to be going to an approved school. Sammy knew that next time Micky was caught he could easily be sent away and he didn't want to find himself there as well. Besides, who would look after Mum?

He turned away. 'I've got to go in now.'

Micky shrugged. 'Don't care, then. I can do better things on me own and I'll keep whatever I get. Might go down Commercial Road and go in Woolworths. There's always stuff you can pinch in there, off the counters.' He sauntered off, whistling, and Sammy looked after him. He knew it was going to be lonely without the other children around and no school to go to, and he thought Micky was feeling miserable too. His best friends, Cyril Nash and Jimmy Cross, had gone as well, so there was no one for him either. It would be good to play with him, but not to go pinching stuff from Woolworths or the allotments.

He went down the back alley and up the narrow garden, passing the sheets of corrugated iron that were supposed to be made into an Anderson shelter. Everyone else had got theirs up but Sammy's father hadn't even got the hole properly dug yet. He said he was going to wait until he knew for certain there was going to be a war. It was daft, doing all this before you even knew it was going to happen.

Dan and Gordon had already left for work at the Camber dock, and Nora was downstairs, washing up the dishes that had been left the previous night. She was half leaning on the sink, working slowly, and her pale face had a yellowish tinge to it. She looked round as Sammy came through the back door and gave him a wan smile.

'There you are, love. Did you see your mates off? Go off all right, did they?'

He nodded and picked up a grubby tea towel to start drying. 'They went on buses. Then they were going to go on trains, but nobody knows where they're going. It's a secret.'

'I know, love. Can't see why it should be, I must say. The blooming Germans aren't going to be worried about a lot of nippers.' She gave him an anxious glance. 'Did you wish you could be going too?'

Sammy looked at her. His mother had changed a lot in the past year. He could remember when she was lively and pretty, playing games or singing to him. She used to sing old songs and nursery rhymes, and she had one favourite that she'd sung to him ever since he was a baby:

> 'Sammy, Sammy, shine a light,
> Ain't you playing out tonight?'

The song was part of a game, a sort of hide-and-seek after dark in which half the children ran off to hide and the rest searched for them. If you thought you knew where a hider was, you had to call out the rhyme and then the hider must show his light – a torch, if he possessed one, or a candle in a jam jar, hidden under his jacket – and if he was caught he had to join the chasers. Sammy's mother, who had lived out in the country with her granny for a while when she was a little girl, said it was best played among the trees and fields, but Pompey children thought the streets and alleyways of the town were best, and they didn't call out 'Sammy'. Their word was 'Dick' and Micky Baxter had sneered at Sammy when he'd first played the game.

'Well, it was Sammy where my mum lived,' he'd retorted, and Micky had stepped forward, his fists raised pugnaciously before Tim Budd stepped in.

'Leave him alone, Micky. It don't matter what name we use so long as we get on with the game. My candle's not going to last all that long, I could only get a bit of a stub.'

Nora still sang to him occasionally, but her voice was weak and tired now, and when she sang the 'shine a light' rhyme her eyes would fill with tears.

She'd started to get ill after Sammy's whooping cough and not long before Gordon had got into trouble, but it wasn't anything you'd go to the doctor for, she said. Just feeling tired and sick and having headaches, or even aching all over. Doctors couldn't do much about that sort of thing and besides, she and Dan didn't have the money. Not for just feeling tired. She'd be better soon anyway.

But she hadn't got any better, some days she didn't get up at all. Sammy could do some of the jobs she couldn't manage, but on the whole most of them were left undone. Getting meals was the only thing that really had to be done, and even then their dinner often consisted of no more than a few pennyworth of chips from the shop in September Street.

He thought about the green fields and trees where the others were going today. He'd watched them getting on the buses; some, like Tim Budd, had been as excited as if they were going on holiday, but others had cried and clung to their mothers.

'I'd rather stop here with you and Tibby,' he said. He leant against his mother, feeling the sharpness of her bones.

She looked down at the dishes. 'I can't finish this now. I'm going to go and sit down for a bit. You do the rest, Sammy, there's a love.'

She went into the back room and lay down in the old armchair they'd brought from the pub when they came to April Grove. She looked worn out and when she closed her eyes the lids looked blue, as if the colour was showing through. There was a small bruise on her cheek that he hadn't noticed before and Sammy looked at it anxiously, wondering where it had come from, before covering her gently with an old blanket.

There was some tea in the pot, left over from Dad's when he went to work. It was a bit cool but Sammy poured some into a cup and added milk. He took it in and gave it to his mother, then went back to the scullery and looked at the scummy water in the sink.

There were only a few cups and plates to wash, and he swished them about a bit with the dishcloth and put them on the wooden draining board. The teacloth was too wet to dry them properly and left greasy marks, but he put them in the cupboard and tipped away the water. It gurgled very slowly down the drain.

Nora was asleep. Tibby was asleep too, on a pile of crumpled washing dumped in the other chair. Sammy lifted him off and pushed the washing aside to sit down with the cat on his knee, watching his mother. After a while he got up and wandered outside, still holding the cat.

The street was empty. Even Granny Kinch had gone indoors. There was no sign of Micky and all the other children must be on the train by now, on their way to the countryside.

Sammy put his thumb in his mouth. He sat down on the doorstep, with Tibby beside him, and waited for the long day to pass.

Chapter Two

In the village of Bridge End, Ruth Purslow had been busy all morning, baking rock cakes and making a big jug of lemonade for the new arrivals. She put them all into a shopping basket, covered them with a clean teacloth, then got ready, washing at the kitchen sink and putting on her grey frock and the green cardigan her niece Lizzie had knitted her for Christmas. It was just the colour of her eyes, she thought, looking in the mirror to brush her soft auburn hair. Over the top she put on her second-best coat and her little green hat with the pheasant's feather in, then popped her head through the living-room door to say goodbye to her father.

'I'm just going down to help with the evacuees, Dad. They'll be arriving this afternoon.'

He looked up from his chair by the window and nodded. 'Evacuees.'

'That's right,' Ruth said, pleased that he had understood the word. 'They're coming from Portsmouth, because of the war. I've made some lemonade and buns.' She straightened the crochet blanket over his knees. 'I shan't be long.'

There was a group of women already in the village hall when she reached it, laying out buns and cups of lemonade on the long trestle tables. Lizzie was near the door, talking to her friend Edna Corner. They'd grown up together, skipping down the lane to the village school and playing by the stream and, later on, dawdling by the bridge on summer evenings to flirt with the boys. Boys and girls must have met on that old bridge for hundreds of years, Ruth thought, casting her mind back to her own courting days.

She'd met Jack there – well, she'd known him for years, of course, all the youngsters knew each other, but when you got to about fourteen or fifteen and started going down to the bridge it seemed different, somehow. Jack, who'd always been just another boy, kicking a ball about and running after girls to pull their pigtails, had suddenly become a tall young man with shy eyes and a nice smile. He was three years older than her and had got an apprenticeship at one of the shipyards in Southampton. When that finished, he'd told her, he was going to join the Merchant Navy as an engineer.

'I want to see the world,' he said, his dark eyes glowing. 'I want to see all these places you read about or see at the pictures. America – Australia – China. I want to see them for myself.'

Ruth had been fascinated. She listened for hours as he talked about the places he would see, wishing she could go too. But girls didn't do that kind of thing. Girls stayed at home and looked after the family, and waited for their sailor husbands to come rolling back from overseas.

'You will wait for me, won't you, Ruthie?' Jack had whispered the night before he went away on his first voyage. He'd got a position as sixth engineer on a cargo ship. It was going to Africa to collect bananas and he was so excited he could hardly wait. Ruth would have felt left out and abandoned if he had not already told her how much he loved her, and how he wanted to find her waiting for him when he came home.

'I wish we could get engaged ...'

'Dad wouldn't let us,' Ruth said. 'I'm only seventeen. He won't let me get engaged for at least another two years.'

'He let your Jane, didn't he? She couldn't have been

much more than nineteen when she and George got married.'

'I know, but that was because . . .' Ruth blushed. Jane's first baby had been born embarrassingly soon after the wedding – a fine, lusty child for a seven-months baby. Ruth, who had been only nine at the time, hadn't been supposed to know about it but there hadn't been any way of concealing the family row that had shaken the little cottage, leaving Jane and her mother in tears while George Warren, not much older, looked white and shaken. The wedding had taken place less than a month later. They'd gone to live in one of the tiny farm cottages and a few months later Ruth had found herself with a niece only ten years younger than herself – the same age difference as there was between her and her sister.

All that had been forgotten by the time Ruth and Jack were courting. Jane had had two more babies, Terry and Ben, and George was hoping to take over as farm foreman when old Simon retired. There had been sadness when Jane's and Ruth's mother, Florence, had died soon after young Ben's birth, and after that Ruth and her father lived alone in the cottage. And that, she knew, was half the trouble.

'Trouble with your dad', Jack said gloomily, 'is that he doesn't want you to get engaged at all – much less married.'

'He doesn't want me to leave him,' Ruth agreed. 'You can't blame him. He'd be so lonely, here on his own, and who'd cook his meals and look after him?' She sighed. 'I don't see how I'm ever going to be able to leave him.'

'Well, you don't have to,' Jack said. 'You could stop here with him. I'm going to be away a lot anyway – it'd be company for you too.'

They'd agreed to talk about it again when Jack came back from this first trip. Her father would be able to see then that they were serious. They'd get engaged and save up to get married two years later. They wouldn't have any children for another two years, to give them time to save for a home of their own nearby – Dad wouldn't want kiddies under his feet and Ruth could still look after him – and then they'd have three children, like Jane, or maybe even four. It was all worked out.

At first it seemed that everything was going their way. Joe Sellers had agreed to their engagement and was pleased that he wouldn't be losing his daughter. He gave them a good wedding in the little village church and what privacy he could in the little cottage, after their honeymoon in Bournemouth. When Jack went back to sea he settled down again with Ruth as if nothing had happened.

Jack came back and went to sea again. On one of his trips he acquired a parrot and brought it home for Ruth, to keep her company and remind her of him. He'd taught it to talk, copying his voice and saying the things he said to her when he was at home. 'I love you, Ruthie. Let me be your sweetheart. I'll be home soon, Ruthie . . .'

And then he'd caught malaria and that was the end of all their dreams. Here she was, a widow woman at thirty-five, she thought sadly, and that was all she had left of him – Jack's voice, a bit croakier than it had been in real life, following her around the cottage. And Dad needing her more than ever before.

It was funny that her niece Lizzie should also have married a lad who went to sea instead of stopping on the land. Alec came from Southampton and she'd met him in the shop where she worked. He was an engineer in the Merchant Navy, just like Jack, and away at sea more than he was at home. Ruth hoped Lizzie's luck would be better than hers, although with this war coming the girl must be worried stiff.

Lizzie looked cheerful enough this afternoon, however, and had done her dark brown hair in the latest fashion, rolling it over her forehead in a bang. She greeted her aunt with a smile.

'Hello, Auntie Ruth. Come to get yourself a slave?'

'Certainly not. I've just brought down a few rock cakes and some lemonade. I suppose you'll be taking a kiddy in, Edna?'

The fair-haired young woman nodded. Plump and motherly, she and her husband Reg hadn't been blessed with children yet, though a better mother and father you'd go a long way to find. Perhaps having a youngster about the place might set them off, you often heard of that. Anyway, Ruth thought regretfully, it wasn't something you could hurry.

She took her basket over to the long tables and set the cakes and lemonade out with all the rest. Then she went back to the other women.

'I wonder what they're going to be like,' Edna Corner said a little nervously. 'There's some awful slums in Portsmouth. My Reg had to go there once, he said it was terrible – tiny narrow streets, all crowded together, and kiddies running around with no backsides to their trousers. And the smell! It was worse than the day they come round to collect the nightsoil.'

'They'll be filthy dirty, all of them,' Mrs Hutchins said. Her mouth tightened, little straight lines splaying out all round her thin lips. 'And we'll be expected to clean up their dirt. It's not right, sending young hooligans from the slums out to decent country folk.'

'I'm sure they won't be that bad,' Joan Greenberry said. 'And at least we're just getting the younger ones here, and the mothers with babies. I've offered a room to someone like that. I'd like another woman about the place.'

'You won't when you see her,' Aggie White, whose husband was the village butcher, said darkly. 'All perm and lipstick, and a fag hanging out of the corner of her mouth as likely as not. I wouldn't want another woman in *my* kitchen.'

'Well, we've all got to put up with something these days, Aggie.' Joan glanced around. 'I must say, I'm surprised to see the Woddis sisters here. I wouldn't have thought two old spinsters like that would want kiddies about the place. They've never been used to children, have they. And they've got some nice furniture in that house of theirs, too.'

'It's a big place, though, isn't it?' Edna remarked. 'I think that's what it is. Anyone who's got the room has to register, whether they want to or not.'

'Are you taking one, Lizzie?' Aggie White asked, but Lizzie shook her head regretfully.

'Not with me and Alec still living at Mum's – when he's at home, that is! There's no spare rooms, see. Otherwise we wouldn't mind at all.'

A small boy raced in, skidding on the wooden floor and panting. 'The train's come! They're here! The 'vacuees are here.' He slid to a stop by his mother. 'Can I have a bun before they get here, Mum, can I?'

'No, you can't, our Freddy! They're for poor little children that've been on the train all day. You had a good dinner not half an hour ago, *and* you licked out the bowl when I made the buns. You leave them alone.' Mary Parker turned to the others. 'Hollow legs, that child's got. Hollow legs. And I suppose these kiddies'll want feeding too, when we get them sorted out. A penny bun and a cup of lemonade isn't going to be enough.'

'That's just the trouble,' Aggie White said sharply. 'They'll eat us out of house and home, you mark my words. Growing children want a lot of feeding, specially the boys. And the few bob we get for putting up with them ain't going to go far, not when you think of all the washing and the ironing, and cleaning up after them. *And* the breakages.'

25

'Well, you've got to make a few allowances,' Edna Corner said. 'They're bound to find it strange, away from home. It'll take them a little while to settle down. What are you hoping for, Mrs Purslow, a little girl?'

Ruth shook her head regretfully. 'I can't take one at all, not with Dad the way he is and me working part-time at the Cottage Hospital. And if it wasn't him, it'd be my in-laws – I'd like to get them out from Southampton, if they'd come. If I did have the room I'd like a little boy, but I don't suppose they'd think a widow suitable for boys. I suppose you'd like one, to help on the farm, like?'

'Reg would like a boy, yes. I'm happy either way.' Edna tilted her head. 'Listen! I can hear voices.'

'It's them, it's them!' Freddy scuttled to the door. 'I can see them! They've got suitcases, and gas masks. What did they want to bring them for? We're not going to need gas masks out here. They're just for towns.'

'Don't be silly, Freddy, you're getting above yourself,' his mother told him sharply. 'You know very well we've all got gas masks and if a war starts we'll have to take them with us wherever we go. Just because we're not in a town doesn't mean we can't get gas. It spreads, like clouds.'

A large, tweedy woman bustled into the hall. She was carrying a folder and had a bossy, efficient look about her. She marched up to the little group of women, eyeing the tables spread with their buns and lemonade.

'I see you've prepared a welcome for the children. They'll be glad of that. They were all up early and their teacher says that most of them ate their sandwiches the minute they got on the train. Now, they'll be here in just a few moments and you'll have a chance to look them over while they have their tea. You'll be able to pick the children you like the look of, but I must warn you that not all of you will get your first choice and those that are left over will be allocated as best we can.'

'I don't want no slum kids,' a fat young woman with straggly hair and a grubby blouse said aggressively. 'I got my own little 'uns to consider.'

The tweedy woman glanced at her and Ruth Purslow hid a smile. The whole village knew Dotty Dewar's children. There were five of them already, running wild, and it looked as if another might be on the way. Ruth was surprised that Dotty was even being considered for an evacuee. Surely there was no room in the dilapidated cottage on the edge of the village, with its scrubby garden full of broken toys, straggling bushes and old motorbikes that were being 'repaired' by Dotty's husband Ned, not to mention the scrawny, ferocious dog that was chained to the front fence. Ruth didn't envy any evacuee child billeted there.

'I want a nice strong girl, about twelve or thirteen, what'll give me a bit of a hand around the place,' Dotty went on. 'I can't be expected to look after a little one, not in my position.'

You just want a servant and one whose keep'll be paid for, what's more, Ruth thought, hoping that the billeting officer would see through Dotty. But she had already turned away as the new arrivals appeared at the door and hesitated, their faces uncertain. Their teacher, a tall, thin, rather harassed-looking young woman, ushered them in and indicated the tables laid with buns and lemonade. There was a pause and then a rush. Two thin, ragged girls began to fight over a plate of buns and it was pulled off the table and smashed.

'Look at that! You'd think they hadn't eaten for a week.' Aggie White pursed her mouth as the teachers scolded their charges and made them form orderly lines. 'You can see they've never learnt any manners.'

'They're hungry and frightened, poor little mites,' Edna Corner said sympathetically. 'I don't suppose any of them have ever been away from home on their own before. I like the look of that little chap there, the one with curly hair.'

'There's two of them,' Ruth said, liking the look of Tim Budd herself. 'I expect they're brothers. Could you manage two?'

'I dare say we could. I'll go and see.' Edna went to speak to the tweedy woman, and a few moments later she and the two Budd boys went off together. The Woddis sisters took Wendy and Alan Atkinson, with evident doubt on both sides, and Rose, whose mother and baby sister were coming next day, went with Joan Greenberry. Gradually, all the children were allocated to their various billets and the village hall emptied. Only Ruth Purslow and a few other women who had come to help were left to clear away the empty plates and cups.

The billeting officer looked at Ruth. 'It looks as if you're one of the lucky ones. Most of the houses have got at least one evacuee now.'

'I wouldn't have minded one,' Ruth said quickly. 'It's just that my father's an invalid and I'm a nurse at the Cottage Hospital as well. But if things were different I'd have been glad to give a kiddy a home.'

'Well, if the situation changes you can let us have your name.' The woman ran her eyes down the list in her hand. 'It's Mrs Purslow, isn't it?'

'Yes, but—'

'Thank you for giving your time, anyway.' The billeting officer snapped her folder shut. 'I must go. I've got to visit all these homes in the next day or so, see that everything's as it should be. Good afternoon, Mrs Purslow.' She gave a quick nod to the other women clearing up and strode briskly out of the hall.

Ruth looked after her, then turned to the others. 'Well! Did you hear that? "If the situation changes!" And just what did she mean by that, do you suppose? If my poor old dad dies, that's what. Not that I expect him to last much longer,' she added sadly. 'That was a really bad stroke he had.'

'Well, I've got to get home,' Dotty Dewar said in a disgruntled voice. 'My old man'll be wanting his tea on the table, and since we're evidently not good enough for Pompey slum kids I don't see why I should clear up after them here. I don't know why they wouldn't give me one, I'm sure. There was a couple of bigger girls there looked as if they could have been real useful and the money would've come in handy too.'

She marched out of the hall, trundling the dilapidated pushchair which had seen her through five toddlers already and been second-hand when it started.

Ruth made a wry face and turned to the only other woman left. 'That leaves just you and me, Mrs Ward. Well, we'd better get on with it.'

Mrs Ward nodded. She was about seventy years old and hadn't been asked to take an evacuee. She lived next door to the hall and looked after it, keeping the keys and sweeping it through once a week. She was quite accustomed to doing other people's chores for them.

'I don't reckon the village'll ever be the same now,' she whispered as she carried a tray full of cups through to the tiny kitchen. She had lost her voice after an illness twenty years before and never been able to talk any louder ever since. 'Everything'll be different now, you mark my words. Country folk and townies never did mix.'

Well, they're going to have to try, Ruth thought, loading up another tray. And it's not the only change there'll be if there really is a war. *Everything*'s going to be different from now on.

Back at Ruth's cottage Joe Sellers was propped up in the old armchair looking out of the window across the green. He could see almost everything that went on from here and people could wave at him as they went by. He could watch Ruth going over to work at the Cottage Hospital and coming home again; he could see kiddies going to school, housewives carrying their bags from the village shop and stopping for a gossip, and the local dogs and cats going about their own business. He knew everyone and knew pretty well what they were all up to.

'Chubbleduck's got a tree,' he said when Ruth came in. The stroke had affected his speech and he now talked a language of his own. Ruth worked hard to learn its grammar and vocabulary, but just when she thought she was getting somewhere it all changed.

She looked at him doubtfully. Yesterday, 'chubbleduck' had meant the ginger cat from next door and it was quite possible that it still did today, and 'tree' might mean exactly what it ought to. She decided to take the risk.

'Ginger's up a tree, is he?' she said, coming to the window. 'I expect he's trying to catch birds. Which tree is it?'

Joe Sellers stared at her. She sometimes wondered if he knew what he had said. Perhaps, in his mind, the words had come out quite correctly and he didn't even know he'd said 'chubbleduck' for 'Ginger'. It certainly seemed, when he looked at her as if she'd taken leave of her senses, as if she were the one whose words were nonsense.

'Never said nothing about train,' he said irritably. '*Chubbleduck*, I said. Got a *tree*.'

'Oh, I see,' Ruth said, her heart sinking as she wondered what he could be talking about. If he just accepted that she understood it would be all right, but if he required an answer it could lead to yet another of those long, frustrating muddles as she tried to work out what he meant and he kept repeating it, getting increasingly distressed.

Poor Dad, she thought sadly. It must be awful having to sit there day after day, unable to do a thing but watch other people and not even able to talk properly. It must be like being trapped in a prison, the worst kind of prison. It was no wonder he got snappy and bad-tempered, and that must make him feel even worse.

'I'm sorry, Dad,' she said gently, deciding that honesty was the best policy. 'I don't really know what you mean. It's not Ginger, is it?'

'Train? Of course it's not train. *Chubbleduck*.' He could still use his left hand, and he raised it now and pointed across the green. 'There. *Chubbleduck*.'

Ruth looked where he was pointing and saw Edna Corner coming out of the lane which led down to the farm where she and Reg, who was the farm stockman, had a cottage. She sighed with relief.

'Oh, you mean Mrs Corner. Edna. Yes, she's got an evacuee – two, actually. Two little boys.'

He nodded, his bad temper gone now that she understood. 'Tree, yes. Two trees.' He smiled, content now that he was understood. 'Nice little trees.'

'They do look nice little boys, yes.' Ruth made a mental note that chubbleduck might now mean Edna Corner, as well as ginger cats, saucepans (which it had meant last Sunday) and the postman (a fortnight ago). Why he should have picked on that word, which he seemed to have made up, she had no idea, and why it was easier to say than 'cat', 'saucepan' or 'postman' was totally beyond her. But Dad had enough to put up with without her trying to teach him the correct words, as the nurse at the hospital had said she ought to do. She was the one who was still fit and well, and she was the one who had to make the effort.

'I'll go and make some tea, and talk to Silver for a bit,' she said. 'He's been in the kitchen by himself all afternoon, he'll be getting lonely.'

Silver was the big African grey parrot that Jack had brought her not long after they'd been married. He'd taught it to say all kinds of things and the parrot repeated them all in Jack's own voice. 'It'll be like having me here with you, Ruthie,' Jack had said and indeed, when Silver murmured that he loved her or asked her to let him be her sweetheart, it was just like hearing Jack's voice. But not, she thought wistfully, like having Jack with her.

Silver had learnt a good many other things during his seafaring days, most of them not fit to be repeated in polite society. Ruth usually covered him up when the vicar called in to see Dad. But she'd also taught him quite a lot herself, so he had a wide repertoire of nursery rhymes and sayings, and he picked up a lot of what other people said too, using their voices. It was quite embarrassing at times.

He was now learning Dad's language and, Ruth suspected, making a better job of it than she was herself. But Dad couldn't stand his squawking for too long, so for a lot of the time he was relegated to the kitchen.

She went through the door and Silver greeted her by dancing up and down on his stand, ducking his head and peering up at her flirtatiously.

'Let me be your sweetheart,' he cajoled her, in what still sounded uncannily like Jack's voice, with half a bucket of gravel thrown in, and then in her father's voice, '*Poor old Joe.*' Dad had taught him that before he had his stroke. He went back to Jack's soft tones. 'I love you, Ruthie . . . You old bugger, you.'

Jack hadn't taught him to say *that*, she could tell by the voice. It was one of the other sailors and Jack had been furious. But it always made Ruth smile to hear the sudden change and she scratched the bird affectionately under the chin.

'It's time you learnt some manners. It's a good thing we're not having an evacuee, if you're going to use that sort of language.'

'If you were the only girl in the world,' he began, but Ruth was filling the kettle at the pump in the corner and his voice was drowned by the squeaking. She set the kettle on the range and handed him a few seeds, saved from the sunflowers she grew in the garden. He cracked and nibbled at them, forgetting to make further conversation, and Ruth started to slice some bread and spread it with fish paste.

As she worked, she looked out through the kitchen window at the neat little garden, with its rows of vegetables and flowers, and its two or three old fruit trees. Dad had looked after it until his stroke, but Ruth managed it herself now. The late afternoon sun was slanting over the crest of the hills beyond and across the woods and fields. The cows were coming back from afternoon milking, lumbering across to their favourite spots, and she could hear a cackling from someone's garden as one of her neighbours fed her hens and ducks. It all seemed very peaceful.

I wonder what those little evacuees are making of it all, she thought. Some of them have never even seen a cow, except in picture books. I hope they won't be frightened when they hear the owls later on. They'll be upset enough as it is, being taken away from their mums and dads like that.

Was there really going to be a war? It didn't seem possible that the authorities would have gone to all this trouble if there wasn't. Someone had said Mr Chamberlain was going to make a broadcast on the wireless on Sunday morning. It looked bad.

The kettle boiled and Ruth made a pot of tea. She finished making the sandwiches and put them on plates, together with a few buns kept back from the ones she'd baked to take to the village hall. She set the whole lot on a tin tray with a picture of a garden on it and carried it through to the front room.

Silver finished his sunflower seeds and looked up in time to see her disappearing through the door.

'Oy!' he cried in the voice Dad used to use when the boy next door had been in scrumping apples from the tree at the bottom of the garden. 'You thieving little blighter! I *love* you, Ruthie. *Poor* old Joe . . .'

Ruth smiled and left the door open so that he could still see her. What with Dad and his chubbleducks, and Silver and his parrot talk, there wasn't much chance of a sensible conversation in the cottage, but at least she was never going to be lonely.

All the same, she'd have welcomed an evacuee. It would be nice to have a bit of young life about the place.

Chapter Three

The rest of the evacuees – the mothers and babies, and the blind people – arrived in the countryside next day. Jess Budd went to Mrs Greenberry's, with Rose, and the two women took to each other immediately. One or two younger women from the September Street area of Copnor settled in with other families and old Mr Crouch from the top of March Street, who walked with a white stick, was put with the doctor. He seemed bewildered, groping his way around the unfamiliar house, tears seeping from his sightless eyes.

'It's a shame, that's what,' Mrs Mudge, the vicar's housekeeper, told Mrs Greenberry when she dropped in for a cup of tea a few days later. 'Poor old man, he doesn't know where he is. Trying to find his way round that great house – it's daft. He ought to be in a small place, like he's used to. And doctor's wife's at her wits' end, frightened to death he'll hurt himself.'

'I'll call in and see him, if that's all right,' Jess Budd said. 'He's a funny old chap, but there's no harm in him. He's never been the same since he lost his sight and his wife went only last year, so he hasn't properly got over that either.'

They sat for a few moments without speaking. Jess was thinking about poor old Mr Crouch, blind and bewildered in a strange place. It was strange enough for her, living in someone else's house, away from her own home and husband, so it must be ten times worse for him. She stirred her tea and sighed.

'So it's war, then,' Joan Greenberry said, echoing her sigh, and the other two women nodded. They'd all heard Mr Chamberlain's broadcast on the wireless on Sunday morning. 'I hoped right up to the last minute that they'd find some way of stopping it.'

'They must have known they couldn't do that,' Jess said. 'They'd never have gone to all the trouble and expense of sending us out here if they'd thought there was any chance . . . And then there was all those Andersons being delivered right back in July. The day my little Maureen was born, that's when they brought ours, and I could have done without all that clatter, I can tell you! But they must have known then. *Months* before then.'

'My Harold reckons they've known for years,' Mrs Greenberry said. 'They've been getting ready for it. Only trouble is, they weren't as ready as the Germans. *They've* been getting ready ever since the last one, that's what he says.'

The women sat in silence for a while. Jess was thinking about Frank, alone in the little house in April Grove. How was he going to manage without her? How was he going to get his meals, do his washing? And how long was she supposed to stop out here, miles away from him?

It's not just people like poor old Mr Crouch who don't know what to make of it all, she thought ruefully, and went to fetch Maureen, who was starting to wake up and cry in her pram just outside the kitchen door.

With war now a reality, the two communities settled down uneasily together. It wasn't easy for a small village to find itself suddenly twice the size and there were inevitable frictions. The children, sharing the small school – evacuees in the mornings, village children in the afternoons – eyed each other suspiciously; some of the village children who had evacuees in their own homes made friends with them, others treated them as enemies. The Portsmouth children drifted together and there were quite a few squabbles between the two groups.

'Those are *our* conkers! They're not for you townies.'

'Yah! Frightened of a few old cows! Didn't even know where milk comes from!'

'*I'm* going back to Pompey, soon as I can. There's nothing to do out here. Nothing but trees and stuff. It's stupid, the country is.'

Some of the children, like Tim and Keith Budd, treated it as one long holiday. They roamed the fields and woods, finding new games to play, and – once they had got over their shock at the size of cows – helped around the farms. There was plenty to do, and when you got fed up with it you could slip off and climb trees or make a den. With school for only half the day there was time for both work and play.

Women like Jess, accustomed to running their own home and looking after a family, found it more difficult. Jess naturally wanted to do her share around the house, but Mrs Greenberry had her own ways and even though the women had quickly made friends there were still occasional differences.

'Oh! I thought I might do some baking—'

'*Tuesday*'s my baking day. I get the range stoked up for it then, see, and then I can heat up the irons as well, to do the ironing while the baking's in the oven. We don't have gas stoves we can just turn up whenever we feel like it, not out here.'

Or: 'Wouldn't it be better if I did my own washing? You don't want to be bothering about my and Rose's things.'

'Best if they all go in the copper together, my dear, so we can get it all done the same day. But I'd be grateful if you could air the baby's nappies somewhere else. My hubby does like to see the fire when he comes in after a day's work.'

It was no easier for Mrs Greenberry, having a woman

and two children – one of them an eight-week-old baby – suddenly foisted on her. Jess, having to wash nappies every day, was almost at her wits' end, trying to keep them out of the family's way. She'd hung them round the range to start with, then in the big living room, then in the bedroom the three of them shared. But they never seemed to be properly aired unless they'd been either out on a line or in front of a fire. She worried about Maureen catching a cold and eventually decided she had to tackle Mrs Greenberry again.

'Suppose I just put them round the range during the afternoon? I'll take them away before Mr Greenberry comes in. I know it's a nuisance, but Maureen did have that sniffle yesterday. And I really do need to boil at least twice a week.'

Mrs Greenberry looked at her, and her face softened. 'I know you do, my dear. I'm sorry. Of course you can air the kiddy's things and we'll stoke the boiler up every other day for you. There's no sense making things harder than they already are.'

Two women in the same kitchen was undeniably tricky. But with goodwill and understanding on both sides it was possible to shake down together and share a lot of the chores. It couldn't ever be like having your own place, though, Jess thought as she wheeled Maureen's pram through the village to visit the boys. And it seemed downright unnatural to be living in a different house from two of her own children.

'They're doing really well,' Edna Corner reassured her. 'You mustn't worry about them at all. They're smashing little boys and Reg is like a dog with two tails, having them to take around the farm.'

Somehow, that didn't comfort Jess as much as it ought to have done. 'It just feels so funny, not having them with me,' she said. 'I can see you're looking after them properly, Mrs Corner, and I'm grateful, don't think I'm not, but it ought to be *me* washing their clothes and tucking them into bed at night.' She sighed. 'I don't know, everything seems to have turned upside down lately. And how long's it going to go on? There hasn't been a sniff of a bomb so far.'

There weren't any bombs at all. The threatened air raids still hadn't happened by Christmas and a lot of the children went back home to Portsmouth for the holiday. It was strange to be back among the narrow streets after the wide open fields and woods of the countryside, and they felt conspicuous and uneasy at first. Some of the few children who had stayed behind were curious to know what life as an evacuee was really like, while others were scornful of the 'runaways'.

'Cowardy-custards. There ain't bin no bombs anyway. Scared of your own shadows, that's what you are.'

'That's all you know, Micky Baxter.' Tim squared up to his arch rival. 'I bet *you* wouldn't walk through a field of cows and bulls like me and Keith have to, to get to school every day.'

'Don't have to go to school,' Micky countered triumphantly. 'They've took it over for a first-aid post and there's no teachers anyway. All run off to the country with the rest of the cowards.' But there wasn't much real malice in his tone. In truth, he'd missed the other children and was glad to see them back, even the namby-pamby Budd boys. With Gordon Hodges at work all day, there'd been only young Sammy left in the whole of April Grove, and Sammy was just a kid, still tied to his mother's apron strings.

Sammy saw the other children too and hung about on the edge of the little group, feeling left out. He listened to them talking about Christmas and wished he could share their excitement. Stockings full of toys – the Budds, it appeared, even had pillowcases! – and parties with the whole family coming round for a big dinner and then a tea, with jelly and Christmas cake; none of these things, he knew, would be happening in the Hodges' household. And worse still, there'd be two whole days with nobody to play with at all, for everyone would be indoors with their own families and not out in the street.

He trailed home, thinking of the present he had bought for his mother. Soon after the evacuation he had started to go round the neighbours and ask to run errands to earn a penny or two. Sometimes he bought his mother a small bar of chocolate, sometimes he spent it on sweets for himself – an everlasting strip or a string of liquorice bootlaces, or some tiger nuts. Sometimes he gave it to his mother to help buy food and just lately he had begun to collect a small store of coins in his drawer, under his collection of old copies of *Film Fun*.

He'd saved for weeks now, hoping to get enough for a larger bar of chocolate. By the time he'd got enough and gone to the little sweetshop on the corner there wasn't all that much to be had, since sweets and chocolate seemed to be disappearing now there was a war on, and people had stocked up for Christmas and against the threat of rationing. But when he'd told Mr Sims it was for his mother's Christmas present the shopkeeper had found a bar of milk chocolate for him and even wrapped it in a scrap of coloured paper. Sammy had put the bar in his drawer, under his comics, and was looking forward to seeing his mother's face when he gave it to her next morning.

The scullery was cold but there was a small chicken lying on the draining board with some potatoes, a couple of onions, a pound or so of carrots and a stalk of brussels sprouts. They were going to have a proper Christmas dinner after all, he thought with delight. He already knew there would be a pudding because Mrs Shaw from the other end of the street had brought one along a few weeks before, explaining that she'd made too many. It had been sitting in the cupboard ever since.

Nora was asleep in her chair when he crept through the

back door. She had bought some strips of coloured paper a week ago and Sammy had spent his evenings making paper chains, sticking them with home-made paste. They hung round the room and Sammy paused for a moment or two to admire them, then tiptoed upstairs to gloat over his little gift.

Gordon, who had got home early from work because it was Christmas Eve, was already there, lying on the top bunk of the narrow iron-framed bed, and as Sammy came in he grinned at him.

Sammy stopped. Gordon was chewing something and there was an unmistakable smell in the room.

'Have you got some chocolate?'

'What if I have?' his brother retorted.

Sammy glanced at the chest of drawers. There were four drawers, two each for the two boys. In those, and the cupboard in the alcove that had been fitted with a hanging rail, they kept their clothes. They seldom had anything new; Nora bought most of their clothes in second-hand shops or was occasionally given them by better-off neighbours. They were not supposed to go to each other's drawers – at least, Gordon objected strongly if Sammy ever went to his and Sammy had assumed that the rule applied equally.

It had never been put to the test because he had never had anything Gordon would want, but when he glanced at his drawer now, his brother laughed.

'What's the matter? Got a secret?'

Sammy saw that there was a scrap of paper on the floor and his heart sank as he recognised it as the paper Mr Sims had wrapped his chocolate in. With a surge of fear and anger, he jerked open his drawer and dragged out his vest, crumpled from the wash. The bar of chocolate had gone.

He wheeled to face his brother, still grinning on the bed. 'You pinched my choclit! You stole it! You bin in my drawer and stole my choclit, what I was going to give to

Mum for her Christmas present. You're a thief, you are, a *thief*!'

'Garn,' said Gordon. 'You never got that for Mum, you got it for yourself. You was going to eat it all on yer own.'

'I wasn't! I *wasn't*! It was Mum's Christmas present and now I got nothing to give her and it's all your fault!' Red in the face, tears pouring down his cheeks, Sammy reached up and snatched at the remainder of the bar, still in Gordon's hand. Gordon jerked back and Sammy gave a howl of rage and dragged at the blanket that covered the thin mattress. His fury giving him strength, he had Gordon half off the bed before the bigger boy could save himself, and Gordon overbalanced and crashed on top of him. They collapsed on the floor in a tangle of flailing arms and legs, the blanket twisting itself around them as they fought.

Already thin, it ripped and Gordon grabbed an end, pulling it into a strip which he wound swiftly around Sammy's neck. 'Take that back! Take back what you said!'

'Let go! You're hurting me!' Sammy's eyes bulged. Gordon wasn't pulling hard on the rag but it was uncomfortably tight around his throat. 'You're *strangling* me!'

'Say I'm not a thief. *Say* it.'

'You *are* a thief,' Sammy cried, struggling. 'You took my choclit what I was going to give Mum, so that proves it. And if you strangle me you'll be a murderer as well and you'll go to prison and *hang*!'

'I won't, because—'

'What the bleeding hell is going on in here?'

The two boys froze. Sammy, half buried under his brother's bigger body, the strip of blanket still wound round his throat, stared up at his father with frightened eyes.

Gordon, grinning uneasily, untangled himself and slid the rag away.

'We was just having a game,' he said nonchalantly. 'Being Christmas an' all.'

His father glowered at him. 'Well, it didn't sound like it. It sounded as if someone was being murdered up here.'

Gordon slid Sammy a warning glance. Sammy sat up, feeling his neck. He was breathing quickly.

'Our Gordon was strangling me because I called him a thief. He pinched something from my drawer.' He gave his brother a defiant look. 'You did, you know you did.'

'Called him a thief?' Dan gave a short laugh. 'What have you got that he'd want to pinch? Unless it was something you pinched yourself.'

'It was my choclit,' Sammy persisted, ignoring Gordon's threatening glare. 'My bar of choclit what I bought Mum for Christmas, and he's *et* it.' His eyes filled with tears. 'Now I got nothing to give her.'

'I didn't know he'd got it for Mum, did I?' Gordon argued in an injured tone. 'How was I to know that?'

'It was in my *drawer*. It was under my jumper, all wrapped up.'

'All right, that's enough,' Dan interrupted, tired of the argument. 'You'd better clear this mess up, both of you, and come downstairs. And no more arguing and fighting, understand? You woke your ma up with all your row. Just when she was trying to get a bit of rest . . .'

He stamped downstairs and Gordon turned on Sammy. 'You'll be sorry you said all that.'

'It was true. You did pinch my choclit, and then you tried to strangle me. I wish you didn't live here. I wish you'd got sent to a proved school, like the judge said.'

Gordon made a threatening move towards him and Sammy backed away. 'Dad said we wasn't to fight any more. It's Christmas.'

They straightened the room in silence, spreading the spoilt blanket over the bed. A pile of old *Hotspur* comics

43

that Gordon had brought home had also fallen off the end and got crumpled, and some of them were torn too.

Gordon looked at them in disgust. 'I hadn't even read those yet.'

Sammy said nothing. He went downstairs and buried his face against his mother's thin breast.

'Sorry about the row, Mum.'

'What was it all about? I thought the roof was coming in.'

Sammy hesitated, but Gordon could still be heard moving about upstairs. 'He pinched my choclit,' he whispered. 'I saved up and bought it for your Christmas present, and now he's *et* it.' He began to cry again. 'I got nothing to give you now.'

'Oh, Sammy.' She stroked his head. 'Don't worry about it, love. It's the thought that counts. Look, we'll pretend you did give it to me, shall we? And don't think about it any more. Gordon didn't know you meant it for me.'

'He didn't ought to have gone to my drawer—' Sammy began, but she put one hand over his mouth.

'Never mind now. It's done and it's over. Come on, Sammy, it's Christmas. He's your brother. We can't have fighting over Christmas, now can we?'

Sammy gazed at her. He saw the thin face that had once been so pretty, the greying hair that he could remember being as fair and golden as his own. He saw the blue eyes that had begun to fade, the skin that looked like yellowed paper. His mum was old, he thought, old and poorly, and she didn't want to be upset at Christmas.

He looked around at the paper chains and thought of the little chicken and the pudding from Mrs Shaw.

'We'll play games,' he said. 'We'll have chicken for dinner and play games after. It'll be a proper Christmas, won't it, Mum?'

'Yes,' she said, smiling at him. 'It'll be a proper Christmas.'

The wireless was playing carols when Sammy woke next morning. One of his mother's old stockings was hanging on the end of his bunk and he pulled it eagerly towards him, feeling the roundness of the orange in the toe. There wasn't much else inside – a few nuts, half a dozen new marbles, a ball and a pair of socks Nora had got for him. There was a puzzle to do, and a tin whistle as well as a Mars bar from Dan. Sammy sat in bed looking at the presents with pleasure.

Gordon hung over the edge of the top bunk. 'Father Christmas been, then?'

Sammy looked at him cautiously, knowing that his brother was going to say that Father Christmas didn't exist. 'I've got a new ball. And a Mars bar. I'm going to give it to Mum.'

Gordon shrugged. 'That's OK, then. Here.' He handed down an old copy of *Film Fun*, which had probably come from Sammy's own collection, but which he didn't mind looking at again because he liked Laurel and Hardy on the front page. 'Happy Christmas.'

'Thanks.' Sammy reached under his bed and found a copy of *Hotspur* that he'd got from Bob Shaw down the road, only a week old and hardly torn at all. 'This is for you.'

They grinned at each other, then Sammy rolled out of bed and pulled on his shirt and grey flannel shorts. He ran downstairs and found his mother making tea.

'Happy Christmas, Mum.' He pushed the Mars bar into her hand and she tried to give it back.

'No, Sammy, that's yours.'

'I wanted to give you choclit,' he said stubbornly, and she gave him a kiss and hugged him for a moment.

'We'll go up to the church after breakfast. I always like the service on Christmas Day.' The family weren't frequent churchgoers, but Nora liked to go on special days – Christmas, Easter, Harvest Festival – and she liked the boys to go with her. Gordon had refused last time, but Sammy enjoyed the singing (though he wasn't so keen on the kneeling down and praying) and he particularly liked the carols, especially those with sheep in them.

Gordon had given up carol singing two years ago when someone in Old Portsmouth had chucked a bucket of dirty water over him. He'd only ever done it for the money anyway and reckoned you could get more going down to the harbour, where you could wallow in the mud for pennies that people threw in from the ferry Hard.

Gordon came downstairs with a bottle of beer for his father and a handkerchief, with her initial embroidered in one corner, for Nora. As Sammy had expected, he wouldn't go to church with them, but when they came home he and Dan had peeled the potatoes and got the sprouts and carrots ready. They put the wireless on for some more music and the King's speech, and Nora cooked the dinner, but the effort left her exhausted. She fell asleep in her chair and Dan, who had been to the pub, dozed off on the other side of the fireplace.

'Dunno what the King was on about, all that stuff about a "family of nations" and the "freedom of the spirit",' Gordon grumbled. 'Anyway, what's it to him, all posh and comfy in that palace eating off gold plates and getting servants to do the washing-up. Let's go out and play football.'

Sammy picked up his new ball and the two boys went out into the street and kicked it about for a bit. After a while, Micky Baxter appeared and joined them.

'Boring old Christmas.'

'Get any good presents?' Gordon asked. 'Our Sam got this ball.'

'It's not bad,' Micky said judiciously and added with a swagger, 'I got my mum and gran gold necklaces.'

The two Hodges boys stared at him. 'Gold necklaces? *Real* ones?'

'Yeah.' He looked cocky and nonchalant, both at once. ''S easy. I know this place, see. They're all left laying about. You can just walk in, help yourself.'

'I'd like to get Mum a gold necklace,' Sammy said enviously.

'Well, you can't, not now. Doors'll be shut, see.' Micky looked at Gordon. 'I could show you, though.'

'Now?'

'If you like.'

The two older boys looked at each other. A glance of understanding passed between them. They turned to walk up March Street, then Gordon turned back towards Sammy. 'You stop here.'

'But I want to get Mum a gold—'

'You heard what I said. And they're not open today anyway, Micky's just said so. You stop here in case our dad comes out looking for you.'

'But what shall I say if—'

'Just tell him I've gone for a walk, all right? You stop here and play with your new ball.' He winked at Micky. 'You're too little to come with us. You wouldn't be able to keep up.'

They walked away rapidly, leaving Sammy staring after them. He felt lonely and disgruntled. Gordon hadn't bothered with Micky Baxter since he'd started work down at the Camber. It was only because it was Christmas Day and there was no one else around, and Sammy had been hoping for attention from his brother for himself for once.

I wanted to get Mum a gold necklace, he thought, kicking the ball uninterestedly along the gutter. Now Gordon'll get her one *and* he ate her bar of chocolate so I couldn't even give her that. It's not fair.

Through every window he could see Christmas decorations and people enjoying themselves. The Budd brothers had come home for Christmas, but they wouldn't be out in the street. They weren't even allowed out to play on

Sundays and anyway, he knew they were all up at their auntie's house, at the bottom of March Street. He'd seen them going up there before dinner, all laden down with parcels and dishes. He sighed and kicked his ball again, but there wasn't much fun in kicking a ball with no one to kick it back. He'd have to go in soon anyway – it was beginning to get dark and people were drawing their blackout curtains.

The door of number 1 opened and Tommy Vickers came out. Tommy was a small, cheerful man who made it his business to know everything that went on in April Grove. He looked at Sammy. 'All by yourself?'

It was just the sort of question grown-ups asked, when they could see the answer for themselves, but Sammy only shrugged.

'Where's your brother, then? Too big to play with a ball now?'

'Gone for a walk with Micky Baxter,' Sammy said and Tommy whistled.

'Well, that's ominous! I bet that lad's not up to any good. You steer clear of him, young Sammy. He'll lead you into bad ways.'

Sammy thought he'd better not mention the gold necklaces. He turned back towards his own doorway.

'How's your mum these days?' Tommy asked, his voice a little softer. 'Mrs Vickers was saying she didn't look too well. She hasn't been properly right since you moved in, has she?'

'She's tired, that's all. She's been tired a long time.'

'I know.' Tommy studied him. 'Well, maybe my Freda'll call in and see if there's anything she can do, once we got Christmas out of the way.' He glanced up at the sky. The first pale stars were peeping through the dusk. 'You'd better go in. It'll be dark soon and you ought to be in by the fire on Christmas Day having a good time. I'm just off on me rounds, see nobody's showing a light.' He chuckled.

'Here, that's a game, isn't it! "Sammy, Sammy, shine a light, ain't you playing out tonight?" Well, those days are over, more's the pity. No playing out after dark and no shining lights, eh?'

He set off up the street on his nightly task of making sure that no lights were gleaming through chinks in the blackout curtains. Sammy watched him go and turned again to go indoors, wondering if his mother and father were still asleep.

Nora had woken, but his father was still snoring. The fire beside which Tommy Vickers had advised him to sit was almost out. Sammy went out to the back shed and started filling the old galvanised bucket with coal.

It could all have been different, he thought, if he'd only managed to get Mum a gold necklace.

Chapter Four

Christmas for the Budds was everything a Christmas should be, with a big family party at Annie Chapman's on Christmas Day and another in the Budds' tiny house on Boxing Day. Annie had managed to get a turkey, and they'd played games like Family Coach and the Jelly Race, and sung songs late into the night. There hadn't been a lot of money to spend on presents, but a lot of thought had gone into their choosing or their making. Everyone was delighted with what they received and Olive Chapman had capped it all by getting engaged to Derek Harker.

'I s'pose that means we've got to go to a wedding,' Tim Budd said glumly as the family went out for a walk on Boxing Day afternoon. He and Keith went on ahead, wearing the new mittens Jess had knitted them. 'Have our hair cut and get all dressed up in our best clothes and go to church.'

'Still,' Keith said, looking on the bright side, 'there'll be cake. It's just the same as Christmas cake, only there's three of them in a pile and there's a stork on top.'

'A stork? Why's there a stork?'

'I dunno. But there was one on top when we went to that christening party once. And someone said the cake was the top off a wedding cake, so there must be.'

'Anyway,' Tim said, 'it won't be for ages yet. Derek's a soldier now, so he's got to go and fight the war first.'

They went back to Bridge End a day or two after that, just in time for the snow. It was a heavy fall and it lay over the fields like a thick white quilt. Everyone turned out to shovel it from the roads to let the horses and carts through, and the children organised snowball fights, built snowmen and took huge delight in stamping their footprints over the smooth white billows. Tim and Keith built an igloo and begged the Corners to let them sleep in it. Reg was half inclined to let them, but Edna put her foot down and was justified when it collapsed during the night.

'I don't reckon this bombing's going to happen after all,' Ruth Purslow remarked to her sister Jane when she tramped up to the farm for some eggs. Jane's husband George was foreman, in charge of up to a dozen workers, and they had a nice house a little way away from the main farmhouse. 'I reckon they just got in a panic.' She put down her basket and took off her hat, shaking out her coppery hair.

'That's not what my Alec says,' Lizzie said. She worked in a shop in Southampton but hadn't been able to get in that day because of the snow. She was knitting beside the fire, but now she produced a letter from her knitting bag. 'I had this letter this morning. He says the German navy's all over the place, chasing our merchant ships from pillar to post. He reckons there'll be food shortages. Well, it stands to reason, don't it? It's as if the Germans have got us under siege.'

'Well, yes, I know it's going on at sea,' Ruth said apologetically. 'You must be worried about him – we all are. But it's the bombing I'm talking about. I mean, we never had much during the last war, did we?'

'They never had the aeroplanes then,' Jane pointed out. She split some fresh scones and buttered them. 'Have one of these, Ruth, they were in the oven five minutes ago. They didn't have the bombs either, not many. But they've been making them ever since and you can mark my words, they'll use 'em. I think Hitler's just biding his time and you can't blame him with the weather the way it is.' She sighed.

'I just hope it doesn't last too long. Our Terry will get his papers before long, I dare say, and Ben's coming up to seventeen, you know, and if they start calling up the youngsters . . . It'll put paid to his college course.' She stared at the scones for a moment without seeing them. 'Still, there's no use looking for trouble. How's Dad today?'

Ruth put a scone on to one of Jane's pretty plates. 'Oh, you know, much the same. Still on about his chubbleducks. Goodness knows what they are today but he got himself proper worked up, trying to explain something to me this morning. Him and Silver, they make a good pair, neither one of 'em knows what they're talking about. In fact, Silver makes more sense than he does at times. I swear that bird does know what some of his little sayings mean, he brings them out so apt.'

'You ought to just leave them to chat away together.'

Ruth smiled but shook her head. 'The squawking gives Dad a headache. He likes Silver, but he can't stand being in the same room for too long. It's a shame he can't get out now. He used to be such an active man. Not that he complains, mind.'

'I know.' Jane poured another cup of tea. 'He's a wonder really, always keeping so cheery. But don't think I don't realise how hard it is for you, Ruth. You know you can always call on me for a hand, or to come and sit with him so you can get out a bit if you need to go into Southampton, that sort of thing.'

Ruth nodded. She could slip out for an hour or so, like this afternoon or to Women's Institute meetings, but she didn't like to leave her father to go out of the village.

'Thanks, Jane, but I don't think I'll be going anywhere much till this snow clears away. It's a good three foot deep across the pathfields, I had to come all the way round the lane. Mind you, the kiddies are enjoying it. I suppose the ones from Portsmouth haven't ever seen it like that, it gets all dirty and slushy in towns. You should see them in the field at the back of my cottage, having a fine old time, they are. I had to dodge the snowballs!'

'You still wish you'd been able to take in an evacuee, don't you?' Lizzie remarked. She had read Alec's letter through again for the tenth time that day, feeling the same lump of anxiety and sadness in her throat each time she did so. People didn't realise what the Merchant Navy was going through ... She put the letter back into her bag and attended to the conversation once more. 'I know I'd have one, if I had a place of my own.'

Ruth nodded. 'Yes, I do, though some of them are little terrors. And some of the people that have got them – well, you've only got to look at those two poor little mites with the Woddis sisters to know things aren't right there. And that little Martin Baker, who was with Mrs Hutchins, he looked so white and frightened all the time, till he ran off. I don't know why the billeting officer didn't do something.'

'She just didn't know, I suppose,' Jane said. 'She's got three or four villages to look after. But you wouldn't think the Woddises would be unkind, would you? Not two old ladies in that big house. They must hardly know the kiddies are there.'

'Well, I don't know, they don't look happy to me. I was talking to Mrs Budd, her that's with Joan Greenberry, about them before Christmas. She lives near their mother so she knows the family quite well. They run a greengrocer's shop. She was telling me there's been a lot of illness. Their mother had a bad fall and broke some ribs, and then it turned to pleurisy and then, to top it all, the grandfather got killed by a car in the blackout. So the kiddies couldn't go home. I don't know what sort of Christmas those two old biddies could give them, I'm sure.'

'Perhaps the billeting lady could move them, now a lot of the children have gone back,' Lizzie said. 'Those two little boys Reg and Edna have got are all right, though. Reg has taught them both to milk and they feed the calves regular.

And they've both got a couple of hens of their own to look after – they sell the eggs to their mother over at Mrs Greenberry's.'

'They *don't*!' Ruth laughed. 'Well, I can't deny I'd like a boy or two like that about the place. But it's out of the question while I've got Dad the way he is.' She glanced at the old grandfather clock standing in the corner. 'And talking of Dad, I'd better be getting back. I promised I wouldn't be too long.'

'It's a shame you'll miss Ben,' Jane said, glancing at the clock on the mantelpiece. 'But he's bound to be late, with this weather. I wondered if he ought to go into Southampton this morning, with the snow so bad, but you know what he is, he won't miss school.'

'Bit different from when he was a kiddy,' Ruth remarked with a smile. 'I lost count of the times I caught him mooching about in the woods.'

'Well, that was all he was interested in, nature,' Jane said. 'Once he got to the big school and started doing proper science there was no holding him. I must say, I never thought he'd want to stop on past fourteen, but look at him now, he's done that School Certificate and he's working for the higher one and planning to go on to college. It'll be a crying shame if he gets called up and has to lose all that.'

'It will.' Ruth got up and began to put on her coat. 'Tell him I'm sorry I didn't see him, and to come in and see me and his grandad over the weekend. The old chap likes to see the youngsters and hear all their news.'

'I'll walk back with you now, Auntie Ruth,' Lizzie said. 'Then I can say hello to him as well.'

They put on their wellington boots for the trudge back through the darkening afternoon. Lizzie wound a striped knitted scarf round her neck and pulled on the old fur gloves that had once been her grandmother's.

'Started snowing again,' she said, opening the door to a

flurry of cold white flakes. 'There's a nasty wind getting up too.'

'Not another blizzard,' Ruth groaned. 'Just as if we haven't got enough snow already! They haven't got half the roads unblocked as it is. Are you sure you want to turn out in this, Lizzie?'

'Course I am. You know I don't mind the snow.' Lizzie slammed the door behind them and stamped footprints in the fresh white layer. 'Mind you, I might not be so pleased tomorrow when I can't get to work! The railways are all to pot too. Did you see those pictures in the paper yesterday? Engines buried up to their funnels in snowdrifts! Over a week ago, that was, and it must be even worse now.'

'There was that one stuck near Bridge End, too,' Ruth agreed, walking slowly so as not to slip. 'Twelve hours before they'd got it dug out. I went down myself, to open up the village hall and fetch in blankets, and give the poor souls cups of tea and biscuits.'

'Well, there's one thing,' Lizzie observed. 'Hitler won't be sending his bombers over in this weather. It must be just as bad in Germany.' She looked up at the heavy clouds and shivered. 'I hope Grandad's all right.'

'He should be. Mrs Perkins said she'd come in and turn on the lamp and make up the fire, and draw the blackout curtains.' Ruth sighed. 'It's not long ago when you could see your way by the lights from all the windows. Now everyone's indoors by four o'clock and it's as dark as the grave at night.'

She opened the front door and they saw a chink of light coming from the living room. The wireless was on, playing some music. Joe liked listening to the wireless, it was one of the few pleasures he had left. With Lizzie close behind her, Ruth closed the front door quickly in case any light escaped and took off her coat and hat before going into the room. She shucked off her wellingtons and pushed her feet into the old slippers she had left by the door, calling out to her father as she did so. Lizzie unwound her scarf and pulled off her own boots before walking on the carpet.

'Hello, Dad, it's only me. Jane sent you her love and says she'll pop in tomorrow, and I've got some lovely big eggs, a couple of their hens have just come on to lay early and she saved them specially for you. And our Lizzie's walked back with me to say hello. She heard from Alec today and he's—'

She pushed open the living-room door and walked in, then stopped short. Lizzie, still struggling with a boot, heard her gasp.

'*Dad!*'

'What is it, Auntie?' A cold dread gripped her and she jerked the boot off and left it where it fell. 'What's happened?'

'It's Dad,' Ruth whispered. 'Oh, *Lizzie* . . .'

Lizzie peered over her aunt's shoulder. Already half prepared for what she would see, the sight of her grandfather, lying on the floor with his neck twisted and his eyes rolled upwards, still came as a shock. She let out a little cry and tried to push into the room, but Ruth was there before her. She ran to kneel beside his body, laying her head to his chest and feeling for a pulse in his wrist. Lizzie, her own heart thudding, stared at her with frightened eyes.

'He's not dead? He's not, is he, Auntie?'

Ruth laid his hand gently on his breast. She looked at Lizzie and nodded, her eyes filling with tears.

'I knew it the minute I saw him. It must have been another stroke – only just after Mrs Perkins had been in, I should think. He's still warm, see. Oh, Dad . . .' She gazed down at him, her lips drawn in and her eyes and nose wrinkled with grief. 'Oh, *Dad* . . .'

'Poor Grandad,' Lizzie said softly. 'Poor, poor Grandad.'

They sat for a few moments, gazing at the old face that had been so familiar to them and so dear. He had been with them all their lives, first as a young, strong father, then as an ageing grandfather but still hale enough to do a good day's work, until the stroke had bound him to his chair. They would miss him dreadfully and so, they knew, would the whole village. Joe Sellers had known everyone and been everyone's friend. Bridge End would be a poorer place without him.

Ruth closed his eyes gently and looked in her purse for two pennies to lay on them. 'I'll have to go and tell the rector. And I suppose I should fetch the doctor in too, since Dad's been under him for the past few months. And there's our Jane, she's got to know, and we'll have to get the funeral arranged. There's a lot to see to . . .'

'And I'll see to it,' Lizzie said quietly. 'I'll go and see the rector and the doctor, and then I'll go home and fetch Mum and Dad. We'll all come down and be with you, and I'll stop the night too, if you want me. We can think about the funeral tomorrow. We'll all help, Auntie, you know that.'

Ruth nodded. 'I know, love. I know. You're a good girl and Jane's the best sister anyone could ever want. But there's one thing I do want to do myself. I'll lay him out.' Gently, as if she were still taking care not to hurt him, she straightened the twisted body. 'It's the last thing I can do for him, poor old soul.'

Lizzie pulled on her boots and scarf again and hurried out into the storm, knowing that for a little while Ruth wanted to be alone with her father. She could sit here beside him, in front of the fire Mrs Perkins had made up, and stroke the thin grey hair and look at the face she had known since she was a baby, and give him her thoughts and her prayers. Soon enough his colour would all have gone and his flesh would cool and harden. But for a little while it would be as if he were just asleep.

As she sat there, Ruth heard Silver scuffle and scratch in the kitchen. He'd be wanting his sunflower seeds, she thought, and was glad she still had one living being to look after. She stroked her father's head and bent to lay a soft farewell kiss on his forehead.

'*Poor* old Joe,' Silver said mournfully from the kitchen. '*Poor* old Joe ... You old bugger, you!'

Chapter Five

As Ruth had said, snow in Portsmouth was very different from in the country, its pristine whiteness quickly rimed with black from the soot of many fires and the dirt of passing vehicles. On the roads it turned to slush and the slush then froze into grubby ridges of ice. The pavements were death traps, and worse where the children turned them into polished slides.

A lot of Portsmouth children didn't go back to the country. There hadn't been any bombs and once they'd come home it didn't seem worth going through all that upheaval again. They roamed the streets, starting up snowball fights and terrorising passers-by. The schools, commandeered for first-aid posts or war offices, were barred to them and although a scheme had begun for holding classes in people's front rooms, it was difficult to pin down the pupils.

Micky Baxter, who had hardly ever gone to school even before the war started, now ignored it completely. With most of the other April Grove children away, he took to hanging about outside number 2, waiting for Sammy to come out to do the shopping, and fell into step with him, kicking his feet in the slush as they walked up October Street. 'What're you going for today?'

'I got to get a cabbage and some potatoes, and then ask Mr Hines for some mince. We're having shepherd's pie.'

'I don't mind shepherd's pie,' Micky said. 'We has that sometimes, with peas. I like the crunchy bits round the edges.'

Sammy said nothing. He and Gordon argued sometimes over those bits, until their father told them to shut up. Usually, Gordon got them but Nora would slip a few bits on to Sammy's plate if she could.

'I'm going down Charlotte Street in a bit,' Micky said, referring to the market street behind Commercial Road. 'I know a bloke there that gives me stuff free – cabbages and carrots, whatever's going. You could come too if you like.'

Sammy shook his head. Nora had told him several times not to go anywhere with Micky Baxter. She didn't like Gordon going with him either, even though Gordon was older, but Gordon didn't take any notice. 'I've got to go home with the meat and stuff.'

'Well, after that then. I'll wait for you.'

'I don't know.' Suddenly, Sammy longed to go. He was tired of having no one to play with and Micky carried an aura of excitement and danger with him. 'What about those gold necklaces? Do you get them down Charlotte Street?'

Micky gave him a sly glance. 'Why, d'you want one?'

'I wouldn't mind. I'd like to give Mum a gold necklace. You said you and Gordon could get some, Christmas Day, but you never.'

'No, well, the place wasn't open, see.' Micky looked consideringly at Sammy. 'Anyway, like I said, you're too little. You'd better tell your Gordon to come down my house when he gets home from work one day.'

'But *I* want to get one.' They were at the butcher's shop now and Sammy stared at Micky. 'Please. I want to give my mum a gold necklace.'

Micky looked at him again, narrowing his eyes. 'Well, maybe you could be useful. Being little – you could get into places—' He broke off abruptly. 'Tell you what. Go and get your meat and stuff, and I'll meet you in half an hour. We'll go down Charlotte Street and p'raps I'll show you the gold necklaces . . . But better not tell your mum, all right?'

Sammy nodded doubtfully. He didn't much like keeping

secrets from his mother, yet the thought that he was doing something secret to get her such a present as a gold necklace made him feel grown-up and powerful. He took his place at the end of the queue standing outside the butcher's shop, his heart thumping a little with excitement.

Mr Hines didn't have any mince and Sammy had to be satisfied with some neck of mutton. He came out and found Micky sitting on a wall, waiting for him.

'Here you are,' Micky said, 'here's your cabbage.' He thrust it at Sammy, together with half a dozen carrots. 'They didn't cost nothing, so we can use the money to buy sweets.'

Sammy stared at him. 'How'd you get them for nothing?'

Micky gave him a scornful glance. 'How d'you think? I went in and arsked, didn't I?' He burst out laughing at the expression on Sammy's face. 'Well, how d'you *think* I got them? Old man Atkinson wouldn't give his grandmother a free carrot, not if she was dying. I *pinched* 'em. It was easy – the shop was full of old women all doing their shopping and I just nipped in and grabbed what I could. I got some apples too.' He took one from his pocket and bit into it.

'But that's *stealing*,' Sammy said.

'So what? Don't tell me you never pinched nothing from a shop.'

Sammy opened his mouth to deny it, then remembered a day, several years ago, when he'd been in the paper shop with his mother and taken a small bar of chocolate from the counter. He hadn't even realised it was stealing at the time but Mr Brunner had noticed and snapped sharply at him to put it back, and his mother had been crosser than he'd ever known her. She'd marched him home and given him a good telling-off, ending up by saying he could go to prison for stealing, and for over a week he'd lived in fear of a policeman coming to take him away. He'd never taken anything since.

Micky was watching him, a sly grin on his face. 'See?

You can't. Anyway, your Gordon wouldn't be so bothered. Catch him passing up the chance of getting something for nothing.'

Sammy looked at him, then at at the cabbage in his hands. A slow realisation crept over him. 'The gold necklaces . . .'

'Well, what d'you think?' Micky threw away his apple core and jumped down from the wall. 'Well, are you coming or not? You'd better take that stuff home first. We'll use the money to go on the bus if it's too far for you to walk to Charlotte Street.'

Sammy looked at the cabbage again. He thought of giving his mother a gold necklace, imagining the pleasure and excitement in her face as she opened the box, and he longed to be able to give her that pleasure. Then he remembered the bar of chocolate in Mr Brunner's shop and the look on her face as she'd scolded him, and his own fear as he waited for a policeman to come, and he made up his mind.

He handed the cabbage back to Micky. 'I've got to do my mum's shopping. She wouldn't like me pinching stuff and Mrs Atkinson's her friend. I can't come with you.'

Micky's scorn deepened. 'You won't get no gold necklace, then. Your Gordon'll get her one, but *you* never won't – 'cause you're a scaredy-cat, that's what you are, a scaredy-cat and a baby!' He grabbed the vegetables and marched away. '*My* mum'll take 'em and be glad of 'em, *she* won't care where they come from. And I'll get her another necklace too. There's plenty of other kids'll come with me.' He turned to sneer at Sammy again. 'Baby! Cissy! Mummy's little darling! Yah!'

Sammy watched him go. He picked up his shopping bag and trailed off to the greengrocer's shop to join another queue. He felt miserable and despised, and the fact that he'd done what his mother would have wanted didn't seem to help at all. All he could think of was that he'd never be able to give her a gold necklace now. He would never be able to put that look of pleasure and delight on her face.

I thought being good was supposed to make you feel better, he thought as he finally reached the top of the queue and asked for a cabbage and a pound of carrots, none of them as good as the ones Micky had offered him. That's what they told us in Sunday School, and the man said it again in church when me and Mum went on Christmas Day. But it doesn't. It just makes you feel even more miserable. And Micky Baxter'll never want to play with me again.

Still, he thought a little more cheerfully as he trudged back down through the frozen slush of October Street, at least there won't be a policeman coming for me. And I won't have to go to prison . . .

Nora Hodges, weaker than ever, spent almost all her time in bed these days and only struggled downstairs in the evenings to get a meal ready for her husband. Sammy did his best to look after her, bringing her thick, uneven slices of bread spread with margarine and fish paste or jam, and cups of lukewarm tea. She tried to eat his offerings but as often as not he would creep upstairs again later to find the teacup still half full and a partly eaten sandwich on the plate. He took them down and finished them off himself by the cold grate, then cleared the ashes out of the fireplace and got the fire going for her to come down to. He still went round all the neighbours every day, asking for errands to run, but now that there were more children at home he found his trade falling off.

Sammy had only one shirt and one pair of flannel shorts, both thin and ragged, and an old woollen jersey several sizes too big which served as a jacket. It wasn't enough to keep out the bitter cold and one day Nora sent him out to get some brown paper. He spent a penny of his errand money to buy some from the rag and bone man; when he took it home, Nora tore it into the shape of a vest and sewed it round his thin chest to wear under the shirt. After that he felt a bit warmer but it wasn't the same as a good, thick coat.

Dan, who was working long hours at the Camber dock and often had to go to sea for a few days to attend to the engines of the cargo boats that used it, seemed to veer wildly between concern and impatience. He was exhausted by his job, panic-stricken by the war and bewildered by his wife's illness. He wanted to come home to a bright fire and a good meal, with a wife who was well and strong and would help him to forget, and the reality came as a constant and bitter disappointment. He did not admit, even to himself, how frightened he was by Nora's weakness. Instead, he took refuge, as he had learned to do years ago, in bad temper.

'What the hell do you ever *do* to get so tired?' he demanded when he came in from work, stamping the slushy snow from his boots, and found her lying in the chair. 'It's not bloody housework, that's for sure. The place hasn't been cleaned since we got here.'

'I just don't seem to have the strength . . .'

'Strength!' Dan echoed. 'What sort of strength d'you need to sweep the floor a bit and make a bloke a cup of tea? I've been working my flaming guts out all day down the docks *and* had to walk most of the way home in the blackout because it's snowing again and the bloody buses aren't running. I need a bit of comfort when I get home. And I need some grub too. What is it tonight, faggots and chips again?' He shrugged off his thick working jacket and hung it on the back door, then pulled off his cap and shook the snow off it in a shower of white. His thick black hair was greasy and needed cutting.

'I sent Sammy up the street for some rations but all he could get was a bit of scrag-end to make a stew with. Don't go on at him, Dan. There's just nothing in the shops.'

'Well, there bloody ought to be. We got ration books now, haven't we? It's all supposed to be shared out fair between everyone. There ought to be meat up the butcher's, and groceries and everything. If our Sam doesn't come back with something decent tomorrow I'll go up there myself and give that bugger Alf Hines what for. He's taking advantage, that's what it is. Knows you're not the ticket and he just palms all the old rubbish off on the nipper.'

'I don't think he does . . .' Nora began, but she was too weary to continue the argument. Dan wouldn't listen anyway. He'd gone out to the scullery to look at the stew, bubbling on the stove. At least she'd managed to put that together, with a few carrots and some swede and potatoes. Dan ought to know how difficult it was to get stuff now. The terrible weather meant that hardly any vegetables could be brought from the farms, even if they could get the stuff out of the ground, and there wasn't much arriving at the docks either. Even if there hadn't been any rationing, even if there hadn't been a war at all, it would still be difficult and she just felt too ill to go up the street herself.

Nora was beginning to think there was something really wrong with her. It wasn't just that she was so tired all the time – there'd been blood on her pillow that morning, although she hadn't cut herself, and when she changed her vest she'd noticed bruises on her body that she couldn't remember getting. I must have walked into the corner of the table, she thought, looking at the mauve stain on her thigh, but how could I have done that without realising it? And where did I get that other bruise, on my chest?

'Where's our Gordon?' she asked as Dan brought the saucepan in and set it on the table. Sammy had laid it before going upstairs, where he always went when Dan was due home. 'Didn't he ought to have come in with you?'

'Stopped on to do some overtime.' Dan peered into the saucepan. The stew smelled all right but looked thin and watery, and the meat was gristly and full of bone. 'Blimey, this looks like bloody dishwater. Can't you do no better than that, Nora?'

'I'm sorry, love.' Her eyes filled with tears. It had taken all her strength to scrub the carrots and chop up the swede. She'd cut her finger doing it too, and the blood had run for ages before it had stopped, making her feel really faint so that she'd had to sit down. 'I'd run out of browning for the gravy and Mr Sims didn't have no more. It'll taste all right.'

'It'd better.' He went to the doorway at the foot of the staircase and yelled loudly enough for the Vickerses, next door, to hear him. 'Sammy! Come down here, your supper's on the table. I dunno what that boy does with himself up there,' he grumbled, returning to the table. 'He ought to be down here, giving you a bit of company and a hand round the house.'

Nora wanted to tell him that Sammy did all he could manage and stayed with her almost until they heard Dan's key in the lock, but he would know then that the boy only scurried upstairs to keep out of his father's way and he'd be more annoyed than ever. Rows and arguments were more than Nora could cope with.

Sammy came slowly down the stairs and slid into the room. He looked at his father with anxious blue eyes and slipped into his chair at the table.

'Well?' Dan demanded. 'Got nothing to say for yourself, then? Cat got your tongue?'

Sammy shook his head, licked his lips and whispered. 'Hullo, Dad.'

'That's a bit better. Now eat your stew, your mum's been busy all day making that.'

He sat down at the head of the table and Nora heaved herself out of her chair and sat opposite him. She ladled stew out of the saucepan and the meat and vegetables lay on the plates in a greyish puddle. Dan attacked his straight away. Sammy picked out the fat and laid it on the edge of his plate.

'Now what's the matter with that?' his father demanded. 'That's good meat, that is. Build you up. No wonder you're such a miserable little runt if you won't eat your dinner. Come on, get it down you.'

Sammy looked at the fat and felt tears come to his eyes. 'I can't chew it.'

'Can't chew it? Of course you can chew it! Got teeth, haven't you? They oughter be sharper than mine, being so new. Get it down you and don't answer back.'

Sammy put a piece into his mouth. It felt like a lump of rubber. He turned it over and over in his mouth, but could make no impression.

Dan stared at him. 'Come on then, swallow. You must have chewed it enough now.'

'I *can't.*'

Dan leaned across the table, his black brows drawn heavily together. He fixed his eyes on Sammy's face.

'I *said*, swallow.'

Sammy gazed at his father. He made a huge effort and gulped the lump of rubbery fat down. It stuck in his throat and he began to choke.

'Oh, my Gawd!' Exasperated, Dan reached across and thumped his son hard between the shoulder blades. The fat shot out and Sammy, scarlet-faced, began to heave and retch. His father jerked him out of his seat and pushed him towards the door.

'There's no need to make yourself sick. You're just playing on it. Get outside, and when you've finished you'd better get back upstairs. No –' he changed his mind '– come back in here and finish your supper. Then you can do a bit of clearing up, help your mother.'

'Dan, don't—' Nora began, but her husband cut her off with a brusque movement of his hand.

'Keep out of this, Nora. Someone's got to discipline the

boy. Seems to me he's doing bugger-all to help you. Place is like a flipping dump. He might as well have been evacuated like the others.'

'You know I didn't want him to go.'

'You said you wanted him at home to help you. Well, he's not doing much of that, far as I can see.' Dan sat down again and attacked his meal once more. 'You not eating that?'

Nora was pushing her food half-heartedly around her plate. 'I dunno, I just don't feel very hungry. You have it, Dan, you've been working hard.'

'Too bloody true.' He wiped his plate clean with a lump of bread and took hers. 'I'll see that boy does the washing-up and then I'll go up the pub for a pint.'

He looked at Sammy as the boy sidled back into the room. 'And you needn't look as if you're frightened to come in. Sit down and get on with your supper, it's getting cold.'

Sammy looked despairingly at his plate. The thin gravy had congealed and when he pushed the surface with his fork it wrinkled. Large tears dripped on to it and he looked imploringly at his mother.

'It's all right, Sammy,' she said. 'You don't have to eat it. I know you don't like the fat—'

'*Doesn't like it*!' Dan roared, thumping the table with his fist. 'What the bleeding hell has *that* got to do with it? It's food, innit? It's all we bloody got. We got to eat it whether we like it or not.' He glared at his son. 'Don't you know there's a bleeding war on?'

'Dan, don't. He's only eight.'

'He's old enough to do as he's told. I had to eat what I was given when I was his age and think myself lucky to get it, never mind *liking* it. He don't know he's born, none of 'em do.' Dan pushed his plate away and leaned close to his son again. 'Listen, I've been working hard to get the money to buy you food and you'll bloody well eat it, see? I'm not

68

seeing good food go to waste. Now, get on with it and no more argument.'

Slowly, Sammy began to fork up the cold vegetables. Each mouthful made him want to retch again, but he dared not anger his father any more. He forced the food down, gulping the fat whole and wishing he dared pass it down to Tibby, and after a long time the plate was almost empty.

His mother took it away. 'That's enough. He's eaten nearly all of it, Dan. I did give him a big helping.'

Dan glowered but said no more. Nora nodded at Sammy. 'All right. You can get down now.'

Sammy slipped out of his chair and hesitated, looking at his mother.

'Clear the table, there's a good boy,' she said. 'Then you can help me wash up and afterwards you can sit by the fire and listen to the wireless for a bit.' She watched as Sammy gathered the plates together and took them out to the scullery, then she turned back to her husband. 'He shouldn't have had to eat all that, Dan. It's cruel, making him.'

'Cruel? I'm not cruel! I'm just trying to get some goodness into the boy, feed him up a bit. Can't you see he needs it, Nora? Can't you see he's not growing like he should? Look at our Gordon, always been a big, strong nipper and now he's nigh on as big as me. Trouble with Sam, you've always kept him tied to your apron strings, turned him into a sissy.' He looked into the fire and added more quietly, 'I'm not being cruel.'

Nora was too weary to argue. She lay back in her chair, wishing she didn't feel so tired all the time. It had been going on for months now and there were other things too – the way her body ached and the funny way things got blurred sometimes, as if her sight was going. She felt sick a lot of the time, too, and she didn't blame Sammy for not wanting his meal. It really wasn't very nice, specially when it got cold.

She thought of the old days, living over the pub in Old Portsmouth. It wasn't much of a place and they got all the rougher sailors and dock workers down there, but somehow, even in the worst times, during the Depression of the Thirties, her dad had managed to find something to laugh at. 'If we can't get the beer to sell, Eth,' he'd say to his wife, 'the customers can't run up a big slate, can they!' Not that he allowed many of them to run a slate anyway. You couldn't, in a place like Old Pompey.

'It's not that I want to keep on at the boy,' Dan said suddenly. 'I just want to see him grow a bit and get a bit more spark about him. He's going to be a *man*, Nora, and he's going to have to do a tough job, like me and Gordon. It won't do him no good to let him grow up frightened of his own shadow.'

It's his father's shadow he's frightened of, Nora thought. She looked at Dan's dark face and remembered what he'd been like as a boy, always been full of laughter and mischief. They'd grown up together in the streets around Spice Island, the bit of Old Portsmouth between the Camber and the entrance to the harbour where cargoes had come from all over the world, and spent hours scavenging round the beach at low tide to pick up driftwood or any other bits of flotsam and jetsam that came in. Some of it was only fit to be used as firewood but now and then you'd come across something that could be cleaned up and taken to the junk shop or the rag and bone man to sell for a few pence. She remembered Dan finding a really good belt once, that he'd got eightpence for. He'd shared it with her and she'd bought a bag of bacon cuttings, an onion and twopenn'orth of suet and taken it all home to her mother, and that night they'd had a meal she'd provided all herself.

She and Dan had always been together. Childhood sweethearts, they'd been called. But then he'd gone off to fight in the Great War and when he came home he was different. Quiet a lot of the time, but with a sudden, frightening temper she never remembered from before. They'd got married and she found that he had nightmares too, horrible ones that woke him up screaming, but he would never tell her what they were about. She just had to hold him in her arms until the shuddering stopped and the sweat gradually cooled.

Over the years the nightmares had grown less frequent but the temper had remained and you never knew quite what would set him off. Since there'd been all this talk of war he'd got worse and the other night he'd woken up shouting again. It was as if he was going back to those dark, secret days of the trenches.

'Sammy'll be all right,' she said now. 'He looks after me during the day, and does the shopping and goes round earning a bit of money doing errands as well. Don't keep on at him.'

Dan turned and looked at her, and she was startled by the look in his eyes, a look of sorrow and bewilderment that reminded her of the Dan who had come home from the war to touch her heart. 'I know, love,' he said. 'I know he does. But when I look at him – and when I look at you – well, I just wonder what's going to become of us all. I mean, if this war really gets going – and I has to go away again. I'm not too old, Nora. I'm under forty still. I got in under age last time because I told 'em I was older, but lies won't wash this time, they got all your records now. It's not Gordon I worry about, it's you, being poorly all the time, and our Sam, only knee-high to a grasshopper . . .' He shook his head, and the anger and frustration and despair came back into his face. 'And I can't bloody do nothing *about* it!' he exclaimed, thumping his fist on his knee. '*None* of us can do nothing about it. We're just – just caught up in it all, like rats in a bloody trap!'

Nora could find nothing to say. For a moment, she had been allowed a brief glimpse into her husband's frightened heart, but almost as soon as she saw it, the shutter came down and she was faced with his familiar anger again, and she understood that he would rather feel angry than frightened. Anger kept him in the present; fear took him back to the horrors he had known twenty years ago, horrors he could not bear to face again.

Sammy finished the washing-up and came uncertainly back into the room, and Dan put on his jacket and went off to the pub. Sammy sat down on the little wooden stool at her knee and rested his head against her.

'I'm sorry, Mum.'

'You done nothing wrong, love,' she said, laying her hand on his hair. 'You been a good boy. I know you can't eat the fat.'

'I'll try and get sausages tomorrow,' he said. 'Mr Hines said there might be some, if I got there early enough.'

Nora looked at him. Dan was right, she thought, he did look thin and small for his age, and he wasn't very clean either. He looked as if no one cared. But I do care, she thought, I do, it's just that I'm so tired. Perhaps I'm being selfish keeping him home when he could be out in the country, getting good food and fresh air.

'Would you rather go away with the other kiddies?' she asked. 'Would you rather be out at Bridge End? I dare say you could still go, if you wanted.'

She saw a series of thoughts pass across his face. He did *half* want to go, she thought. He missed the other kiddies, even if he didn't know them very well; there was no school now, and only Micky Baxter for him to play with, and anyway Micky'd been more Gordon's friend – for what good that had done them. But almost as soon as the longing had been there, it passed and he leant his head on her knee.

'I'd rather stay here, Mum. I'd rather help you.'

Poor little nipper, there wasn't much he could do. Nora was too tired out to bother much about the house, which had already been in a poor state when they'd moved in. She couldn't find the strength to brush the threadbare carpet every day, or wash the step like most of the other women in the street did. She knew they thought she was letting April Grove down – she'd seen the look on Annie Chapman's face one morning, as she went by on her way to see her sister, Jess Budd.

Well, you try it, she thought, you try being chucked out of the pub you've lived in all your life; you try sorting out all the stuff your mum and dad had before they died and haggling a price for it out of the rag and bone man; you try shifting the few bits you've got left on a handcart all the way up to Copnor because you couldn't find anywhere else to rent; you try coping with a boy like Gordon who was always into mischief and getting worse, and a man like Dan who was tormented by his own past . . . you try doing all that, when you've had four miscarriages, two of them in the past two years and feel like death warmed up, and *then* see if you still feel like whitening a doorstep or cleaning windows so the neighbours can see in easier!

She'd done her best, and Sammy did his best too, but he was only eight, for cripes' sake, you couldn't expect him to do much. And he was getting more and more scared of his father.

'I want you here,' she said to the little boy. 'But not if you'd be better off out in the country. If the bombs come . . .'

'I'd rather stay here with you and Tibby,' he repeated and she didn't urge him. I know I'm being selfish, she thought. If the bombs come he could be killed. We could all be killed. For herself, it didn't matter. It wasn't going to make any difference either way. But for little Sammy . . .

She tightened her fingers in his fair, matted curls. I can't let him go, she thought. I can't. If I do I might never see him again . . .

Gordon came in at about ten o'clock. He was looking excited and pleased with himself, and there was something under his coat. Nora, who would have gone to bed hours ago if he'd been home, roused herself from her chair to ask where he'd been.

'Working,' he said, and gave her a sly look. 'Didn't Dad tell you I was on overtime?'

'Yes, but I didn't think you'd be this late. Your stew's gone cold hours ago.'

'Don't want it,' he said carelessly, sliding towards the scullery door. 'Had a couple of pies down the dock.'

'What's that you've got under your coat?' she asked. 'You haven't been pinching again, I hope.'

'I was give it,' Gordon said in an injured voice. 'Bloke gave it me, down the dock, said he didn't want it no more.' He produced an object from under his jacket and Nora stared at it.

'That's a silver cup!'

'It's a goblet,' he said. 'That's what they call it, a goblet. I can get a good price for this in the junk shop.'

'Let me see it.' She held out a thin hand. 'That's not junk. That's new and it's real silver. You *have* been thieving.'

'I never! I told you, this bloke *give* it me. I done a bit of work for him, see – bit of extra. It's not down the dock, it's a shop. I do a bit of heavy work for him sometimes of an evening or in me dinner time. He give me this instead of money. Straight up, Mum.'

Nora stared at him. He was making it all up, she was sure. 'You've never mentioned this bloke before.'

'No, well, I didn't think you'd like me working extra hours. Look, what's it matter? We need the dosh, don't we? You're always saying that. I can get a good price for it and I was going to give you half, what about that?'

Nora wanted very much to believe him. She looked at the goblet again. 'Is that all you got? Or has he been "giving" you other things?'

Gordon shrugged. 'Bits and pieces. Coupla bits of silver,

few trinkets – rings and stuff like that.' He felt in his pockets, unable to resist the urge to show off, and dragged out a handful of jewellery.

Nora caught her breath. 'Gordon, I don't believe you! Nobody would give a boy things like this for a few hours' work. What have you been up to? Tell me!'

'I have told you –' he was beginning sulkily, when they heard Dan's key in the door. He stumbled in and glowered at them.

'Whass goin' on here?'

'It's Gordon—' Nora began, speaking at the same moment as her son but falling silent under his loud voice.

'It's our mum. She won't believe me. I told her, Dad, I told her I been doing jobs for a bloke on Spice Island and he give me these things 'stead of money, but she won't believe me, says I've been thieving.'

Dan stared at his son, then at the pile of gleaming rings and necklaces and the silver goblet on the table. He put out an unsteady hand and lifted them, letting a necklace pass through his fingers. He looked again at Gordon.

'She's bleeding right, too, ain't she? You *have* been thieving.' He advanced on his son and cuffed him sharply over the ear. 'You little sod! D'you want to get sent to prison?' He dealt another blow, which sent Gordon spinning across the room. He came up hard against the table and yelled out. Dan advanced again, his fist raised, but Nora caught his arm and, weak though her grip was, it was enough to make him pause for a moment. He glared at his son and subsided, glowering.

'Well, what if I have helped meself to a few things that were left lying about?' Gordon said sulkily. 'How else is people like us ever going to get anything decent? Seven and six a week, that's all I'm getting down the docks, and Mum has five bob for me keep. I want a motorbike. I'm saving up for it. There's a bloke I know got one he'll let me have for three quid. I could get that for this lot, easy.' He slid a glance at his mother. 'I could get enough to buy Christmas presents and all, better'n socks and gloves.'

'Not with stolen money, you won't!' Nora said sharply, surprising all three of them with the sudden strength in her voice. 'And you won't be buying no motorbike with it, neither. You'll take it all straight back, Gordon, first thing in the morning.'

He stared at her. 'Don't talk daft, Mum, I can't do that. They'd have me down the nick before you could say Jack Robinson.'

'They would, too,' Dan said, sitting down heavily. He seemed to have sobered up a bit. 'And you know what the magistrate said last time. It'll be an approved school for you. Or Borstal. That's prison, as good as, and you'll have it against your name for life.'

'Gordon, how could you be so blooming silly?' Nora asked. 'We might be hard up, but we've never had that sort of trouble in the family. I know my dad's pub was in a rough area, but we never got the wrong side of the law. I thought when we came to April Grove we were going to better ourselves a bit, but it just seems to have got worse.' She stared at the glittering heap on the table. 'It would kill me if either of you boys ever got sent to prison, it would straight, it'd *kill* me.'

'I'm not getting sent to prison. And it's the war that's making it worse, not me,' Gordon said truculently. 'Bloody rationing and restrictions. Blackout. Can't get this, can't do that. I tell you, I'm fed up with it already and it hasn't even started yet, not properly.'

'That's nothing to do with it. You're just taking advantage of the blackout to get up to mischief. Well, if you won't take these things back, I will.' Nora stared at them, her blue eyes almost black in her white face. 'Tell me where you got them.'

Dan gave her an irritated look. 'Don't talk stupid, Nora. You're not fit to go anywhere. And all you'd do is get the

76

police round here anyway. The boy's right, he can't take them back so we might as well get a bit of good out of them.' His eyes returned to the glittering heap on the table and he stretched out a hand.

'No!' Nora cried and tried to struggle out of her chair. 'No, I'll not have it! They got to go back. If you won't take them open and above board, then at least wrap 'em up and leave them in the doorway. You can do it on your way to work in the morning; nobody'll be about then. Just bundle them up in a bit of sacking. And make sure you put it all in, every bit. I won't have no stolen goods coming to this house.' She sank back, ashen-faced, struggling for breath. A harsh, wheezing sound came from her chest and she flailed an arm, her eyes suddenly frightened.

Dan left the table and flung himself to his knees beside her. 'Nora! Nora, what's the matter?' He threw his son a swift glance. 'Look what you done now, made your mother ill . . . Nora, what is it? Don't just stand there like a dummy, boy, get her some water . . . *Nora*!'

He stared at her, his hands moving uncertainly over her body. What did you do when someone couldn't breathe? Artificial respiration, as if they were drowning? But he didn't even know how to do that, not properly . . . Gordon shoved a cup of water under his nose and he took it and held it to her lips. They were almost blue, he noticed with alarm. '*Nora*!'

She managed a sip and drew a shuddering breath. The blueness began to fade, but her face was still as white as Annie Chapman's front step. She lay, breathing now but still very shallowly, and her eyes met his. Her eyelids flickered and her tongue moved tremulously over her lips. She's dying, he thought in panic and pulled her half out of her chair against him. *Don't die, Nora, don't die*. He put the cup to her mouth again, trying to ease the water through her shaking lips.

'I feel so queer,' she whispered. 'I feel—' She slumped

suddenly to one side, her eyelids flickering down over her eyes, so blue that they seemed transparent. Gordon and his father stared at her in dismay and then, hearing a sound behind them, turned to see Sammy standing in the doorway, his shirt unbuttoned, the brown paper vest showing underneath.

'I heard Mum shouting.' His eyes went past them to the slumped figure and he started forward in terror. 'What's the matter with her? What's the matter with my mum?' His voice rose to a shriek of fear. 'She's *dead*! You've *killed* her! *My mummy's dead*!'

Chapter Six

Joe Sellers's funeral was held amid deep snow. All the village was there, for he'd been a well-liked man and everyone had known him. He'd worked as a stockman on the farm where George worked now, and when he retired he'd helped out in busy times and done gardening jobs all over the village. You could always be sure of spotting him, trimming a hedge or clearing out a neglected garden, whenever you walked along the lanes.

Even after his stroke he'd still kept in touch with the neighbours by sitting at the window and lifting his good hand in a wave whenever anyone went past, and he'd insisted that Ruth kept up his tradition of carrying a few broken dog biscuits in one pocket and toffees in the other for distributing as appropriate when she went out.

Ruth, following the coffin into the church with Jane and George at her side and Lizzie and Ben just behind, felt her eyes brim over at the sight of the packed church. We'll miss him so much, she thought, kneeling in her pew. The whole village will miss him. But I'll miss him more than anyone else.

Even with Silver to keep her company, the cottage was going to seem emptier than it had ever done before.

While most of the village was at the funeral, the evacuee children were left to their own devices. With the village children at school that afternoon, they were free to roam unmolested and Tim and Keith set out into the snow-covered fields, feeling like birds let out of cages. They met Brian Collins in the lane and stood discussing what to do.

'I'm Scott of the Antarctic,' Tim Budd announced. He had brought Moss, the Corners' sheepdog, with him, a bit of washing line tied to his collar. 'I've got a husky dog with me and a sledge –' he brandished Edna Corner's tin tea tray '– and we're going to the South Pole.'

'Well, you can go on your own, then,' Brian Collins said. 'He never come back, did he? Died of cold.'

'*I* shan't,' Tim said, only momentarily disconcerted by this fact, which he had forgotten. 'I'll find the South Pole and come back and be the winner. Let's have an expedition.'

Moss, who wasn't used to being on a lead, barked suddenly and Keith looked at him.

'He shouldn't be barking like that. He's supposed to be husky, isn't he?'

'It's not that sort of husky, dopy,' Brian said scornfully. 'It's the name for dogs that pull sledges. Anyway, expeditions are boring. I think we ought to have a snowball fight.'

'We did that yesterday.' Tim was determined to remain in charge. 'We won't be able to have Moss again because Mr Corner has him on the farm. I've only got him today because he's at the funeral. And we can't go to the South Pole without a husky, so this is our only chance.'

'Well, where is this South Pole, then?'

'It's Mrs Corner's washing pole,' Tim decided. 'We'll tie Moss to the tray and go through the woods and over Top Field. That'll be far enough. Keith can ride on the tray, 'cause he's smallest, and I'll drive and shout "Mush".'

Brian looked grumpy. He and Tim always vied to be in charge and now he could see his chance of leadership slipping away from him. He cast about for a better idea.

'I wanted to go and watch the funeral. I've never seen a dead body being buried before.'

The others, already starting to tie Moss' lead to the tray, stopped and looked at him. Keith saw an expression of longing on his brother's face, mixed with jealousy that Brian Collins should have thought of it. He hesitated, glancing at the tray and Moss, waiting to become a husky.

'We'll never get the chance to see a funeral again,' Brian said cunningly.

Tim bit his lip, then made up his mind. 'Tell you what. Mr Sellers can be Scott and we're the rescue party, going to find him, only we're too late. That's what really happened. And they had to take huskies and sledges and things, so we can still use Mossy. And we'll still go over Top Field because it goes right down to the churchyard and they'll all be in church singing.'

'I want to look in the grave,' Brian said. 'I saw old man Barford digging it yesterday but he chased me off.'

'It was ever so hard to dig,' Keith chimed in. 'Mr Corner was talking about it and he said the ground was so frozen Mr Barford couldn't get his spade in. They thought they were going to have to keep Mr Sellers till it got a bit warmer.'

'But he'd have gone bad,' Tim said. 'Like that dead fox we found in the ditch. I bet he'd have smelt horrible, too.'

'Well, they got it dug anyway,' Brian said, 'and I want to see it before they put Mr Sellers in.'

They decided that there would just be time to do this if they set off quickly enough, and finished tying Moss to the tray. Keith sat on it and Tim shouted 'Mush', startling the dog so much that he leapt into the air and began to run in circles, frightened by the tray which clattered after him. The washing line got tangled round his legs and Keith fell into the snow and scratched his arm on a hidden branch. He yelped almost as loudly as Moss, who began to lick his face, tangling the line further as he did so.

'He thought I was shouting his name,' Tim said, convulsed with giggles as he tried to unwind the rope.

'Stand *still*, Moss, while I get it off your legs. And stop yelling, Keith, you're not hurt. It's only a scratch ... I don't think we'll bother with a sledge. We'll be an advanced party. But we'll still have to take the husky, of course.'

Once again they set off, with Moss now freed from his bonds and trotting beside them. He knew the boys well now and was especially attached to Tim. They plunged into the little wood where Tim and Keith had collected nuts and mushrooms with Reg Corner, and climbed the hill to Top Field. From here, they could see down into the churchyard.

'They're all inside the church,' Brian said. 'The funeral's at two.'

'It's five past,' Tim said, screwing up his eyes to look at the church clock. 'We've just got time to get down and look at the grave. How long do funerals take?'

'Oh, about two hours, I think,' Brian said. 'Mr Knight said they'd be back by four, for milking. They'll be in there for ages, singing hymns and praying. You have to do that or the person goes to hell.'

'Mr Sellers wouldn't go to hell,' Tim argued. 'Mrs Corner says he was the nicest man you could ever wish to meet and he always had dog biscuits in his pockets. Sweets, too, sometimes.'

'Just because he liked dog biscuits—'

'He didn't eat them himself, stupid. He gave them to dogs. It just shows what a nice man he was, that's all.' Tim was growing tired of the argument. 'Anyway, are we going to go and look or not? I'm getting cold.' He dragged the tin tray into position at the top of the slope. 'I'm going to toboggan down.'

'That's not fair –' Keith began, but Tim was already careering down the hill, yelling at the top of his voice, with Moss racing beside him barking wildly. The other two followed, Keith still grumbling because he'd been the one to carry the tray all the way from the farm, and Brian scowling because he hadn't thought of bringing one himself. At the bottom of the slope the tray hit a stone and tipped Tim sideways into the ditch, where he lay, rubbing his head and trying to stop Moss licking his face.

'Serves you right,' Brian said unsympathetically. 'Come on, we can climb over the wall here, where it's a bit broken down, see.'

'I bet I'll have a bump as big as an egg,' Tim said to Keith, but the smaller boy shrugged and turned away. They followed Brian into the churchyard and across the snow-covered hummocks to the newly dug grave, and stood looking down into it. From inside the church came the sound of muted singing, and the doleful tones of the organ.

'It's a bit creepy, isn't it?' Keith murmured, moving a little closer to Tim. 'I mean, there's going to be a dead body down there soon.'

'There's dead bodies all over the place in here, you twerp,' Brian said, a little over-loudly. He glanced around at the headstones, as grey as the clouds that loomed above. 'Tell you what, they look a bit like dead bodies themselves, don't they? All wrapped up in shrouds, waiting to jump on you . . .' He raised his arms, bending his hands forwards in imitation of a ghost, and began to moan. 'Ooh-ooh . . . I'm coming to get you . . . Oooh-ooooh . . .'

Keith shrieked and stumbled backwards. Tim shouted out in alarm, and Moss barked and cavorted around them as Keith, with an even louder shriek, lost his balance and toppled into the grave. Tim stared in horror, then grabbed Moss and smacked his nose to stop him barking. Brian let out a guffaw of nervous laughter and the two boys peered down, half expecting to see Keith's dead body lying at the bottom of the hole.

'You all right, Keith?' Tim asked anxiously after a moment.

To his relief, Keith's voice replied, sounding more cross and frightened than hurt. 'No, I'm not! I'm at the bottom of a grave and it's miles deep and they're going to put Mr

Sellers in here soon, on top of me . . . Get me out, Tim, get me *out*!'

His voice rose in panic and Tim looked around helplessly. The grave was at least six feet deep, its sides hard and slippery with ice, and Keith's face was like a pale, scared moon staring up at them. He had no idea how they were to get Keith out, and the thought of his still being there when the coffin was carried out of the church made him feel dizzy with fear. Reg and Edna won't want us any more, he thought. We'll be sent back home, and Dad will go mad. He'll *kill* us. And then, because his sense of humour always came to the surface at the worst possible moments, we might as well stop here in the grave anyway . . .

'We need a ladder,' Brian Collins said, jerking him out of his stupor. 'There's one in old Barford's shed, I saw it one day. Come on, before they come out of church.'

'Don't leave me here by myself!' Keith shrieked as they turned to go. 'It's horrible! I might get buried alive! *Tim*!'

'I'll have to go. Brian can't carry the ladder by himself. I'll leave Mossy here on guard. Stay,' Tim ordered the dog, but Moss didn't have the respect for Tim that he had for Reg Corner and bounced after him, ignoring Keith's frantic cries. He leapt about the two boys, barking joyously and getting under their feet as they ran over to the shed in the corner of the graveyard, and Brian cast an anxious glance towards the church.

'Can't you shut that dog up? Someone'll be out in a minute.'

'Quiet!' Tim hissed, but Moss ignored him. As far as he was concerned, Tim and Keith were no more than puppies and this was a holiday afternoon full of fun and games. He was thoroughly enjoying himself, and when a dog was enjoying himself he just had to bark.

To their relief the shed door was unlocked and they found the ladder, lying along one side. They dragged it out and back across the graveyard to where Keith was in tears, convinced that they had abandoned him to be buried alive. As soon as the ladder was lowered into the hole he scrambled out, muddy and tear-stained, and got as far away as he could from the rim.

'I'm never going to be buried, never. It was horrible down there.'

'You'll have to be, when you're dead. Unless you want to be cremulated.' Brian and Tim began to haul the ladder back out of the hole. 'Come on, we've got to get this back in the shed before anyone comes out.'

'What's cremulated?' Keith, determined not to get near the grave again, made no move to help them.

'Burnt,' Brian said tersely. 'My grandad had it done. They put you in a big sort of furnace and set light—'

'No! No!' Keith screamed and put his hands over his ears. 'Stop it! It's not true, you're making it up. I don't want to be cren—cren—'

The sound of the organ's playing sounded suddenly louder and Tim glanced across at the church. '*They're coming out*!' Panic-stricken, he dragged at the ladder and it jerked up out of the hole. 'Come on, we've got to get this back before they see us! Come *on*, Keith! Oh, I wish we'd never done this – I wish we'd gone to the South Pole instead, like I wanted to – I wish . . .' Half sobbing, the three of them stumbled across the graveyard, with Moss repeating his delighted performance and the ladder catching on the headstones so that they tripped and fell. Tim looked back again and gave a sob of terror. 'The vicar's coming out! I can see the coffin! Oh – oh – *oh*!'

'Leave it here,' Brian commanded. 'They won't see it on the ground. Let's just get away – we'll go round behind the church, we can get out that way – nobody'll ever know it was us. Come on!'

Tim grabbed Keith and they scuttled out of sight just in time, as the mourners came solemnly out after the coffin.

Behind the church they stopped, clutching each other and breathing hard. Keith was still crying.

'I don't want ever to come here again. It's all your fault, Brian Collins, pretending to be a ghost. Tim, I want to go home.'

'It's all right. They didn't see us and you're not hurt, and Brian's not a ghost, he's just a stupid twerp.' Tim and Brian had never liked each other and this was the sort of talk that usually ended in a scrap, but for once Brian didn't rise to the bait. Instead, he gave Tim a sly look.

'What did you do with that old tray? Did you leave it in the field?'

Tim stared at him. He glanced around, as if expecting to see the tray come round the corner of the church by itself. Moss, panting but still joyous, leant against him. Briefly, he considered sending the dog to retrieve the tray and immediately rejected the idea.

'I must have dropped it by the grave.' He stared at the other two, the picture of dejection. 'They'll know it was us now.'

Brian grinned evilly. 'They'll know it was *you*,' he pointed out. 'It wasn't *my* tray.' He began to walk off, swaggering a little and pretending to whistle. 'Wouldn't be in your shoes when they finds out. And it won't be no use sneaking on me, see – I'm too much use round the farm. *I* won't get sent back to Pompey!'

Left alone, Tim and Keith looked at each other miserably.

'Well, we can't go and get it now,' Tim said. 'We'd better go back home. Maybe we could start the milking or something, to get Reg in a good mood.'

'I don't care what happens,' Keith said, still sniffing. 'Just as long as I don't have to go and fetch the tray. I tell you, Tim, I'm never going near a grave again – not as long as I live!'

*

'He'll be sorely missed,' Joan Greenberry told Ruth as they walked slowly away from the graveside. 'They don't make many like that any more, you know.'

'That they don't,' agreed Mr Knight, the farmer Joe had worked for, coming up on her other side. 'Reckon they broke the mould when old Joe was born. Mind you, your brother-in-law doesn't do a bad job,' he added with a small wink as George Travers came to take his sister-in-law's arm. 'And young Terry, too – chip off the old block, he is.'

Ruth sighed. Terry was away now doing his basic training and it didn't look as if Ben was going to be a farmer. She looked at him, walking beside his mother, very tall and slender in his dark suit. He'd taken the day off school for his grandfather's funeral but he'd be back on the Southampton bus next day, his satchel bulging with books. Sometimes Ruth thought he overdid his studying. You hardly ever saw him round the village with the other lads now.

Once this war was over, she hoped that Lizzie and her Alec would be able to settle down properly and raise a family, so that there might be more sons to follow on in the farming life.

'Whatever was all that noise in the churchyard?' Jane asked. 'It sounded like a riot – people yelling and screaming, dogs barking. And the snow was all trampled too – heaven knows what was going on out there.'

'It was some of those evacuee children, I'll be bound,' Aggie White said. 'Ours are all at school – anyway, they'd have more respect. Shouting and yelling round a church-yard when a funeral's on – or any time, come to that. For two pins I'd tell the policeman, if we knew who it was.'

Edna Corner heard her and looked guiltily at the tin tray she'd picked up not far from the grave. It was hers, she knew it by the picture of a bowl of roses and the dent in one corner, but how it had got into the churchyard was a mystery – a mystery she felt could probably be solved by

Tim and Keith. And that had sounded very much like Mossy's bark she'd heard, too.

I'll find out what they were up to, she thought, but whatever it was I don't believe it was lack of respect.

'Will you come back to the house for a glass of sherry or a cup of tea?' Ruth asked the vicar. 'I've made a bit of fruit cake – not that there's much fruit about these days, but people have been ever so kind letting me have some of their own rations and one or two have brought some leftover Christmas cake – and there's a cut of ham off the joint Mr Knight sent round. Joe would have liked to know you'd be there.'

'I'll be very pleased to, thank you, Mrs Purslow,' Mr Beckett said. 'I want to pay my respects in the proper way.' He smiled down at her. He was tall and thin, with long arms and legs like a stick insect. 'It's time I had a word with that parrot of yours, too. I suppose he's still got plenty to say for himself?'

'Too much,' Ruth said wryly. 'He's even learnt a few of the words Dad's been coming out with lately.' She dabbed her eyes with her handkerchief. 'Things that didn't make any real sense, you know. I suppose I ought to be used to it, but it seems really queer, hearing him say Dad's words. And he's got the voice off to a T. Sometimes I really think it's Dad himself, and then – then I remember.' Her voice shook a little and she wiped her eyes again. 'I'm sorry – it just comes over me at times.'

'Of course it does,' Joan Greenberry said. 'You were with your dad a long time. You're bound to feel it.'

They reached the cottage and went indoors. Lizzie had come round to help her aunt tidy the cottage and set out the sliced ham, with some pickles and chutneys made from Joe's own onions and tomatoes, some bread freshly baked in Jane's Rayburn, and the fruit cake. Glasses of sherry were ready for the mourners, who stood at the door stamping the snow from their boots and pulling off their gloves. Lizzie, her eyes red, took their coats and Ruth went out to the kitchen to put the kettle on.

'Come in, come in!' her voice cried impatiently. 'Born in a field?' And then, in a rougher tone, 'You old bugger, you!'

If it hadn't been for the change in tone from Ruth's to that of the unknown sailor who had presumably been a shipmate of Jack Purslow's, they would have thought it was Ruth herself chiding them. But Silver's raucous cackle gave the game away completely, and they looked at each other and laughed.

'That bird!' Ruth exclaimed, popping her head through the door in embarrassment. 'He'll be the death of me yet!' She stopped, her hand at her mouth, hardly knowing whether to laugh or cry. She looked apologetically at the vicar. 'I'm ever so sorry. I'll put his cover on.'

'Don't do that, Mrs Purslow,' Mr Beckett begged. 'It'll do us good to hear him jabbering away. And he's right, too. Get that door shut, George, before we let all the heat out. Now, did someone say something about a glass of sherry? Just what we need to keep the cold out on an afternoon like this. Oh, and what a nice fire you've got going.' He shrugged out of the long black overcoat and stood in his cassock, stooping his long thin body to come through the door into the living room.

There were only a dozen or so of the throng who had attended the funeral, but they were enough to fill the tiny room. They found seats or stood about, holding plates of ham and pickle, and reminiscing about Joe and, inevitably, their talk turned to the war. Most conversations did end up that way these days.

'Dad was in the first lot, of course,' George remarked. 'Looked after the horses, he did, pulling the gun carriages. He was a wheelwright too, that's how he come to be so good with the farm carts. He never talked much about it, though.'

'They didn't, none of them,' said Ruth's friend Joyce

Moore, who lived along the lane. 'Just wanted to get home and forget it, if you ask me. My uncle was the same. Mind you, he was never the same man after he come back, so my mum told me. Quiet as a mouse most of the time, then used to fly into terrible tempers, all over nothing. Shell-shock, it was called.'

'What d'you reckon's going to happen in this lot, Mr Knight?' Joan Greenberry asked the farmer. 'It all seems pretty quiet so far, apart from all the rationing coming in and the evacuees being sent out to the countryside. I mean, there's been hardly any fighting.'

'Well, I don't know what you think's been going on at sea, then!' Lizzie said sharply. 'There's been plenty of ships sunk. My Alec says the Germans are following the convoys all the time, trying to get close enough to torpedo them, and there's been any amount lost. People don't think of that until they can't get the rations and even then they just blame the government.' She felt the tears come to her eyes again and turned away, angry with herself for being so sharp. 'Sorry, but it gets my goat when people forget that.'

Jane Travers moved to her daughter and put an anxious hand on her arm, and Mrs Greenberry bit her lip. 'I'm sorry, Lizzie, I spoke without thinking. Of course we're all worried about the boys at sea and we know how brave they are. It must be worst of all for chaps like your Alec, not even armed.'

'Well, they're not trained to fight, are they,' Lizzie said, only partly mollified. 'They never joined the Merchant Service for that. They're just sitting ducks.'

There was a short, embarrassed silence. Then Ruth said, 'I suppose if my Jack was still alive I'd be saying the same. But it seems to me it doesn't matter what the men are involved in, it's just as bad. And if the bombing starts . . .'

'The bombing's not coming here,' Mr Beckett said firmly. 'And our job in the country is to produce as much food as we possibly can, so that men like Alec don't have to take more risks than are absolutely essential, and to look after the children we've been entrusted with.' He turned to Edna Corner. 'How are you getting along with your two little lads?'

'Oh, Tim and Keith are smashing little chaps. Settled in as good as gold, though they're a lively pair. But they like helping Reg on the farm and they're interested in everything. You should hear some of the questions they ask! We're hard put to it to give them the answers sometimes.' She glanced doubtfully towards the corner where she'd put the tin tray and thought there were one or two questions she'd like answered too, as soon as she got home.

'Mrs Budd says they've always been an active pair,' Joan Greenberry said. 'She's a nice little body too, and so's young Rose. We've been lucky getting that family – specially when you look at some of the others.'

There was a general murmur of agreement and they began to talk about the other evacuees – Brian Collins, who was big for his age and strutted about trying to bully the village boys, and little Martin Baker who had run away. And there were the Atkinson children, who had been put with the Woddis sisters and were hardly ever seen playing with the others.

'I don't know about them, I'm sure,' Joyce said. 'It hardly seems right, two maiden ladies like that suddenly having kiddies to look after. I mean, what do they know about children? That little Wendy, she looks like a worried little old woman sometimes, and Alan doesn't have a word to say for himself.' She sighed. 'I'd have taken them in myself if I hadn't already had four of my own.'

'They're probably just shy,' the vicar said. 'But I'll call round and see them one day soon.' He set his sherry glass on the table and bent his long thin back to go through the doorway again. 'I must be going now, Mrs Purslow. Thank you again for the sherry. Now, you will let me know if there's anything you need, won't you, and I'll call in again soon for a chat.' He put his hand on her shoulder for a moment and smiled down at her. 'You did everything possible for your father,' he said, 'and you looked after him well. He wouldn't have wanted you to mourn for too long, you know.'

Ruth smiled back, but her eyes were full of tears and she could find nothing to say. The same did not, however, apply to Silver. When the vicar went out to the kitchen to give him a crumb of fruit cake, they heard his voice again.

'You thieving blighter,' he said disgustedly. 'You old bugger, you.' And then, in the quavering voice of an old man, 'Chubbleduck . . .'

They were all gone at last, except for Jane and Lizzie who had stayed to help clear up. They washed up and put away all the crockery and glasses, and then came back into the living room where the fire was just glowing. Ruth put on a couple of logs and stirred it into life.

Lizzie was carrying a tray of tea and she set it down on a small table. 'At least Silver can come back in here now,' she remarked. 'I must say, it did seem queer without him. He's been in this room as long as I remember.' She bit her lip, thinking of her grandfather who would never sit here again. I'm going to miss him so much, she thought. It's like a hole being torn out of my life.

'I'll bring him in tomorrow,' Ruth said. 'I'll keep the room as it is for tonight. It seems a bit like pushing Dad out to change things too quick.'

They sat for a while sipping their tea and gazing into the fire. Outside, it had begun to snow again and the flakes danced and fell softly against the window-panes. It was one of the coldest winters anyone could remember, with some of the lanes filled to the tops of the hedges with snow and the ground so frozen that poor old Bert Barford, the gravedigger, had had to use a pick and shovel to dig Joe's grave. It reminded him, he'd said, of his old grandad's tales about Dartmoor, where he'd grown up. Bodies had to be taken miles for proper burial and they'd had to be kept for months sometimes, before the journey could be made. 'Didn't smell, though, 'em didn't,' he'd added reflectively. 'Cold kept 'em nice and fresh, see.'

'Well, we're not keeping my dad till spring comes,' Ruth had told him tartly, 'so you just stop leaning on that shovel and get on and dig him a proper grave at the proper depth, as is fitting.'

'What will you do now, Auntie Ruth?' Lizzie asked after a while. 'You'll be lonely with just Silver to keep you company.'

Ruth laughed a little. 'I'll never be lonely with that old rapscallion! It's like having a whole crowd of people in here when he gets going in all his different voices. But you're right, he's not like proper human company. It won't be the same without Dad.' She sighed. 'I'd like to bring Jack's parents out from Southampton, but they won't budge from their own home.'

Lizzie thought that even Grandad hadn't been what you'd call *proper* human company just lately, what with never being able to find the right words, but she didn't say so. Auntie Ruth had always insisted his mind was all right, it was just his tongue that had the problems, and once you'd learned what his words meant you could have a sensible conversation with him. What made it difficult was that they were liable to change, so you were kept forever on the hop. And he'd always had a smile on his face and kept his interest in the village.

'I'll miss Grandad too,' she said softly. 'He was a sweet old man. I remember when I was little and he used to let me plant beans in the garden. He always gave me one to grow in a jam jar, so that I could see the roots. And I remember when that swarm of bees settled in the school playground and he came to fetch them away. We were all scared stiff but he just walked up and scooped them into his basket, and they went like lambs. I felt really proud of him.'

'It was a good funeral,' Jane said. 'You could see how well liked he was. The church was full right up. I thought with the weather being so bad not many would have managed it, but they all got there somehow.' She finished her tea. 'Well, I must get back. George will be getting on with the milking and wanting his supper when he comes in. You coming, Lizzie?'

'I'll sit here a bit longer,' Lizzie said. It didn't seem right, leaving Auntie Ruth all by herself. It would have to happen soon, of course, but only half an hour or so ago the cottage had been full of people and it was going to seem very empty when they'd all gone. She poured another cup of tea for them both and sat back in the armchair.

'When d'you expect Alec home again?' Ruth asked. 'He's been away getting on for six months now.'

Lizzie shrugged. Her mouth turned down despondently. 'Haven't a clue. The convoys are dodging about all over the place, trying to shake off the Germans and half the time they don't even know which port they'll be docking at. If they get low on fuel they just have to put in anywhere that can take them. It's chaos.'

'It must be. But he'll be home soon, surely. You were expecting him for Christmas.'

'I know. I just hope it won't be too long.' Lizzie looked at her aunt. There was a special bond between them, both having been married to merchant seamen, and sometimes Lizzie thought Ruth was the only person who really understood. Other women had husbands who were either already in the Forces or expecting to be called up, and seemed to think the Merchant Navy had it easy, not having to fight. But that didn't mean you couldn't be attacked. And that was on top of all the usual dangers to be faced at sea.

'This weather doesn't help,' she said. 'Imagine what it

must be like out there, Auntie. Blizzards and huge waves, and everything covered in ice, and it's not as if the ships had any comfort. I wish he'd give it up and get a shore job, I really do.'

'I know. I used to think the same. But once the sea gets into a man's blood . . . well, you just can't fight it. He'll tire of it in the end and be glad to settle down.'

'If he's not killed first,' Lizzie said bitterly. She got up suddenly and loaded the tea things on to the tray. 'I'll just wash these up for you and then I'd better get back. There's another three inches of snow come down while I've been sitting here.'

She went out into the kitchen. As soon as he saw her, Silver began to shift from foot to foot on his perch, tilting his head to one side and looking hopeful. She grinned at him and scratched his neck.

'You're an old scoundrel, you are. I suppose you want something nice to eat.' His bowl of sunflower seeds was on the table and she put two or three in the little bowl fixed to his perch. He winked at her and picked one up delicately in his big grey beak.

'Humpty-Dumpty sat on the wall,' he said conversationally. 'Who pushed him in? You old bugger, you.'

'You old scallywag, you,' Lizzie said, unable to help smiling. No wonder Auntie Ruth said she would never be lonely with Silver for company.

'Splice the mainbrace,' he suggested in a gravelly voice. 'Sippers or gulpers. I love you, my darling. Let me be your sweetheart.'

'He sounds more like my Jack every day,' Ruth said, coming out to the kitchen and regarding him with affection. 'That's what Jack wanted, you see. He taught him all those things so that when he was away it would be like him talking to me. Trouble was, he learnt a lot of other things too, while they were on their way home from the Far East!'

Lizzie giggled. Some of the things that Silver had

learned had brought a blush to her mother's face and caused her father to threaten not to allow Lizzie, Terry and Ben to visit their aunt if the bird's language couldn't be moderated. But Auntie Ruth had taken no notice. Parrots always swore, she said, it was part of their nature, and the children didn't have to repeat what they heard. They wouldn't even have known the words were bad if George hadn't pointed it out.

'No,' he said, 'they'd just go out and use them in the street or at school, and it'd be me that'd get the blame.' And, giving his son and daughter a severe look, 'Just don't repeat *anything* that bird says, you understand? Then there won't be any risk of you saying something you shouldn't.'

The result was that for years Lizzie and Ben had been under the impression that expressions such as 'splice the mainbrace' and 'sippers or gulpers' were some of the rudest swear words in the language, and only repeated them in whispers in the corner of the playground. Even later, when they realised that 'splice the mainbrace' merely meant serving out an extra rum ration and 'sippers or gulpers' referred to the way you drank it, the family continued to use them as a joke; so that when she dropped her mother's milk jug or Ben stubbed his toe on the fender they exclaimed, 'Oh, sippers and *gulpers*!' and when surprised by something they would remark, 'Splice the mainbrace, is that really true?'

When Jack had died a few years ago, of malaria, Jane had wondered if her sister would be upset to hear his voice repeated in the parrot's croaking tones, but Ruth had continued to find it a comfort. It wasn't any different from someone having a recording of their husband's voice, she said, except that Silver was alive and well, and looked like keeping her company for a good many years yet.

'Parrots can live till they're a hundred years old. He'll see me out, the old rascal.'

'I wish I had something like Silver to keep me company

while Alec's away,' Lizzie said. 'So that I could go on hearing his voice, like you can hear Uncle Jack's. I'm sure it'd help.'

'What you want is a baby, not a parrot,' Ruth told her. 'And when your man comes home you ought to do something about it. Don't leave it too long, like Jack and me.'

Lizzie looked at her. 'I know. I keep thinking about it. But – it seems such an awful world to bring a baby into. Suppose we get invaded. You hear such terrible things about the Germans. I couldn't bear to see my baby hurt, or killed. Dotty Dewar told me the other day that they *eat* babies. It doesn't bear thinking about.'

'And I don't suppose it's true either,' Ruth said. 'I wouldn't believe anything Dotty Dewar told me. I know we don't have any time for Hitler and the Nazis, but most of the Germans are ordinary Christian people, same as us. I don't believe they'd do anything like that.'

'Yes, but it's the Nazis who are in charge now, isn't it, and look what they've been doing to the Jews. Making them live behind brick walls and wear yellow stars on their sleeves, and taking all their money away and everything. They've been treating them like animals.'

'Well, there's lots of people don't like the Jews,' Ruth said. 'Mind, I've nothing against them myself, but I know there are plenty who think they ought to go back to their own place. That's the trouble, you see, they've spread all over the world and they seem to make money wherever they go. It's bound to cause trouble.'

Lizzie stared at her. 'But that's just jealousy! If everyone worked as hard as Jews do, they could all make the same money. And they can't go back to their own place – they haven't got one.'

'Well, I don't know,' Ruth said. 'I don't know what the rights or wrongs of it are. *Why* haven't they got their own country? I've never understood it all. All I know is wherever there's Jews there's trouble, and it can't always be everyone else's fault.'

They seemed to have strayed a long way from parrots and babies, and Lizzie decided it was better to leave it there. She went out into the tiny hallway and wrapped her long scarf round her neck, pulled on her hat and shrugged into her coat. She gave her aunt a kiss on the cheek.

'Don't you get cold, now,' Ruth said. 'We don't want you going down with your chest.'

'I'm warm as toast. And these mittens you knitted me are lovely and cosy.' Lizzie held her hands up like woolly red paws. 'I've got my old gloves on underneath them too. Now, are you sure you're going to be all right, Auntie? You could always come and stop with us for a few days, you know, Mum told you that. You could have Ben's bed, he could sleep downstairs on the settee – he wouldn't mind.'

'Thanks, but I'd rather be here with my own things. And I've got plenty of clearing out to do – that back bedroom's cluttered up almost to the ceiling with all Dad's old junk. I used to tell him he must have been a magpie once, but he always reckoned it would come in useful some day. Well, so it might, but it'll be someone else getting the use of it, because I'm clearing out the lot. There's stuff in there going back years.'

'Well, you don't need to do it all on your own,' Lizzie told her. 'I'll come and give you a hand. Now don't you stand on the doorstep letting in all the cold.' She gave her aunt another kiss. 'I'll see you tomorrow and I dare say Mum'll come along too. Night-night.'

She slipped out into the darkness and was lost instantly in a whirl of snowflakes. Ruth watched for a few seconds, then closed the door quickly. It was impossible to believe that there might be a German plane above them now, looking for a light to show it where to bomb, but the blackout was law and you had to keep to it. She went back into the living room and made up the fire again, then stood for a moment or two, irresolute.

'I think I'll bring that blessed bird back in here now after all,' she said to herself. 'It does seem ever so quiet, now that everyone's gone.'

She went out into the kitchen and fetched the perch with Silver clinging to it, then went back for the big domed cage. She set both down in their accustomed places and she and the bird looked at each other.

'Well, that's it, then,' she said with a sigh. 'Just you and me again. Back to the way it's always been.'

'Two for tea,' the parrot said cheerfully. 'You old blighter, you.' He cocked his head to one side and winked his bright eye and then said, very softly and tenderly, 'I love you, Ruthie.'

Lizzie trudged home through the snow, head down against the driving wind. Despite her assurances she could feel the wind slicing through her thick coat and she jammed her woolly hands deep into her pockets. Every now and then her foot skidded on the packed ice that lay beneath the snow and she slithered and almost fell. Once she skidded to lie in a heap on the snow, but it was so soft and deep that her fall was cushioned and she had to struggle to get back on to her feet.

'My stars above, whatever's happened to you?' Jane exclaimed as her daughter came through the kitchen door at last. 'You look like a snowman.'

'I fell in a drift. You just can't see where to put your feet.' Lizzie pulled off her mittens, which were plastered with snow, and put them beside the range. She hung her coat on the back of the door and held out her hands to the glowing coals.

'Your auntie all right, is she?' Jane asked, leaning over to stir the large saucepan which was simmering on the top of the range. 'It'll seem queer to her, now she's on her own again.'

'I think she's all right. I said I'd go in tomorrow, help her clear out some of Grandad's things.'

'She doing that already? Seems a bit quick. Still, I suppose she might as well get on with it, no point putting off jobs like that. I'll go down with you.' Jane sighed. 'I must say, it's going to seem funny down there without Dad. I mean, I know it's a few days now, but we've had the funeral to arrange and all that. It's only now that it sort of comes home to you.'

'I know.' Lizzie thought of the little cottage without her grandfather in his armchair at the window, watching the world go by. 'Still, it won't exactly be quiet, not with Silver squawking his head off.'

Jane smiled. 'He's like a baby to our Ruth, that bird is. Shame she never had her own kiddies.'

'She told me they'd left it too long,' Lizzie said quietly. 'Said me and Alec didn't ought to do the same.' Her mouth twisted a little. 'Chance'd be a fine thing! And yet – well, I said to her, it don't seem any sort of a world to bring a baby into. Not with this war going on, and nobody knowing what's going to happen. I mean, suppose they do invade. You hear such awful things about what they've been doing in Poland. Even in their own country . . . I don't think I want to have a baby, Mum, not till the world's a bit more settled.'

Her mother moved the saucepan to the side of the Rayburn, where it could be left to simmer. George had been allowed to stay at home during the last war, working on the farm, and she hadn't had to face the prospect of losing him. There hadn't been the fear of invasion then either, so having a baby seemed the right and natural thing to do. But things were different now and she couldn't blame Lizzie for feeling the way she did.

'It'll all come right in the end,' she said, hoping her

words were true. 'You and Alec will get your chance, Lizzie. This war hasn't come to all that much so far, and maybe it never will. It might all be finished with this time next year, then we can all settle down to a proper normal life again.'

'I hope so,' Lizzie said. She had started to lay the table, spreading the cloth over it, but now she paused to stare at the pattern as if she'd never seen it before. 'I really do hope so.'

Chapter Seven

Nora was not dead. But she was very ill and Dan had sent Gordon racing up the street to telephone for a doctor. He came an hour later to find Nora conscious again and in bed, with Dan beside her and the boys hovering anxiously at the foot of the stairs. Gordon let him in and he brushed past them without a word, not pleased to have been called out on such a cold, snowy evening to a house where there was obviously no money for paying doctors' bills.

'How long's she been like this?' he demanded abruptly, taking Nora's pulse and pulling down her lower eyelid. He moved the sheet and opened her nightdress, laying his stethoscope on her chest. 'Where did she get this bruise?'

'I dunno,' Dan said defensively. 'She keeps on knocking herself on things. I don't knock her about, if that's what you're thinking.' He stared belligerently at the doctor. 'Anyway, she bin tired, and not had much go about her, for quite a while, but I dunno as I'd have said she was actually ill. I mean, there's bin nothing else to notice, apart from that, and some days she seems all right, able to get up the street, do a bit of shopping, wash the clothes, you know. I thought she was getting better.'

'And how old is she?' the doctor asked, as if Nora were unable to speak for herself.

Dan thought. 'She's a coupla years younger'n me, so that makes her thirty-five, coming up to thirty-six.'

'Good God, man, only thirty-five years old and you think she's *better* when she manages to do a bit of shopping! You've been talking as though she's a woman of seventy.'

'Well, she's never bin all that strong,' Dan argued. 'And she's had a few miscarriages; they pulled her down. And then there was the brewery saying we couldn't stop on at the pub after her dad snuffed it, and young Sammy's whooping cough and our Gordon's spot of bother ... I just thought she was a bit run down, that's all.'

'Your wife's more than run down,' the doctor stated, putting away his stethoscope and folding Nora's nightdress over again, with another sharp look at the bruise on her right breast. 'She's ill. I suspect she's got anaemia – quite severe, possibly even pernicious, but we'd need to have her in hospital for some tests to know for sure. She needs iron and she needs good food to build her up. I dare say she's not been eating much lately, has she?'

'Ain't bin much to eat,' Dan said grumpily. 'They said it'd be better when we got the rationing but I don't see no improvement. And Nora knows I need meat to do me job. It's me what brings the money home.'

'So she's been giving you the lion's share.' The doctor nodded, knowing this was no uncommon story. He looked down at Nora and spoke directly to her for the first time. 'Well, you must make sure you get a better plateful in future. Get some liver, and eat it raw. As much as you can get hold of – a pound a day is what she really needs, but obviously there's not much chance of that ... Beef tea will help too. And get these iron tablets from the chemist.' He handed Dan a prescription. 'You know what anaemia is, I suppose?'

'It's to do with the blood. But I dunno what that other sort is – per—per—'

'Pernicious,' the doctor said. 'It's the most severe form. If your wife has that she'll need more treatment than just iron pills. But we'll try these first. If she doesn't improve, I want her in hospital for tests.'

He turned to go, then glanced back over his shoulder. 'Those boys downstairs. Why haven't they been evacuated?'

'The bigger one's at work,' Dan said defensively. 'And young Sammy – well, his mother didn't want him to go. Wanted to keep him with her. And a lot of nippers have come home now, what with there not being any bombing.'

'Hm,' the doctor said. 'Well, he'd be better off out in the country. He looks peaky himself.' He glanced disparagingly around the bare little bedroom with its iron bedstead, damp-stained wallpaper and threadbare curtains. 'It's a pity your wife can't go too. She'd get good fresh food there.'

He departed, leaving Dan and Nora together. She looked up at him, her eyes huge in her white face, and he snorted and shook his head.

'They live in a different world, doctors! How could we afford to send you out to the country? It's bad enough having to fork out for iron tablets. I mean, if it was me, being a worker, he could put me on the panel and we'd get them for nothing, but there's nothing like that for you or the kids . . . And saying you've got to have better food! Where's it going to come from, eh? Tell me that.' He dropped on to the bed beside her and took her thin hand. 'Oh, I'm sorry, love, it ain't your fault, I know that. I know you're poorly and if it's this per—per – anaemia thing, you got to have the right sort of medicine to put you right, and if you got to go to hospital for these tests we'll manage it somehow. But holidays in the country and beef dinners – well!'

'I know, Dan. Don't you worry about it.' Nora smiled at him. She was feeling better now she was in bed and the doctor had been. 'And anaemia's not all that serious. It just means run down, like you thought in the first place. Once I've had a few of these pills I'll be right as rain, you see, though I'm not sure I fancy raw liver! And I couldn't eat a pound a day even if we could get it. I've just let things get on top of me, that's what it is.'

'Yes,' Dan said, gazing at her and trying to see the bright-faced girl he had known in this thin and weary woman, old before her time. 'Yes, that's all it is.'

Downstairs, Sammy made an effort to tidy the room and clean up the kitchen. Gordon, who had scooped up the jewellery and goblet when the doctor was called, sidled up the stairs with his haversack. He gave Sammy a warning look.

'Don't you say nothing about this, see. They've forgot all about it. There ain't no need for you to go putting it back in their heads.'

Sammy watched him and turned back to scrubbing the draining board. He didn't for one minute believe that Gordon had been given the things as a reward for helping. And he remembered Christmas Day, when they'd met Micky Baxter in the street and Micky had boasted of giving his mother and gran gold necklaces.

Sammy remembered his mother's words, that if either of the boys ended up in prison it would kill her, and he felt sick.

No more was said about the jewellery for a few days. Nora stayed in bed most of the time, taking the iron pills Sammy had fetched from Mr Driver's chemist shop in September Street and drinking Oxo. Sammy had also managed to get some stewing steak from the butcher, and he put this into the saucepan and boiled it along with some carrots and turnips.

Mr Hines had been sympathetic when Sammy told him of his mother's illness and promised to help when he could. 'Liver's not on ration so you can have as much as you like. I'll put a pound by next time it comes in.'

Sammy hated liver. It was like strips cut from the bottom of shoes, just as tough and just as tasteless. He accepted it reluctantly and took it home, staring in distaste at the floppy, dark red mass.

'I'll have mine raw, like the doctor said, and casserole it for the rest of you,' Nora said, coming downstairs to go to the lavatory. 'It'll be all right with an onion or two.'

Tommy Vickers had kept his word and asked his wife Freda to look in, and she popped in most mornings when she'd done her own work, and offered to do any shopping or a bit of washing. Her own house was like a new pin, Sammy knew from having run errands for her, and she looked around Nora's living room as if she'd like to give it a good spring-clean. She offered to sweep through, or put something in the oven for their supper – a nice shepherd's pie, perhaps, like she was making for herself and Tommy. But Nora shook her head.

'We're all right, thanks very much, Mrs Vickers. Sammy's a big help to me and I'd rather do me own work. I don't like being beholden.'

'You wouldn't be beholden,' Freda Vickers said. 'It's just a neighbourly gesture, that's all.'

'I'd feel beholden,' Nora said stubbornly. 'If I couldn't do nothing in return, it would always hang over me. Thank you all the same, Mrs Vickers.'

Freda sighed. 'Well, as you please. But don't you be too proud to ask if there's anything you do want. You've only got to send young Sammy round, or just knock on the wall. Me and Tommy are always pleased to lend a hand.'

Nora nodded and closed her eyes. The iron pills and liver didn't seem to be making her any less tired. Freda looked at her uncertainly and tiptoed out. Her face was set in worried lines and when her husband came home from work she gave him a cup of tea and told him she thought poor Mrs Hodges was really ill.

'It's more than iron, if you ask me. She looks like a ghost, you can just about see right through her. And the house is in such a mess! It's like a slum, it is really. Not like April Grove at all. Why, I don't think even Granny Kinch and her Nancy live in such a pigsty as that.'

'Well, if she's as poorly as you say I suppose she can't do the work,' Tommy said, taking off his boots. He looked around their own living room, which he'd papered only last summer. It was bright and cheerful, with nice cushions that Freda had embroidered herself, a coloured rag rug in front of the fire, the furniture shining with polish and everything in its place. The houses in April Grove were only small – two rooms up and two down, with the scullery tacked on the back and an outside lavatory – but they were well built and didn't have to be slums. 'And it can't be easy with two boys dragging in all the dirt. We've only got our Eunice and she's just about grown up now anyway.'

'Eunice never brought in dirt even when she was little,' Freda said a little sharply. 'But even if we'd had boys, I'd have kept the place a bit better than Mrs Hodges is keeping hers. It don't look as if there's been so much as a duster passed over that room for months. It *smells* dirty. Give me them boots and I'll put 'em in the scullery . . . But it's not that I'm so bothered about,' she went on, coming back into the room. 'It's her state of health, and it's that little Sammy. She can't look after him properly, Tommy, and he's being neglected.'

'He looks pretty scruffy,' Tommy agreed, taking a long swig of tea. 'But some boys are like that, Free. Doesn't matter what you do, within five minutes they look as if they've been mudlarking down the harbour.'

'Sammy Hodges looks worse than that. You know he does. Shoes all broken, clothes torn and ragged. I don't think he's got a coat to his name. And he doesn't look as if he gets enough to eat either. I tell you what I think, Tom. I think he ought to have been evacuated. Sent out to the country, where he'd have got some good food and fresh air. That's what he ought to have been.'

'Well, a lot of those that were have come back now,' Tommy said. 'And not all of 'em seem to have thought much of it out there. Look at that little Baker lad. But there's nothing we can do about it, anyway. It's not for us to say what the Hodges do about their boys. And Dan Hodges is a funny bloke, he could turn nasty if he thought anyone was interfering.'

Freda refilled his cup. Her mouth was turned down. 'I know, and that's another thing. He's been hitting her, Tommy, I'm sure of it. There was a big bruise on her shoulder, I saw it before she had a chance to cover it up, and I wouldn't be surprised if she had a black eye coming too. *Hitting* her, in the state she's in! It don't bear thinking of. But that don't stop me thinking about it, all the same. They're our neighbours and we're here to help each other, that's what I always say.' She sighed. 'Well, I'll keep popping in anyway. She might let me do a bit of sweeping out one day, you never know. And at least I can keep an eye on the nipper.'

'It's not him wants keeping an eye on,' Tommy remarked. 'It's that brother of his. He's been getting thick with Micky Baxter again and I heard they'd been seen down Commercial Road, hanging round the backs of the shops. They won't be up to no good neither, not if I knows anything.'

'I hope they don't get into trouble again,' Freda said. 'It would just about kill that poor woman. As if she hasn't got enough to put up with!'

She took Tommy's cup out to the scullery. He heard the oven door open and close, and got up to sit at the table. A few minutes later she came back with a steaming shepherd's pie.

'My, that looks good,' he said, smacking his lips. 'All brown and crispy on top, just how I like it. You're a smashing cook, Freda. And that's a real compliment, coming from me.'

She laughed. 'Go on, just because you were a cook in the Navy!' She plunged a spoon into the pie and rich brown gravy oozed up around the mashed potato. 'It's a shame Nora Hodges wouldn't let me make her one too. It's only mince and potatoes, after all, and she could have got the meat with her ration. But there you are, you can't help someone that doesn't want to be helped.'

'You can't,' Tommy agreed, holding out his plate. 'But we can still do a bit where we can, Free. And we'll keep an eye on them. Nobody'll be able to say we never took an interest.'

While Tommy and Freda Vickers were enjoying shepherd's pie and Dan Hodges was coming home to faggots, Gordon and Micky Baxter were down in Commercial Road, Portsmouth's main shopping street. Gordon, who worked in a different area of the dock from his father, had said he'd be doing some more overtime. Instead, he left just a few minutes after the other men on his shift and slid through the shadowy backstreets from Camber, meeting Micky by the war memorial soldiers who knelt at their guns at the entrance to the park.

'I found a way into the second-hand shop,' Micky greeted him. 'There's a lavvy window left on the latch. I reckon I can get through there and let you in the door. We can go through the whole place and nobody'll know.'

Hidden by the blackout, they scurried down the back way. The alley was filled with slush and rubbish but there was a dustbin conveniently near the window. Micky climbed up and pushed the window fully open, then dragged himself through it. There was a moment when he thought he was stuck, but Gordon pushed hard on his backside and then he was through. A scrabbling sound and a splash indicated that he had been right about the nature of the room inside.

'Bugger it, my foot's all wet . . .' Gordon waited for a

few minutes and then the door beside him opened. 'Come on. They've done the blackout, so we can put the lights on and see what we're doing.'

Gordon slipped through the door and closed it behind him. The light snapped on and Micky grinned triumphantly from the far corner. They looked around to see where they were.

The second-hand shop was actually an antique shop, keeping quality goods. To Micky and Gordon it was just a jumble of old furniture and china, but they could read a price label and knew that they could pass the stuff on for at least a quarter of the price. It was enough to make an evening's work worthwhile.

'It's an old bloke keeps it,' Micky muttered. 'He'll never miss anything out of all this lot. I bet he doesn't even know what he's got!'

'We'll just take small stuff, though, like we did from the other place,' Gordon said. Their previous expedition had been to a similar shop in Arundel Street. 'Rings, and necklaces and things, and maybe some silver. Nothing that'll break.'

They had both brought old sacks and began to fill them, shovelling stuff in at random. It didn't matter too much what they took – it would all go to another junk shop in Southsea. The thin, ferret-faced man who ran it had given them five pounds for their previous haul, and they hoped for at least the same amount this time.

'It's good stuff, this,' Gordon said, looking critically at a chain necklace set with dark-red stones. 'That's real rubies, that is. You can get hundreds for rubies.'

'Old Ratface won't give us hundreds,' Micky said. 'He'll diddle us, same as he diddles everyone. I reckon we oughter find someone else to take it—'

'And *I* reckon', a different voice said, 'that you ought to come down the station with me. I'd like to have a little talk with you about all this. *And* about Old Ratface.'

The two boys spun round. A large policeman was blocking the doorway, arms akimbo, watching them with a sardonic expression on his grim face. They dropped the sack and made for the back door, but it had locked as Gordon pulled it behind him. The window through which Micky had scrambled was out of the question. Micky would never get through it in time and Gordon wouldn't get through it at all. They turned this way and that, but there was no way out. The policeman had them trapped.

'I thought there was something up when I saw you two skulking down the alley,' he went on. 'So I followed you and saw which window you went through. I got the keys to most of the shops along here – ah, didn't know that, did you? Anyway, we don't want to stand here nattering all evening, do we? Much warmer down the station, they'll have a nice fire going there. You can bring the sacks along too.'

He grasped each boy by the collar and pushed them through the door. But Gordon was a big boy, and the work he did in the docks had built up his muscles. As they reached the front door of the shop, he twisted away and took to his heels, scuttling off into the darkness and leaving Micky with his bag of plunder still in the grip of the policeman.

Micky let out a whimpering cry of anger and panic, and the policeman shook him.

'Not much of a mate, is he, leaving you to face the music? Still, don't you fret. We'll catch up with him. It'll be easy, because you're going to tell us who he is and where he lives – aincher? When we get back to the station, you're going to tell us all about it. You're going to spill so many beans we could set up a blooming canning factory.'

He set off at a rapid stride and Micky stumbled beside him, still dragging the sack. He was starting to cry.

It would be all Gordon Hodges' own fault if Micky told on him. He shouldn't never have run off like that.

Once Micky had told the police all he knew, Gordon's fate was sealed. He'd been warned the last time he came before the court, the magistrate told him severely, and he'd thrown his chance away. He would be sent to an approved school for three years and if he were a sensible boy he would take the opportunity to mend his ways. He could learn a proper trade while he was there and could come out at seventeen ready to take a responsible place in the world.

Gordon listened sullenly. He was furious with Micky for spilling the beans and glowered at the younger boy. He knew perfectly well why Micky had done it. It wasn't under torture, as Micky had claimed, nor because they'd threatened to come after his mum, though they could easily have done that. Nancy Baxter had been up in front of the court herself more than once, and if she hadn't had a young baby she'd have been in jail for soliciting. But it wasn't family feeling that had loosened Micky's tongue. It was the promise that the police would get him put on probation instead of being sent away with Gordon, as he should have been. He'd given his mate away just to keep his own freedom.

'It was him went through the window,' Gordon had complained to his mother and father when the policeman had finally left after bringing him home that night. 'It was him hung about round the shop and found out when the old man went home and all that. I'll bash his head in next time I see him, see if I don't.'

'Don't talk like that, Gordon,' Nora begged, and Dan cuffed him sharply round his own head.

'You'll get into more trouble doing that. Leave the boy alone. You're the oldest and you oughter known better. Now I got to take another day off work and if you get sent off we'll lose your wage as well. Never thought of that, did you?'

Sammy sat in a corner, saying nothing. He remembered the day Micky had tried to persuade him to go down to Charlotte Street, promising to show him the gold necklaces, and when he thought that it might have been him the policeman had come about, and him having to go to court, he felt sick.

Dan and Nora both went to the court, Nora paler than ever and as thin as a shadow. Maybe they'll look at her and feel sorry for us, Dan thought, without much hope, but if the magistrates did feel compassion towards the mother who was so plainly ill they expressed it by taking Gordon off her hands, and Nora and Dan said goodbye to him outside the courthouse and went home on the bus without him.

'Bloody stupid fool,' Dan growled. 'I thought I drummed it into his head that other time that I wouldn't have him thieving.'

Nora looked at him. 'That was the night you got the doctor to me, wasn't it? What did he do with those things, Dan?'

'Well, he took 'em back, didn't he? That's what I *told* him to do.'

They sat in silence for a few minutes, staring out at the grey streets. The snow had almost gone now, leaving small grimy lumps on the edge of the pavements. Nora glanced uneasily at her husband.

'We don't *know* he did, though, do we? The magistrate did say they'd sold stuff before.'

Dan scowled. He was fed up with Gordon and wanted nothing more than to go to the pub with his mates, have a few beers and a game of darts and forget all about it. He was sick of having coppers come to the door, sick of Nora crying, sick of his son's self-righteous complaints about Micky Baxter. And Sammy didn't help either, clinging to his mother all the time and looking as frightened as if he thought the coppers were coming for him as well. I dunno why we ever had kids, he thought as they reached their stop and got off the bus. Nothing but bleeding trouble.

'I don't see that it matters now,' he said as they walked slowly down March Street. 'The boy's got his punishment and we're being punished alongside him. That's five bob a week you won't see now, nor his rations neither.'

'Well, he's not going to need feeding, is he?' Nora stopped and put her hand to her side. 'Oh Dan, I've got an awful stitch.'

'A stitch? You ain't done nothing to get a stitch. You ain't hardly walked more than four miles a fortnight, let alone run anywhere. How could you have a stitch?'

'I don't know, but it hurts something chronic.' She leant against him. 'I don't know as I can walk home, Dan.'

He stared at her. 'Come on, Nora, it's only a step. We're nearly halfway down March Street. You can walk that bit.'

'I can't . . .' She sagged against him and he grabbed her as he felt her body begin to slide to the pavement. Suddenly, she was a dead weight and he let her down to lie on the paving stones before looking wildly up and down the street. There was nobody in sight and he looked down at her again and picked up her hand, holding it against his cheek.

'Come on, Nora – wake up, for Gawd's sake wake up. You can't lie here on the pavement, it's all ice, you'll catch your death—' He caught the words up, feeling sick. '*Nora!*'

'What's up, mate?'

It was Frank Budd, from the other end of the street. He and Dan had been in the Army together in the '14–'18 war, and it was Frank who'd told him there was a house for rent in April Grove. He stood beside Dan, staring down, his cap pushed to the back of his head. 'Missus been took poorly?'

'Well, she ain't having an afternoon nap!' Dan snapped,

then cursed himself as he saw Frank's expression. 'Sorry, mate, but she's just collapsed and I'm at me wits' end. Could you – could you give me a bit of an 'and? Just to get her down the street and indoors, like.'

'Course, mate.' Frank helped Dan pick Nora up and carry her down the street. 'You going to get her to a doctor?'

'I just want to get her back home,' Dan said tersely and they staggered on. It was a wonder, Dan thought, how heavy a little wisp of a thing like Nora could be when she was out for the count. To tell the truth, he was a bit taken aback by how thin she was now. It was a long time since he'd held her in his arms, she was always too tired or too sick just lately, and she only seemed to be half the woman he remembered.

They came to number 2 at last and Dan poked his hand through the letter box and pulled out the key that hung on a string behind it. He unlocked the door and said, 'It's all right. I can manage now.'

'I'll just help you get her inside,' Frank said, not noticing Dan's reluctance to let him over the doorstep. Together they hauled Nora along the passage, past Dan's bike that had had a puncture for the past month and past a sack of potatoes he'd brought back from the Camber one night, and into the back room. Frank helped lay Nora down in the armchair, then straightened up and looked about him.

Dan looked too, seeing the room for the first time through someone else's eyes. He saw the dreary wallpaper, stained from where he'd chucked a plate of half-eaten dinner at Sammy one night when the kid had been playing up over his food. He saw the chipped paint on the door of the cupboard under the stairs and the splintered hole in one of the panels where Gordon had put his boot through it in a fit of temper. He saw the table, covered with sheets of newspaper dated two weeks earlier instead of a tablecloth, with dirty crockery strewn over it and Sammy standing beside it with a tin of cold baked beans which he'd been eating with a spoon. He saw the battered armchair with its stuffing oozing out and the scrap of threadbare mat on the floor in front of the cold embers in the fireplace.

'Yeah, all right,' he said, knowing what Frank was thinking. 'It's a bloody mess, but she ain't been too clever lately, see. I can manage now, thanks.'

'Yes, OK, mate,' Frank said, dragging his eyes away and thinking what Jess would say if she could see it all. He caught Dan's look and turned towards the door, then hesitated again. 'Look, if there's anything we can do – Jess and me – I mean, we know you've had a bit of bother and what with your missus being poorly as well.'

'I said I can manage,' Dan said. 'Thanks.' He said it as if it meant 'get out', and Frank nodded, shrugging his shoulders as he turned away again.

'All right, mate. It was just a friendly offer. If you change your mind –' he paused but Dan said nothing and he went through the door. 'All right, then, cheerio.' The front door opened and closed. There was silence in the room.

'Is – is Mummy dead?' Sammy asked at last in a small voice and his father's head snapped up.

'No, of course she's not dead! Why d'you always keep on about her being dead? She's just fainted a bit, that's all – look, she's coming round already. Well, don't just stand there – get her a drink of water. And shut that bloody front door, Frank Budd's left it half open, there's a draught like the flaming Arctic coming down the passage.' He sat over Nora, rubbing her hands and whispering to her as Sammy scuttled out to the scullery and poured a cup of water from the tap. 'Nora, Nora,' he whispered, 'wake up, for Gawd's sake. Don't go and die on me, *please*. I can't manage it all without you. Nora, *please* . . .'

Sammy came back with the water. Dan held it to his wife's lips and, her eyelids fluttering, she sipped it, choked a little, then drank some more. She gave them both a weak, tremulous smile.

'Oh, Nora,' Dan breathed. 'Thank Gawd. Thank *Gawd* . . .'

He sat quite still beside her, holding her hand. Sammy wriggled his fingers into the palm of the other and she squeezed it gently. The three of them sat together in the cold room, silent and unspeaking, for a long time.

Chapter Eight

The phoney war, as those first months were called, came to an abrupt end in June 1940 when the British Expeditionary Force – almost the entire Army – was driven back to the beaches of Dunkirk and the survivors had to be rescued by a flotilla of ships, from the greatest battleship to the humblest dinghy. After that, with France occupied together with most of the rest of Europe, it seemed only a matter of time until Britain too went under the iron heel.

The war then took to the air as the Battle of Britain was waged up and down the Channel and over the south of England. In cities and towns, in hamlets and villages, people took cover, or stood and stared as British and German aircraft tore the skies apart. Every small boy became an expert in identifying Spitfires, Hurricanes, Messerschmitts and Dorniers. Every one dreamed of capturing his very own parachutist.

Evacuees who had come home after Christmas began to filter back to the countryside, but it wasn't until the bombing began in July and August that many parents started to take the idea seriously again and the billeting officers found themselves busy once more.

'You could have an evacuee now, Auntie Ruth,' Lizzie said when she dropped in to see her aunt one afternoon. Now that she didn't have Joe to look after any more, Ruth was working longer hours again at the Cottage Hospital just over the village green. She often took Silver with her and stood him on his perch near the front door to entertain visitors. He learned to imitate the nurses and added a few more words to his repertoire.

'Nurse!' he would squawk in an uncanny imitation of Matron's voice. 'Nurse, come here at once!' After being caught out a few times, the nurses stopped taking any notice, then found themselves in trouble when Matron really did call them and they ignored her.

Ruth split some scones and spread a thin layer of butter over them. Even in the country, you had to be careful with the rations and they'd formed a new tradition of having butter only if you weren't having jam or some other spread. Nobody liked margarine much, but Ruth's home-made blackberry-and-apple jam was famous in the family and its rich flavour concealed the taste.

'I know. I've been thinking about an evacuee. I've heard they're starting to come out again. There was a new batch sent out from Gosport last week but they all went out Fair Oak way. One of the doctors told me. I suppose if there were any from the district our evacuees live in they'd be brought out here, so that they could go to the same school.'

'Well, you'd better make sure they've got your name, then,' Lizzie said. 'But could you manage one, Auntie? I mean, what about when you're working nights?'

'Well, I thought the kiddy could come with me and sleep in that little side ward. It's never used.' Ruth's brown eyes softened. 'Poor little mites, they need a bit of comfort. Torn away from their mums and dads. It's enough to break your heart.'

'They're a bit rough, though, some of them,' Lizzie said. 'I mean, ones like the Budds are all right, but some of them come from real slums. I've heard they're riddled with lice and fleas, and don't know how to use a knife and fork, or what a bar of soap's for, or anything. You want to make sure you get a decent one, Auntie.'

'I'll take whatever the good Lord sends me,' Ruth said.

'I'm sure me and Silver can manage. He won't stand any nonsense, will you, Silv?'

'Stuff and nonsense,' the bird said. 'Oompah, oompah, stuff it up your jumper.'

Lizzie grinned. 'He might even learn a few new words. Or the evacuee might! But honestly, Auntie, you want to be careful. Ask for a nice little girl who'll be a bit of help to you.'

'I'd rather have a boy who'd be a bit of life. That's what I'd have wanted if me and Jack had been blessed. A houseful of boys, like Joyce Moore.' Ruth's face saddened. 'But there, it wasn't what the good Lord had in mind for us, so maybe He's giving me another chance now. And that's why it's not for me to choose, same as it wouldn't have been for me to choose if He had decided to send us our own. Take what you're given and be grateful, that's what I always say.'

Lizzie spread some jam on her scone and bit into it thoughtfully. Auntie Ruth had always seemed as bright as a wren, bustling cheerfully through life and even when Uncle Jack had died she had never imposed her grief on other people, but had gone back to nursing almost as if nothing had happened. Yet she talked about him constantly and indeed, with Silver croaking words Jack had taught him in Jack's gravelly voice, he would have been impossible to forget.

'D'you know when the evacuees will come?'

'Well, I think they're sending them out more or less all the time, as the parents decide to let 'em go. And the authorities are going round trying to persuade them that don't want to that it's for the best. They say people on the coast are on edge all the time, waiting to hear the church bells ring to say the Germans have arrived.'

Lizzie nodded. 'Those raids they've had in Portsmouth and London sound awful. People killed, buildings smashed to bits . . . and they say it'll get worse. It's no place for kiddies.'

'And that's why we've got to give a home to them,' Ruth said. 'You're right, it doesn't bear thinking of, little children being bombed out of house and home. We've got to do all we can for them. Even if they *are* crawling with lice and fleas and don't know what a knife and fork are for,' she added. 'It's easy enough to give a child a bath and any youngster can learn table manners.'

Lizzie gave her a rueful look. 'I know, Auntie. You're right and I'm glad you're having an evacuee. I hope it'll be a nice one, that's all. And it'll be fun to have a kiddy in the family. You'll have to bring it over to tea with us.'

'Tea for two,' Silver said, evidently feeling that he had been silent for too long. 'I'm a little teapot, short and stout, here's my handle, here's my spout, when you fill me up you'll hear me shout –'

'We hear you shout all the time,' Ruth told him. 'We don't have to fill you up to hear that. Have a piece of scone and be quiet. And now tell me what news you've got of Alec,' she said to Lizzie. 'Surely to goodness he'll be back in Southampton soon and get a few days' leave. It's months since you saw him.'

'Nearly nine,' Lizzie agreed ruefully. 'It's all that dodging about in the convoys, trying to keep out of the Germans' way. But I think there's a chance he'll come back in the next week or so. I hope so. If he stops away much longer we won't recognise each other!'

'Oh, you'll recognise each other all right,' Ruth told her with a reminiscent smile. 'That's the best thing about being a sailor's wife – it's just a series of honeymoons!'

They settled back into their chairs for a good gossip, assisted by Silver until Ruth lost all patience with him and draped his red cover over the cage. After that, they were able to talk in peace, interrupted only by an occasional meaningful snore. Silver was no more asleep than they were, but even in darkness he couldn't keep completely quiet.

Lizzie recognised her husband very well when he came swinging up the garden path a few days later. She was standing at the sink peeling potatoes and stared, transfixed, with the knife in her hand as he thrust open the gate. He saw her and bounded across the vegetable patch, grinning, to thrust his head through the open window and deal her a smacking kiss.

'Alec! *Alec*! Why didn't you let me know?'

He withdrew his head and a moment later burst into the kitchen and swung her into his arms. 'Couldn't. We only docked a couple of hours ago – if I'd stopped to send you a telegram I'd have missed the bus, and even then I'd probably have got here before it arrived. Oh, Lizzie, Lizzie, I just couldn't wait to see you. I've missed you so much!'

'I've missed you too,' she declared breathlessly as he kissed her again and again. 'It's seemed like years . . . How are you, Alec? Are you all right? Shall I put the kettle on? Did you have any breakfast? There are some new-laid eggs . . . Oh, it's so *lovely* to see you!'

They stared at one another, each taking in all the details of the other's appearance. He was thinner, Lizzie thought, and he'd grown a moustache. And he looked tired. But he was still her Alec, and her heart turned over as she looked into his intense dark eyes and saw the passion in them.

'Gosh, you look better than ever!' he exclaimed. 'You've got a suntan too. I expect you're helping out on the farm – well, it's better than having to be a Land Girl, I suppose!' He laughed, and then the intense expression returned as he smoothed her hair back from her forehead. 'Oh, Lizzie, if you knew how I've dreamed of being back here with you – able to touch you and kiss you and smell your lovely hair – d'you know, it doesn't just look like chestnuts, it *smells* like them! All sweet and brown and woody.'

'That's because I've only just finished cleaning out the range,' she told him. 'And who said you could grow a moustache? I don't remember you mentioning it in any of your letters. I suppose you think it makes you look like Ronald Colman, specially with your hair slicked back like that.'

He grinned and glanced in the mirror at his smooth black hair. 'Well, I thought you might like a film star for a husband. Don't you like it? They say kissing a man without a moustache is like eating an egg without salt, don't they?'

'Do they?' Lizzie retorted and grinned. 'Well, maybe I should try it out again . . .' They gave the moustache a thorough testing and then she drew back once more and pretended to consider. 'Mmm – well, it tickles a bit, but I suppose it's quite nice, really . . .'

'Perhaps it needs a bit more attention,' he murmured wickedly, one eye on the staircase door. 'Is anyone likely to come in?'

'Yes – Mum. She's only gone down the garden to pick some beans.' Lizzie rubbed the moustache with one fingertip. 'It'll have to wait till later. Oh – how long have you got? You're not going back straight away, are you?'

He shook his head. 'Four or five days. I'll have to go back on board tomorrow to see to a few things, but then it's over to the maintenance boys and the stevedores. We can have a bit of a honeymoon. D'you think you can get a few days off from the shop?' He winked. 'Say it's for passionate leave!'

Lizzie laughed. 'I'll have to go in on Monday morning,' she said. 'But I'll ask. They might give me a day or two.' She gazed at him and thought of her Aunt Ruth, saying how being married to a sailor was a series of honeymoons. And how if she wanted a family, she shouldn't leave it too late.

We've got a chance now, she thought. We could start our family now, if we were lucky. But is that what I really want to do? Is it really right to bring a baby into the world, the way things are now?

'I'll put the kettle on,' she said, withdrawing herself from his arms. 'And I'll fry you a couple of fresh eggs and a bit of bacon. And when we've had dinner we'll go for a walk. The countryside's looking lovely now.'

Alec flung himself into Jane's old rocking chair and stretched out his legs. 'That'll be smashing. I tell you what, Liz, I don't really mind what we do. It's just so good to be home again. It's so good to be with you.'

The time passed all too quickly. There were old friends to see, old haunts to rediscover. Alec had been away for almost a year, far longer than anyone had expected. Everyone wanted to see him and hear his stories, but Lizzie didn't want to share him with anyone else. She wanted to hold him close and keep him all to herself.

'Four or five days!' she said bitterly. 'After you've been gone all that time. It's not fair.'

'There's a war on,' he reminded her, but she sniffed and tossed her head.

'So there might be, but *you're* not fighting it! You're supposed to be unarmed – neutral.'

'The country's depending on us to bring in food and supplies. We're fighting it as much as anyone in the Armed Services. Same as you are, on the land, and all those people growing beans and taters in their gardens. We're all in it together, Liz.' He drew her close. 'I feel just the same. I want to stop here with you for ever. But I can't leave the Merchant Navy now – and if I did, I'd just get slung into the other lot! At least I'm not in armed combat.'

'You could still get torpedoed, or bombed,' she said gloomily. 'Oh, I know, Alec, we don't have any choice, none of us. It's just so *unfair*. One man in Germany decides he wants to rule the world, and the rest of us have to turn to and give up our own lives to stop him. Why? How was he ever allowed to *get* to that position? Couldn't anyone have stopped him?'

Alec shrugged. 'No good asking me that, Liz. In any case, it's too late now. And that's what we're doing, isn't it – stopping him. At least we're having a go now.'

'If we haven't left it too late,' she muttered. 'He could be invading at this very minute. Sending ships full of soldiers to the beaches. Planes full of bombs. Oh, Alec, Alec –' She turned in his arms and gripped his shoulders. 'Alec, I'm scared. I'm frightened of what might happen to you – what might happen to us, here at home. And it's not just me – everyone's frightened. Even if they don't say so, you can see it in their faces. It's why we're all so snappy. We hardly know where to put ourselves sometimes, we're all so scared!'

Alec held her closely. 'I know.' He had seen it for himself – the fear in people's faces, tightening the skin around their eyes, drawing deep grooves between their brows. He had seen the shadows under their eyes that told of sleepless nights, heard the tautness in their voices. And he understood it, for he too had felt the fear during the long months at sea in the convoys, trying to dodge the German vessels that hunted them like whales, hearing the gunfire as their naval escorts fought them off, seeing the smoke and flame of the explosions as ships from both sides went down . . .

'I know,' he said. 'I know.'

Chapter Nine

Gordon's appearance in court and his being sent away to an approved school seemed to have been the last straw for poor Nora Hodges.

Frank Budd had told Tommy how he'd found Dan Hodges almost frantic, with his wife collapsed on the pavement as if she were dead and how, although Dan swore they could manage, Frank had sent his wife Jess, who had come back from the evacuation to be with him, to offer a hand.

By the time she had arrived Dan was in no state to refuse help and he hadn't lifted a finger to stop Jess as she bustled about, sending Sammy out for the doctor and making a pot of tea, clearing the scullery and living room as she did so. It would take more than an hour's cleaning to get that place up to scratch, she'd told Freda later, but at least by the time the doctor had arrived the place didn't look as if the rubbish men had just made a delivery.

The doctor had looked grim as he examined Nora's thin body. He looked at the yellowish tinge of her skin, at the bruises that kept appearing so inexplicably and at her puffy ankles, and told Dan that he ought to have been called sooner. Mrs Hodges was very sick indeed. 'I'm not sure there's even any point in sending her to hospital,' he concluded, putting away his stethoscope.

Dan and Jess stared at him.

'What d'you mean? What're you saying?'

'I'm saying your wife is very ill indeed,' the doctor said, speaking slowly as if to make his meaning clearer. 'She's got a serious illness. And she's had it for some considerable time, by the look of her.'

'What sort of illness? What are you talking about? I *did* call the doctor – the other one came, the old one with white hair. He said it was anaemia, he gave her iron tablets and said she ought to have liver. Alf Hines, up the shop, he put some by for her every week. And you mean to say it's not done no good? All them pills and that blooming liver we all had to eat, it's not done no good at all?' He stared at his wife. 'D'you mean my Nora – my Nora's going to d—?'

'Ssh!' Jess cried. She pulled Dan out of the room and they stood at the top of the stairs. 'You mustn't say that, not where she can hear you.' The doctor had followed them out and they filed down the narrow stairs into the scullery. 'That's not what you mean, is it, Doctor?' she appealed to him. 'She's not really that bad?'

'I'm afraid she is. It's rather more than anaemia. Not possible to say for certain without tests, of course, but it looks to me like leukaemia.'

They stared at him. 'Leukaemia?' Dan repeated at last. 'And what the bleeding hell's that when it's at home?'

The doctor glanced at him with distaste. 'Your words are all too appropriate. It's a serious blood disorder. A kind of cancer, in fact.'

'*Cancer?*' Jess gasped. She had barely ever spoken the word, or even heard it spoken aloud before. It was a word you whispered behind your hand or mouthed silently. More often, you'd say it was a 'growth'. Yet how could you get a growth in your blood?

'I'm afraid so. Has your wife been very tired, Mr Hodges? Fainted at all? Complained of aches and pains? Blurred vision? Excessive bleeding if she cuts herself?' He gave Dan a sharp look. 'She's showing signs of bruising, but—'

'We don't know where those bruises come from!' Dan broke in. 'They keep on coming. Nora swears she don't remember hitting herself on anything, but you needn't think I been knocking her about. I've never laid a finger on her, not that way.'

The doctor looked as if he doubted that, but he said, 'Well, that's another sign. Bleeding, bruising – it's the blood, you see, breaking out of the circulation system. And the swollen ankles – that's fluid.'

'My granny had that,' Jess said. 'Dropsy. Her whole legs came up like balloons—' She glanced at Dan and broke off, biting her lip.

'Just so,' the doctor said. 'It's because the heart is beginning to fail and fluid's building up. Now, what I'd like to do is take your wife into hospital for a few tests, so that we can be sure – but I have to tell you that if it *is* leukaemia the outlook is very poor. There's nothing we can do for it.'

'Nothing?' Jess whispered. 'Nothing at all?'

Dan stared at him. His face was white under his dark stubble. 'But I just thought it was the way she was naturally. I mean, she's never been properly strong, and she's had a few miscarriages. And she always reckoned it must be her age or the worry over the war or – or our older boy. He's been in a spot of bother with the police, see. Fact, we just come from the court now, he's bin – well, he's bin sent away. Approved school.'

'I see. Well, you may have to ask permission to have him home again. Just for a few days. Not immediately – but in a few weeks, I think. And meanwhile—'

'Hold on a minute,' Dan broke in. 'What d'you mean, have him home? They won't let us do that – not unless it's an emergency.' He caught the doctor's eye and his shoulders sagged. 'All right, Doc, I get your drift. You don't have to say no more.' He turned away for a moment and leant over the sink, his hands gripping the white rim. Jess gazed at him, pity welling up in her breast. She had never known him well, it was Frank who'd known him in the last war, but she'd tried to make friends with Nora and felt sorry for her. But now her heart went out to the big man, looking so lost and bewildered. He really does love her, she thought. For all his bad temper, for all his bluster and shouting that Tommy Vickers says he and Freda can hear through the wall, he really does love her. And she remembered what Frank had told her, about Dan being shell-shocked.

'There isn't nothing at all?' he said at last in a husky voice. 'You can't do nothing to help her?'

The doctor shook his head. He seemed a little more sympathetic now, as if his original assessment of Dan had changed when he saw the man's obviously genuine distress. 'I'm sorry. As I say, we can take her into hospital and carry out some tests, but I don't really think there's much doubt.' He paused, then went on. 'I can't really tell you how long it will be. It could be just a few weeks – it may be a few months. If it does prove to be leukaemia, she might as well return home. I'll come and see her regularly, of course, but there's really very little I'll be able to do besides give you a prescription for some tablets to help the pain. I'll get the district nurse to call in every day to do whatever's necessary. Other than that . . .' He sighed, then glanced at his watch. 'I'm sorry, I'll have to go, I have a surgery . . . I'll send an ambulance to take her into hospital. Do you pay any insurance? To a Friendly Society or anything?'

'Yeah.' Dan straightened his shoulders and turned back to them. 'Yeah, we pays a penny a week, Sammy takes it to the old woman round Carlisle Crescent. I s'pose it'll pay . . .' He wiped the back of his hand across his face and eyes. 'Thanks for coming. We'll manage. We always do, one way or another.'

The doctor hesitated, glanced at them both, then nodded and walked quickly through the living room and along the passage to the front door. Jess looked uncertainly at Dan and moved to put a hand on his arm.

'I'm ever so sorry,' she said. 'I really am. You – you

know we'll do whatever we can, don't you? Me and Frank –
and Ted and Annie, and Tommy Vickers and Freda next
door. We'll all do whatever we can. You've only got to say
the word.'

Dan looked down at her. She thought briefly that he
must have been a good-looking man when he was young,
before hard work and worry and drink had taken their toll.
Before the so-called Great War. Frank always did say he
used to be different, that he'd never been the same again
after he'd been in the trenches. And he was a good-looking
man still, when you looked behind the tiredness, the
anxiety, the grief. Tall, dark, well set-up – you couldn't
ever destroy those sort of looks.

A sound at the door made them both turn. Sammy stood
there, framed in the doorway, his face white beneath its
shadowing of grime. His blue eyes were enormous.

'I heard what you were saying,' he said in a trembling
voice. 'She *is* going to die, isn't she? My mummy – she *is*
going to die . . .'

Early in July the terror they had all been waiting for came
at last, with the first of the daylight raids. Eighteen people
were killed at Kingston Cross and one of the gasholders at
Rudmore was set on fire. Frank Budd had got caught on his
way home from work and told Tommy Vickers he'd seen
dead bodies at Drayton Road School, which was being used
as a First Aid post. It wasn't casualties that had been
brought in, though, it was the First Aid people themselves.
The school had been completely destroyed.

Sammy didn't know what to do. He sat beside his
mother, trembling, wondering how to get her down to the
shelter. She was too weak to get out of bed, now, and had to
be helped to sit on the chamber pot that was kept under the
bed. The noise overhead was terrible, worse than any
thunderstorm. He could hear planes roaring and screaming
above him, and the crashes of the exploding bombs. The

house shook and rattled about his ears, and he crouched beside the bed, terrified. He pictured Germans landing in the street outside, forcing their way into the house and storming up the stairs to get him.

Nora's blue eyes stared down at him, almost black, like holes in her paper-white face. It looked like a mask of terror. 'Go down the shelter, Sammy,' she whispered urgently. 'Go on.'

'I can't! I can't!' He was too afraid to move, too afraid to leave the house and venture into the garden. The thought of being exposed to the planes that thundered overhead was too much for him. They'd see him, they'd drop a bomb on him. And even if he had been able to pluck up the courage, he couldn't go without his mother . . . 'I can't leave you here by yourself.'

Nora's mouth twisted wryly. She had spent three days in the hospital, suffering the discomfort of various tests, and knew that she was dying. It didn't seem to matter very much now whether it was the illness that carried her off or a German bomb. The bomb would at least be quick . . . 'Go down the shelter, Sammy. Please. For me.'

But he shook his head and climbed up on the bed, burrowing his head against her. Nora wrapped her thin arms about him and held him there, and they lay close together, listening to the screaming of the aircraft and the thunder of the bombs; until the skies fell silent at last and the lonely sound of the 'All Clear' signal, rose like a lament for those who had died.

Nora sighed. She was exhausted by the noise, by the fear and by the effort of keeping awake for Sammy's sake. She wanted nothing more than to drift into sleep.

'Make us a cup of tea, there's a love,' she whispered into her son's ear. 'They've gone now. They won't come back today. You can go downstairs now, can't you, and make your mum a cup of tea.'

Sammy lifted his head. His face was white, and stained

with tears and dirt. He sniffed and wiped his nose with his sleeve.

'Is the war over now, Mum?' he asked. 'Have the Germans come to get us?'

She looked at him and realised how difficult it was for a child to understand. They were told so little. All these other countries, squabbling over each other, were beyond them. They had no idea what war could be like, or how long it could last.

'No,' she said, 'the war isn't over yet. But the Germans haven't come to get us. We've sent them away, see. Now, get me that cup of tea, there's a good boy.' And as Sammy went downstairs, still cautiously just in case there might be a German lurking behind the scullery door, she lay back and closed her eyes.

I'm not going to see this war through, she thought, with a cold feeling around her heart, and for the first time she was glad that Gordon had been sent to the approved school, where he would at least be safe.

But what was going to happen to Sammy?

As the doctor had promised, the district nurse came every day and washed Nora's body and gave her the tablets the doctor had prescribed. Gordon had been brought home, sullen-faced and silent, and then taken straight back to Drayton. He sat beside her for a while, but she didn't wake up and his face was set with misery when he had to leave.

For Sammy it was a bad dream, a dream that went on and on, and from which there was no awakening. He roamed aimlessly through the days, spending as much time as he could beside his mother before being sent outside 'to play' by the district nurse or the neighbours. But he was afraid to go far away, in case there was another air raid, and anyway there was nobody to play with – only Micky Baxter and a couple of his mates who hadn't gone back to the country, and Sammy was afraid to be friends with Micky.

There were a few girls – Rose Budd and her friend Joy from the papershop, and two or three others – but they were much older than Sammy and wouldn't have dreamed of playing with him. Rose didn't even like talking to him, and he'd heard her grumble to her mother once when Jess had brought her up to number 2 to see Nora.

'It's a horrible house. It's all dirty and it smells.'

'Mrs Hodges is very ill and can't do her housework or cooking. That's why me and your Auntie Annie and Mrs Vickers are helping out. It wouldn't do you any harm to give a hand too, Rose.'

Rose wrinkled her nose in disgust. 'I'll get the shopping, but I'm not coming in the house. And I'm not taking that kid, he's got nits.'

Sammy did have nits. He was very rarely without them. When he'd been able to go to school and the 'nit-lady' had come round to examine the children's heads, he had been regularly sent home with a bottle of black tar shampoo and told to ask his mother to wash his hair. He'd had to sit at a desk separate from the other children too, along with the other 'nits'. It made another excuse for the bigger ones to jeer at him in the playground.

It wasn't just nits, either. His legs and sometimes his body were peppered with flea bites. Tibby's fur was full of fleas and sometimes the cat nearly went mad with them, leaping about all over the place as if he were a flea himself. You couldn't get rid of them so you just had to get used to them.

'We're going to have to get that cat destroyed,' Dan said. 'The government's been on about it long enough. They want all pets done away with. It's for their own good,' he added, seeing Nora's horror. 'I mean, what's going to happen to them in the bombing raids? You can't keep an animal down the shelter, specially as we ain't allowed proper doors. He'll run off and we'll never see him again.

He might get bombed himself. Or the place'll be overrun with cats and dogs all gone wild.'

'Yes, but he's all Sammy's got now. We can't take his cat away from him. Anyway, he was all right in that raid we had the other week, he must have hid somewhere and he came in same as usual, wanting his supper.'

But she had no energy for argument. She slipped back into sleep and Dan looked at her and shook his head. One of these days, he knew, she'd slip away from him altogether, and then *he'd* have nothing. What was a cat beside a wife like Nora?

The weeks slid by and Nora faded a little more each day. She had to be given more and more of the painkilling pills the doctor prescribed, then it had to be injections given by the nurse. She moaned and muttered, crying out that there were eyes watching her, hundreds of staring eyes, or that she could hear animals scratching at the door. She seemed to think she had just given birth to a baby and begged for it to be put into her arms. She stared at Dan as if he were a stranger and tried to push him away, and one day she told Sammy he was a nasty little boy and she didn't want him in the house again.

'She doesn't mean it,' Freda Vickers said, coming in to find him sobbing broken-heartedly on the bottom stair. 'She doesn't know what she's saying. You know she loves you.'

'Not any more,' he wept. 'She doesn't love me any more. Nobody loves me now.' He gripped the cat hard against him. 'Only Tibby.'

To Freda's relief, Nora woke next morning almost like her old self, and called for Sammy to come and give her a kiss before he went to school. He didn't remind her that there was no school now, but buried his face against her thin breast. She stroked his head, asking what had upset him so much, but he couldn't tell her and after a few minutes she slipped again into her uneasy sleep.

There was another raid in the middle of August, exactly a month after the first. Old Portsmouth got it bad and Dan said you could see the Harbour Railway Station on fire from Camber dock. After the last raid he'd moved the bed downstairs to the front room, and he came home to find that Freda Vickers and Annie Chapman had managed to get Nora down to the shelter and stayed there with her and Sammy. He thanked them gruffly but Nora begged them to leave her where she was next time. 'It hurts too much, being moved, and I feel so sick . . . So long as my Sammy's all right . . .'

'I don't see how we can do that,' Freda said to Tommy. 'I couldn't sit easy in the shelter, knowing she was all by herself in the house. I don't know what we're to do, I'm sure.'

Sammy went to the shops every day. He was getting used to doing the shopping now and knew what to ask for. He spent hours standing in queues, hoping that whatever he wanted would still be available when he finally reached the counter and sometimes getting shoved to the back before the shopkeeper noticed him and called him over. Mr Hines, the butcher, had a soft spot for him, as he did for all children, and glared angrily at the other customers when they pushed past Sammy, telling them they ought to be ashamed of themselves. 'This nipper's ma's ill in bed, has been for weeks,' he said. 'She's only got him to get the groceries and you lot can't do no better than push in in front of him. You don't deserve no rations.'

'We thought he was with someone,' one or two said in aggrieved tones, but most of them did look ashamed and one said she was after a nice bit of oxtail, but if the nipper wanted it he could have it. 'It makes a lovely gravy, oxtail does. That'll build his mum up.'

Sammy had the oxtail, and a bit of bacon too that Mr Hines had put by, and then ran down October Street, watched all the way by old Mrs Kinch who was standing as usual at her front door, and along to his own house. He flung himself in through the front door, dropped the shopping on the table and scurried upstairs.

'Mum! Mum, I'm back. I've got some oxtail, a lady said it would make gravy to build you up, and Mr Hines give me a bit of bacon knuckle and – Mum?' He stopped by the bed, staring down in panic.

Nora was lying very still and white. Her eyelids fluttered and she opened her eyes. There was still a flicker of life in them, but he knew that it was fading fast.

He fell to his knees, gripping her thin hand.

'Mum,' he whispered. 'Mum, don't . . .'

Her eyes flicked over his face. There was the faintest ghost of a smile about her blue lips. A breath of sound escaped and he heard the words she had sung to him as a baby.

'Sammy . . . Sammy . . . shine a light . . .
Ain't you playing out tonight?'

There was a tiny pause. Her fingers moved, as if she were trying to lift them to his face. Almost without knowing what he did, he brought her hand to his cheek and held it there, cold and bony.

'My Sammy,' she whispered. 'My angel . . .'

Her eyelids fluttered a little, then closed. The last soft breath escaped her lips in a sigh and her head lolled to one side.

Sammy stared at her. He shook her hand gently. He touched her face and kissed her. And then, with the tears rolling silently down his cheeks, he climbed up on the bed and lay beside her cooling body.

136

Chapter Ten

Nora was buried in the churchyard of St Lucy's, the little church at the top of the street, where she had taken Sammy on Christmas Day. The funeral was attended by Dan and his two sons, and a few neighbours. Frank Budd, who had known Dan for years, took a couple of hours off from the dockyard and came in his best suit, and Jess stood beside him in her grey coat and hat with a black band round it. Tommy and Freda were there, together with Ted and Annie Chapman, and Peggy Shaw who lived next door to the Budds. There were others from April Grove and March and October Streets as well – Florrie and Jim Parkinson, the Hackers and old Mr Cornwell leaning on his two sticks. Nobody knew quite why he had come, since he had never spoken to Nora and it was doubtful that he even knew she existed, and Tommy muttered to his wife that he'd probably seen the little procession walking up the street and thought it was Sunday.

The coffin looked ridiculously small as they stood in the church, singing a wavering and uncertain hymn that none of them knew. 'Day of wrath! O day of mourning!' Freda sang and thought how frightening it sounded. She glanced at Sammy, in the pew in front of her, and wondered what he was making of it. 'Oh, what fear man's bosom rendeth.' Perhaps the words would be too difficult for him; she hoped so, anyway. Gordon, standing beside him, had a sullen look on his face that might mean he was trying not to cry, but could just as easily be fury at being brought home just for this, knowing he had to go back to the approved school at Drayton immediately afterwards.

He hadn't seen his mother since the time they'd realised how ill she was and brought him home to visit her. It seemed cruel, Freda thought. He was still no more than a nipper and, no matter what he'd done, he ought to have had the chance to be with his mum at the end. It was enough to set him against authority for life.

But there was more to worry about than funerals and boys like Gordon, who was at least being well looked after. There had been another raid a couple of days earlier, the worst so far, with over a hundred killed, so it was said, and hundreds more hurt or bombed out of their homes. One of the cinemas had been hit, right in the middle of the children's Saturday morning pictures, and the Baptist church next door to it badly damaged too. Luckily, not many of the kiddies were hurt but it brought it home to you how dangerous it was for them in Portsmouth now.

After the funeral the raids grew even worse – one or more almost every day. Hilsea gasworks was hit and a lot of houses round about. That was getting a bit too close to home, Freda said to her husband as they ate salt cod for their supper.

'I know. It's looking bad.' Tommy chewed for a minute or two and then said, 'Blimey, what do they do to this stuff, Free? It's more like cottonwool than cod. No disrespect to your cooking, mind.'

'It's got to be soaked for about three days to get the salt out, so Mr Perkins up the fish shop says. He says he's got a sinkful of it.'

'Well, it might get the salt out, but the blooming flavour goes with it. Still, if it's all there is . . .' He chewed again. 'How's that boy getting on? Young Sammy next door.'

Freda sighed and helped him to more cabbage and mashed potato. 'Have a bit more veg, love, there's plenty left for bubble and squeak tomorrow. I don't know what to do about the poor kiddy and that's the truth. D'you know, I went in yesterday and found him trying to fry an egg. Whole – in its *shell*! There was nearly an explosion.'

'He ought to be out in the country,' Tommy said. 'All on his own all day in that house, in the state it's in. It's not right.'

'I know, but what can we do? You can't interfere with a father's rights,' Freda said. She looked at the piled plates and sighed. 'I wonder what they're having for their tea.'

'God knows. Half a pound of nothing on toast, I expect. Can't you slip the nipper a bit of dinner now and then, Free?'

'I do. I think he'd starve if I didn't. I mean, Mr Hodges isn't even *there* half the time – he's off on ships for three or four days on the trot, leaving the kiddy to fend for himself. I mean, a little chap like Sammy can't manage, it stands to reason. He'll set fire to the place one of these days, that's what he'll do.'

They sat eating silently for a few minutes, thinking over the events of the past few weeks. Since Nora's death, things next door had gone steadily downhill. Dan had withdrawn into himself completely, curtly refusing all offers of help. He'd bitten Jess Budd's head off when she suggested that Sammy should be evacuated, and Frank Budd had come storming up the street and demanded an apology, which Dan had refused. Since then, Frank had forbidden his wife to have anything further to do with the man, even though they'd been friends of a sort before.

Sammy crept about like a shadow, his cat either at his heels or clutched in his arms. He'd been grubby enough before, but now he looked as if he never washed at all and his clothes were little more than tatters. He looked half scared and half starved, and the air raids terrified him almost out of his wits.

'I take him down the shelter with me and I give him a bit of dinner every day,' Freda said. 'But it's not enough,

Tom. The poor little chap's missing his mum, and Mr Hodges don't look after him at all. It breaks my heart.'

'Well, I think we ought to do something about it,' Tommy said decidedly. 'With winter coming on he'll either die of cold and starvation or set the place on fire like you said. Either way, it's up to us to see that something's done.' He pushed away his empty plate. 'I'll go down the billeting office, see if they can't talk Dan Hodges round. I know what you said about not interfering, Free, but we'd never be able to forgive ourselves if something happened to the nipper.'

'I know,' she said, taking the plates out to the scullery and coming back with a fruit tart. 'And he's not a bad little chap, you know. Not like that brother of his. I've never had a minute's worry he might pinch something when he's been in here, and I reckon if he was given a good wash and some decent clothes to wear he'd look quite nice.'

'Well, we'll see what we can do. I'm fed up with Dan Hodges jumping down my throat whenever we offers a hand. That nipper needs help and if his own father won't give it then it's up to us.' Tommy gave her a firm nod and looked at the dish she'd brought in. 'Blimey, Free, what the flipping heck's that?'

'It's bird's nest pudding,' she said. 'It's apples and blackberry jam and tapioca, baked in the oven. I got it off Gert and Daisy on the wireless.'

'Bird's nest pudding!' Tommy said. 'Well, we had bird's nest soup once when I was out in Hong Kong, but even they never made a pudding out of it! Never mind, we'll have a go at it. Give us a good plateful, but mind you don't put any birds in with it. I never could abide feathers in me throat!' He spooned up the pudding and looked pleased. 'Here, that's a bit of all right, that is! Better'n that salt cod, anyway.' He nodded again. 'That's what I'll do, Free. I'll go down the office first thing in the morning. I'll get that kid out in the country, away from the bombs, if it's the last thing I do.'

Tommy was as good as his word and next morning he took the opportunity to slip into the council offices. Tommy's job with the council took him all over Portsmouth, checking street lights (a job he didn't need to do now there was a blackout), repainting street signs and generally helping to keep the city tidy. Since the bombing had started, he said to Freda one day, there was a hell of a lot more tidying up to do. But he liked the work. He was out of doors a lot of the time and he was more or less his own boss. It also gave him plenty of opportunities to chat to passers-by and keep his finger on the pulse of the city. There wasn't much that went on in Pompey that Tommy Vickers didn't know about.

It was easy enough to find a reason to visit the offices and he found the tiny room that had been allocated to the evacuation authorities. He knocked on the door and went inside.

'Yes?' The woman at the desk was one of those volunteer women by the look of her – the wrong side of fifty, a bit stout, wearing a dark green jumper and cardigan, what they called a twinset, with a string of pearls round her neck. But she looked friendly enough, if a bit harassed by the pile of papers on the desk in front of her. 'Can I help you?'

'Well, it's not me that needs help, as a matter of fact.' Tommy gave her his saucy grin. 'Not that you wouldn't be the first person I'd come to if I did, mind! But it's the nipper next door I've come about.'

'If he's causing trouble, it's the school authorities you should speak to. Unless it's serious enough to warrant the police—'

'No, no, it's nothing like that. Poor little blighter, he don't need no more trouble. It's just that me and the missus – well, we wondered if you couldn't do something about getting him evacuated. He's all on his own, you see. Dad away half the time and don't hardly look after himself properly, let alone the kid. My missus, she slips him a bit of dinner most days or he'd get nothing at all, but you know what it's like, our rationing don't hardly stretch to feeding another mouth. Specially a growing boy. Not that he *is* growing much – what with his whooping cough and then his ma going the way she did, he seems to have stopped where he was the past year or two. Not that we knew him before that, being as the family—'

'Stop!' The woman raised her hand like a traffic policeman calling a halt to the cars around Piccadilly on *In Town Tonight*. 'Let's take it a bit more slowly, shall we? Now, what exactly is the problem with this little boy?'

Tommy stared at her. 'Well, I just told you. He needs to be evacuated.'

'All the children need to be evacuated,' the woman said wearily. 'And thank heaven most of them are. But there are still a few around the town and mostly it's because their parents don't want them to go, or perhaps because they already have been and their billets have proved unsatisfactory. Tell me about this little boy. What relation is he to you?'

'Well, he's no relation. He just lives next door.'

The woman put down her pen. 'I can't do anything about evacuation simply on the word of a next-door neighbour.'

'No, but you could go and see his dad and talk him round,' Tommy said, beginning to feel exasperated. 'I tell you, it's not right, a nipper living the way he is. He's not looked after. He's half starved, he's filthy dirty, he's left on his own for days at a time . . . He's going to have an accident one of these days. Set fire to the house, or gas himself.'

'I see.' She picked up her pen again. 'Well, I'll take some details and see what we can do. Now, what name is it . . . ?'

*

It was a different billeting officer who came to see Dan Hodges that evening. Neither Tommy nor Freda saw him, but they heard the voices through the wall and knew it was someone upper-crust. They also knew that Dan was angry about the visit.

'I dunno who been sticking their noses into my business,' Dan said in an aggrieved tone when Captain Whiting had come through to the living room and stated his business. 'I know it ain't what you're used to, the way we're living, but me and Sammy's all right, ain't we, Sam?'

He dragged Sammy to him, holding him against his side, while Sammy stared at the visitor with anxious blue eyes.

The captain looked thoughtfully at them, then sat down on one of the wooden chairs that stood by the old kitchen table. He had a briefcase with him, with papers inside. Dan glanced at it uneasily and sat down opposite him. He glowered at his son. 'You ain't been getting into trouble, have you? You know what happened to your brother.'

'Sammy's not in any trouble,' the captain said quickly. 'And what did happen to his brother? I understood there was just the one boy here.'

'Sent to approved school,' Dan said sullenly. 'You can look it all up in the records. It was nothing to do with Sam.'

'I see.' The captain looked at him thoughtfully. He was about sixty, had retired from the Army several years ago, and had taken on this work as part of his voluntary service. He also helped with the Home Guard and had a number of other small jobs he didn't talk about. He wore his uniform, the ribbons on it showing that he had seen distinguished action in the Great War. 'I understand you lost your wife recently, Mr Hodges.'

Dan flushed a dark red and looked down at the table. There was a deep groove in it, which Gordon had cut once, meaning to carve his initials until Dan had come in and sent him flying with a cuff on the head. 'What's that to you?'

'I'm sorry. I don't want to cause you any distress. But it

does mean that Sammy is here on his own for a lot of the time, doesn't it?'

'Well, and what about it? He's all right. Looked after his mum when she was poorly and if he could do that I reckon he can look after himself now. I always leave him some food, make sure he's all right.'

'But don't you work at Vosper's? You're away at sea sometimes, for two or three days at a time.'

'Here, how d'you know that?' Dan let go of Sammy and half rose to his feet. 'You been sniffin' round Vosper's? Look, I work hard down Camber, I do me job, I don't want no busybodies ferreting about getting me into trouble—'

'There's no question of getting you into trouble, Mr Hodges. It was just a matter of confirming certain pieces of information—'

'Yeah, and that's another thing. Who's been telling you things about me? Who's been sticking their nose in where it's not wanted? It was that nosy Annie Chapman, I'll lay. Or that bitch Ethel Glaister what can't bear to walk the same side of the street as me. Or Tommy Vickers, next door, him and his missus are always on about Sammy not getting enough to eat. Well, whoever it was, you can tell 'em where they can put their long noses. Me and Sam's all right.' He glared belligerently at the captain and looked round for Sammy, who had crept into his mother's old armchair in the corner.

'Are you sure?' Captain Whiting asked quietly. 'When you're at work and Sammy's here on his own, and there's an air raid? Are you sure your little boy's all right then, Mr Hodges?'

Dan flushed and looked down again. 'He knows what to do. We got a shelter.'

'But he's only a little boy, Mr Hodges. Eight years old. He can't be left alone in these circumstances. Suppose something happened to him – suppose he *didn't* go down to the shelter and the house were bombed. How would you feel, knowing that you'd left him alone? Don't you worry about him at all? Don't you wonder, when there's a raid and you're not here, don't you even *wonder* if he's safe?'

Dan sat down again. He didn't look up. 'His mum didn't want him to go,' he muttered. 'The other kids in the street, they went – 'cept for the Baxter boy. But Nora – well, Sammy was all she had, see, they was always close, proper mummy's boy he was – and she didn't want him to go. So he never went. He stopped here and looked after her.'

'But she's not here now, is she?' the captain said gently. 'There really isn't any reason why he can't go now.'

Dan looked up at him and the captain was shocked by the dark misery in his eyes. 'He was all she had,' he repeated, as if it were a lesson he had learnt by heart. 'She used to say that – her Sam was all she had. She used to say this rhyme, see – "Sam, Sam, shine a light, ain't you playing out tonight?" And after our Gordon went away—'

'Yes, I understand,' Captain Whiting said quietly. 'But Sammy's alone in the house now. He doesn't have his mother for company. And it's dangerous for him. He really would be much better off in the country.' He glanced over at Sammy. 'Wouldn't you like to be in the countryside, Sammy, with the other children?'

There was a long silence. Sammy, curled up in the chair, stared at the two men. He understood what was happening, but he had no idea what he wanted. He did not know how miserable he was. He was used to being at home and he couldn't imagine what it would be like in the countryside. From what the other children had told him on their occasional visits home, it sounded a fearsome place, full of huge animals with horns roaming vast empty fields and dark, dangerous forests.

'*He* don't know what he wants,' Dan said. 'It's no good asking him.'

'He'd be much safer,' the captain said. 'And I think he would be happier.'

'How d'you know that?' Dan demanded. 'Look at the way some of them country people treats our kids. Look at that Baker kid, washed down with a hosepipe when he was bad with appendicitis – he could have died! And those two nippers from the greengrocer's shop up the road, shut in a cupboard. How d'you know my Sam wouldn't go the same way?'

Captain Whiting bit his lip. The treatment some of the city children had received was a subject of considerable distress to him. He felt responsible for the problems that had been encountered and determined to see that they didn't happen again.

'We keep a very careful eye on the evacuees.'

'You can't do,' Dan stated. 'There's hundreds of 'em – thousands, when you looks at London. And now they're talking about taking youngsters from Southampton and Bristol and Liverpool – all the places they said wouldn't be bombed. How can you keep an eye on all of them?'

Captain Whiting sighed. 'I agree, it's a difficult situation. All I can say is we do our best. And as for Sammy – Mr Hodges, you *must* see that it would be better for him to be safe in the country. The bombing's getting worse. *You* know how badly London's been hit. We could get that sort of treatment here – even worse than the raids we've been getting. Saturation bombing that goes on and on for hours, destroying huge areas of the city. Buildings flattened – shelters buried.' He curled one hand into a fist and thumped it on the table. 'You *can't* leave a child of eight by himself during that kind of attack. You *can't* let him look after himself, sit all alone in an air-raid shelter with no one to look after him and comfort him. It's inhuman. It's neglect. It's sheer, selfish, bloody-minded *cruelty*.'

There was a long silence. The captain bit his lip and looked down at the table, already regretting his outburst. He'd always tried in cases like this to use gentle persuasion rather than loss of temper and what amounted to nothing short of abuse. And he was uncomfortably aware that a lot of what Dan said was true. They *couldn't* look after all the evacuees properly.

At the same time he was desperately anxious to get little Sammy Hodges away from the squalor of this hovel, away from the lonely life he led and, above all, away from the dangers he faced every day, all on his own.

A child of eight, he thought. It's not right. It's like something out of Dickens.

'All right,' Dan said at last. He didn't look at the captain. 'All right, you win. He can go.'

Captain Whiting stared at him. 'You mean it? You'll agree to his being evacuated?'

'I said so, didn't I?' Dan got up suddenly, almost knocking his chair backwards. 'I said he can go. Make the arrangements. Take him off, wherever he's got to go.' He looked down at his son and back at the captain. 'I don't want nothing to happen to him,' he said in a thick, husky voice. 'I don't want to be – what you said – *cruel*. I just been doing me best, that's all. But if you reckon he'd be better off out in the country – well, you take him. And make it snappy, because we got a big job on down Vosper's and I'll be at sea for the rest of the week after Wednesday.'

The captain looked at him. He glanced at Sammy, who had not moved from his curled position in the chair. Then he took some sheets of paper from his briefcase.

'There are a few forms to fill in. It won't take long. If we do it now, I can make the arrangements tomorrow and Sammy can leave on Wednesday morning.' He hesitated. 'I'm sure you won't regret this. You're doing the right thing.'

Dan grunted. He came back to the table and went rapidly through the forms, barely glancing at them before adding his signature. Once it was done, he remained silent, waiting for the captain to go.

Whiting stood up and looked at Sammy. 'I'll come

myself on Wednesday morning,' he said kindly, 'and take you to the railway station. Pack all the things you want to take with you and don't forget your gas mask. Have you got a warm coat for the journey?'

'I ain't got no coat,' Sammy whispered, and Captain Wilding glanced at Dan.

'I expect we'll be able to find something. The Lady Mayoress has set up a clothing fund. We'll be able to provide Sammy with anything he needs.'

Dan nodded and the captain hesitated another moment, then turned towards the door. He walked quickly down the passage and out of the front door. They heard his footsteps marching away along the street.

Dan moved towards his son and Sammy, still curled in the chair, stared up at him.

'Well, that's it, then,' Dan said gruffly. 'Your mum never wanted you to go away, but it looks like you're going to. And maybe it's for the best after all. Maybe you'll be better off out in the country, with trees and fields and animals all round you.' He put out his hand and laid it awkwardly on Sammy's head. 'I promised her I'd do me best to look after you and I ain't made much of a job of it, have I? Better let someone else take you over.'

He looked down at his son, then around the room with its peeling wallpaper, its battered table and sagging chairs, the pile of dirty overalls in one corner and last night's fish and chip paper still on the table.

It seemed cold and empty without Nora, but it came to him then that it was going to seem even emptier without Sammy.

Chapter Eleven

Ruth prepared for the arrival of her evacuee as if she were a pregnant mother expecting her first child. She had to remind herself that this wasn't her child, never would be, that its stay would be only temporary and she might not even like it. Of course I'll like it, she argued back as she unfolded fresh white cotton sheets and made up the narrow bed in the small spare room. It's a kiddy, isn't it, and it's been taken away from its own home and family. Poor little scrap. It'll be lost and bewildered, and it'll need some love and comfort. And that's what I'm going to give it.

Only Jane knew how much Ruth had longed for children of her own. It wasn't Ruth's way to visit her griefs on other people. She'd learnt that through being a sailor's wife. But she had thought there'd be children to fill the gap, and although she and Jack had certainly done their best when he was at home – she smiled at the memory of Jack and herself doing their best – it hadn't happened. And those long absences had made it even less likely.

The chance had gone for ever when Jack died. It wasn't that Ruth was too old, she was only thirty-five, but she'd just never fancied another chap after Jack. Will Prosser from Fair Oak, whom she'd known at secondary school, had been keen but Ruth hadn't fancied moving out to Fair Oak. It was a nice enough village but too far away from all her friends and family, and you couldn't get the train into Southampton like you could in Bridge End. And she hadn't liked the way Will laughed, a loud, honking noise that Silver would have picked up in no time. She couldn't face the thought of living with that laugh, honking through the house even when Will wasn't there.

Albert Newton, from Church Street, was a nice enough chap and they got on well. But he was fifteen years older than her and Ruth thought that was too big an age gap. And there was Blackie, his cat. How would Silver take to having a cat about the place? He wouldn't, Ruth thought. He'd hate it and the cat wouldn't be too thrilled either.

And that was another thing. Any man she married would have to live with Silver, which meant, more or less, living with Jack. What man would want to listen to his predecessor's voice asking to call Ruth sweetheart and saying he loved her?

I've learnt to do without men, Ruth thought, arranging a few books on the shelf. But I've never really learnt to do without kiddies.

The room was ready now and she stood with her hands resting on her hips, looking around it with satisfaction. The white curtains were patterned with apples, and she'd spread an apple-green coverlet over the bed to match and put a cheerful rag rug on the brown linoleum floor. There was a small wooden chair by the bed and a washstand with a marble top and a mirror. The shelf that ran along one wall bore the children's books that she'd had for years – a battered *Grimms' Fairy Tales* that she'd had when she was girl, which had half frightened her to death, and some Enid Blyton *Sunny Stories* books that Jane had handed on to her when Lizzie had grown out of them. Ruth had taken them to the hospital to read to children who were having their tonsils out, but she'd always kept them at home.

She glanced out of the window. The autumn sky was clouding over and the light was fading rapidly. Time to light the fire, or Silver would be complaining. He hated the cold, even after all these years in England. She went downstairs and gave his neck an affectionate scratch as he squawked a greeting.

'Goodnight, sweetheart. I love you, Ruthie.'

'I love you too,' she told him. 'Time for tea now.'

'Tea for two. I'm a little teapot –'

'You're a little flirt,' she told him as she knelt to put a match to the fire already laid in the grate. 'You think if you're nice to me now I'll give you a bit of cake. Well, you've got another think coming. There isn't any. It's Wednesday, see, and we only have cake at the weekends.'

'Splice the mainbrace,' he suggested and she laughed.

'And there's definitely no rum, you old scallywag.' She watched for a moment as the flames licked around the kindling and then caught. 'But I'll make some tea and we'll have it by the fire. I've got a couple of crumpets in the breadbin. It'll be a good thing to have a kiddy around the place,' she told the bird as she went out to the scullery. 'You might learn to copy him as well as you copy my Jack.'

And then she'd have the child's voice for company even after he – or she – had gone back home again, when all this was over, she thought. She could even get him to copy other youngsters, like he'd already copied things Lizzie had taught him. A whole family, all wrapped up in one grey bird.

'Goodnight, you old scallywag,' she heard coming from the other room in her own voice. 'Go to sleep now. See you in the morning.'

Ruth laughed. It didn't matter how much she pretended to grumble to other people about the bird, they'd only to listen to her voice coming tinnily from his big grey beak to know the truth. You couldn't keep anything secret with a parrot about.

The room was ready, yet no evacuee came. It seemed as if the second wave, brought by the reality of bombing, had stopped and there must be no children left in the cities. Or if there were, they weren't going to be evacuated.

Ruth went into the bedroom and looked sadly at the

apple-green coverlet and the curtains. It just didn't seem as if she was ever meant to have a child, even for a little while. I ought to offer to have a woman, she thought, someone who's on her own like me and hasn't got anywhere else to go. But anyone like that was likely to be either old or unwell, and although Ruth told herself she was being selfish, she just didn't want to have to do more nursing at home as well as at work. She wanted someone lively and young, someone who would fill the empty space in her heart.

Autumn was fading into winter. Nobody could call the war 'phoney' now. Every day brought news of more bombing, more people killed and injured, more people homeless. In London they called it the 'Blitz', after Hitler's 'blitzkrieg', meaning 'lightning war'. And it was like lightning that the bombers came, flashing across the skies to deliver their thunder on the cities below, and it was like lightning that the searchlights flung their bright spears upwards to spotlight them for the gunners.

London was bombed night after night. The people took to sheltering in the underground stations after dark and the authorities began to encourage them, providing bunks and making space for the Women's Voluntary Service to set up tea urns and even small lending libraries. People said it was like a big party down there sometimes – a party that ended, all too often, in tears when the revellers came up in the morning light and saw the devastation of their streets and homes.

'It's not just London, either,' Ruth said to Jane when they met in the village shop one day. 'Portsmouth's been getting a lot of raids too. Some of the evacuee kiddies must be worried stiff about their mums and dads.'

Jane nodded. 'I think they are, though people try not to talk about it too much in front of them. I know Reg and Edna do their best to give Tim and Keith Budd a proper childhood. Not everyone takes the same trouble, though, as we well know.'

The two women were silent for a moment, thinking of the little Atkinsons, Wendy and Alan, who had been billeted with the Woddis sisters. You wouldn't have credited that two old spinsters could be so unkind and the village was still ashamed that it had taken Jess Budd, herself an evacuee, to see what was going on and put it right. And her such a meek and mild little woman too! And then there was old Widow Hutchins and Martin Baker. It was no wonder some of the city parents didn't want to send their children away.

'I'd have given them a home,' Ruth said regretfully. 'Any one of 'em. But I can't blame them for not wanting to take the chance again.'

A few days later they heard the news of the raid on Coventry and were shocked to see in their newspapers the pictures of the cathedral, reduced to piles of rubble. Almost the whole of the city had been destroyed and there were heartbreaking reports of the survivors trekking hopelessly away from the ruins, carrying what few possessions they had salvaged. It seemed as if the Germans must be winning and the fears of invasion grew.

It was Liverpool's turn next, then Bristol. And then, at the very end of November, Southampton.

The inhabitants of Bridge End could see and hear it all. They stood in their gardens and watched with horror as the skies turned the colour of blood and the thunder of aircraft, gunfire and exploding bombs shook the ground. Jane sent George down to fetch Ruth up to them, saying she mustn't be there on her own; but Ruth had already gone to the Cottage Hospital in case casualties were brought in. Lizzie, white with fear, sat at her window staring at the surging glow of the fires, ignoring all her mother's pleas to come away.

'If there's a blast you'll be cut to pieces. Please, Lizzie. You don't *know* that Alec's ship was in dock tonight.'

'It could have been. He's due in some time this week. He might be down there now, burning—'

'Lizzie, stop it! It doesn't do any good to think like that. And suppose he comes home and finds you cut to bits by flying glass. You're being stupid and obstinate!'

Ruth tended the patients who were already in the hospital, reassuring them with calm words, but her mind was in the stricken city with Jack's parents who still lived in Southampton. They were both in their eighties and she'd begged them over and over again to come out to Bridge End, but they had steadfastly refused. 'We've lived in Southampton all our lives,' her father-in-law said, 'and this is where we'll die. Anyway, 't ain't right for folk our age to take up spaces what ought to be kept for younger folk.'

That was all very well, Ruth thought, but it didn't seem as if she was going to be allowed to have a youngster. The room was going begging but nobody seemed to want it.

She switched on her wireless next day to hear the news. Southampton (referred to merely as a 'town on the south coast') had received what was called 'sustained bombard-ment'. Nearly a hundred and fifty people were feared to have died and hundreds more injured. Theatres, cinemas, hotels and the newspaper office were all burnt out.

It took Lizzie most of the day to find out if Alec's ship had been in dock, but in the end she found that it was still at sea. Ruth, almost out of her mind over the Purslows, was in two minds whether to go into Southampton and see for herself when a telegram arrived. She had a moment of fear, as she stared at the little brown envelope, then sagged with relief as she read the brief words.

'They're all right. Oh Jane, they're all right.'

'Thank God for that,' her sister-in-law said. She had come down after dinner to see if there had been any news and they were standing in the little hallway together. 'D'you think they'll come out to Bridge End now?'

'Oh, I shouldn't think so for a minute,' Ruth said, half annoyed, half admiring of the old people's defiant courage. 'They'll stay there and let me worry every time a plane comes over, just for devilment! They're Jack's mum and dad, when all's said and done, and he'd have been just the same.'

'They're talking about evacuating from Southampton now,' Jane said, scanning the paper. 'About time too. You'd have thought they'd have known a big port like that would be in danger. I suppose they thought it would be just military ports, like Portsmouth. Well, perhaps you'll get your evacuee after all.'

'Perhaps,' Ruth said, seeing her out. 'But I reckon they've crossed me off their list.'

She shut the door quickly so as not to show a light, then went upstairs and looked again at her spare room. No kiddy was ever going to sleep here now, she thought sadly. There's something about me the billeting people don't like. Perhaps Mrs Hutchins gave widows a bad name, perhaps it's because I work at the hospital so couldn't be here all the time. But even if they do bring the women and children out of Southampton, like they're saying they should, they won't bring any of them here. It's just me and Silver, and always will be. I might as well just give up hope.

She wasn't even thinking about evacuees when she crossed the road from the hospital the next afternoon to find a woman in a brown hat and coat standing on her doorstep. It was a cold day, with a bruised look to the lowering clouds and a raw nip in the air.

'Mrs Purslow?' The woman consulted a sheet of paper. She wore fur gloves and a woollen scarf, but her nose still looked blue with cold. There was a small car parked a little way off along the muddy lane.

'That's me,' Ruth said warily, wondering who she was.

She looked official, as if she'd come to complain about rent arrears or some other unpaid bill, but Ruth knew she'd paid all her bills. It was a matter of pride to her that she didn't owe a penny to anyone.

'I believe you've expressed your willingness to offer hospitality to an evacuee,' the woman said, looking at Ruth with some doubt.

'I've said I'll take in some poor kiddy, yes,' Ruth agreed, when she had sorted out what the woman meant. 'But I didn't think I was getting one after all. I thought they'd come, all those that wanted to.'

'Most of them have. But we do have this particular case. A child whose parents . . .' The woman looked down her nose and evidently decided not to say any more about the child's parents. 'Evacuation seems to be the best answer . . . I'm afraid it's a boy. Would you still be able and willing to take him?'

'Yes, of course I would.' Ruth's heart gave a tiny leap. 'I don't mind a boy at all. I get on well with boys. When will he come? What's happened to the poor little mite's mum and dad?'

The woman ignored the last question. 'He'll be arriving some time in the next few days. I can't say exactly when – travel's difficult at the moment. I believe you work in the hospital?'

'Yes, it's only just across the road. It won't be any problem. And he'll have Silver for company too.'

'Silver?' The woman looked at her papers again. 'I understood you were a widow and childless. Do you already have a lodger? The rooms—'

Ruth laughed. 'No no, Silver's my parrot. He's very friendly,' she added hastily. 'Children love him. He talks, you see. My hubby brought him back for me years ago, to keep me company when he was away. Jack was a sailor, he was away a lot.' She knew she was babbling but there was something about the woman that made her feel nervous.

'He died a few years ago. Silver and me have been on our own ever since – except for having Dad with us, of course. But I love kiddies, I nurse them a lot in the hospital, you see, when they have their tonsils out and that sort of thing. And we deal with more serious cases too, of course. I'd be able to look after the little boy. He wouldn't be any problem.'

The woman gave her a dubious look. 'He's a city child, you know. From Portsmouth. They're different from country children.'

'They're children just the same,' Ruth said stoutly. She was getting a little tired of being patronised by this woman in her brown coat and hat and fur gloves. Probably never had any kiddies of her own, Ruth thought, never wiped a snotty nose or bathed a grazed knee. 'You just bring him along when he arrives,' she ordered. 'His room's all ready for him, and Silver and me'll look after him like he was our own. He'll be safe with us.'

The woman gave her a few more details, about the billeting fee, schooling and so on, then departed along the icy street. Ruth unlocked her door and went inside.

She never even asked to see the room, she thought. Never showed any interest in how I lived. That's all they care about these poor evacuees. They could be putting them with just anyone, anyone at all.

She went into the back room and opened the door of Silver's cage so that he could hop out on to his perch. 'We're going to have our evacuee soon,' she told him. 'A boy. Something wrong with his mum and dad, poor little scrap. You mind and be nice to him now, no swearing, see?'

'Bugger me,' the parrot said in a tone of astonishment and then, changing to rebuke, 'Language! Language!'

'I should think so too,' his mistress said severely, giving him a scratch on the head. 'I said *no* swearing. We've got to set a good example. Make the poor little mite feel at home. And now I want to listen to the wireless while I get my tea ready, so you just eat up your sunflower seeds and be quiet for a bit.'

She put on the kettle and went upstairs to look at the room she had got ready for the evacuee. It looked fresh and clean and tidy. Soon it would be strewn with a child's belongings – a few clothes, a toy or two, maybe some books. She felt a surge of pleasure and excitement, and reminded herself sternly that the child wasn't coming for her benefit, but for his own safety.

Well, he'll be safe enough here, she thought. He'll be safe with me and Silver.

Chapter Twelve

Ruth's evacuee arrived on her doorstep the very next day. She hadn't been told exactly when to expect him and was taken aback to find the billeting officer in her brown coat and hat standing there once more when she crossed the road after her shift at the hospital.

'You were out,' the woman said accusingly. 'We were just about to give up.'

Ruth looked at her and at the small boy standing at her side. He looked about seven years old and he was wearing a thick tweed coat, tied round the middle with string, and grey flannel shorts that drooped beneath his chapped knees. His socks were wrinkled round his ankles and his boots were split and worn down at the heels. He had dirty hair that might, she thought, be quite fair when it was washed, a grimy face and large blue eyes, and Ruth's heart went out to him at once.

'I was at work,' she said, fitting her key in the lock. 'Let's get inside, out of the cold. It's starting to snow.'

Inside the narrow passage they stamped their feet and the little boy blew on his fingers. He looked pale and unhealthy, Ruth thought, accustomed to the ruddier complexions of country children, and she made up her mind at once to feed him up.

'Come into the parlour,' she said, aware of Silver's presence in the back room. She didn't want his remarks and language causing the woman to change her mind about Ruth's suitability as a foster-mother. She took them into the room kept only for best, with its polished sideboard and family portraits, and invited the billeting officer to sit down on the horsehair sofa.

The woman spoke briskly. 'There are just a few formalities. I need your signature here, on this form, as a receipt for the child. This is his ration book and here's his identity card. If you have any problems, call on me at this address – I'm Mrs Tupper – and here's the office telephone number. I'll come round in a week or so to see how you're getting on.' She began to get to her feet.

'Wait a minute,' Ruth said. 'Aren't you going to give me his address in Portsmouth? And why's he being evacuated now, all by himself? There aren't any other children coming here as far as I know. It all seems a bit queer to me.'

Mrs Tupper looked at her with irritation. 'We're in the midst of a national emergency,' she said as if explaining to a child. 'Ours is not to reason why. You expressed yourself willing and able to take in a child, and here's one who needs a billet. And I'm sure he knows his own address, don't you?' she added, turning to the boy, who stared at her with wide, frightened eyes and backed away slightly.

'Of course I'm willing to take him in,' Ruth said quickly, half afraid that the woman would march him out of the house again. 'I just think I ought to know a bit more about him. You haven't even told me his name.'

'Gordon Hodges. It's on his identity card.' The billeting officer sounded impatient. 'I'm sorry, but I have to go. Despite what you seem to think, there are other children to be placed and a mountain of paperwork to be done. There's a war on and we all have to do what we can. All *you* need to do is look after this child.' She made it sound as if Ruth were the lucky one with no responsibilities, while others took on the real work. 'You have all the information you need and I'll call again next week. Now I'm afraid I really must go.' She was properly on her feet now, looming like a brown tweed mountain in the crowded room. Ruth got up too and put her hand on the boy's shoulder, feeling the bones through the material of his coat. She felt him flinch slightly. 'You'll be a good child, won't you –' Mrs Tupper consulted her papers '– Gordon.'

The boy stared at her. She tutted impatiently. 'A little lacking, I'm afraid. Anyway, you're a nurse, you'll know what to do for the best. I'll leave you now, Mrs Parker. He may need something to eat and drink before bed – some bread and milk, perhaps.' She was at the front door, brushing aside Ruth's attempts to speak. 'I dare say the most important requirement is a good wash. You may find you have some little visitors.' She lowered her voice and mouthed the next word. '*Fleas.*'

'I can soon deal with them,' Ruth said firmly. One of her jobs had been to tour schools examining the children's heads for nits. 'But—'

The billeting officer had the front door open now, letting in a swirl of snowflakes. The wind snatched Ruth's words away, or perhaps Mrs Tupper just didn't want to hear them. Perhaps she'd had a hard day as well and was longing to get back to her own fireside. Ruth decided to leave it as it was. If there was anything else she wanted to know, she could ask next time the woman called.

Mrs Tupper thrust her way out into the storm and marched along the street towards her Baby Austin. Ruth closed the door and turned, almost trampling on the boy as she did so.

'Good heavens, I didn't realise you were right behind me.' She regarded him in the dim glow of the hall light and he stared back at her, his eyes enormous. 'Well, you are a little scrap, aren't you?' she said, bending towards him. 'Now, I'm your Auntie Ruth, see? And your name's Gordon, is it?'

He shook his head and she realised that so far she hadn't heard him utter a word. Not that he'd had much chance, with that tweed elephant of a woman talking the minute she'd got into the house. Ruth waited, then repeated her question.

'What's your second name, love? You do know it, don't you? Gordon what?' It would be on his ration book, of course, but Mrs Tupper had hinted he might be a bit simple, and if he didn't know his name it didn't look likely that he would know his address either, although of course that would be on his ration book too.

He shook his head again, more violently this time, and opened his mouth. Ruth bent lower to hear what he was saying.

'Not Gordon,' the boy whispered. 'I ain't Gordon. Gordon's my brother.'

'Your *brother*?' Ruth stared at him. 'So where's he, then? Has he come to Bridge End too? Why didn't they keep you together?' But to her dismay she saw the huge blue eyes fill with tears and she added hastily, 'Never mind that now. You can tell me all about it tomorrow. So what's your name, if it isn't Gordon? And mine isn't Parker, by the way,' she added, remembering what she'd been trying to tell Mrs Tupper. 'It's Purslow. So she got both our names wrong, didn't she? Now you tell me yours and we'll be equal, see?'

The boy swallowed back his tears, but she knew they weren't far away and she bent again to catch the whisper. Poor little chap, she thought, he's tired, cold and scared to death. And he needs something hot inside him. I'd better get him straight into the living room and light the fire, and give him a nice wash and some supper.

'Sammy,' the boy whispered. 'Me name's Sammy. Sammy Hodges. It's me brother what's Gordon. Me *brother*.'

'All right, I understand that,' Ruth told him. 'And we'll find out about your brother tomorrow, see if he's anywhere near. Now you come along with me and see what I've got in my living room.'

She opened the door as she spoke and switched on the light. Silver, who had been waiting impatiently at the door to his cage, let out a squawk and danced up and down on his perch. He saw Sammy and stretched his neck, turning his head sideways in the way he had when something had taken him by surprise. Then he squawked again.

Sammy stopped dead in the doorway. His eyes, already enormous, looked as if they were about to pop out completely. He stared at Silver and then at Ruth. He started to back away, his face white.

'Blimey!' he said in an unexpectedly deep, gravelly voice. 'It's a bleedin' eagle!'

It was much later that evening when Ruth finally sat down alone, with Sammy asleep at last upstairs.

The sight of Silver had frightened him badly and she'd had a hard time of it to persuade him that the parrot was not only harmless but friendly.

'No, Silver's not an eagle,' she told him as he started to back out of the doorway. She drew him into the room, disturbed by the thinness of his shoulders. 'He's a parrot and he won't hurt you. He can talk.'

Sammy removed his stare from Silver and fixed it upon her. 'Birds can't *talk*.'

'Parrots can. Listen.' She went over to the cage and scratched Silver's neck. 'Hello, Silver. Hello, my boy. Say something to Sammy. Say "I'm a little teapot".'

Silver turned his head sideways and shuffled along the perch, his beak firmly closed. Ruth tried again. '"The grand old Duke of York, he had ten thousand men . . ." Come on, Silver, be nice now. Sammy's come to stay with us. How about "Run, rabbit, run"?' He's only just learnt that,' she added, turning to Sammy. 'He learns very quickly. You'll be able to teach him things too.'

Sammy looked round a little anxiously. 'Where's the lav?'

'Oh, you poor boy! Of *course* you need the lavatory – you don't want to stand there while I chatter to this silly bird. Come with me and then I'll get you some tea. Silver will talk in his own good time.' She led Sammy out through the kitchen into the yard and showed him the door to the lavatory, then returned to set a match to the fire. She put the kettle on and began to cut some bread.

Sammy came back while Ruth was making the tea. A pile of bread and margarine was ready on a plate with a pot of home-made jam beside it, and she was looking in the cupboard for something more substantial. She poured some warm water from the kettle into the sink and handed him a scrap of soap from the jam jar on the windowsill.

'There you are, wash your hands and dry them on the roller-towel behind the door. You may as well give your face a bit of a treat as well,' she added as he swished his hands doubtfully in the water. He rubbed them over his face, leaving dirty streaks, then wiped himself on the towel. I'd better have that off and wash it next, she thought, observing that he had not so much washed himself as dirtied the towel. The billeting lady was right – he did need a good wash. But he would do for now, and in Ruth's opinion the most important things were a good hot meal inside him and a smile on his face.

'D'you like beans on toast? I always think they're nice if you're cold and tired. Tasty, and give you a bit of comfort.' She took out a tin and looked at him enquiringly.

'I has them at home,' Sammy confirmed. 'They're all right.' Apart from his remark about the eagle, he had reverted to a whisper. It was as if he was afraid to speak and he kept glancing nervously around the room. He's as frightened as a kitten, she thought pityingly.

Relieved that she had found something he would like to eat, Ruth opened the tin and tipped the contents into a saucepan. She lit the grill of the little gas stove and put a couple of fresh slices of bread underneath.

'So tell me a bit about yourself,' she said to Sammy, warming some milk in a pan. 'How old are you?'

'I'm eight,' he whispered. 'I had a birthday before – before –' he stopped and blinked hard, then went on '– and I was seven before that, so I must be.'

'Eight!' Ruth had thought him at least a year younger. 'And how old's your brother?'

Sammy looked away. Alarmed, she saw tears in his eyes again and hastily changed the subject. 'Where do you live, then? Portsmouth?'

He nodded. 'Can I go and see that eagle again?'

Ruth smiled and tipped the warm milk into a cup. 'Of course you can,' she said, adding a spoonful of sugar. 'But he's not an eagle, he's a parrot, remember? And his name's Silver.' The toast was done and she put it on two plates and tipped hot beans on top. Sammy had already gone through to the living room and she followed him with the two plates. 'No! *Don't* do that!'

Sammy was standing by Silver's cage, poking the bird with the brass toasting fork Ruth kept by the fire. Silver was backing into his cage, squawking with annoyance. As Ruth snatched away the toasting fork he began to swear. Sammy cringed away.

'Bugger me! Sod the little buggers. It's a bleedin' eagle. It's a bleedin' eagle.'

Sammy stared at the parrot, jerked out of his nervousness by astonishment. 'That's what *I* said! See, it *is* a neagle, it says so itself. And it doesn't like me.'

'It isn't an eagle, it's a parrot. And he's just copied you. He already knew some of the words, so it was easy.' Ruth didn't say which ones he knew. 'And he doesn't mean you, when he says that. He learnt some of those words when he was on board ship coming home from Africa. They used to get cockroaches . . .' She looked at Sammy, wondering if he understood what she was saying, but he nodded.

'We had cockroaches too. My dad used to hit 'em with his boot.'

And probably used the same words while he did it, Ruth added to herself. She wondered who was going to learn most, Sammy or Silver.

'Come on,' she said, 'sit up to the table and have your tea. I've warmed you some milk as well.'

He eyed it dubiously. 'I haven't never had *hot* milk before.'

'Well, try it now.' She picked up her knife and fork and began to eat. Sammy watched her for a moment and then picked up his fork and, using it like a spoon, began to shovel beans into his mouth.

Ruth watched him for a few moments. He was ravenous, she thought. Poor little mite. She remembered Mrs Tupper's words. 'And I think you'd better have a bath before you go to bed.'

Sammy looked at her suspiciously. 'A bath?'

'Yes. You'll have to help me bring it in from the yard.' Ruth normally got one of the neighbours to help her drag in the old zinc bath that hung on a nail outside. 'We can put it in front of the fire.'

He looked at the fire. 'Bring it in here?'

'That's right. What do you do at home? Do you have a bathroom indoors?' It didn't seem likely, but you never knew. Ruth seemed to remember hearing some comment about people with bathrooms keeping coal in the baths.

Sammy stared at her. 'We ain't got no bath. Mum took us down the municipal sometimes. But it costs sixpence, see. Dad said we ain't got money to pour down the drain.' His blue eyes filled again and his lower lip shook, but at least he was speaking in a more normal tone now instead of that fearful whisper.

Poor little mite, he's missing his mother, Ruth thought. She took away his empty plate and put the bread and jam

166

on the table. Sammy looked at it doubtfully and Ruth spread a slice for him.

He glanced at her. 'Is that for me too?'

'Yes, of course. You need something more than baked beans. You must be hungry after coming all that way.' He touched the bread, still uncertain, and she added encouragingly, 'Come on, eat it up.'

Sammy lifted the bread and then, as if suddenly afraid it would be snatched from him, crammed it into his mouth, pushing until it was all in and his cheeks bulged. He chewed desperately, his eyes still fixed on her face, then swallowed.

Goodness me, Ruth thought, perhaps the people who say evacuees have no manners are right. Or perhaps he was really hungry. She debated whether to give him some more, but before she could decide he had slid down from his chair and begun to back into the corner again, his eyes fixed on Silver, who had recovered from his annoyance and shuffled out of his cage to sit on his perch. He leant forward and swung his body from side to side, muttering to himself, while Sammy watched from a safe distance.

'Do you have any pets at home?' Ruth asked. 'A dog, or a cat? Or maybe you've got a canary. Lots of people have canaries.'

The boy shook his head and to Ruth's dismay his eyes filled with yet more tears. 'I had a cat but Dad said it got run over. I reckon he drowned it really, 'cause of the bombing. He said the gov'ment said dogs and cats had to be des—destroyed.' His voice trembled. 'I wish you had a cat.'

'I don't think Silver would like me to have a cat,' Ruth said, thinking of Albert Newton's Blackie. 'But I'm sure your dad didn't drown yours. I expect it just died peacefully of old age.' She decided to change the subject. 'Whereabouts do you live, in Portsmouth?'

'Copnor. We used to live in Old Portsmouth, till we got chucked out of the pub. Then we moved to Copnor.'

'Oranges and lemons,' Silver said, deciding to join in. 'Bells of St Clements. Ding-dong bell, pussy's down the well, who pushed him in –'

Sammy stared at him. 'That's nursery rhymes.'

'He knows lots of them,' Ruth said. 'All sorts of songs and things, he knows.' She wanted to ask Sammy more about his home and family, but he was looking suddenly white beneath the grime. He's worn out, poor little chap, she thought. He needs to be put to bed, but he can't go in that state. She got up and began to clear the table.

'I'll bring the bath in now.' She went out to the backyard.

The bath wasn't a full-length one. It was a short, oval tub, just big enough to sit in. Ruth took it down from its nail and between them they manoeuvred it through the door and into the living room. She then fetched a galvanised bucket and began to fill it with hot water.

Sammy stood looking at it, doubt in every line of his body. 'Have I got to get in that? With no clothes on?'

'Yes, of course. You've had baths before.' Presumably by the 'municipal' he meant public baths. 'And I'll wash your clothes and hang them round the fire so they're clean and dry for you in the morning.'

He looked at her. 'But you'll see me bare.' The anxiety was back in his face and voice.

'Well, that doesn't matter. I'm a nurse. I see people without clothes on all the time.'

'Boys?' he asked unbelievingly.

'Lots of boys,' she assured him. 'Look, there's nothing you've got that I haven't seen a hundred times.' She poured in the last bucket of water and tested it with her hand. 'There, that's just right. Now, you take off your clothes and get in and I'll fetch a nice new bar of soap to wash you with. You'll feel a different boy when you're clean.'

She went out into the kitchen and got a bar of Lifebuoy from under the sink, returning to find Sammy very slowly unbuttoning his shirt. Ruth knelt in front of him and helped him, talking soothingly, as if he were one of the frightened children who had come into the hospital to have their tonsils out. She peeled off his shirt. 'Hullo, what's this brown paper for?'

'It's me vest,' Sammy said. He'd struggled to cobble it together himself, remembering how his mother had done it for him the year before. 'I always has a brown paper vest in winter.'

'I see.' Ruth had heard of such things before – some of the country children, years ago, had been 'sewed into' their flannel underclothes for the entire winter. But Sammy's paper vest didn't seem enough to keep a flea warm – though it was obvious he'd had plenty of them – and it was sewn badly and ruckled around him, tearing in places. She sighed and then looked in dismay at the thin body.

Why, it looks as if he's never had a square meal in his life, she thought, touching the prominent ribs, and went out to the kitchen, feeling like weeping. Dirt she'd expected, fleas and nits she'd been prepared for, but starvation she had not even considered. The child had been really neglected and nobody seemed to have done anything about it. What sort of a mother had he had? What about his teachers at school? Had nobody realised what was happening to this poor child?

She went back into the living room. Sammy was standing where she'd left him, looking uncertainly at the bath of water, while Silver watched from his perch, quiet for once.

'Come on, then,' she said gently. 'Get in and sit down.'

'Sit down?' he repeated.

'Yes. What did you do at home?'

'Mum used to wash me face with a bit of flannel. And sometimes she'd make me stand in the sink so she could wash me bum. We never had a bath we could sit in.'

'Well, we have here,' Ruth said firmly, 'so now you can

sit down. It's all right, it's not too hot. Try it with your foot first.'

Distrustfully, he lifted one foot and dipped it in the water. With a wary eye on her, he stepped in and stood for a moment, thin and shivering – more with nervousness than from cold, Ruth thought – and then, with an air of someone going to his doom, sat down.

'It's *hot*.'

'It only feels hot because you're a bit cold from having no clothes on. It won't scald you.' Ruth knelt on the rag rug beside the bath, picked up her flannel and dipped it in the water. She dabbed it gently over his narrow shoulders and he gasped.

'Don't do that!'

'It's all right. You have to be wet, to be washed. When I've soaped you all over, I'll bring in a bucket of clean water to rinse you with, and then I'll wash your hair.' She soaked the flannel in the water and rubbed the bar of Lifebuoy on it, then began to wash him. He squirmed away from her and she continued to talk to him in a soothing voice. 'It's all right, Sammy. I'm not going to hurt you. Just let's get this dirt off you. It's nice and warm here, in front of the fire, a nice place for a bath. Afterwards I'll wrap you in the towel and you can sit in front of the fire for a bit, while I find you something to wear in bed. Or have you got your own pyjamas?'

'I dunno. I dunno what pyjamas is.'

'Well, I'll find you something for tonight, and maybe tomorrow we can get you some.' Ruth wondered if you could ask the billeting office for clothes or if you were supposed to provide them yourself. It didn't seem right that children should be sent to foster homes without the right clothes, but Sammy didn't seem to have anything with him, other than a paper carrier bag which had shown some suspiciously greasy stains. Perhaps Mrs Tupper will bring his case tomorrow, she thought, and wondered again what kind of home he came from. Not a loving one, that seemed certain. And where was his brother Gordon?

She moved her hands over his body, washing every part with the flannel, aware that his tension was slowly dissolving under her firm, gentle touch. He was so thin, she could almost count his ribs. More milk for you, my boy, she thought, more milk and butter and eggs, that's what you need.

'You're tickling me,' he complained and she smiled.

'Look at this water! You've turned it almost black. Now for your hair. Have you ever had your hair washed?'

'Only when I had nits. They give us black stuff to wash it with. It stings,' he said, stiffening again. 'It hurts me eyes.'

'Not if you keep them tightly closed.' She fetched a bucket of fresh water and rubbed the soap into a lather. 'Shut them tight now, and don't open them till I say so. Here goes.'

Hair-washing was not easy. At the first touch of soap on his head, Sammy began to roar and squirm. The soapsuds poured down his face and into his open mouth, and he choked and yelled and wriggled all the more. Water slopped over the side of the bath and spattered into the fire, and Silver, shocked by the noise, joined in with his own increasingly panic-stricken squawks.

'Bugger me! Bugger *me*! What shall we do with a drunken sailor? Pussy's down the well. I'm a little teapot. Goodnight, precious bird. Sod the little buggers. Bugger me! Bugger *me*!'

'Be quiet, Silver!' Ruth panted, trying to keep a grip on the slippery body. 'Sammy, keep still. It won't go in your eyes if you just keep them closed. *And* your mouth. Just keep still, now, and let me rinse it off.' She reached with one hand for the enamel mug and dipped it into the bucket. 'Hold still. I'm going to pour some nice clean water over your head. *It won't hurt you*. Keep *still*.'

It was done at last. Sammy sat in the bath, red-faced and sobbing. Ruth lifted him up to stand in the bath while she dipped the flannel into what was left of the clean water and gave his body a final rinse, washing away the dirty scum that clung to his skin. She set him on the rag rug.

'You should have had two baths to get that lot off.' She wrapped him in the big towel that had been warming in front of the fire, and folded it close around his body. 'There, doesn't that feel better?'

Sammy drew a deep, shuddering breath. 'There's water all over me.'

'I know. But it's clean water and the towel will dry you.' She picked up a smaller towel and began to rub his head briskly. 'Goodness me, your hair's really fair. Now, you sit here on the rug, in front of the fire, and I'll find something for you to wear.'

She went upstairs, wondering what she had that was suitable for a very small, thin boy to wear. An old blouse, perhaps. Or something of Jack's.

Ruth had kept Jack's civilian clothes in the spare-room cupboard. There weren't many – he'd only needed them when he was home on leave – and she'd never been able to bring herself to throw or even give them away. But now, without hesitation, she went to the cupboard and looked among the clothes folded there. A few blue working shirts, soft from much washing – one of those would do for him in the morning, if she cut it down a bit. And a pair of pyjamas with blue stripes. She took out the jacket and held it against her cheek.

'I know you wouldn't mind, Jack,' she whispered. 'I know you'd want the poor little mite to have a bit of comfort.'

She stood for a moment with it in her hands, then took it downstairs to where Sammy was sitting, still wrapped in his towel, in front of the fire. Gently, she lifted the towel from his thin shoulders, gave him a few final dabs to make sure he was properly dry and hung the pyjama jacket round his shoulders.

It fitted him like a nightshirt, reaching to below his knees. She looked at him, as thin as a reed, his hair almost white and as soft as a rabbit's fur, his eyes even larger in a face that, cleansed of its grime, was as pale and smooth as ivory, and her heart seemed to move in her breast.

'You poor little soul,' she said, gathering him gently in her arms. 'You poor, dear little soul . . .'

The bedroom took Sammy completely by surprise.

'Is it for me?' he asked, staring at the neat bed with its apple-green coverlet. 'Me to sleep in, all by meself?'

'Of course it is,' Ruth said with a smile. 'Who else did you think was going to sleep in it?'

'I always had to sleep with our Gordon, till – till he went away. I thought there'd be another boy here.'

'Well, there isn't. There's just you and you can have the bed all to yourself. It's nice and warm,' she added. 'I put in a hot-water bottle while you were sitting by the fire.' She drew back the sheet to show him the stone bottle, wrapped in a knitted cover. 'That'll keep you warm for hours. And you've got a nice soft pillow, look, with feathers in.'

'That eagle's feathers?'

'No, not Silver's feathers, and I've told you, he's a parrot, not an eagle. The feathers in the pillow are from a chicken, or perhaps a duck. Come on, now, get in. You're tired out, you'll be asleep in no time.'

Sammy eyed her dubiously. 'Where will you be?'

'I've got my own bed in the next room,' Ruth said. She wondered if he was frightened at the idea of being left alone. 'Look, I'll show you.'

In the front bedroom he stared at the double bed and the bow-fronted chest of drawers. 'Is this where you sleep? In that big bed, all by yourself?'

'Well, there's no one else living here,' Ruth said with a smile.

'My mum had a bed like that,' he said. 'She slep' in it with me dad.' He closed his mouth firmly.

'Well, I used to sleep in it with my hubby. He was called Jack. He was a sailor – it was him brought me Silver. Now, you know where I'll be if you need me. If you want anything, or you feel a bit scared or lonely, you just come in and wake me up, all right? Let's get you into your own bed, now. You're half asleep on your feet.'

Sammy allowed her to lead him into the small bedroom. She pulled the covers back again and he lay down, his head a pale gold against the white cotton pillowcase. Ruth pushed the bottle close to his feet and drew the bedclothes up to his neck. She tucked them in gently and touched his pale cheek with her finger.

'Goodnight, little boy,' she whispered. 'Sleep tight. Sleep safe. You'll be all right with me. You'll be all right with Auntie Ruth.'

Sammy slid his thumb into his mouth. For a minute or two he gazed up at her, before his eyelids drooped. They were so fine that it seemed she could still see the blue of his eyes, glowing through the translucent skin. Then he gave a small sigh and turned his head away, already asleep.

Ruth stood very still for a moment. She touched his cheek gently with one fingertip, feeling the softness of his skin. Why, he was little more than a baby; a lost and lonely little boy; the child she had longed for, sent to her at last.

She gazed down at him until the tears blurred her vision. Then, with a sigh, she turned away and slipped quietly out of the room, leaving the door ajar in case he woke and was frightened.

Downstairs in the scullery she washed his clothes and hung them round the fire to dry before starting work on the shirt she was going to alter to fit his thin body. His socks needed darning too, there was more hole than sock, and she put them closest to the fire so that they would dry quickly.

Poor little boy, she thought. Poor little neglected, half-starved boy.

'Poor old Joe,' Silver said sorrowfully. 'Hear the bugle calling, poor old Joe.'

Ruth looked at him, startled, and realised she must have spoken aloud. 'You're too quick, you are,' she told the parrot. 'Only got to say one word and you're on to it like a cat on to a mouse. You've got to learn to be a bit more tactful, see?'

'We joined the Navy,' Silver said obligingly, 'to see the world. But what did we see? We saw—'

'Oh, shut up,' Ruth said and threw one of Sammy's socks at him.

Chapter Thirteen

Having an evacuee wasn't, Ruth discovered, simply a matter of feeding, clothing and sending off to school.

That first night had been punctuated by nightmares. Three times Sammy had woken, screaming and sobbing, and Ruth had hurried in to hold him in her arms, wake him gently and reassure him that he was all right. In the end she'd had to stay until he was asleep again, his hand in hers, and when she'd crept away to her own room she'd barely nodded off when he was calling out again.

In the morning, after an uneasy sleep, she woke to a familiar pungent smell and the sound of muffled sobbing. Annoyance swept through her; not with Sammy, but with herself. I ought to have known he'd be a bedwetter, she thought, pushing back the blankets and feeling for her slippers. Her old camel dressing gown was hanging on the back of the bedroom door; she wrapped it round herself and hurried into the other room.

'Oh, *Sammy*.'

He had pulled the wet sheets from the bed and heaped them on the floor. Jack's pyjama jacket, soaking wet, was piled on top of them and Sammy, wrapped in the eiderdown that seemed to be the only dry thing in the room, was huddled on the floor by the window, weeping bitterly. When he looked up and saw her, Ruth was appalled to see the fear in his eyes and the way he tried to cower even further out of reach.

'I'm a bad boy,' he said miserably in his hoarse voice. 'I'm a dirty, bad boy.'

'Sammy, you're *not* bad.' Ruth crossed the room towards him and bent to take the thin, cringing body in her arms. 'You're not bad at all. You're just little and frightened. And this happens to lots of boys. *Lots* of them.'

He shook his head. 'Only bad ones like me.'

'No. It's nothing to do with being bad. It's just something that happens. You can't help it.'

'Dad says I can. He says I do it out of devilment. He says I'm a wicked little bleeder.'

'Well, your dad's wrong,' Ruth said firmly. She didn't believe in taking a child's side against its father, but in this case . . . 'Your dad's *wrong*.'

There was a moment's silence. Perhaps I shouldn't have said it, all the same, Ruth thought. A kiddy wants to think well of its father. It could upset him all the more. 'If you don't stop crying soon,' she said lightly, 'you'll flood the whole house out. And Silver can't swim! Don't you think there's enough water to be going on with?'

The joke fell on stony ground. Sammy sobbed harder than ever and Ruth sighed and lifted him in her arms. 'Come on, let's get you downstairs and light the fire. You'll need another bath – it's lucky we didn't put it outside last night, isn't it! And your clothes will be dry by now. Let's try and get you nice and smart before Mrs Tupper comes round with your luggage.'

'I ain't got no luggage,' Sammy said, sniffing and wiping his nose on the eiderdown. 'I brung all me stuff in the bag. They give me some clothes from the mayor's fund but I left 'em on the train.'

Ruth had looked in the carrier bag after he'd gone to bed last night. It had contained a grubby shirt, a pair of ragged short trousers and a tin of sardines. The sardines had gone into the cupboard and the shirt and trousers into the wash with the rest of his things. 'Is that all you've got? There's no more to come?'

'No, miss. I left 'em on the train. I forgot them. They wasn't mine anyway, they was from the mayor's fund.'

'No, *Auntie*,' she corrected him. 'Auntie Ruth, that's what you call me, remember? Well, we'll just have to see what we can find for you then. I don't know what clothes they'll have in the shops, they're as empty as everywhere else. Talking about putting clothes on ration, they are, like food, and goodness knows how that will work out. I'll see if I can borrow a few things from my friend Mrs Moore, she's got four boys so there's bound to be a few bits and pieces she can spare.' They reached the bottom of the stairs and she set Sammy down in her armchair, still wrapped in the eiderdown. 'Now, you just sit down here while I light the fire and get some hot water on the go. You'll feel all the better for a wash.'

'I had a wash last night,' he objected. 'I had a *bath*. It's not good for you, too much washing, it can wash all your skin away.'

'I don't think there's much risk of your skin being washed away,' Ruth said dryly. 'You've got a bit of catching up to do first.' She raked out last night's coals and ashes, and carried them out to the bin in the backyard. Returning with some kindling, she noticed that Silver's cage was still covered up and hastily pulled off the red cover. 'Goodness me, that's the first time I've ever come down without uncovering His Majesty first thing! And how are you this morning, my bird?'

Silver shook out his feathers and eyed her balefully. 'Poor old Joe. *Poor* old Joe.'

'Poor old Silver, you mean. Not used to not getting all the attention, are you? Well, you'll have to wait a few minutes while I see to young Sammy here. His need is greater than yours.' She knelt to lay the fire and within a few minutes flames were licking round the kindling and catching at the small coals she had laid on top. Ruth regarded it ruefully. Coal was getting scarce already and keeping a fire in all day was impossible. She generally took Silver over to the hospital during the winter, much to the delight of the patients. Now it looked as if she'd have to take Sammy as well.

'Still, you'll be at school in a week or so,' she said, washing him down with warm water as he stood in the bath; since it was only for a wash, she'd poured in no more than a couple of inches. Gently, she dried the bony body. Then she wrapped him in Jack's old blue shirt and sat him in the armchair.

'Have to do some washing next,' she told him cheerfully. 'I'll get the fire lit under the copper before we have our breakfast, otherwise it'll take all day. And it doesn't dry in this weather, no use at all in hanging it out. How does your mum manage?'

There was no reply. She glanced at him and saw the tears trickling down his cheeks. There's something very wrong there, she thought as she went out to the little brick wash-house in the backyard, and what about that brother he talked about too? Maybe I should ask Mrs Tupper when she comes.

'That fire's just about right for making toast,' she said when she came back. 'We'll have some for our breakfast, shall we? You like toast, don't you?'

'I dunno,' he said listlessly, wiping his nose on his sleeve.

'Yes, you do. You had some last night, with your baked beans. Look, I'll just cut a slice of bread and put it on this fork –' she picked up the brass toasting fork he'd been teasing Silver with '– and hold it out to the fire, and it'll be done in no time. Didn't you ever do this at home?'

He shook his head. 'Won't it burn?'

'It'll toast. Look, it's turning brown already. We'll take it off and put it on the other way round, see, and do that side. You can have a go in a minute if you like.'

How can a child grow to eight years old and not know how to make toast, she wondered, spreading it with margarine and putting a smear of Marmite on top. She put it on a plate and handed it to him, and he sniffed it dubiously.

'Smells funny.'

'It's nice. Try it. It's good for you.' She watched as he nibbled the edges, and then went upstairs to collect the wet sheets. Poor little chap, she thought, gathering them up, I suppose he gets smacked for this at home. As if he can help it! As if any child would want to wet the bed deliberately.

A sudden scream nearly made her jump out of her skin. She dropped the sheets and hurried down the narrow stairs, almost falling down them as she smelt burning. She pushed open the door to the little staircase and gasped. The room was full of smoke and Sammy was holding a blazing toasting fork, waving it about wildly and screaming at the top of his voice. Silver was squawking with terror and trying to get back in his cage. At any moment, she thought in panic, the flames were going to catch on the curtains and the whole house go up.

'Let me have it! Give it to me! *Sammy*!' She snatched the fork away from him and dunked the flaming mess into the bath, where it hissed virulently before going out. 'Goodness me, child, whatever were you doing?'

'I was trying to make toast,' he sobbed between his coughs. 'I wanted to make you some toast.' He collapsed on to the floor and lay there shaking with sobs. 'I told you I was bad! I told you! You'll hit me now, you'll have to!' His voice rose to a scream. 'The house is burning down! The house is burning down!'

'Nonsense. It was only a bit of toast.' Ruth opened the window and went through the scullery to open the back door as well. 'I'm sorry about the cold, but we've got to get this smoke blown out. It's bad for Silver . . . Now get up, Sammy, and stop crying. Are you all right? You haven't hurt yourself?'

She picked up the trembling boy and set him on his feet.

He shook and shuddered in her hands. He's really frightened, she thought, he's terrified.

'It's all right,' she said soothingly. 'It's all over now and nothing bad has happened. Ssh, now, you can stop crying, no one's cross with you. Everything's all right. You're not hurt, are you?'

'I got a bit of blood on the bread,' he said, snivelling and showing her a nick in his finger. 'The knife's sharp. But it don't hurt,' he added bravely.

'You cut the bread?' She looked at the loaf with its ragged edge, and at the thick, uneven doorstep that was floating in the bathwater. 'Sammy, you mustn't do that. You mustn't do anything until I've told you it's all right, do you understand? Not until I know what you're capable of.' She looked at him through the last wisps of smoke. 'Now let's make sure Silver's all right, shall we? He's not used to all this excitement.'

Together they looked at the parrot, who was sitting on his perch again looking distinctly ruffled. Ruth stroked his feathers down and spoke to him as soothingly as she had spoken to Sammy. 'Poor old chap. Poor old Silver. What a morning, eh? And you haven't had your breakfast yet, have you? You haven't even had one single sunflower seed. Poor old boy.'

'Poor old Joe,' Silver agreed mournfully. His hoarse voice softened. 'I love you, Ruthie.'

Ruth felt a lump in her throat. Jack's voice was speaking to her again, as he'd spoken to her during those long nights at sea when he'd been bringing Silver home. So long ago, she thought, and yet hearing his voice coming from the parrot's beak made it seem like yesterday. If he'd lived they might have had their own little boy like Sammy. Only he would never have been as timid and frightened as Sammy seemed to be.

She looked down at the boy at her side. His sobs were

quietening and he was gazing up at Silver with wonder. She thought of the soaked sheets upstairs and the blazing toast.

Having an evacuee wasn't going to be as easy as she'd thought. But already she was committed to making it a success. She and Silver together.

Luckily, Ruth's duty didn't start until ten and she was able to clear up the house, get the washing done and even slip along the lane to her friend Joyce Moore to borrow a few bits of clothing for Sammy.

Joyce was sympathetic and helpful. With four boys of her own there were enough spare clothes to put together an outfit of sorts for Sammy, and she gathered them on the table and found a bag to put them in.

'Couple of pairs of underpants, those old flannel shorts of our Johnny's, Joe's shirt and Fair Isle pullover what are too tight for him now, and some socks. I can't do nothing about a coat, I'm afraid. Will you be able to manage with this?'

'He's got a coat. He says he was given some clothes from the mayor's fund, whatever that is, but he left them on the train. Perhaps that Mrs Tupper will bring him a few more things when she comes. I mean, they can't expect the families to turn round and start kitting the kiddies out, can they? With the best will in the world . . .' She sighed. 'I don't know what sort of a home he's come from, Joyce. He doesn't seem to have ever been washed properly, let alone had a bath, and he eats with his fingers as much as with a knife and fork. Come to that, I haven't seen him pick up a knife yet, except to cut bread, and then he nearly took his finger off.' She leaned closer and whispered, aware of the boys squabbling over some Meccano in the corner of the room, 'If you ask me, he's probably been knocked about a bit. He more or less *told* me I should smack him when he wet the bed.'

'Knocked about?' Joyce whispered back. 'Poor little

tacker. Still, perhaps he deserved it. He seems to have set your place by the ears. I know what boys can be like.'

Ruth shook her head. 'He's not bad, Joyce, just a bit unlucky. He was only trying to help when he set the toast on fire.' She gathered the clothes up quickly, wondering suddenly what Sammy might be doing now. 'I'd better get back to him. Goodness knows what I'm going to do with him while I'm on duty.'

'Send him down here,' Joyce said. 'One more or less don't make no difference to us. So long as he don't set *our* house on fire.'

'He won't do that. Thanks, Joyce. It'll be better when he can go to school, or I can take him over to the hospital with me. He can make himself useful there. But I don't like to do that, not till we've got a bit more used to each other.'

She set off along the narrow lane, carrying her bundle of clothes. It was good of Joyce to let her have these; with four boys money was tight and everything was handed down in the end to the youngest, Billy, who was only three. Mentally, she ran through a list of other bits he'd need. Gloves – you couldn't expect a kiddy to go out in this weather without gloves – and a couple of warm vests to replace that brown paper. She could alter another of Jack's warm working shirts, but he really needed some more trousers. Those he'd arrived in were nothing more than rags and although the pair Joyce had lent were infinitely better, they were still old.

I'll see Mrs Tupper as soon as I can, she thought. I'll pin a note to the door when I go on duty, so she'll know she can come over to the hospital. We've got to get a few things sorted out – like why he starts to cry every time I ask him about his mum and where that brother of his has been sent. And why they're not together, for heaven's sake. Brothers ought to be kept together.

Joyce's husband Olly was a farmworker, like Reg Corner, and the cottage they lived in was a little way along the lane

183

from the middle of the village. The rooms were tiny, with uneven stone-flagged floors. It always seemed crowded in there with the four boys, but warm and cheerful too. It would do Sammy good to go there, she thought, and be part of a family.

Back at the house, Sammy was huddled in the armchair where she'd left him, with Silver on his perch cracking sunflower seeds and muttering to himself. Ruth dumped the parcel on the table and gave him a smile. 'There. That's a few more clothes for you to wear. See – a new pair of trousers, a nice shirt and this lovely pullover, that'll keep you warm.' She held it up for him to see. 'What do you think of that?'

Sammy stared at it. 'It's all different colours. Didn't they have enough wool?'

Ruth laughed. 'It's meant to be all different colours! It's Fair Isle. Ever so hard to knit. I tell you what, this blue will look lovely with your eyes and fair hair.' She regarded him. 'It's gone curly! Why, you're a really nice-looking little boy.'

'I look like a bleeding girl,' he said, putting his hand up to the fair curls. 'A bleeding sissy, Dad says.'

Ruth found that she disliked Sammy's father more every time she heard his name mentioned. 'Well, *I* don't think you look like a girl,' she said firmly. 'I think you look like a very nice little boy. Though I think it would be better if you said "blinking" instead of "bleeding". It isn't good for Silver to pick up any more swear words . . . Now, you're going to spend today with some other boys at my friend's house, while I'm at work. They've got some Meccano.'

'What about him?' Sammy, asked, looking at Silver.

'He comes with me, while it's so cold. I don't usually light the fire in the mornings, see. Coal's getting so short, with the roads being as bad as they are and even the trains can't get through half the time.'

'We gets our coal in an old pram,' Sammy said. 'Mum

used to go up the station yard . . .' His voice faded and to Ruth's dismay she saw the tears begin to form again. Poor little fellow, he's missing his mum dreadfully, she thought, and hastened to distract him.

'Let's get you into some of these clothes and then you can help me wring out the washing before we go out. I don't think we'll get your sheets dry today, but at least I've got a change of them for tonight. And I'll borrow a rubber sheet and a draw-sheet from the hospital to save the mattress. Matron won't mind.'

The Cottage Hospital was small, with only two wards, and the atmosphere there was more relaxed than in a big city hospital. Matron was a plump, homely woman who ran a tight ship but knew all her staff personally and took an understanding view of domestic problems. It was nothing unusual to see small children rolling bandages in the office or pushing a meal trolley round the wards, and often one of the patients would be the child's own mother or father. Children were not, of course, allowed by hospital regulations to visit, but nothing had ever been laid down about their helping the nurses, and if Matron chose to decide that there was therefore no rule against it nobody was going to argue with her.

However, Matron would not tolerate any bad behaviour and Ruth knew that she must be sure of Sammy before taking him to work with her. She could not risk any accidents such as they had already had at home.

She went out into the backyard and set up the mangle, then took the zinc bath into the wash-house and piled the wet sheets into it from the copper. Rinsing was hard and heavy work, and her fingers were frozen before she decided that the soap had been thoroughly washed out. She dragged the bath out into the yard and began to feed the sheets through the rollers of the mangle.

Sammy appeared in the doorway, arrayed in his new clothes.

'Oh my, you do look smart,' Ruth told him, panting. 'I knew that colour would suit you. I'll just button the shirt up properly – see, you've got an extra button at the top and an extra buttonhole at the bottom! How do you suppose that happened, I wonder.'

'I dunno,' Sammy said, looking down. 'I thought it'd been made wrong.'

Ruth smiled. 'Well, it's easy to put right, see . . . Now you can help me. Lift the sheet up from the bath and just let it go through the mangle, while I turn the handle. But don't let your fingers go with it!' she added hastily, remembering how accident-prone he seemed to be. 'We don't want you coming over to the hospital with me as a patient.'

'It's squeezing all the water out,' Sammy said, fascinated.

'That's right. It helps the washing dry quicker, see, and we can hang it up indoors round the fire on wet days. We couldn't do that if it was still dripping, could we. Doesn't your mum—' She remembered the tears that formed whenever his mother was mentioned and stopped herself. 'Haven't you ever seen a mangle before?'

He shook his head. 'We don't wash sheets much.'

I don't suppose they've even got any, Ruth thought pityingly. She had heard about the London slums but never realised that the same depth of poverty existed in Portsmouth as well. She finished her work in silence, speaking only to encourage Sammy in his efforts to help.

He really is a dear little boy, she thought as they carried the damp sheets indoors and arranged them on the wooden clothes horse around the dying fire.

Wicked little bleeder, indeed! I know who the wicked bleeder was in *that* house and it wasn't little Sammy.

Chapter Fourteen

Lizzie Travers was feeling restless. The raids on Southampton and her anxiety over Alec had made the war seem
very close and very real. She had given up working in the
shop and went out into the fields every day with her father,
pulling carrots from the frozen ground or piling up wurzels
for the animals' feed, but it still didn't seem to be enough.

'I wish I could join one of the women's Services,' she
said to her mother as they sat in front of the fire one
evening, knitting navy-blue balaclavas. 'I feel as if I'm
skiving, just stopping at home.'

'Of course you're not skiving. You work as hard as any
man and your father needs you. If you weren't here, Mr
Knight would have to apply for another Land Girl, so what
use would it be to the war effort, you joining something
else?'

'They probably wouldn't let me anyway,' Lizzie said
gloomily. 'They'd say the same as you, I've got to stop
where I am.'

'So it's no good fretting about then, is it,' her mother
said a little tartly. She'd heard a lot about the women's
Services, and not much of it good. Young girls, leaving
home and let off the reins too early, they were bound to let
it go to their heads. There'd be a good few of those nice
smart uniforms suddenly not fitting any more, she thought.
And it wouldn't do a young woman like her Lizzie, only
married a year and a half and missing her husband, any
good to be mixing with all those men, either.

'I just wish I could do more,' Lizzie said. 'There's my

Alec out at sea, with German U-boats and torpedoes and God knows what, and I never know what might be happening to him, and I'm just stopping at home—'

'Doing war work. Farming's war work. It's important to grow food.'

'But it's *what I've always done*!' Lizzie cried, throwing down her ball of wool. 'It doesn't *feel* as if I'm doing something important. I want to do something *different*.'

Jane looked at her. Lizzie had always been hot-tempered and liable to fly off the handle. There wasn't any use in getting hot under the collar yourself. She started a new row of purl stitches and let a minute or so go without speaking.

'They're taking men off the farms,' Lizzie said. 'The ordinary farmworkers aren't reserved. Why can't I go?'

'Because you're a woman,' her mother said quietly. 'The men are going to fight. You wouldn't – you'd just do what another woman could do. And that would mean *another* girl coming here to take your place on the farm. It doesn't make sense, Lizzie.'

There was another short silence. Lizzie sighed and bent to pick up her ball of wool. She turned it over and over in her hands, staring at it.

'I'm not even knitting for my own husband. Some other woman's man will wear this balaclava. That doesn't make sense, either.'

'You've knitted plenty of things for Alec,' Jane pointed out. 'He's got more than enough. What we're knitting for is men who *haven't* got women of their own to knit for them.'

Lizzie pulled her lips in but nodded. She started to knit again, staring into the log fire as she did so. I split those logs myself, she thought. I dug the potatoes and pulled the carrots we had for dinner, and fed the pig whose bacon we had for breakfast. I milked the cows and fed their calves, I went out to look at the sheep in the fields, I took corn out to the hens and shut them up for the night – there's no end to the jobs I've done and I'll do them all again, or different ones, tomorrow. And it's what I've done all my life. Ever since I could walk, I've been chucking corn to hens and swill to pigs. In between school, in between working in the shop, I've been planting and sowing and weeding and harvesting ever since I can remember. I *know* it's essential work, but it doesn't *feel* like it. And I'm not a farmer's wife. I'm a *sailor*'s wife, and I don't even live by the sea!

'If I just had a kiddy of my own,' she burst out. 'I feel as if my life's standing still, Mum, that's what it is. When me and Alec got married, I thought we'd got a future to look forward to. We were going to get a place in Southampton, so we could be nearer the ships. I knew he'd be away a lot, but it was only ever supposed to be short trips. Now I never know when he's coming home, and when he does he has to turn round and go back after about five minutes, and I'm always afraid – I'm afraid he'll – oh Mum, I'm so *worried* about him. Out there at sea, dodging about all over the place in those convoys, trying to keep ahead of the Germans. He could be dead *now*, for all I know. I can't sleep at night for thinking about it all.'

Jane put down her knitting and reached out a hand. 'Oh, Lizzie. My poor little girl.'

Lizzie stared at her. Her dark brown eyes were huge with misery. She shook her head and drew in a deep, shuddering breath.

'That's just it, though, isn't it, Mum? I'm not your little girl any more. I'm a grown woman with a man of my own, and I ought to have my own home and family to look after, and it's all been just *stopped*. And I know it's not only me. Because of one stupid madman in another country, *everyone*'s lives have been stopped. And instead of having what I ought to have – and it isn't much to ask for, is it, a home and family? – I've got to stay at home and knit balaclavas for other men.' She looked down at the navy-blue wool in disgust. 'I ought to be knitting *baby clothes*.'

Jane hardly knew what to say. Everything Lizzie said was

true, but the girl was doing herself no good railing against it all.

'I thought you'd decided it was wrong to have a family with the world the way it is now,' she began, but once again Lizzie's anger broke out.

'That doesn't mean to say I wouldn't still *like* one! It doesn't mean I don't wish I *could* have a baby! It doesn't mean I don't still feel my life's being *wasted*!'

Jane sighed. 'Well, it's the same for us all, Lizzie. Even people like me. *You* might think my life's over, with my children more or less grown up and off my hands – even though you are still living at home for the time being – but it doesn't feel like it to me. My life's been stopped as well.'

'I don't see how,' Lizzie muttered. 'The war doesn't seem to be making much difference to you. You'd still be here, running the house and looking after Dad and going round the village, whatever happened. I don't see that it's changed anything for you.'

'Well, I haven't got any grandchildren for a start!' Jane flashed and then caught herself up. 'I'm sorry, Liz, I didn't mean to say that. But it *is* different, that's all. There's all the worry – and remembering last time – and all the evacuees round the village, making everything different. And wondering what's going to happen next and if he will invade. And worrying about Ben and if he'll get called up. He's got his exams next summer and he could be going on to college, but he'll be eighteen in July. I know they're not taking boys that age yet, but they're bound to if the fighting gets really bad.'

'I still wish we could have an evacuee,' Lizzie said. 'If we had just one more room . . . I'll walk down and see Auntie Ruth tomorrow, see how she's getting on with hers. He's been there a few days now so he should have settled in. Perhaps I'll bring him back here to tea.'

'That's good idea,' Jane said, relieved that Lizzie had

found something else to think about. 'You do that. It'll be something, if we can just give Ruth a hand.'

Lizzie went down to her aunt's cottage the next afternoon. Ruth had decided to ask for a few days' leave from the hospital, just while Sammy was settling in, and she was pleased to see her. More snow had fallen during the night and the cottage was warm and cosy inside.

'Tell your dad I was really pleased to find a new load of logs stacked outside when I looked out this morning,' Ruth said, leading her niece into the living room. 'He must have come down first thing. It's meant I can have a nice fire for Sammy here, when it's so cold outside.'

Lizzie looked at the little boy sitting on the rug in front of the fire and her heart went out to him. He looked like a picture from an old book, she thought, with his fair curls and his big blue eyes. He was wearing an assortment of clothes that were too big for him, like a waif out of a Dickens story, and he looked up at her as anxiously as if he expected to be smacked just for being there. He was sucking his thumb.

'Why, you dear little thing!' she exclaimed, dropping down beside him. 'So you're Sammy! My name's Elizabeth, like the Queen, but everyone calls me Lizzie.'

'You could call her Auntie Lizzie,' said Ruth, who didn't approve of children calling grown-ups by their first names, but Lizzie shook her head.

'Lizzie'll do, unless you want a new auntie. I expect you've got some real ones at home, haven't you?'

Sammy gazed at her. He still hadn't come to terms with all that had happened to him in the past few months and to him Lizzie was just another of the string of strange women who had passed through his life, taking him away from all he knew. He said nothing.

'Have you?' Lizzie persisted. 'Got any real aunties at home, I mean?'

He took his thumb from his mouth. 'I did have one. She was called Auntie Betty.'

Lizzie smiled. 'What a deep voice you've got. And where does Auntie Betty live?'

He shook his head. 'I dunno. I didn't see her again, not after we was put out of the pub.'

'Oh.' Lizzie glanced at her own aunt for clarification of this remark, but Ruth shrugged and shook her head. 'And what about your mum and dad? Are they still in Portsmouth?'

To her consternation the blue eyes filled with tears. She glanced at Ruth again and Ruth clucked with annoyance and beckoned Lizzie out into the kitchen. They stood in the cramped little space, whispering.

'There! I should have warned you – there's something about his mother that upsets him. I wanted to ask the billeting lady, but she's never been back yet. Not that she can be much of a mother anyway, the child was half starved when he arrived. Thin as a rake, all skin and bone, and didn't look as if he'd had a wash for months. I don't think he'd ever had a proper bath at home, though he did say they'd been to the "municipal" once, but his father said it was pouring money down the drain. To tell you the truth, I can't understand it, the other children from the Copnor area seem decent enough, though there's one or two obviously not so well looked after as the others. But it's not a really poor area, not from what I can make out.'

'It's a pity Mrs Budd isn't still here,' Lizzie said. 'She seemed to know most of the families around there. She might have been able to tell you a bit. Perhaps we could ask Tim and Keith.'

'I don't know. It seems like asking them to tell tales.' Ruth turned away to fill the kettle. 'I do think it's a bit much, leaving the kiddy here with me not knowing a thing about him, but that Mrs Tupper seemed in such a rush when she came. I suppose she's got a lot of other little ones to think about too . . . You go in with him now, Lizzie, while I make a cup of tea.'

Lizzie returned to the living room and sat down again beside Sammy. They looked into the fire together without speaking for a while, listening to the hiss of the flames and the companionable sound of Silver scratching in his bowl of sunflower seeds.

'How do you like living with a parrot?' Lizzie asked after a few minutes. 'Have you taught him any new words yet?'

Sammy looked at her, startled. 'He knows all his words.'

'He can still learn new ones. All you have to do is say something a few times and if it's a sound he likes, he picks it up. He likes rhymes best.' And swear words, she added silently. But if Sammy came from a poor area, he probably knew a good many already.

As if reading her thoughts, Silver cackled wickedly from his stand behind them and squawked, 'Splice the mainbrace, it's a bleedin' eagle! It's a bleedin' eagle!'

Lizzie turned to stare at him and then looked at Sammy. He was gazing at her, his blue eyes huge, and she burst out laughing. 'You see! You've taught him something already! And you can't pretend you didn't, because he's copied your voice too.'

'That's not *my* voice,' Sammy said indignantly, but Lizzie laughed again.

'None of us thinks it's our voice when he copies us, but everyone else always says it is. That's you all right, Sammy. You'll have to be careful what you say to him in future.'

'We're all careful what we say round here,' Ruth said, coming into the room with a tray. 'The only one who isn't careful is Silver himself. Here you are, Lizzie, here's your tea, and here's a cup of cocoa for you, Sammy. He learnt that the minute the child arrived,' she went on, nodding towards the parrot. 'Only said it once, but that blessed bird caught on to it in no time. It's always the same when it's something you don't want repeated. I know people say he doesn't understand what he's saying, but I reckon he does. He does it for devilment.'

'Still, you get a lot of fun out of him. We all do.' Lizzie sipped her tea. 'I remember when Dad told us not to repeat anything that bird said in case it was something bad, and we all thought "sippers and gulpers" and "splice the main-brace" must be really wicked words – and said them whenever we thought Dad wouldn't hear us! We told our friends too. Half the school was using parrot-swear at one time.'

'Sammy'll be going to the village school after Christmas,' Ruth said. 'I'm going to see the headmaster soon. Of course, he might say Sammy should start straight away, even though there's only a week or so to go before they break up.' She looked at him anxiously. 'I just hope he'll be all right with the other children,' she added in a lower voice. 'He seems so timid. I don't know what sort of a home he came from, I'm sure.'

'Well, he'll be all right here with you,' Lizzie said. 'Won't you, Sammy? And Christmas is coming. You'll enjoy that.'

Sammy looked up at her. He remembered last Christmas and the ball his mother had given him. He thought of the Christmas dinner she'd struggled to cook, the gloves and socks she'd bought them with her savings, carefully gleaned from the housekeeping money, and the Mars bar his father had given him. That reminded him of the chocolate he'd meant to give his mother, that Gordon had found in his drawer and eaten, and of Micky Baxter's boast about gold necklaces. Perhaps if they hadn't gone out that afternoon and met him in the street, Gordon would never have gone off thieving with him and got caught and sent away. Perhaps Mum wouldn't have got even more ill and died.

It had all started at Christmas, he thought. It had all gone wrong then.

He thought of his cat Tibby, who – his dad had told him

– had got run over only a day or two before he'd come away to the country. Mum wouldn't have let that happen. He thought of his mother, thin and weak and tired, yet always ready to give him a smile and a cuddle, calling him her sweetheart, her angel. He shut his eyes and tried to imagine her arms about him once more, and suddenly Nora was there beside him, almost touching him, and he felt a rush of grief so strong that his mouth turned down at the corners and his eyes filled with tears. He struggled for a moment but it was no use; he couldn't stop the huge sobs forcing their way up from his chest, into his throat, and out through his trembling lips. As the two women watched in horror, he sank down in a heap on the rag rug and began to weep as if his heart would break.

'Sammy!' Ruth cried, dropping to her knees beside him and drawing him into her arms. She rocked to and fro, his head cradled against her breast. 'Oh Sammy, Sammy, whatever is it? Whatever's the matter?'

Lizzie stared in dismay. All she'd done was mention Christmas. Whatever could have happened to this little boy that the mention of Christmas, of all things, could upset him like this?

She felt suddenly ashamed of her own grumbles. This poor little fellow's seen more of the war than I've got any idea about, she thought. He's been through air raids and bombing, and God knows what, and now he's out here without anyone he knows, and he just doesn't know what to make of it all. And all I've got to worry about is myself. Even though my Alec's at sea and could be in danger all the time, I'll still never see what this little chap's seen.

'Come on, Sammy,' she said, taking out her handkerchief and dropping to her knees beside Ruth. 'Let's wipe those eyes of your before you drown us all. And blow your nose – no, not on your sleeve, use this hanky. And then drink up this lovely cup of cocoa Auntie Ruth's brought for you.

You're frightening Silver, look. He's all upset because you're crying.'

Slowly, Sammy's sobs eased and turned to sniffles. He blew his nose as directed and heaved a deep, shuddering sigh. He looked at Lizzie and then at Silver, preening himself unconcernedly on his stand.

'He ain't upset,' he said in his hoarse voice. 'He ain't upset at all.'

Silver stopped preening and looked down at him. 'Bleedin' eagle,' he said conversationally. 'Bugger me, it's a bleedin' *eagle*.'

'Well, as you know, we share the school with the village children,' the headmaster said to Ruth. 'They have it in the mornings and we have it in the afternoons. It's a squash even so, but he can come to school for the last week of term. It would help him to settle in after Christmas, and he'd have the fun of helping to decorate the school and coming to the Christmas party.'

'Oh, that's kind of you,' Ruth exclaimed. 'He only knows a few of the other children – apparently the family hadn't lived in the area for long and before that he was ill. I gather he never actually came to your school.'

The headmaster frowned. He was uneasily aware that he ought to know more about Sammy Hodges, but with fifty or so children in each class, and all the upheaval of evacuation coming at the very beginning of the autumn term, he hadn't even been aware of the child's existence.

'The family must have moved to Copnor some time during the summer,' he said. 'I understand there's an older boy too, but he'd left school before they moved. I really don't know any more than you do about them, Mrs Purslow. However, we know about Sammy now and he'll be welcome to attend school with the others every afternoon. In fact, he *ought* to.'

It was hard to tell whether Sammy was pleased or not

when Ruth told him the news. He looked at her with his huge blue eyes, and she felt a rush of warmth and pity. I'd just like to scoop him up and put him in my pocket, she thought. Keep him safe. He's been through too much already, poor little mite.

'You'll like being at school,' she told him. 'You'll be able to play with the other children and make friends. You liked playing with the other children in Portsmouth, didn't you?'

'Some of them,' he said. 'Some of them picked on me.'

'Well, if anyone picks on you here you're to tell me,' she said firmly. 'And you'll do lessons as well, of course. You'll learn arithmetic and reading and writing, and – and all sorts of things. You'll enjoy it.'

Sammy looked doubtful and went off to the village school next afternoon with an air of resignation. Ruth watched him go anxiously. I hope the others won't pick on him, she thought. They'd better not, or they'll have me to reckon with! But she knew that interference in the children's lives didn't really do any good. They were better left to work things out for themselves. Anyway, it was only a week until they broke up for the Christmas holidays and many of them were going home then. By the time school began again he'd have found his feet a bit more.

He came home for tea looking a little more confident, with Tim and Keith Budd on either side of him. Ruth went to the gate and thanked them for bringing him home.

''S all right,' Tim said nonchalantly. 'Sammy's from our street. We used to play with him.' He strolled off with his brother, whistling, and Sammy came indoors, pulled off his wellingtons and coat, and went straight to Silver's cage.

'Say you're an eagle. Say you're a bleedin' eagle.'

'I'm not sure I want him saying that too much,' Ruth observed, pouring him a cup of warm milk. 'Why don't you teach him something new? Aren't there any different rhymes you know?'

Sammy looked at her blankly. 'I can't think of any. He knows them all.'

What an admission, Ruth thought, that a parrot knows more rhymes than an eight-year-old boy. But she smiled at him and said, 'Well, I expect Silver will think of something and then it might remind you. Here's your milk. I'm going to have a cup of tea.'

'Time for tea,' Silver said at once. 'Tea for two. I'm a little teapot, short and stout –'

'There you are,' Ruth said. 'It only takes one word he recognises to start him off. Now look, I've been shopping. See what I've got.' She picked up a paper bag that had been lying on the table and produced some coloured paper strips. 'We're going to make some paper chains. Have you ever had paper chains at Christmas?'

He nodded. So he'd had some sort of Christmas at home, she thought. 'Mum used to get bits of paper like that. I put 'em all round the room. They looked pretty.'

'Good. We'll make this room look pretty too. I've made some flour and water paste to glue them together with. But don't let Silver get his beak into that bowl, I don't think the flour would be good for him.'

Sammy gazed at the bowl, then regarded her solemnly. 'He likes flour. He likes *sun*flower.'

There was a moment's silence. Ruth looked at him carefully, not quite sure if he knew what he had said. Then she smiled and laughed.

'You clever boy! You've made a joke – a really good joke.' She looked at him again and this time she saw a distinct gleam in his eye before he began to giggle. With a sudden rush of warmth and love she caught him against her. 'Oh, Sammy, if you only knew how good it is to hear you laugh. If you only *knew* . . .' She held him away and looked into the blue eyes. We're getting somewhere, she thought with a surge of relief. We're really, really getting somewhere.

They spent the evening making paper chains and as they worked she told him how Christmas had been before the war started.

'We always went carol singing, with lanterns and candles. We'd go round all the cottages and the big houses, and some of them used to invite us in and give us mince pies and mulled ale. We collected money to give the old folk a party, or take things to them at home. And then we'd go out into the woods and dig up a Christmas tree and bring it home and decorate it. We're going to do that again. Uncle George and Auntie Jane are going to have a big one, and Uncle George says if you want to go with them you can help get a little one for us.'

'A tree just for us?' he said, looking round the little room. 'To have here?'

'Yes,' Ruth said, 'and what's more I've got some fairy lights to put on it! And with the paper chains you've made as well it's all going to look really pretty.'

Sammy gazed at her and she feared for a moment that he was going to start crying again, as he had when Lizzie had talked about Christmas. But although his eyes were very bright, no tears fell. After a while he sighed and looked deep into the fire.

'What are you thinking about, Sammy?' she asked gently.

'I just wish my mum could be here,' he said, and there was a world of sadness and longing in his hoarse voice. 'I wish my mum could be here and have Christmas too.'

The mystery of Sammy's home and family troubled Ruth and a few days later, when the billeting officer returned to see how he had settled in, she asked what was known about them.

Mrs Tupper shook her head. 'There's no need for you to know about that. All you're required to do is look after him.'

'But how can I do that, if I don't know what's upsetting him?' Ruth asked. 'He looks so miserable and I know he cries at night.'

'Most of them do. It's only natural. They miss their families.'

Ruth pursed her lips. 'It's more than that with Sammy. He seems really upset about something – something to do with his mother. And you ought to have seen the state he was in when he first came here. Thin as a rake, covered in flea bites and looked as if he hadn't been washed for weeks.'

Mrs Tupper gave a short laugh. 'That's nothing unusual, I'm afraid. He came from a rough area, you know. There are plenty like that, and worse.'

'But he doesn't come from a rough area,' Ruth said. 'There are other children in the village who come from the same part of Portsmouth. The two little Budd boys, they're from the same street, and they're not neglected. And he seems so upset about his mother. And there's a brother somewhere—'

The billeting officer shook her head again. 'I don't know anything about a brother. And plenty of children his age are upset about leaving their mothers. It's unfortunate, but it's more important that they're safe. The best thing to do is take no notice. They get over it.' She looked at the sheaf of papers in her hand. 'I'm sorry, I have to get on. I've got other children to see . . . So long as he has enough clothes for his needs, and you've got his ration book and identity card, there's nothing more I need do here.' She gave Ruth a sharp nod and bustled away along the lane.

Ruth looked after her. Enough clothes for his needs! she thought angrily. Ration book and identity card! A little boy taken away from his parents needs more than that. But if he did, it was clear that Mrs Tupper didn't consider it a part of her job to attend to it.

Well, it might not be her job, Ruth thought, but I reckon it's mine. It's easy enough to look after a kiddy's clothes and make him a few meals, but that doesn't mean to say he's *happy*. And if you ask me, being happy's every bit as important as being safe.

Chapter Fifteen

Once again, a good many of the evacuees were going home for Christmas. Tim and Keith Budd were to go, not knowing how much their mother had pleaded to have them back and how hard it had been to persuade their father. They looked forward to it, anxious to see their parents again and their baby sister Maureen. Tim was also secretly pleased at the thought of seeing Micky Baxter. He wasn't really allowed to play with Micky, but the bad boy of April Grove had an aura of glamour he found hard to resist.

'Most of them that are staying have got presents and cards from home,' Ruth told Joyce Moore when she went round to collect Sammy after the school carol service. It was the last day of term and she'd hoped to go to the service in the little church, but she had been working afternoon shifts at the hospital, now that Sammy was at school. 'But there's nothing come for Sammy. Poor little mite. Doesn't anyone back there love him?'

'You still haven't found out anything about his family, then?'

'Well, no. It seems so queer. I asked that billeting woman, but all she would say was that he came from a rough area. But he doesn't. He lives in April Grove, you know, same as where those Budd boys live, but even they don't seem to know all that much about him.'

'Tim told Edna Corner the family hadn't been there long,' Joyce said. 'They came from Old Portsmouth. I got the impression that that's a much poorer area than Copnor.'

'Well, that could explain a bit, I suppose,' Ruth agreed.

'But it's not just that. I've written to his mother and got no answer. I wondered if they might've gone away too, but surely they'd have let the billeting people know.'

'Well, I don't know, you hear some queer things . . . Someone told me about a little girl they'd heard of, she went to school one morning and when she got home that afternoon the family had moved! Without even *telling* her. The neighbours found her sitting on the steps crying her heart out. You can't credit anyone doing that to their own kiddy, can you.'

'Goodness, I hope Sammy's family haven't abandoned him like that,' Ruth said, shocked. 'Perhaps Tim Budd might have some news when they come back. Anyway, we'll give the poor little chap a good time. Anything to bring a smile to his face!'

'I'd have thought that parrot of yours would do that.'

'Yes, he thinks the world of Silver, now he's got used to him and stopped calling him a bl— an eagle. And Silver seems to have taken to him too. It makes me laugh, hearing them chuntering away together in the back room while I'm in the kitchen. They're like two old men, thinking they're having a proper conversation when really neither of them's listening to a word the other one says.'

'It does seem funny that he never talks about his mum or dad. Most little boys are so proud of their dads.'

'I don't think his dad's much to be proud of,' Ruth said grimly. 'But I'd say he thought the world of his mum. I still haven't got anything more out of him, you know. I wondered if he might have said anything to your boys.'

Joyce shook her head. 'It's only Davie he plays with all that much. John and Joe are older and Billy's not much more than a baby. And whenever I've heard them talking, it's only been about that blessed Meccano, or aeroplanes, or pretending to be soldiers. You know what boys are. If they were girls, now, they'd have each other's life histories in the first five minutes.'

Ruth smiled. 'Well, I suppose they're like men, aren't they?' she said. 'Can't talk about anything but football. I'd better be getting on home, Joyce. Thanks for having him after school. It's a big help.'

'I'm surprised really they let you have a boy,' Joyce remarked, following her to the door to pick up Sammy's coat. 'Seeing as you're on your own and at work, I mean. Not that you don't look after him a lot better than some people you hear about, but I wouldn't want one of my boys to go off to someone who wasn't going to be there all the time. No offence,' she added hastily, 'but these mothers, they don't know what people are like, do they? They just don't know where their kiddies are going to end up.'

They shook their heads. Ruth called to Sammy and he left his game with Davie and came at once. The other boy came with him. 'Can I come and see your parrot?'

'If your mum says you can.' Ruth helped Sammy button his coat. She looked at him. 'Would you like to bring any of your other friends at school?'

He looked worried. 'I haven't got no friends.'

'Oh, surely—' Ruth began in distress, but Davie butted in before she could finish.

'It's because nobody knows him much, only Tim and Keith Budd. But if they could see his *parrot* . . .'

Ruth noticed with some amusement that Silver seemed to have stopped being her parrot and become Sammy's. Well, that's all right if it helps him make friends, she thought. He's got Davie, of course, and the Budd boys look out for him, but he needs more friends than that, boys who will play with him and not pick on him because he's smaller and quieter.

'When you're at school properly, after Christmas, you can bring two different boys every day,' she said. 'You can choose them yourself but you must tell them they're not to poke Silver or pull his tail. Tell them he can bite hard with his beak.'

The two boys looked at each other. Davie's eyes were sparkling and he quickened his steps. Sammy looked up at Ruth and she winked.

She might never have had any of her own, but she was rapidly learning just what little boys liked.

The whole family set themselves to give Sammy a happy Christmas.

'Poor little mite,' Lizzie said, knitting furiously to make him new mittens for Christmas. She had unpicked an old red jumper of her own specially to use the wool. 'I don't reckon he's ever had a proper Christmas in his life. Well, it's up to us to make sure he gets one, at least. He might not be here next year.'

'I hope he is,' Ruth said. 'I want to keep him as long as the war lasts. Not that I want it to last that long, of course,' she added hastily. 'Though he'll have to go back when it does end . . . oh dear, it *is* difficult!'

'Well, there's not much point in wondering about all that,' Jane declared briskly, coming in from the kitchen with tea on a tin tray. 'We just have to live for the day. It's *this* Christmas that matters now, and like Lizzie says, we'll make it as good as we can for Sammy. Are you getting him a present, Ruth?'

'Of course I am! He's getting a stocking too, on the end of his bed Christmas morning. Just a few bits and pieces, you know – a couple of those puzzles with balls you have to jiggle about to get into the right holes, and a few crayons and a colouring book, and an orange and some nuts. I found a jigsaw puzzle up in the loft the other day, one of Jack's that he used to take to sea with him, he can have that, and then there's an old compass. Boys like that sort of thing. And I'll get him something new as well – a book, I thought. I've been reading to him from *Treasure Island*, he loves that, specially the bits about the parrot!'

'That sounds lovely,' Jane said. 'We'll give him something too. I wonder if he'd like a *Rupert* book? He's not too old for that, is he? And Ben's making him a wooden aeroplane. A Spitfire.'

'And I've seen a ball I'm going to get him,' Lizzie said. 'A really nice, big red one.'

They went on talking about Christmas presents. There wasn't all that much in the shops, but Jane had unearthed an old leather coat and was using it to make George and the boys new gloves, and Lizzie had her eye on it for a pair for Alec. She was knitting him a new pullover too, for best when he came home. The whole family had clubbed together to buy Terry a really good mouth organ, and Ben a gramophone and some records – one of Winston Churchill's speeches, Harry James playing 'Feet Dragging Blues' and some Victor Silvester dance music.

Terry had just finished his six weeks' basic training and was home on a few days' leave.

'You wouldn't believe how he's changed,' Jane told her sister. 'I don't know how the Army does it, but in six weeks they've managed to achieve all the things I've struggled to do for twenty years! He's so tidy now you don't dare to put anything down for a minute, or he'll either put it away or polish it. He won't let me iron his trousers, and he gets the creases so sharp he could kill Germans with them. He looks after his uniform as if it was made of gold leaf. And his hair's been cut so short he looks like a convict!'

Ruth laughed. 'That's the Services for you. Teach 'em to look after themselves and be smart into the bargain, and you can teach 'em anything. Of course, they know there's not many young chaps have ever had to look after themselves in that way anyway, they've all come straight from home and had mothers to do it all for them.'

'Well, I dare say he'd soon slip back if he was at home for long,' Jane said. 'Anyway, he's pleased enough to take your little lad out to kick that old football about for a while. More tea, Ruthie?'

The back door opened and Terry came in, Sammy at his heels like an adoring puppy.

'We played football,' Sammy cried, running to Ruth's side. '*I* played football. Terry says I could be a footballer if I wanted, he says I kick really well.'

'Well, isn't that lovely.' Ruth beamed at him and put out a hand to stroke his fair hair. He beamed back and she gave him a hug. 'Thanks for taking him, Terry.'

'It's all right.' Terry was in old clothes and looked like his old self, except for his very short hair. His eyes gleamed when he saw the scones and he picked one up and handed it to Sammy before taking one for himself. He grinned at his aunt and fetched a couple of cups from the kitchen, pouring tea for himself and milk for Sammy.

'Mm, home cooking,' he said, his mouth full. 'That's what I miss most!'

'I hear you've been learning to wash and iron your own clothes,' Ruth said to him teasingly. 'I thought you were supposed to be training to be a soldier, not a washer-woman!'

'A smart soldier's an efficient soldier,' Terry said, obviously repeating what one of his officers had said. 'And the enemy wouldn't be very frightened by a crowd of scruffy oiks.'

'So how are you enjoying it, then? Think you'll like being a soldier?'

'Yes, I do, as a matter of fact. I didn't think I would, really – I volunteered because it seemed the right thing to do – but I'm in with some really good blokes, and once we're through our training and we can get out there and start putting the Jerries to rights, we'll be able to feel we're really doing something. And it's interesting learning to fire a gun and use a bayonet and all that. We were throwing grenades the other day. I tell you what, you don't make any mistakes with those.'

'Real grenades?' Jane asked in horror. 'You mean they could have exploded?'

He nodded. 'That's the idea of them, Mum! Once you've pulled out the pin, you throw as hard as you can. That's why it's good to teach little nippers like this youngster –' he indicated Sammy, who was watching him with wide blue eyes '– games like cricket and football. Teaches 'em the skills they're going to need, see.'

'I hope he's not going to need them for fighting,' Ruth said sharply. 'I hope it'll all be over by the time he's your age.'

'It will be,' Terry said confidently. 'We're going over the Channel soon and we'll sort it all out then. But we're always going to need an army, Auntie. There's always going to be wars.' He finished his tea and leapt up. 'Come on, young Sam. Let's go and have that boxing lesson.'

'*Boxing*?'

'It'll be good for him,' Terry said. 'Learn to stand up for himself. Little blokes with yellow hair get picked on a bit. And he's a plucky little chap. Doesn't matter what it is, he'll have a go.'

'What have you been doing with him?' his mother asked sharply. 'You were supposed to be playing football, not doing basic training.'

Terry looked at her. 'We've all got to be able to take care of ourselves, Mum. And even if this war's over when young Sam's grown up – and it *will* be, because we're going to knock the living daylights out of Jerry when we get over there – there'll be others. There'll always be wars, Mum, and they'll always need men to fight 'em.'

He pulled Sammy to his feet and propelled him out of the door. They could hear Sammy's voice as the back door slammed and he sounded more excited than Ruth had ever known him.

The two sisters looked at each other. 'I suppose he's right,' Jane said sadly. 'There'll always be wars. It's human nature, isn't it? But I don't suppose there's ever been a mother yet who's really wanted her own boys to go and fight.'

Ruth looked out of the window at Terry and Sammy, sparring in the backyard. I haven't got any boys of my own, she thought, and I know Sammy will go back to his own family in the end. But I know how Jane feels. Just the thought of that little chap going to fight a war turns me cold all over.

There must be mothers all over England who were feeling just the same.

All the same, she thought as she walked back to the cottage, I'm looking forward to Christmas more than I have for years. It's having a kiddy to think about and do things for, it makes such a difference. She felt a pang of sadness for the years she'd missed, years that could have been filled with her and Jack's children, but almost immediately she pushed them away. I've been sent Sammy instead, she thought, Sammy who doesn't seem to have had a proper Christmas ever, even though he did know about paper chains and Christmas trees. And since this might be the only Christmas I do have him, I'm going to make sure it's a really good one. We all are.

She went indoors and started to teach Silver to sing 'Jingle bells'.

Having realised that he was to have a 'proper' Christmas, Sammy wanted to do it all.

'Can we go carol singing, Auntie Ruth? Can we send Christmas cards? Can I write a letter to Father Christmas and put it up the chimney? Can I really have a real stocking? One of yours?'

Ruth laughed. 'So long as you don't make the holes

worse! Stockings are getting harder to come by these days. Now, what presents are you going to give?'

Sammy looked at her.

'For everyone else,' Ruth said. 'Auntie Jane and Uncle George, and Terry and Lizzie.' She hesitated. 'And your mum and dad of course, and your brother.'

Sammy said nothing.

He turned his head away and Ruth moved slightly so that she could see his face. There were tears in his eyes.

'Sammy,' she said gently, 'can't you tell me about your brother? And your mum and dad? Why is it they never write to you?'

Sammy gave her a swift glance and then looked down at his feet. The room was very quiet. Even Silver seemed to be listening.

'I haven't got a mum,' he said at last in a very small voice. 'My mum's dead.'

Ruth stared at him. '*Sammy*!'

'It was my fault,' he went on, trying to sound matter-of-fact although his voice was shaking. 'I was too long up the shops. I was in a queue and they wouldn't let me through, and I was gone *hours*, and when I got back—' His voice wobbled again and the tears began to roll down his face, huge, fat tears that seemed to have been growing through all the weeks he had been with Ruth. He tried to wipe them away with his sleeve, with the back of his hand, but they still kept coming and after a minute or two he gave way and began to cry properly, great tearing sobs that wrenched their way up from his chest and burst out in a long chain of sound, a howl of pain and misery and unbearable loss.

Ruth stared at him, horrified, then pulled him into her arms. 'Sammy! Oh, you poor, *poor* little soul! Sammy, don't cry like that.' And then she hastily amended her words. 'No, you cry all you want to. Cry as long as you want. I'm here to hold you. Ruth's here. You just stay with me and cry as long as you like.'

She held him against her, the fair head cradled against her breast, and as he wept her own tears began to flow too. The poor, poor little boy. His mother dead, his father and brother goodness knew where, lost and bewildered, brought to this strange place where nobody knew a thing about him. Surely they knew, she thought angrily, surely the billeting people knew, surely that Mrs Tupper had known when she brought him in so hurriedly that cold afternoon. Why on earth had they not told her?

Sammy stopped crying at last. He lay against her for a little longer, his body still shuddering with leftover sobs, and then he slowly raised his head. Ruth put her hand under his chin and lifted his face towards her, her heart twisting at the sight of his ravaged face, his puffy, red-rimmed eyes, his running nose.

'Here,' she said, feeling in her sleeve for her handker-chief, 'have a good blow. That's better. Now, I'm going to make you a nice cup of cocoa and you can have a couple of the biscuits I was saving, and then if you feel like it you can tell me about your mum. Do you think you can do that?'

He nodded and Ruth went out to the kitchen to fill the kettle. Sammy was left alone in the room with Silver. They looked at each other.

'I'm a little teapot,' Silver suggested in an unusually subdued voice. 'Humpty-Dumpty sat on the wall. Poor old Joe . . . Let me be your sweetheart . . .'

Sammy got up and went over to his perch. He held out a sunflower seed and Silver took it delicately in his beak. He cracked it, keeping one eye on Sammy, and Sammy bent closer and began to talk to him.

'Sammy, Sammy, shine a light, ain't you playing out tonight . . . ?' His voice wobbled again and he turned away, feeling the skin of his face tighten. He heard Ruth coming in and returned to his place on the hearthrug.

'There,' Ruth said, setting the tray down. 'That's cocoa for us both, and biscuits with chocolate on. I was saving them for Christmas, but it won't hurt to have a couple now. Did I hear you talking to Silver?'

'He was talking to me,' Sammy said, eyeing the biscuits. 'I told him a rhyme but he didn't say it back.'

'Well, he usually needs to hear it a few times before he'll do that.' Unless it's something you don't want him to repeat, she thought ruefully, remembering the 'bleeding eagle'. 'But you just say it to him every now and then, and I expect he'll pick it up. What rhyme was it?'

Sammy shrugged, staring at the fire. 'It was just something my mum used to say.'

'I see.' Ruth gave him a quick glance. He was still looking into the flames, his shoulders heaving a little every few moments, but he seemed to have got over his outburst of grief. Perhaps now was a good time to get him to talk. 'Would you like to tell me about your mum?' she asked gently. 'Anything you like. What she looked like. Games she used to play with you. What you did together. That sort of thing.' There was another pause. 'I'd really like to know, Sammy. I really would.'

For a moment she thought she had gone too far. He was sitting immobile, as if frozen, before the fire. He didn't turn his head to look at her, didn't move at all. The only sounds were the crackling of the flames and Silver's movements on the perch behind them.

She offered Sammy the biscuits and he took one and bit a piece off. Then he drew in a deep sigh and turned at last to look up at her, and she knew he was going to talk at last about all the griefs that had been shut away inside him during all these weeks.

It took a little while, even so, to get him started, and after a minute or two she prompted him gently.

'Was your mum poorly for a long time?' she asked. 'Did she have to stay in bed?'

He nodded. 'She was all right when I was little. She used

to work in the pub then, with Gran and Grandad. Me and Gordon used to have lemonade. But then Mum missed and that made her poorly.'

'Missed? What did she miss? Did someone go away?'

'No. I don't know,' Sammy said, frowning. 'I just heard Gran talking about it once, she said that was the second miss Mum had had in a year, and she wouldn't ever be the same again. I couldn't see no difference, mind, but she didn't play with us as much after that and when she worked in the pub she got tired.'

'Oh, I see.' Miscarriages, Ruth thought. Two in a year, and possibly bad ones too. No wonder poor Mrs Hodges hadn't been well. But that wasn't enough to explain her dying.

'Gran died and then Grandad, so we couldn't stop in the pub any more. That's when we moved to April Grove, only I got whooping cough and Mum got tired again too, and she fell over one day when Gordon brought the necklaces home, and the doctor said she'd got enema in her blood.'

'Enema?' Ruth said, trying to make sense of the confused story. 'D'you mean anaemia?'

'Yeah, that's right,' he said. 'Enema. And he said she'd got to have iron, you can get it in little tablets, so she had to take them and she stopped in bed a lot. I got her liver at the butcher's because it's got iron in, but I don't think the liver I got had any, it was all soft, and it never made her any better. She was just as tired, see. And then Gordon went to the proved school and she fell over in the street on the way home and another doctor came and he said it was enema too, only a different sort of enema.' He frowned again. 'There was someone in the Bible had the same name, they told us about it at school once, he's in a prayer.'

'The same name as anaemia? What d'you mean, what sort of name? What prayer?'

'You say it when you go to bed,' he said. 'Mum used to

say it to me. Matthew, Mark, Luke and John, that's it. It's one of those names.'

Ruth stared at him. Matthew, Mark, Luke and John. *Luke*. She felt a chill run through her.

'Was it *Luke*?' she asked quietly. 'Was it *leukaemia*?'

'That's right,' he said. 'Leukaemia. Is that a very bad sort of enema?'

'Yes,' she said. 'It's a very bad sort, Sammy.'

There was a brief silence. Sammy had crept closer during the tale and was now leaning against her knee. She put her hand down and rested it on his head, and they both stared into the fire for a moment or two without speaking.

Leukaemia. There was no cure for leukaemia. If you had it, you died. You faded away. There was nothing anyone could do.

'Oh, Sammy,' she said. 'I'm so sorry.'

'I don't know why she had to get it,' he said in a muffled voice. 'I don't know why she had to die, when she'd got two boys to look after.'

That reminded Ruth of his brother. 'What happened to Gordon?' she asked. 'Why was he sent away? Did you say he was at a school somewhere?' If it was an approved school, as she suspected, he must have done something pretty bad.

'He got in a shop,' Sammy said. 'He took necklaces and stuff. It was him and Micky from up the street, Micky said they could get Christmas presents only it was after Christmas when Gordon went, so they were going to sell it instead. They'd have got *money*,' he said with a touch of indignation, 'and we could have got Mum some better medicine.'

'Well, yes, but it was stealing, wasn't it?' Ruth said gently. 'You know stealing's wrong, don't you?' If the child's mother had said prayers with him at bedtime, surely she would also have taught him right from wrong. 'So were Gordon and Micky both sent to the approved school?'

'Not Micky. Only Gordon, because he was older. He's fifteen.'

'But Micky wasn't evacuated, was he? I don't know any Mickys in Bridge End.'

'No, he stopped home, with his mum and gran. And I stopped home too, with my mum. She didn't want me to go away, see. She –' he caught his breath and his eyes filled with tears again '– she wanted me to stop with her, she said I was her – her *angel* and she wanted me to be at home.'

'Oh, Sammy.' Once again, Ruth cradled his head against her. 'You don't have to tell me any more now if you don't want to.'

'She stopped in bed nearly all the time after Gordon got sent away,' he went on, as if he hadn't heard her. 'I did the shopping and things, only I couldn't cook very well and Dad used to bring in chips from the shop. Mrs Vickers next door used to come and help, and Mrs Budd from down the street. And one day I went up the shop and got stuck in the queue, and I was gone ever such a long time, but I got some oxtail, they said it would be good for her – and when I went back, she'd gone all white. She always was white, but she was sort of blue as well. And I thought she'd – she'd died, but she hadn't, she opened her eyes and looked at me, and – and she – she just said I was her angel, and then – then . . .'

His faltering voice stopped. Ruth drew him up on to her lap and he huddled against her body, quivering. She wrapped both arms round him and held him close.

'It's over now,' she whispered at last. 'Your mum's in heaven now, with Jesus. She's not tired or hurting any more. She's well and happy, and she can look down and see you, and she wants you to be well and happy too.'

'Does she?' he said, glancing up at the ceiling.

'Of course she does. She called you her angel, didn't she? Well, now your mum's a real angel and she loves you even more. She's never really left you, you know,' Ruth said gently, thinking of how she'd felt when Jack had died, how she'd seemed to feel his presence all about her, almost as if he'd wrapped his arms about her for ever. 'I know that when someone dies we never see them again, but that doesn't mean they've stopped loving us, any more than we stop loving them. You still love your mum, don't you?'

'Yes,' he said warily, 'but Dad said she'd gone and not to talk about her any more.'

'Well, you can talk about her to me!' Ruth felt another quick surge of anger towards Sammy's father. 'I shan't mind how much you talk about her. I'd like you to tell me all about her. Not all at once – just whenever you feel like it. And I know she still loves you. I *know* she does.'

They sat quietly for a few minutes. The fire was dying down, and Ruth eased him off her lap and got up to put on some more wood. The flames leapt up, lighting the room with warmth, and Silver, who had been unnaturally quiet all this time, suddenly squawked into life behind them.

'Bugger me! Bugger *me*! Splice the mainbrace. Sippers and gulpers. Bugger me, it's a bleedin' *eagle*.'

Sammy giggled, rather waveringly but a giggle nonetheless, and Ruth laughed. She ruffled his hair and looked at the empty cups. 'I think we could do with another cup of cocoa, don't you? And then I'll read to you from that book Lizzie brought round. *The Wind in the Willows*. You like that story, don't you?'

Sammy nodded, and Ruth went out to fill the kettle again. She pumped up the water and stood thinking as it poured slowly from the tap.

There were still questions to be answered. His brother, his father and what was to happen to the little boy who seemed so neglected, so unloved.

He can't go back there, she thought. Even when the war ends, he can't go back.

'Can you credit that anyone could be so cruel?' Ruth said to her sister. 'It's not just his father, it's the authorities. Taking him away like that and not telling me what had happened. And the poor little chap's got no idea where his brother is.'

'But why won't they tell him that?' Jane asked. 'I don't see why he can't know.'

'I don't suppose it's a case of *won't*, it's a case of *haven't bothered*. Nobody seems to have given a thought to his feelings. It's never occurred to them that he probably never knew the address. He's only eight, for heaven's sake. How would he know? His mum wrote the letters and posted them. All Sammy knew was that it was a "proved school" as he calls it, he's no idea where it is.'

'*Someone* must know. His father must.'

'But I don't know how to get in touch with him. That Mrs Tupper's no help at all. She hardly ever comes near us and she's always in a hurry, and she just ignores me when I ask questions. As if it's none of my business,' Ruth said indignantly. 'And I'm supposed to be looking after the child! How can you give a kiddy proper care when you don't know he's only just lost his mum?'

'All they're concerned about is keeping them safe from any bombing,' Jane said. 'I suppose they think that's enough.'

'Well, it's not,' Ruth said shortly. 'Kiddies need to be looked after in more ways than being fed and washed and kept safe. They need to feel cared about as well.' She paused and then said, 'They're still worried about this invasion, aren't they? It's nowhere near over.'

'No, it's not. There's barbed wire going up all round the coast, so I've heard, and people standing by to ring the bells to let everyone know if the Germans come.' Jane shook her head. 'It doesn't seem much, to stop an army that's overrun all those other countries already. I mean, it's like standing in front of a tank and trying to push it back. I don't want to sound defeatist, Ruth – we're supposed to try to keep cheerful, aren't we – but honestly, I do wonder sometimes if we're not just banging our heads against a brick wall.'

'I do too.' Ruth was silent for a moment, then shook her head a little and drew in a deep breath. 'Still, there's nothing you and I can do about it, so we might as well do what the song says and keep smiling through. And make Christmas as good as we can. It's up to us, Jane, and that's something we *can* manage.'

Her sister nodded and smiled. 'You're right, Ruth. The best Christmas we can manage. And that's a promise!'

They did everything that Sammy wanted to do at Christmas.

'You don't need a lantern to go carol singing,' Lizzie declared when Ruth and Sammy went up to the house to have tea. 'There's the moon and stars. And people don't need to open their doors to listen – just to pass out the money! We'll all go and we'll get Edna Corner as well, it'll cheer her up – she needs it, what with Reg being called up and her not being able to keep the Budd boys any more because of the baby coming. And you can ask Joyce Moore and her boys, and anyone else who wants to come.'

'Not too many,' Ben put in, spreading Marmite on toast. 'If the whole village turns out, there won't be anyone left to sing carols to.'

Lizzie made a face at him. 'I'll work out a route. We'll go round by Mr Knight's farm and down the lane to Middle Bridge, and we'll go to Bridge End House, they're going to have a big party there, I've heard. Everyone's determined to have a good Christmas and they'll be really pleased to have carol singers coming round.'

'I think they will,' Ruth agreed. 'It'll be like old times. We'll go on Christmas Eve, when everyone's at home.'

'I wonder if the Germans will let us *have* Christmas,' Jane said to her in a low voice as they went out to the kitchen to make more tea. 'You hear about that truce they're supposed to have had in the last war, but we can't be sure they'll do the same this time. I wouldn't put it past them to send bombers over on Christmas Day itself, just to be nasty.'

The bombing had been going on all through December. London had been getting the worst of it, with almost continuous raids, both day and night, but other cities had been hit as well. Birmingham, Liverpool, Bristol, Southampton, Plymouth – all had been attacked. It seemed as if every city in Britain must be at risk and even in the countryside you weren't completely safe. The sound of a lone German plane, droning overhead on its way home after a raid, was one of the most frightening that Ruth had heard. It might still have bombs aboard and no pilot was going to go back to Germany with unused bombs. Better to drop them at random and hope to hit some small rural settlement, a village, farm or even church. Better to kill one person than no one at all.

It seemed, during the last few days before Christmas, as if Jane was right and the Germans weren't going to allow a Christmas holiday from the bombing. Liverpool was badly hit again and Manchester had its first big raid. The idea of all the families who had lost their homes and possessions, even their loved ones, wrenched at Ruth's heart. It was impossible to help them all. But she could help Sammy and she knew that already she had taken the motherless boy to her heart. What would happen when the war ended she didn't know and couldn't do anything about, but while he was with her he would know what real family life could be.

Christmas Eve came and it was as if the world held its breath. No planes droned overhead. The air-raid sirens stayed silent. The sky was dark, a canopy of black velvet, spattered with stars, as the little crowd of carol singers made their way around the village. The sound of their voices rising into the clear air brought people to their doors to listen – mindful of the blackout, just in case – and when they said their collection was to be used to give both evacuee and village children a party, coins were dropped willingly to chink into their tins.

'That was a good idea of yours,' Ruth said to Jane, shaking her cocoa tin to hear the satisfying rattle. 'I know a few people were saying the evacuees were getting a lot done for them – and so they should, poor little mites – but it's a good thing to give our kiddies a party too. It's not easy for them, having to share everything with strangers.'

They went up the drive to Mr Knight's farm and gathered outside the big front door. Sammy walked close to Ruth, slipping his hand into hers. She looked down at him and smiled.

'Have you seen the stars, Auntie Ruth?' he asked in his hoarse little voice. 'Look, there's millions of them. All over the sky.'

Ruth lifted her eyes. The stars of the Milky Way were clearly visible, so many and so tiny that they seemed to merge into one another to form a broad path of light across the heavens. Why, it's really beautiful, she thought, and wondered why she hadn't looked up at the night sky for so long.

Jack used to tell her about the stars at sea, she thought. He used to recite a poem to her. She tried to remember it.

'I will make you brooches and toys for your delight,
Of birdsong at morning and starshine at night . . .'

'I've never seen them like that before,' Sammy whispered. 'We had the street lights in Portsmouth, till the blackout, and I had to be indoors then. Are there always that many?'

'Yes. There must be,' Ruth said softly. 'But you don't always see them like this . . .' They were both quiet for a moment, gazing upwards, then she looked at him again. 'Are you enjoying the carol singing?'

He nodded. 'It's smashing. I like "While Shepherds Washed their Flocks" best. It's like me having a bath on Saturday nights, to be ready for Sunday.'

Ruth opened her mouth and closed it again. Why correct him? she thought. The picture of shepherds sitting on the hillside earnestly washing their sheep so as to be ready for Christmas was rather a nice one. She might even get him to draw a picture of it.

Sammy had begun to show quite a knack for drawing. He'd made cards for all the family, most of them pictures of fat robins sitting on uncomfortable-looking holly twigs, and he'd sent one to his father and brother too. Ruth had wondered if his father might want to come and see him at Christmas, but there'd been no word. However, a card had arrived containing a brief scrawled note hoping he was being a good boy and a postal order for five shillings. Sammy had stared at it as if he'd never seen such a thing before – well, probably he hadn't, Ruth thought – and it had been quite difficult to get him to hand it over at the post office in exchange for money. She'd suggested he use the money to buy himself something he really wanted, but he'd shaken his head and as far as she knew he still had it.

The sound of 'Silent Night, Holy Night' rose into the clear air. It seemed especially poignant tonight, during this brief reprieve from the bombing. Nobody doubted that the mayhem would break out again after Christmas, over London and over other towns as well, but just for a night or two it did seem that there was to be a lull. The Germans kept Christmas as well, after all, so it was probably intended as a holiday for them rather than the British, but it was a relief just the same.

The Knights' farm was their last call. They sang three carols, then the door was flung open and they crowded into the passageway, cramming together so that it could be closed before the lights were switched on. Mr Knight was there, his red face beaming, and his wife bustled out to urge them all into the big kitchen. There, laid out on the big table, were platters of mince pies and jugs of steaming mulled ale, with lemonade for the children, all to be served in an assortment of tankards, glasses and cups.

'It's just like old times!' Ruth exclaimed in delight. 'It's just like before the war.'

'It's a real Christmas,' Jane agreed. She looked down at Sammy, almost swamped by his brown coat, his fair hair hidden by the cap he'd borrowed from Ben and his blue eyes wide. 'And all because we wanted to give this little chap a good time. It's turned into a good time for us all!'

Mr Knight filled their glasses and rapped on the table for silence. He looked around the little crowd.

'We've been listening out for you all evening,' he said. 'We went upstairs and opened the window, and we could hear you singing all round the village, and I don't mind admitting it brought a bit of a lump to my throat. Like Ruth Purslow here just said, it was like old times. And I dunno what you all think, but it showed me that it don't matter what the Germans do to us, they won't stop us living the way we've always lived. The country's been through a bashing lately and it'll go through more before this lot's over, but they won't stop us singing carols. They won't stop us keeping Christmas the way we've always done and they won't stop us being good, God-fearing British folk. Because that's nothing to do with bombing and fighting, that's what's inside us and nobody can change what's inside you. Not even Hitler.' He stopped, looking slightly embarrassed. 'Well, that's all I want to say and more than I meant to say, and all I want to do now is wish you all a Merry Christmas.' He lifted his tankard and everyone echoed his words: 'Merry Christmas.'

They drank and then turned to each other and began to chatter and laugh. The mince pies were handed round and glasses refilled. For an hour or so, and for the first time in months, the war seemed very far away.

Nobody wanted to leave. They sang carols again and then moved on to other songs – songs like 'Run Rabbit Run' and 'Who Do You Think You Are Kidding, Mr Hitler?' that were becoming popular, and others like 'Keep the Home Fires Burning' and 'It's a Long Way to Tipperary' that came from the last war. They went even further back and sang songs from music halls – 'Daisy, Daisy, Give Me Your Answer, Do' and 'Two Little Girls in Blue' and 'Only a Bird in a Gilded Cage'. They sang 'Tavern in the Town' and 'The Ash Grove' and 'What Shall We Do With a Drunken Sailor?' It seemed that they would never run out of songs to sing.

'We'll have to go,' Ruth said at last. She looked at Sammy, almost asleep in a corner of the settle in front of the big log fire. 'It's been lovely, Mrs Knight, thank you so much. I don't think this young man's ever had such a good time in his life.'

'Poor little chap,' the farmer's wife said, looking at the sleepy face. 'Well, whatever happens to him in the rest of his life, Ruth, you know he'll never forget this. You've given him one good country Christmas to remember.'

'And it's only just started,' Ruth said with a smile. She touched Sammy's shoulder gently and he stirred and looked at her. His smile broke out over his face and she felt her heart turn over. How am I ever going to part from him? she wondered.

'Come on,' she said. 'Time to go home. You've got to be in bed fast asleep with your stocking hung up before Father Christmas comes.'

Chapter Sixteen

Christmas had been celebrated in April Grove as well. Most of the evacuated children had come home and although there was a shock when one bomber came over, late on Christmas Eve, and demolished almost an entire street, there were no other raids. It was awful for the Conway Street people who had been bombed out, but they'd all been taken in by friends or relatives and there was no point in everyone else letting it damp down their enjoyment.

Tommy and Freda Vickers celebrated with their daughter Eunice and Tommy's sister Molly and her husband Ron and son Clifford, who lived in Fratton. It wasn't too far to walk, and they arrived just before dinner and all sat down together to a turkey that Tommy had managed to obtain, and a Christmas pudding that was as much vegetable as fruit, with mashed potato, grated carrot and cooking apple added to the sultanas and raisins their rations had allowed.

'It's a lot better than you'd expect,' Tommy declared, holding out his plate for a second helping. 'Nearly as good as pre-war, in fact. I reckon there's something to be said for these new recipes, you know.'

'The silver threepenny pieces are just as good anyway,' Ron said, scraping pudding from the one he'd found in his helping. 'Nearly cracked my teeth on this little beauty.'

There were six coins in the pudding, and somehow or other Freda managed to see that each person got one. Cliff was last to find the treasure and his freckled face turned almost as red as his hair with delight. He winked at his cousin. 'What's your New Year resolution, Eunice? Going to volunteer?'

Freda looked annoyed and answered before her daughter could speak. 'Let's get Christmas over first, Clifford, if you don't mind. I suppose you're like all the boys, can't wait to get into uniform.'

Clifford had already volunteered and was due to go off to join the Army early in January. He nodded, his blue eyes bright with excitement. 'We've all got to do our bit, Auntie. Can't stand by and let old Hitler smash us to ruins.'

'Maybe so, but I don't see that we've got to talk about it now,' his mother said sharply. She was trying not to think about Clifford going into the Army. 'It's Christmas Day and we ought to be celebrating and happy, not talking about war.' She turned to her sister-in-law. 'What's happened next door? Has that little boy been evacuated after all?'

'Oh yes, he went off several weeks ago. He's out at Bridge End, where the Budd boys are. Living with a widow, so Jess Budd told me.'

'Well, I hope she's treating him better than that woman treated poor little Martin Baker. He could have died of that appendicitis, you know. I saw his mother in the street only the other day. She says she'll never let him go away again, no matter what happens.'

'I think Sammy's all right. It's his dad we've got to worry about now. Hardly ever there, letting the house go to rack and ruin—'

'Well, he don't have much chance to do anything else,' Tommy broke in. 'I mean, be fair, Free, he's out at sea most of the time from what I can make out, and when he does come home he looks like a ghost. If you ask me, Frank Budd's right when he says the poor bloke never got over what happened to him in the first war. And now he's lost his wife and both his kids are away, what comfort's he got?'

'Well, yes, I feel sorry for him, of course,' Freda said a

little uncomfortably. 'But that don't excuse him coming in drunk when he is here. I'm sorry, Tom, but you know I've never liked him, and he treated Nora and those boys like dirt. That's the truth of it and I don't mind who hears me say it.' She looked defiantly round the table.

Tommy didn't think it was the truth, not really, but he didn't want an argument at the Christmas dinner table. He pulled the pudding dish towards him and began to scrape off the last few shreds, knowing that Freda would tell him off, and when she did he gave her his cheeky grin.

'Sorry, Free. I'll never learn me manners, no matter how hard you try to teach me.'

'And that's true, too,' she scolded him, but she smiled as well, knowing perfectly well why he'd done it. 'All right, since it's Christmas ... And once we've cleared up, we'll have a game of Monopoly, shall we? We gave Eunice a set for Christmas and she's dying to play it. And we've asked young Kathy Simmons from October Street over for tea. It's a shame for her to be all on her own with the kiddies on Christmas Day.'

Kathy Simmons and her two little daughters had been bombed out of their home in Porchester Road during one of the earliest raids last summer. Her husband Mike was in the Merchant Navy and away most of the time, and Kathy had given birth to her third child during the raids in November. She had gone into labour early and Tommy had been the only person available to help her. It had been a nightmare at the time, for he'd never seen a baby born before and scarcely knew what to do, but between them they'd managed and Kathy had called the baby Thomas after him. The two families had become friends, and Freda would have had Kathy and the children over to dinner as well, but Kathy had shaken her head.

'We'll stop home for dinner, but we'd like to come over for tea, if that's all right. It's a bit lonely in the evenings.'

So it must be, Freda thought, in that dark little house.

The old lady who'd lived in number 16 before Kathy hadn't had electricity put in, so there was only gaslight downstairs and upstairs they had to use candles. All the houses in the area had been like that till a few years ago, but now almost everyone had electric light, apart from houses, like Dan Hodges' next door, which were rented out. Freda couldn't imagine living without it now.

Tommy went across to fetch Kathy and the children just before darkness fell. He swung Stella and Muriel into his arms and admired Stella's *Rupert* book and Muriel's new rag doll. Then he leant over the baby's pram and chucked him under the chin. 'He gets more good-looking every day. Just like his mum.'

'Oh, Tommy!' Kathy gave him a shy smile. The night of Thomas's birth, with bombs exploding all around, seemed almost unreal now, like a dream – or even, at times, a nightmare – yet it was an experience she and Tommy had shared. You couldn't be stiff and formal with someone who'd been through that with you, yet it was embarrassing too. Best not to dwell on it, she thought, and Tommy seemed to think the same.

He winked at her as he lifted the baby from the pram. 'Let's get this little chap over the street and into the warm. Freda's got the kettle on and there's jelly for tea.'

'Jelly!' Muriel gave a skip of delight. 'What colour jelly? Is it red? I like red best, but Stella likes green.'

'You'll both be pleased then, because we've got both. *And* a pink blancmange rabbit.'

A pink blancmange rabbit . . . The girls' eyes lit up and they scurried across the street and along to number 1. Tommy and Kathy followed more slowly, and as they stopped by the front door they saw a tall figure making its unsteady way round the corner of March Street.

'That's Mr Hodges, isn't it?' Kathy murmured, and Tommy nodded. He handed her the baby and felt in his pocket for the door key.

'Bit the worse for wear, by the look of it.' He raised his voice. 'All right, Dan?'

The figure stopped and stared at them. It was almost dark now and it was impossible to see his face. He swayed a little and put one hand out to steady himself against the wall. 'That you, Tommy Vickers?'

'It is,' Tommy returned cheerfully. 'Been celebrating in the pub, then?'

'If that's what you call it.' Dan Hodges put his hand through the letter box and drew out the key on its long string. With some difficulty he fitted it into the lock and turned it.

Tommy, opening his own door to let Kathy and the girls go in first, felt suddenly sorry for him. 'Why don't you come in with us and have a cuppa?' he suggested. 'It's Christmas. No time to be on your own.'

Dan turned and looked at him, and Tommy remembered a little guiltily that it was partly through his doing that Dan was alone this Christmas. If he hadn't gone down to the billeting office . . . But he'd done right, he told himself. It had been no place for Sammy either. The nipper was better off in the countryside.

'No thanks,' Dan said. 'I've been working all this week. I need to get some sleep.'

He went indoors and shut the door. Tommy looked at it for a moment, then shrugged and went into his own house. He wasn't all that sorry Dan had refused and he knew Freda wouldn't have been best pleased, though she would never have said so, not on Christmas Day, but he still felt sorry for the man. It wasn't much of a Christmas, half of it spent in the pub and half on your own in an empty house.

He went inside to draw the curtains and put up the blackout. All the other houses in April Grove and March and October Streets were doing the same, so that when night fell there was no light showing at all. Yet nobody walking along them could have been in any doubt that it was Christmas, for from almost every darkened window you could hear the sound of music, singing and laughter. Everyone was determined to enjoy themselves. Everyone was determined to prove that even Hitler and his war were powerless to prevent that.

For Dan Hodges the sounds brought an even more piercing loneliness. As he let himself into his cold and empty house, a house with no wife and no sons, with no smell of cooking, no sputtering gaslight or crackling fire, he felt his loss sweep over him in a giant wave of hopelessness and yearning. Maybe it was poor, maybe the furniture was shabby and the floor dirty, maybe it was the sort of home Annie Chapman or Freda Vickers would turn up their noses at, but with Nora and the boys there it had been home just the same. And they might have argued and shouted at each other at times – well, he'd been the one to do most of the shouting, he acknowledged ruefully – but they'd been a family for all that. And all families argued sometimes. They'd stayed together, that was the important thing, they'd looked out for each other. Bugger it, he thought as he slumped into the broken armchair and stared with hopeless eyes at the empty fireplace, they'd *loved* each other.

And now it was all gone. Gordon sent away to that approved school, his apprenticeship gone down the drain. Sammy, out in the country, learning different ways, forgetting his dad. And Nora – his Nora – dead.

Nora, gone for ever. And nothing for him to do but work, work like a slave on the ships that Vosper's built and maintained. Work till he was dog-tired, too exhausted to stand, because it was only that way that he could put it all out of his mind for a while.

That's what he'd been doing today, Christmas Day. He knew that Tommy Vickers thought he'd been in the pub, he knew he looked drunk, but he hadn't touched a drop all day. He'd been working on a new patrol boat, getting it ready to be handed over to the Navy, and the job still wasn't finished. He'd have stuck at it longer only the foreman had told him to go home. Liable to make mistakes, that's what he'd said. Go home and get a bit of kip, come back in the morning.

Dan got up and looked at the mantelpiece. There was just one card there, from Sammy, a card he'd obviously made himself. It had a crayoned picture on it of shepherds on a rocky mountain, apparently dipping their sheep in a tin bath, while all around them the skies were criss-crossed with searchlights. What could have been a parachutist with his head on fire was hovering above them.

I suppose it's meant to be an angel, he thought, taking it from the mantelpiece and examining it. Poor little sod, he's got all mixed up with the war as well. He don't hardly know what it's all about, any of it.

Dan would have liked to have Sammy home, or to have gone out to Bridge End to see him, but how could he do that, when he was out at sea half the time, going out to repair engines and keep the ships on the go? Before the war it hadn't mattered, you knew when you'd get back. Now, you never knew – you never even knew if you *would* get back. A mate of his had been killed only a week or so ago by a German plane strafing the ship he was on out in the Channel.

Sammy was better off without him, anyway. He'd never managed to be much of a father. Even Gordon, in the approved school, was better off without him. Best leave them where they were, both of them.

He looked at the card again, his fingers moving over the upturned faces of the shepherds and the struggling sheep. Funny, the more you looked at it, the more lifelike it seemed. You could see those sheep were struggling, somehow. The nipper'd got quite a knack.

He put the card back and sank into his chair again. Through the party wall he could hear sudden bursts of laughter from the Vickers family. Had other people in too, by the sound of it, probably Ron Weeks, and his wife and boy, Clifford, and there was that young woman from October Street and her youngsters. They were singing now, singing at the tops of their voices, loud enough for the whole street to hear them. He buried his face in his hands, but the sound still reached his ears.

'Pack up Your Troubles in Your Old Kitbag, and Smile, Smile, Smile . . .'

There wasn't a kitbag big enough to pack Dan Hodges' troubles in. And he couldn't remember when he had last felt like smiling.

Chapter Seventeen

The respite didn't last long.

It was as if the Germans had spent Christmas loading their planes with the biggest cargo of bombs yet. The day after Boxing Day they were back, hurling destruction on London. The newspapers were filled again with pictures of burning buildings and shattered streets. Big Ben itself had been damaged, and there were countless reports of lucky escapes and unlucky encounters. A man escaped unhurt while his wife and friends were killed beside him. A cat was released from a crushed dustbin. A woman dug her baby and badly injured husband from the debris of their home. Others, buried under mounds of rubble, cried out for help until their desperate rescuers managed to dig them out, or until their cries faded and stopped.

The rescuers were still at work when the Germans struck again, with the worst raid yet. The bombing went on for three hours and fires raged through the streets until it seemed as if the entire city must be in flames.

'Look at that, Tommy,' Freda said, staring in horror at the pictures in the *Sketch*. 'They say it was a deliberate attempt to set fire to the city. There's been seven churches destroyed and God knows how many other buildings ruined. They're calling it the Second Great Fire of London. It's dreadful.'

'It is, love, but look at this picture on the front of the *Daily Mail*.' Tommy held out his paper. It was the most dramatic photograph of all – the dome of St Paul's rising clear of a huge cloud of smoke and lit by the flames that burned all around. 'It's like one of those old paintings you see, with God looking down out of the clouds. I reckon he was looking after his own there, don't you?' He looked at the photograph again. 'It sort of gives you heart, somehow, thinking that even with all that bombing a place like St Paul's can get through without being damaged.'

'He didn't look after the other seven churches, though, did he?' Freda said in a shaking voice. 'Nor all those other buildings. It's dreadful. It's *wicked*. All those poor people . . . And it'll be our turn next, Tommy, here in Portsmouth. We must have had getting on for thirty raids already, but we've not had anything as bad as that yet. But we will – they'll do the same to us, see if they don't. They won't be satisfied until every town in England is flattened.'

Tommy put his arm round her. As he did so, they heard the slam of the front door of number 2 and looked at each other.

'That's Dan Hodges going up the pub again,' Freda said. 'I saw him coming home dinner time, he was so drunk he could hardly walk. And there's people getting killed fighting to save the skin of men like him, Tommy. It's not fair. It just isn't fair.'

Dan wasn't going to the pub. He had a couple of days off from Vosper's in lieu of all the overtime he'd done up till Christmas and he was entitled to his relaxation. But relaxing was something he just couldn't do these days and sitting in the pub on his own, drinking himself senseless, made him feel worse instead of better.

He was going back to work. He didn't have to go, not till the next day, but he couldn't stand being alone in the house any more. At least when he was at work he could feel he was doing something. At least he could feel there was some sense in his being alive.

The Blitz didn't end with that massive raid. It went on and on, with new raids every night, on Bristol, Liverpool and

Manchester as well as other cities and London itself. It seemed that the enemy was determined to hammer the country into the ground, and the New Year opened to a dread that all the courage in the world could not quite dispel.

'We're giving as good we get,' Tommy said to Freda as they sat in their shelter at the bottom of the garden. The siren went every night now, for Portsmouth lay close to the path of the bombers, wherever they were headed, and you never knew when it might be Pompey's turn. Some people refused to go down to the shelter, saying that if a bomb had your name on it, it would find you no matter where you were. Tommy scorned that. He didn't believe in bombs 'having your name on them' and he wanted his wife and daughter safe in the shelter while he went on his rounds, firewatching and making sure there were no lights showing.

'Our boys are over there, bombing them just the same way,' he went on. 'The RAF are giving them what for. Blasting their cities to bits, they are.'

'Good thing too,' Eunice said, but Freda shook her head. She had brought her shopping bag down as usual, filled with all the things the family might want during the night, and now she took out her knitting and examined it to see if she'd finished on a purl or a plain row before putting it away. There was a flask of cocoa in there as well and a few broken biscuits in a paper bag. Broken biscuits were a bargain, sold cheaply, and you never knew what sort you'd get. In this lot, she knew, there were two custard creams.

She began to knit, still thinking of the German women who were probably doing just the same, sitting in shelters and knitting as they waited to be bombed. 'I know they're the enemy, but it doesn't seem right all the same. I mean, we're killing kiddies and old people just like they are. I thought wars were supposed to be between *armies*.'

'Everyone's in the army now,' Tommy said. 'In a

manner of speaking, I mean. The Home Front, they're calling us, you know that.'

'Anyway,' Eunice said, 'those old people you're so sorry for, they probably killed our boys in the first war and have been egging Hitler on ever since. And the children, they'll grow up to be just as bad. I think it's right what people say – the only good German's a *dead* German.'

Freda said nothing. She didn't want them arguing down in the shelter, when they might be blown to bits at any moment. All the same, it *didn't* seem right, bombing kiddies, no matter who they were. And what about Heinz Brunner who used to run the newspaper shop in September Street? He'd lived there with his wife Alice for years, everyone knew him and a nicer, kinder man you couldn't wish to meet. He was almost certainly dead now, first interned and then torpedoed on his way to Canada, so perhaps Eunice would consider him a 'good' German at last. But he always had been good and Alice – who wouldn't believe he was dead – was just fading away without him.

'A lot of people are trekking out over the hill every night,' Eunice went on. 'My friend at work's got an auntie at Denmead and she goes there straight from work. She only goes home at weekends now. Her mum goes back in the daytime, of course,' she added.

Freda nodded. 'I know. And they're talking about digging tunnels under Portsdown Hill, so that people can shelter there like they do in the underground stations in London.' She shuddered. 'I don't fancy it much myself. It seems awful, somehow, hiding away in caves. At least we've got this place a bit cosy and we're only a few yards from the back door.' She looked around at the bunks and the camp bed, and the old rag rug she'd put on the floor. There were a few pictures on the walls too, cut out of *Picture Post* magazines and stuck to the curve of the corrugated iron, and there was a soft light cast by the hurricane lamp. It was a hole at the bottom of the garden all the same and it was cold and cramped, and far from being ideal, but she still thought it was a lot better than being in a tunnel under the hill.

'Bit like shutting the stable door after the horse has legged it,' Tommy said. 'You know what the council's like, it'll take them a good couple of years to talk about tunnels, let alone dig them. How long do they think it's going to go on for, for goodness sake? It's now we need them, not in 1943.'

'Maybe they think we'll still need them in 1943,' Freda said sadly.

Eunice gave a scornful laugh. '1943! There'll be nothing left to bomb by then, if they go on at this rate. The war's never going to last that long. Someone'll have to win before then.'

'I'm not so sure,' Tommy said. 'The last one went on for four years, remember. Anyway, they've got to make plans, haven't they?'

Freda started a purl row. 'Well, I don't think it's going to be over for a long time. If you ask me, they're just getting into their stride. And I can't believe we won't get another dose ourselves. All these other places being blitzed – it's bound to be Pompey's turn again soon.'

It came only a few days later, on 10 January. And, just as they had feared, the raid that blasted the city apart that night was every bit as bad as those on London.

It began at just seven o'clock in the evening. It was a Friday and Eunice had come home early, determined to go to the pictures with her friend Sheila. The family had argued about it all through tea.

'There hasn't been a raid over Pompey since just before Christmas. It's London they're going for, you know it is.'

'*And* other places,' Tommy said. 'Your mother's right, we're bound to get another attack and the longer it goes on, the more likely it is. Those cinemas are death traps.'

'They always tell you when the siren goes. You can get out if you want to.'

'Yes, and suppose everyone decided to get out at the same moment?' Freda demanded. 'Have you thought about that, Eunice, two or three hundred people all trying to squeeze through half a dozen doors? And suppose there's a direct hit? Why don't you ask Sheila round here? We can sit by the fire and have a game of cards.'

'We don't *want* a game of cards,' Eunice said, exasperated. 'We want to go to the *pictures*! It's *Rebecca*, with Laurence Olivier and Joan Fontaine. It's ever so romantic and if we don't go this week we'll miss it. It's some Western or other next week.'

'Nothing wrong with a good Western,' Tommy declared, getting up from the table. 'Anyway, it's gone six o'clock, time I was off on my rounds. What's it to be? I'll walk round to Sheila's with you, if you like, and then see you both back here.'

Eunice looked sulky. 'I told you, we don't want to come back here. We're going to the pictures. Look, I'll be back by ten o'clock. Nothing's going to happen before then. We haven't had a raid since before Christmas.'

Tommy glanced at his wife. 'Up to you, Free.'

Freda sighed. 'Well, if you're that set on it I suppose we can't stop you. But mind you come straight home afterwards, all right? Your dad'll come to meet you, won't you, Tom?'

'I'll be outside waiting for you,' he promised. 'You can tell Sheila's dad I'll see her home as well, save him turning out. It's a cold night. And I'll walk round there with you now, like I said. Don't like you being out on your own in the blackout.'

Eunice gave him a look but said no more. It wasn't too late for her mum to change her mind and say she couldn't go to the pictures. She ran upstairs and got her new scarf, the red one her Auntie Molly had knitted her for

Christmas, and came down looking bright-eyed and excited. Freda, looking at her, wondered if she and Sheila were going to meet a couple of boys, but there was nothing she could do about that. The girls were nineteen after all, old enough to start a bit of courting.

'Come on, then, if you're coming,' she said to her father. 'The picture starts at half past six and we don't want to be going in halfway through.'

'That'll only be the little picture. It doesn't matter if you miss a bit of that. It's a Western, isn't it? Thought you weren't bothered about Westerns.'

'I'm bothered about having a good night out,' Eunice said coldly. 'And we won't have that if we only see half the picture and can't make out what it's all about. Anyway, I don't like going in when it's dark, you can't see where you're sitting.'

Tommy wound his own dark blue scarf round his neck and jammed on his air-raid warden's tin hat. 'All right then, come on. I'm ready now.' He bent over Freda in her armchair and gave her a kiss. 'Now, you mind you get down the shelter straight away if there's a warning, see. No fussing around saving stuff. Got your bag ready?'

'Yes, and the tin box with all the papers in. I'll be all right, Tom. Anyway, I expect our Eunice is right, there won't be a raid. You go off now and I'll have some cocoa ready when you get back.' She picked up her knitting and settled down to listen to the wireless.

It was very quiet after they had gone. There was a music programme on, to be followed by a recording of *Hi Gang!* with Bébé Daniels and Ben Lyon, then a concert. It was a shame Eunice hadn't stopped at home, they could have enjoyed it together, but there, the girl was young and naturally she wanted to be out with her pals. Once again Freda wondered if one of them might be a young man.

I'd better do the washing-up in a minute, she thought, before I get too settled in this chair. She wondered if

London might get another attack tonight. They'd had a nasty raid last night, which must have been horrible for all the poor souls still trying to put things straight after that terrible Blitz at the end of December. And they'd said on the news that Manchester had had a bad raid too. It was awful to think of. Yet folk still seemed to manage to carry on. There'd been pictures in the *Daily Mail* of people scrambling over all sorts of rubble to get to work, and it was the same in Pompey when they'd had those raids before Christmas. The local *Evening News* had pictures of people carrying on as usual, right alongside those of firemen battling against burning buildings.

I hope they don't come here tonight, she thought, laying down her knitting. Not while our Eunice is out and Tommy on his rounds. She hadn't forgotten that night when Kathy Simmons' baby had been born and Tommy with her in the shelter, while Freda herself had been too bad with flu to go and help. She'd been in the Anderson shelter with Eunice, all wrapped up in blankets, listening to the scream of the bombs without any idea that Kathy was screaming too, with the pain of birth. All she'd known was that Tommy was out in it somewhere, perhaps being bombed himself, perhaps buried under some ruined building. She didn't want to go through that again.

The comedy programme finished and she realised she'd heard barely a word. She glanced at the clock on the mantelpiece. It was just on seven. Then her heart was gripped with icy fear and she never knew afterwards whether it was because she heard the first note of the wailing air-raid siren, or whether she had some strange, unearthly knowledge that the Germans were on their way, and that death was coming with them.

Tommy left Eunice and Sheila at the cinema and went back to his patrol area, whistling. It was a fine, clear night with a bright moon just coming up, and he glanced at it and felt his mouth twist. Bombers' moon, he thought, they'll be coming over tonight, that's for certain. He wondered where their target would be.

Tommy had been in a good many air raids now, some during the day and some at night. He'd been down in Old Pompey when Pickfords had been hit, and he'd shepherded a crowd of people into a street shelter and got them singing to keep their spirits up. He'd been in Copnor when St Albans church was hit, and all those houses round about smashed and damaged. And then there'd been the one when little Thomas Simmons had been born.

You never got used to it though, not really. You never knew when this one might have the bomb aimed at your house and when you went out of your front door you never really knew if it would still be there when you got back. But it didn't do to think that way, you'd go mad. You just took it for granted that you and yours would come through OK, and did your best to help them that needed it. And when you'd done that and found you were still alive, you went home and hoped for the best.

Tommy wasn't doing his ordinary rounds in Copnor tonight. Along with other wardens, he was due to report to ARP Control in the Guildhall for a lecture on incendiary bombs and to collect orders for a special training session. He walked quickly through the darkened streets to the city centre, keeping a sharp eye open for any flicker of light and shouting the familiar 'Put that light out!' whenever he caught a glimpse of one. Those four words had made the ARP wardens more unpopular than any other, he thought, but you had to do it. The Germans might be up there now, too high to be heard, looking down for a clue that might tell them where to drop their bombs. And there were fifth columnists all over the place, so he'd heard, traitors and spies ready to flash a signal. You couldn't take any chances.

The Guildhall stood, grand and imposing in the growing moonlight, at the top of its broad flight of steps, flanked by the somnolent lions that no small boy could resist climbing up on. The soft, cold light gleamed on their marble flanks and Tommy felt a sudden desire to climb on them himself, sitting astride the big bodies and pretending he was an emperor of the jungle. He grinned and joined the throng of men entering the Guildhall through the side door.

The Guildhall was Portsmouth's grandest building. It housed the City Council, ARP Control had its offices there and the Lord Mayor himself had moved in to live there as soon as the war began, saying he wanted to be on the spot when anything happened. It was the nerve centre of the city.

Tommy and the other ARP wardens went into one of the meeting rooms. There was a small stage at one end and rows of chairs facing it. They filed into place, a murmur of voices as they talked to each other about the war, the Blitz on London and whether they would ever be lucky enough to see Pompey football team play again. It seemed a very long time ago since they'd won the FA Cup, only a few months before war broke out.

The siren went only moments after they had settled themselves down. Almost immediately, before anyone had a chance to move, they heard a tremendous explosion and all the lights went out.

There was instant pandemonium.

'Blimey! What the bloody hell . . .' 'They've hit the electricity, must have.' 'Isn't there no emergency lighting? Who's got a torch?' A score of lights flickered into action. 'They must be overhead already. We'd better get out there.' 'No, some of you get up to the roof, we'll need fire watchers.' 'Ain't there any up there already? Don't say we was all down here, listening to this bleedin' lecture.'

'Where was Noah when the lights went out?' Tommy muttered and gave the answer himself. 'In the *dark*.' But there was no time for jokes, and he was already making for the stairs to the top of the tower. If the *Luftwaffe* was already over the city, men would be required up there to see just where help was most needed and to guard the Guildhall itself from incendiaries. Just one or two of them up there could set the whole place alight.

He emerged on to the narrow parapet, beside the big copper cupola. Here, two hundred feet above the square, he could look right out over the city, stretching north to Copnor and Hilsea, with the dark bulk of Portsdown Hill like a rampart behind them. To the east he could see the dark lines of the streets towards Eastney and Langstone Harbour, to the west was Portsmouth's own great harbour, filled with shipping, and to the south lay the crowded buildings of Old Portsmouth, and the smart shopping streets and hotels of Southsea. He could see them clearly, even in the blackout. They were lit not by forbidden street lights or careless windows but by fire.

'Blimey,' he said to Bill Rogers, who'd followed him up, 'that's Palmerston Road, look. Going up like a flaming torch . . . And that's the electricity station, they must have hit that first. There won't be an electric light on in the whole of Pompey. Bloody *hell*, what was *that*?'

'They're bombing the whole bloody place,' the other man said. 'They're giving us the Blitz, same as they did London. This is the end of Pompey, Tom. The bloody end.'

The roar of the aircraft drowned any other words. There must be hundreds of them up there, Tommy thought, flinging himself flat as a bomb exploded somewhere close. The sky was a web of silver as searchlights flung their beams towards the stars, and somewhere under the drone of the engines and the thunder of the bombs you could hear the rattle of ack-ack guns from the emplacements at Southsea and on the hill. But what use were they against a raid of this size? They could bring down a few planes, perhaps, but they could never destroy an armada like this.

The bombs rained down. From their vantage point

242

Tommy and his mate could see the fires springing up all over the city. Palmerston Road was alight from end to end, its shops surely ruined, and barely had this thought crossed his mind than a shower of bombs fell close by. When he raised his head again he saw the stores of Commercial Road – Littlewoods, British Home Stores, the Landport Drapery Bazaar – beginning to blaze. There won't be a shop left in the place, he thought, and grabbed a fire extinguisher as a stick of incendiary bombs fell on the roof just below him. Blimey, if the Guildhall itself caught alight he'd be fried up here like a sausage on a stick . . .

When he next looked out from the tower it was to see a blazing inferno at his feet. Everywhere in Portsmouth seemed to be on fire. Tommy, who knew the city like the back of his hand, stared in horror and felt his body grow numb. That must be the Eye and Ear Hospital there. And that, in the other direction, was Clarence Pier. Down Queen Street, that was the Royal Sailor's Rest, and there in Lake Road the Sally Army citadel. And the old Hippodrome, that was on fire, surely, and silhouetted by flames he could see the towers and spires of churches, and the ornate frontages of cinemas built during the twenties and thirties, cinemas he'd been in and out of ever since he was a boy . . . *Cinemas*!

He'd seen Eunice to the cinema himself, her and her friend Sheila, laughing and giggling the way girls do, looking forward to seeing – who was it? – Laurence Olivier and Joan Fontaine in some romantic picture or other. His Eunice . . .

He turned and glanced north, towards Copnor. Freda would have gone down the shelter as soon as she heard the siren, he was sure she would. But what if there'd been a direct hit? Even Andersons couldn't survive that. And she was all on her own, as well . . .

'Tommy! *Tom*! Look behind you – *look down there*!' Bill

Rogers's voice was high with panic. 'The Guildhall's on fire – the whole bleeding place is alight! We've got to get out!'

Tommy stared down at the main roof. Bill was right. A mass of incendiaries had sprinkled themselves all over the building and were burning fiercely. He could feel their heat on his face. There was nothing anyone could do about it and the fire watchers were evacuating their positions. Bill was already making for the door which led to the tower stairs. Tommy flung one last wild glance around and followed.

Chapter Eighteen

The Guildhall was gutted. Tommy, Bill and the others had barely reached the ground floor when a high-explosive bomb hit the roof they had been staring at from above and it fell in with a crash that shook the blazing walls. Everyone in the building was on their way out, the Lord Mayor and ARP personnel last. They got through the doors just in time and ran from the ruins, looking back in horror at the inferno behind.

'Bloody hell,' Tommy breathed. 'We could've bin toast in there.'

Mr Daley, the Lord Mayor, was standing beside him. Dirty and dishevelled, looking more like a dustman than a lord mayor, he watched grimly as the firefighters arrived with their hoses and began to direct streams of water on to the flames. He turned to Tommy and shouted above the noise of fire, water and yet more aircraft, yet more explosions.

'You're ARP. Where from?'

'Copnor,' Tommy yelled back. 'I come down for the lecture.'

The Mayor nodded. 'You'll be anxious about your family – better try to make your way back, though I dare say you'll find plenty to do on the way. God knows what it's like out there, the whole city seems to be on fire.'

Tommy nodded. 'My missus will have gone down the shelter. It's my girl I'm worried about, she went to the pictures . . .'

The Mayor nodded again and put his hand on Tommy's

shoulder, giving him a light push. 'You're doing a good job. All of you.' There was a crash from the burning building and they both jumped back. 'Go on. We haven't got time to stand here. We'll be relocating the ARP to Cosham. Good luck!' He turned away and was lost in a billow of smoke. Tommy stared after him for a second, then looked again at the blazing Guildhall. He turned away, feeling sick at heart.

It took Tommy Vickers the rest of the night to get back home. You just couldn't do it, he told Freda when he finally stumbled in as daylight broke next morning, revealing a city devastated by the attack. There was too much to do – people buried under rubble, people searching for their families, people hurt and dying. There were fires everywhere, too many for the fire brigades to deal with, you just had to turn to and give a hand. There was a kiddy he'd found, you wouldn't believe it unless you saw it, with one arm torn clean off his poor little body, yet still staggering about crying out for his mother. There were mothers and fathers screaming for their children, old men and women bewildered and dazed, cats and dogs mad with terror. And around them all the time there were buildings on fire, the sky lit red as blood with the flames, and more and more bombs falling all the time, more and more explosions, more and more of every bloody thing.

'I wanted to get to the cinema where Eunice was,' he said, sinking into his chair as Freda put a cup of tea in front of him. 'I couldn't get there, Free. I couldn't get through, the streets was all blocked, there was piles of bricks and big broken planks of wood, and smashed glass . . . I couldn't even make out where I was half the time. And people yelling out for help – you couldn't just walk by. I kept thinking about her, trapped in the one-and-sixes . . . And when I tried to get home, it was just as bad, every road in the city was closed except for Copnor Road and I didn't know what was happening up here, you could have been

246

buried just the same. I tell you what, I never thought I'd find you here in your own kitchen, making tea as if nothing had happened. After all I saw last night, I never thought that.'

'Well, I am,' Freda said, putting three spoonfuls of sugar into his cup. They'd both started using saccharin months ago, but saccharin wasn't any good for shock, not like proper sugar was, and Tommy had had a lot of shocks. 'I went straight down the shelter when it started and that's where I stayed. I was frightened all the time about you and our Eunice, but it wasn't any good me doing anything else, so I stopped there. And thank God, Eunice got back before it got too bad. The picture stopped first thing, when the electricity went, and everyone came out. She was in the shelter with me from eight o'clock, so we were both safe, and I can't tell you how thankful we were when the All Clear went at last and we could come back indoors again – nearly as glad as when you walked in the door, that's how!'

Tommy managed a faint grin. 'Well, I'm glad to know I'm appreciated. And the damage doesn't seem too bad round this way. I reckon we got off light, in comparison.'

They smiled at each other, deeply grateful to be still alive. But their thankfulness was short-lived. As the flames leapt from Guildhall tower where Tommy had kept watch and the copper plates of the cupola softened and fell away, as the ruins of the shops and offices and homes of the city were revealed in the harsh January daylight, and as Portsmouth began to try to pull itself out of the ashes, so the names of the people who had been killed began to be recovered.

Among them were Tommy's sister Molly and her husband Ron, who had sat in the Vickers's living room only a fortnight ago, singing songs. And among them, too, were Kathy Simmons and her baby son, Thomas.

Chapter Nineteen

Dan Hodges had spent the night of the Blitz over Portsmouth out on the streets.

As a shipworker with erratic hours, and often out at sea, he hadn't joined either the Home Guard or the ARP. He served as a fire watcher both at work and when he was at home, where he possessed two large red fire extinguishers and a tin hat, but that amounted to no more than standing outside in the garden keeping an eye out for incendiaries. Nobody, on the night of 10 January could leave it at that.

In any case, he wasn't even at home when the *Luftwaffe* struck. He was down in the Vosper workshops at Camber dock, finishing work on a new engine which was to be fitted in a fast patrol boat next day. He had just knocked off and, exhausted after a day's work which had begun at seven that morning, was on his way out of the yard when the siren went and he heard the almost simultaneous roar of the aircraft.

Dan stopped and glanced up. The sky was already a silver web of searchlight beams. High above, caught in the criss-cross of white light, he could see the black shapes of the raiders. There was a burst of anti-aircraft fire from Southsea Common and, immediately following that, a huge, thundering explosion so close that the ground shook and Dan found himself knocked off his feet by a hot, gritty blast that felt like a punch from a giant fist.

He lay for a moment or two, fighting for breath. In the seconds since the siren had begun to wail all hell had broken loose. The sky seemed to be filled with planes and the city was shaking with repeated explosions. People were running, shouting, screaming, crowding into the street shelters, rushing past with fire extinguishers, uncertain of where to go, some crying in panic, some with set, angry faces.

Dan staggered to his feet. A woman blundered into him and he caught and steadied her. She looked up into his face, her eyes wild. 'They've hit the electricity. Everything's gone off.'

That must have been the first mighty explosion. The big electricity station, serving the whole of Portsmouth, stood only a few streets away. That meant no lights, no electrical equipment running, no anything. And any gaslights that survived would be put out soon too, he thought grimly. Gas and water mains were fractured regularly in the raids.

'Where d'you live, missus?' He had to yell to make himself heard over the noise. Another explosion shook the earth and a crack seemed to open up in the road beneath his feet. He staggered sideways, still clutching the woman.

'Gosport. I work out Southsea. I was on me way home – I go across the floating bridge.'

The floating bridge was a big, flat-bottomed craft that was pulled across the neck of the harbour on chains. It carried cars, saving them the fifteen-mile journey around the top of the harbour, and although it arrived in Gosport close to the ordinary ferry, its departure point in Portsmouth was in the old part of the city.

'You'd better get in a shelter,' Dan bellowed. 'They might not be working the floating bridge in this.'

'But I *got* to get home! I got my dad waiting for his tea – he's in a chair, see, he can't do nothing much for himself. Mrs Green next door slips in with a bit of dinner for him, but she'll be down her own shelter.'

'I expect she'll look after your dad,' Dan cut brusquely across her scream. 'Look, missus, if the ferry ain't running there's nothing you can do about it. You'll have to go in a shelter, unless you want to swim for it.'

'I'll go and see,' she bawled, pulling away from him. 'I'll go and see. They might not have stopped it yet—'

She was off, running through the streets. Dan watched her for a second, then turned away. Bombs had been dropping and exploding all over the area. People were still running about, but they were different people now. They were firefighters, police, ARP wardens and Home Guard, arriving in fire engines, vans and old lorries, reeling out hoses, trying to find the fire hydrants in which to plug them, while overhead the planes circled the city, hurling down yet more bombs, killing, injuring, destroying.

Dan turned and raced back into the yard, his exhaustion forgotten. As one of the fire watchers he had a post to go to, ships and workshops to look after. As he reached his post an incendiary dropped at his feet. He leapt back, grabbed the extinguisher and banged the handle down, directing the jet of water at the fire that had already begun to burn. No sooner was it dowsed than another sprang up, then another and another, as incendiaries fell like scalding rain all over the yard. He thrust the extinguisher towards them, using it like a gun, and for a few minutes longer it worked and the fires began to die down. Then it ran out of water.

Dan felt his temper rise, his own personal fire flaring in his breast. He yelled and stamped, almost forgetting the extinguisher in his fury. 'You bastards!' he screamed. 'You bloody, fucking bastards! Set us alight, would you? Well, I'll be *buggered* if you will. I'll see you in hell, the lot of you, see you rot in hell for what you done to us. Kill me if you can, kill me if you like, but I'll take you with me, I'll take you all with me, you sodding, bloody swine, you – you – you—'

He was standing amidst the flames by now, glaring up at the sky with mad eyes, shaking both fists at the planes that flew uncaring overhead. Tears poured down his cheeks, scalding the skin as the heat evaporated them, and as yet another incendiary crashed just feet away a flame licked out and caught at the leg of his trousers.

'Hodges! Hodges, what the hell's the matter with you?' Nobby Clark, the foreman, was beside him, beating at the flames, shaking his arm. He picked up another fire extinguisher and shoved it into Dan's arms. 'Can't you see you're on *fire*? Get *on* with it, for God's sake. The whole bleeding place is going to go up if we don't do something.'

'The bastards,' he said in a shaking voice, thick with tears. 'They're bashing everything to bits. There won't be nothing left. Why? What's it all for? What *good* is it going to do?'

'I dunno, mate, and I ain't going to stand here talking about it,' Nobby said curtly. 'Get that fire extinguisher going again, and when you runs out of water get another one. Or a bucket of sand – anything. We ain't going to let them get the yard. Them ships have got to go out tomorrow and help win the bloody war, so shut your mouth, Hodges, and just bleeding well *get on with it*.'

He was gone, and Dan looked at the fire extinguisher and then at the flames that were already springing up again all around him. He felt their sudden heat and his mind seemed to click as he realised again what was happening. With a yell, he started the extinguisher and directed it with grim determination, not wildly as he had done before, but concentrating on one fire at a time. That's one for *you*, Hitler, he muttered savagely as one incendiary after another spluttered and died, that's one for *you*, Goebbels, and *you*, Rommel, and *you* and *you* and *you* . . . You're *not* going to beat us. Do your bloody worst. We're British, and you're bloody well *not* going to beat us.

Afterwards, that long and dreadful night was no more than a patchwork of scattered memories. He had been on a lorry, he could remember that, he'd been out at Clarence Pier when that went up, helping to fight the fires, helping to drag the bodies away. He'd been in streets he'd never known existed – and Dan Hodges would have said he knew Old Pompey like the back of his hand – helping people from their bombed houses, getting them into shelters while the raid continued almost till daylight. He'd staggered into First Aid posts and wardens' shelters with men and women who were hurt by shrapnel, by flying bricks and glass, by blast, and once or twice he'd been given scalding tea to drink by girls no older than Eunice Vickers next door, dressed in boiler suits and tin hats, weary and pale, yet still with cheerful grins on their dirt-streaked faces.

He came home at last as dawn streaked the sky with a different kind of red. Fires were still burning all over the city and streets were closed or impassable. The flames that were consuming the Guildhall could be seen for miles, leaping high into the sky. There were hoses and firemen everywhere, clambering over great heaps of rubble, and there were people scrambling over the same rubble, tearing at it with their bare hands as they searched for their families, for their friends and neighbours. There were other people, shocked and bewildered, just wandering aimlessly, sometimes calling out a name; or sitting on stones, staring sightlessly into their own nightmares, too stunned to know where or even who they were.

Dan stumbled past. Why he was going home at all he didn't know. There was nobody there to worry about, nobody he cared for who might need him. If only Nora could be waiting for me . . .

Nora would not be there and yet he felt that she had been with him; through all that bitter, frenzied night she had been by his side. She hadn't left him, not really, and he hoped she knew now what he'd never been able to tell her while she lived – that he loved her.

Nora, he thought as he staggered blindly through the ruined city. Oh, Nora . . .

*

Out at Bridge End they listened to the news in horror.

'It sounds as if there's nothing left of Portsmouth,' Ruth said to Jane when she collected Sammy after her afternoon shift. Normally Sammy went home with Joyce Moore after school, but today she had taken her boys over to Romsey to see their grandparents. 'I mean, there were planes over all night. Matron at the hospital's got an auntie there, she was out at Denmead for the night but she rang Matron up on the telephone and she says the whole city's on fire. The Guildhall's still burning, you can see the flames for miles, and there's almost nothing left of the shops out at Southsea and in Commercial Road. The poor evacuee kiddies must be frantic.'

'So are their mothers,' Jane said. Several of the mothers had gone back to Portsmouth, as Jess Budd had done, but a few whose husbands were in the Forces were still at Bridge End. 'They don't know if they've got homes to go to and most of them have still got family there, you know. Old people, and brothers and sisters and that. That young Mrs Burton with the twins, she's nearly out of her mind, spent all day trying to find out what's happened to her mum and dad.'

'You'd think they'd get a message through somehow, wouldn't you?' Ruth said, but Jane shook her head.

'There's nothing working. There's no electricity and hardly any telephones, and you can't get into the post offices to send telegrams. It's like the city's been cut off.'

Ruth sighed. 'It's terrible.' She lowered her voice, even though Sammy was out in the garden playing football with Ben. 'I've been wondering about Sammy's dad. He works down the docks, you know. Suppose something's happened to him – what'll become of little Sammy? And there's that brother of his too,' she added as an afterthought.

'I don't know,' Jane said. 'When you think of it, there must be a lot of kiddies that's happening to. Losing their mums and dads. I suppose they get put into children's homes and orphanages.'

'Orphanages!' Ruth said, horrified. 'Oh, I wouldn't want my Sammy to be put in one of them places. I mean, I'm sure they look after the kiddies all right, make sure they're washed and fed and that, but it's not like a proper home, is it. And Sammy needs a home, he's a quiet little boy, he needs to be *loved*. He'd never manage among all those children, specially the bigger boys, they get so rough.'

Jane looked at her. 'You've got fond of that little chap, haven't you?'

Ruth bit her lip. 'I suppose I have. He's such a loving little boy and he's had such a sad time. I still don't think I know the half of it, you know. I've never even seen his dad, he's still never been out to visit him and he hardly ever writes . . . I suppose it's never having had one of my own too. It's as if Sammy was sort of sent to me, if you know what I mean. As if I was meant to have him.'

Jane looked at her doubtfully. 'D'you think it's a good idea, Ruthie? Letting him get into your heart like that. I mean, you're not going to be able to keep him for ever, are you? He's going to have to go back some day.'

Ruth looked obstinate. 'I could adopt him.'

'Well, maybe, but I don't think it's as easy as all that. The billeting people have got his name on their records, they'll want to know what's happening to him. Then there's his dad. He might not be doing much at the moment, but we don't really know why that is, do we, and he's going to want him back eventually. There's the brother too.'

'Well, I'll cross that bridge when I come to it. Sammy's mine for the time being, anyway. We'll see what happens when the war finishes, and by then he might be able to have a say too.'

Jane sighed and then said, 'Our Terry's gone overseas, you know. Africa. They say there's going to be a lot of fighting there. I can't sleep for thinking about it.' A tear trickled down her cheek.

'Oh, *Jane*.' Ruth stared at her sister in dismay. 'Oh, I *am* sorry. Why ever didn't you tell me straight away?'

'Well, you were worried about Sammy.' Jane wiped her eyes. 'We've all got worries now, it seems. We just have to take our turn.' She tried a little laugh but her mouth twisted it into a sob. 'I know it's unpatriotic of me,' she said tremblingly, 'but I can't bear to think of our Terry fighting, and in all that heat as well. He's never liked hot weather . . . And God knows how they'll be living, it'll be just tents, and that's if they're lucky. You see these things on the pictures – men having to sleep in holes in the sand, and there's all sorts of horrible things, scorpions and spiders and God knows what else. I can't *bear* to think of my Terry like that. I know he's nearly twenty-three but it don't seem five minutes ago that he was a baby in his pram, or a little boy coming home from school with his socks all falling down and a hole in his jersey.'

Ruth moved to sit beside her, patting her arm. She thought of the tall, generous young soldier who had played with Sammy at Christmas. Terry had always been a cheerful, willing boy, working hard on the farm yet still ready to do chores for his mother or help his father with jobs like wallpapering and painting. He'd been a good son, like many other young men of his age, and he'd had a good future to look forward to.

Now, it seemed as though that future might be taken away from him.

'He wanted to do it,' she said at last. 'Even if the worst happens, Jane, you can always be proud of him.'

Jane nodded. She found a hanky and blew her nose.

'I know,' she said, 'but I could have been proud of him without that. I didn't need a war to make me proud of my boy.'

Chapter Twenty

Gradually news filtered through. Jess Budd sent a tele-gram to the vicarage, where the boys were now billeted, to say that they were safe. Snow had fallen during the night and Tim and Keith, who had been disgruntled at first to find that they were going to come back to Bridge End after Christmas to live with the vicar, were out building a snowman with Mr Beckett. With his long, thin legs encased in woolly longjohns and black trousers, the vicar looked like a lanky spider as he loped about the garden scooping up fresh snow. He stopped to take the telegram and read it with relief.

'Your mother and father and sisters are all safe,' he told the boys, who had come to see what the telegram said. They'd been aggrieved at not being there during the raid, but although it hadn't consciously occurred to them that their family might be in danger, they were pleased to know they were safe. Especially Mum and the baby, Maureen. Dad would be all right, of course, because he was a man and the biggest dad in the street, and they weren't bothered about Rose one way or the other, but Maureen was just a baby and it wouldn't be right if she got bombed.

'Oh, that's all right, then,' Tim said carelessly and scampered off to finish the snowman, kicking up snow as he went. 'Can we borrow your black hat, Mr Beckett? And one of your pipes?'

'Certainly. A snowman must have a good hat and a pipe to smoke.' The vicar stood for a moment looking at the telegram in his hand. It said nothing except that the family was safe, yet he felt a twinge of discomfort, as if behind the straggling capitals there was another, darker message. Something bad had happened, he was sure of it.

He would find out soon enough. The last word of the brief message was 'writing'. In the next day or two – as soon as they managed to get the postal service working again – a letter would come from Mrs Budd. And he felt horribly sure that it was going to bring bad news as well as good.

He wondered just who it would be about. One of the other children from the area around September Street, he thought, and wondered if it would be little Sammy Hodges.

When the news came it wasn't about Sammy, but about Kathy Simmons and her two little girls, Stella and Muriel. The vicar met Ruth in the churchyard, where she was placing some fresh leaves on Joe's grave, and told her about it.

'It's a terrible tragedy. The mother had only recently had another baby – Tim and Keith say he was born during one of the earlier raids, actually in an air-raid shelter – and both were killed. One of the young woman's friends had come across to take them to her home, and she and the little girls were knocked over by the blast, but the shelter where poor Mrs Simmons and the baby were got a direct hit.'

'Oh, that's dreadful!' Ruth exclaimed. She had cleared away a small patch of snow from the grave and filled the metal urn with holly. Its berries gleamed like little red lights. 'What will happen to them now? Will the father be able to manage?'

'He's in the Merchant Navy, like young Alec – hardly ever gets home. They'll be evacuated, I suppose.' Mr Beckett rubbed his long thin hand across his face. 'I don't think there are many billets left in the village. I'm thinking of offering them room with me.'

'Well, that sounds a good idea. The Budd boys already know them, so they'd feel easier than if they were with strangers. But could you manage?'

'Oh, I think so,' the vicar said, his face breaking into a smile. 'There are plenty of rooms spare, you know, and Mrs Mudge seems to like having the little ones about the place.'

She's not the only one, Ruth thought, hiding a smile as she watched him lope away across the churchyard. Everyone had seen the enormous snowman standing guard in the vicarage garden and they'd heard the noise of the snowball fights Mr Beckett had organised too. It's a shame he never got married and had a big family of his own, like vicars are supposed to, she thought. You could see that's what he wanted.

Sammy too had had a letter that morning. It had come in a brown envelope, the address scrawled in uncertain capitals. Sammy had stared at it in astonishment.

'A letter for *me*?'

'Yes, see, it's got your name on it. I expect it's from your dad.' Ruth looked at him, hoping it didn't bring bad news and wondering if she should read it first. 'Open it up, now, and see what it says.'

His lips caught in his teeth, Sammy pulled open the envelope. The piece of paper the letter was written on looked as if it had been torn from an old exercise book. He read it, following the words with his finger.

'It is from Dad. He says he's all right and I've got to be a good boy.' Sammy looked up at her. 'I am being, aren't I?'

'You're being a very good boy,' Ruth assured him. 'Does it say anything else?'

'He says there were a lot of bombs. And he's coming to see me as soon as he can.'

Sammy folded the letter and put it back into the envelope. His voice had trembled a bit as he spoke the last words and Ruth wondered whether it was joy or something else at the thought of seeing his father again. She looked at him, but he had turned his face away.

'Well, that'll be good, won't it,' she said. 'You'll be able to show him all the places you know, your school and the church and the village green and everything. And you'll be able to show him Silver.'

'Yes,' Sammy said. 'I'll go and put this in my bedroom.'

He went out and Ruth sighed. It was so hard to fathom what was going on in that little fair head. Sometimes, she felt she knew just what he was thinking, but at other times he was a mystery, a closed book. There's still a lot I don't know about him, she thought. Perhaps, if his dad does come, it'll make things a bit clearer.

He might have talked to her in the evenings, during the quiet hour they spent together before he went to bed. Ruth set that hour aside for reading to him – they had finished *Treasure Island* now and were reading *The Coral Island*, one of Terry's books that Jane had found and brought down for him. Sammy seemed to enjoy hearing sea stories and gradually Ruth found herself talking to him about Jack and recounting some of the tales he had brought back from his voyages. He listened, enraptured, and begged her to take him to Southampton one day, when the war was over, to see the big liners there. The berth where the *Queen Mary* and *Queen Elizabeth* docked was so close to the road, you could almost touch them as they loomed overhead, and you could watch them steam majestically down the Solent too, setting up a bow wave that roared up the beaches nearly half an hour after they had passed.

'I'm going to be a sailor,' Sammy said. 'Like Uncle Jack and Alec. I'll be a cabin boy like Jim in *Treasure Island*,

and see bananas growing and coconuts.' He looked wistful. 'Dad used to bring coconuts home, sometimes. And bananas, from the dock.'

Sammy was back at school now, but he still hadn't really settled in. The two Budd boys played with him occasionally, but Tim was older and Keith followed his brother as much as he could. Joyce Moore's boys went at a different time of day from the evacuees, so although Sammy played with them at home he didn't see them at school. He found himself wandering alone at the edge of the playground.

Some of the bigger boys noticed him there and came over. They formed a ring around him.

'I know you,' Brian Collins said belligerently. 'You live down April Grove. Your mum died and your brother's a thief, got put in jail.'

'He's not in jail,' Sammy said, his lips trembling. 'He's at a school, a proved school.'

'Same thing. It's a jail for kids. He'll go to Borstal next and then it'll be proper jail. I 'spect you'll go there too.'

'I won't! I never stole nothing.'

'Bet you did,' Brian Collins said. 'Bet you did and bet you will.' He turned to the others. 'Better watch your stuff. He's a thief, all the Hodges are.'

'I'm not!' Sammy stamped his foot. 'And nor was my mum and nor's my dad, neither. And it wasn't our Gordon, it was Micky Baxter what started it, it was all *his* fault.'

'So why ain't he in jail too?' Brian Collins demanded. 'Garn, it was your Gordon, a blooming thief he is and so are you. Thief, thief, thief!' He turned to the other boys, urging them on, and they all took up the chant. 'Thief, thief, thief!'

Sammy felt the tears sting his eyes. They brimmed over and slid down his cheeks, and the boys saw them and increased their jeering. He stood in the middle of the circle, crying and rubbing his nose on his sleeve.

'Cry-baby! Thief! That's you, Sammy Hodges – thief and cry-baby! Yah, look at him, crying for his mummy. Only she's dead, ain't she! Your mummy's *dead*.'

'No!' Sammy shrieked, turning wildly this way and that to find a way out of the circle. But there was no escape. The boys pressed closer upon him, their chanting louder, the yells ringing in his ears, the words hammering at his brain. 'Thief, thief, thief! Cry-baby, cry-baby! Jail! Dead, dead, *dead*!'

'No! No, she's not dead, she's not, she's not! She's coming for me, she's coming today! Let me out – let me out!' He beat frantically with his fists, blows landing at random on the nearest boys who yelled loudly and punched him back. Within seconds the taunting had become real violence, a scrambling mêlée of boys pummelling each other, but with Sammy at the bottom of the pile and receiving the most blows.

'Oy, what're you doing?' Tim Budd, who wasn't averse to a fight himself, had arrived on the edge of the group. He'd seen the boys gather round Sammy and approached a little warily. Brian Collins was his own arch enemy but he was a lot bigger than Tim. Still, you couldn't let him bash up a little kid like Sammy Hodges. He grabbed the collar of the nearest boy and pulled him over. 'What are you doing? Why are you all getting on to Sam Hodges?'

Nobody took any notice. The boy Tim had dragged away shook himself free and aimed a punch at Tim. It hit him glancingly on the shoulder, which gave Tim the right to join in, and he threw himself into the fray, yelling at the top of his voice.

'Leave the kid alone! He hasn't done nothing to you. Leave him alone!'

'You mind your own beeswax, Tim Budd!' Brian Collins panted. He stood up, forgetting Sammy for a moment, and glowered at Tim. 'Nobody asked you to come butting in.'

'Well, I come without being asked, then. Fight someone your own size.' Tim stood pugnaciously, his fists clenched. 'Or else fight me. Unless you're scared,' he added with a sneer.

Brian Collins laughed contemptuously. 'Scared? Scared of you? You couldn't fight a blooming flea!'

'Try me, then.' Tim squared up as his father had taught him. Frank Budd had done a bit of boxing himself when he was in the Army, and had taught both the boys to defend themselves. He'd always impressed on them that they weren't to start fights, but if they were hit first then it was all right to retaliate. Remembering this, Tim lifted his head and stared Brian Collins challengingly in the eye.

'All right then you asked for it!' He threw a punch and hit Brian squarely on the nose. Brian yelped and backed off, his hand to his face, and Tim saw blood run from between his fingers. Surprised, impressed and a little shocked, he looked down at the hand that had dealt the blow and staggered back as Brian flew at him, flailing punches around his head and almost knocking him to the ground.

Caught off balance, Tim stumbled for a moment, but recovered and ducked his head to rush in under Brian's guard. He caught the bigger boy a hard blow just under his ribs and Brian yelled again and doubled over. Tim followed swiftly with another punch that winded the bigger boy and a quick jab to the jaw. Brian's fists were windmilling wildly and Tim, who had now got into his stride, danced around him, ducking and weaving, just out of Brian's reach, then dived in and struck one more hard blow to the jaw, which sent him spinning. He felt quite disappointed when Brian fell to the ground and lay there, panting and glaring, but making no attempt to get up.

'Come on!' he shouted, hopping from foot to foot and

jiggling his fists in front of him as he'd seen boxers do at the pictures. 'Come on! I haven't finished yet!'

'Oh yes, you have,' a grim voice announced and the boys all looked up, startled, to see Mr Wain, the headmaster, standing over them. How long he'd been there none of them knew, but his face was like thunder as he gripped Tim's collar to yank him away and bent to jerk Brian Collins to his feet. 'I don't know what that was all about, but I'll have no fighting in my school. You'd better both go home now and get yourselves cleaned up. Then you can come and see me in the morning. I'll have a few words to say to you. And as for the rest of you –' he cast a stern eye over the circle of children who were watching, subdued, as he shook the two combatants by the scruff of their necks '– you'd better not start this again. I mean it – any more fighting or bullying and there'll be severe punishment for all of you. *Very* severe punishment.'

Nobody spoke. They knew what Mr Wain meant by severe punishment. They knew, too, what would happen to both Brian and Tim next morning. A caning for the pair of them, never mind who had started it. One or two of them turned and looked at Sammy, who had got up and brushed himself down, and a faint mutter went round them as to whose fault it really was.

'Please, sir—' Sammy began, but Mr Wain turned and frowned at him. 'Please, sir – it wasn't—'

'That's enough! I don't want to hear any more about it. I've told you, there's to be no more fighting, d'you understand?' He looked again at Brian and Tim. 'I'll see you both in the morning.'

He stalked away and the children watched him silently. They glanced at each other and shifted their feet. Then Tim shrugged and said loudly, 'Well, I don't care anyway. I was winning. And you're a bully, Brian Collins, a rotten bully. You leave this kid alone in future, all right? Or you'll have me to answer to.'

He took Sammy by the shoulder and marched him away to join Keith, who was standing on the fringe of the circle. With the eyes of the others following them, they walked out of the playground and went down the lane.

Brian Collins wiped some more blood from his nose and felt it tenderly. It seemed to have swollen to at least twice its usual size and he was pretty sure he'd have a black eye as well. He could feel it throbbing. He wouldn't be surprised if that Tim Budd hadn't nearly knocked out some of his teeth.

'I'll get my own back,' he said viciously. 'You see if I don't.'

But the others had begun to drift away. Tim's performance had impressed them. He'd been like a real boxer, dancing about and punching properly, while Brian had just flailed about with his fists, hitting at random and relying on his size to win the fight. Just as he'd always relied on his size to be boss of the playground.

Brian found himself standing alone. His face hurt all over and there was still blood trickling down his chin. He sniffed and turned away quickly before anyone could see the tears in his eyes. He stamped out of the playground and turned in the opposite direction from Tim. 'I'll get my own back,' he muttered to himself. 'You see if I don't.'

What with the excitement of the snow and with Ruth working afternoons, there didn't seem to have been time for Sammy to bring Tim and Keith home to see Silver, but Ruth had changed shifts that week and could be home after school, so while they were having tea that evening he asked if he could bring them next day. He knew that if it hadn't been for Tim he could have been really 'bashed up' by Brian Collins, and it was the only way he could think of to thank his rescuer.

'Of course you can bring them home. I'll make some

rock cakes and cocoa. Just the two, mind,' she added. 'I don't want the house full of boys.'

Sammy did as she'd suggested and brought Tim and Keith home the following afternoon. The visit was a great success, making up for the caning Tim had received for fighting, and next day Sammy Hodges' parrot was the talk of the playground. Boys crowded round him, asking questions, or pretending not to believe that there was a parrot at all, every one of them desperately anxious to be invited. Sammy found himself the hero of the school.

'I can take two a day,' he said. 'Auntie Ruth says she can't have no more.' He glanced sideways at Brian Collins, hanging around the fringe of the group, pretending to be indifferent, and chose two of his biggest rivals. 'Freddy Shaw and Dick Powell, that's who I'll take today.'

Ruth saw them coming down the lane and hurried to put the kettle on. She watched them with some surprise. They were big, rough-looking boys, not at all like Tim and Keith who had come yesterday and been polite and well-behaved, and thanked her for having them when they went. She asked them in, nevertheless, making them wipe their feet on the mat, and then gave them the rock cakes and cocoa. While they were consuming these she delivered her lecture about Silver.

'He's an African grey parrot. They all have this nice red breast –' the boys sniggered and she fixed them with an eye of ice '– and a big beak. Don't touch him, because he can bite very hard with that beak and he doesn't like to be touched by anyone he doesn't know well. He came home on a ship with my husband, who was a sailor, and my husband and the other sailors taught him a lot of words. Swear words, some of them.' She gave them a stern look. 'I don't want you going home and repeating any of these words and saying you learnt them at my house, you understand?'

'Really *bad* swear words?' Freddy Shaw asked, in a tone that suggested nothing could be too bad for him to repeat.

'Really bad words.' Ruth nodded. 'Doesn't he, Sammy? In fact, *we're* not allowed to use the words Silver can say.'

The boys looked scornful. Ruth thought they probably knew all the words Silver could teach them. She wondered if Sammy had chosen the roughest boys in the class because they were the ones he most wanted to impress. She hoped it wasn't because they were the ones he liked best. She knew Freddy Shaw. He came from one of the poorer Portsmouth streets. He had arrived with the second lot of evacuees and was billeted at the other end of the village with Dotty Dewar, who seemed to live in a permanent state of chaos and had really wanted a nice strong girl to help her with her own brood.

Ruth didn't know the other boy's name, but she knew he came from the same area and lived in Milly Minns' cottage, next door to Dotty. Both boys looked scruffy, with holes in their clothes, and didn't look as if they'd shown their faces a flannel or their hair a comb for a week. But then, all Dotty Dewar's children looked like that. Milly Minns didn't have any children, but Ruth thought that if she had they wouldn't have been much different.

'Silver doesn't talk all the time,' she went on, just in case he decided to have one of his rare silent days. 'But if I give him something nice like a sunflower seed, he'll probably say something. He imitates noises too, like the kettle whistling –' if she'd known that when he first came, she wouldn't have had a whistling kettle '– and birds singing outside. And when he learns new words he says them in the voice of the person talking to him.'

'Like a ventriloquist,' Freddy said. He was a big boy, looking at least two years older than Sammy, the sort of boy who would crook his arms to show off his muscles. 'I heard one on the wireless.'

'Ventriloquists *throw* their voices, stupid,' the other boy said. 'It's depressionists that imitate people.'

'*Im*pressionists,' Ruth said. 'But Silver can throw his voice too. When he does a kettle, it sounds just as if it was out in the scullery.'

'Well, he hasn't done nothing yet,' Freddy said scornfully and turned to Sammy. 'You said he could say all sorts of things.'

'He can,' Ruth said, not liking the threatening tone in his voice. 'I've told you that, and I've also told you he doesn't talk *all* the time.' Just whenever you don't want him to, she thought with a bitter look at the silent parrot, and never when you do want him to. She took a sunflower seed from the bowl and held it out to him. 'Come on, Silver, come on boy, it's teatime. What do you say at teatime, then? I'm a little teapot? Come on, Silver, clever boy, clever bird.'

The parrot eyed her suspiciously. He cocked his head and looked sideways at the sunflower seed. Then he shuffled along his perch, closer to Sammy. The boys waited sceptically. Ruth gave the sunflower seed to Sammy and he held it out.

Silver reached out his neck and took the seed in his beak. He cracked it, tilted his head sideways and whistled loudly.

'Sammy, Sammy, shine a light,' he said in Sammy's voice. 'Ain't you playin' out tonight?'

The boys' mouths fell open.

Ruth stared at Sammy in amazement. 'Did *you* teach him that?'

'I just said it to him a few times,' Sammy said proudly. 'I didn't know it was enough for him to copy, though.'

'He picks things up easy as winking from people he likes,' Ruth said. 'He likes you, Sammy, that's obvious.'

The two boys stared at Sammy and back at the parrot. 'What else can he say?'

'Well, I've sung to him a bit,' Sammy said, reddening when the boys laughed.

'Sung? What've you sung – love songs?' They burst into giggles, their hands over their mouths.

'Course not. Proper songs – "Run, Rabbit, Run", and "I've Got Sixpence, Jolly Little Sixpence".'

'I've got sixpence,' Freddy continued, 'to last me all my life. I've got tuppence to spend –' they were all singing now '– tuppence to lend, and tuppence to take home to my wife!'

Ruth clapped, laughing as they finished. The boys gazed at Silver again.

'What else have you taught him?'

'Nothing else,' Sammy said. 'I didn't even know he could say all that.' He looked flushed and pleased, and Ruth gave him an approving smile.

'You'll be able to teach him all sorts of things now he's started,' she said. 'He's got your voice off to a T.'

'Sammy, Sammy,' Silver said again, 'shine a light, ain't you playin' out tonight?'

The boys looked at each other and giggled.

'I ain't heard it swear yet,' Freddy said, with an accusing look at Sammy. 'You told Dick and me it could swear.'

'Bugger me,' Silver said obligingly. 'Sod the little buggers. I'm a little teapot, short and stout.'

'There, you see,' Sammy said, but Silver was now in full spate and they flapped their hands at Sammy to shut him up and listened in awe.

'Splice the mainbrace. Sippers and gulpers. Here's my handle, here's my spout, when you fill me up you'll hear me shout, lift me up and *pour me out.*' He shuffled back along his perch and stretched his neck out towards Ruth. 'Give us a bite to eat then, Ruthie. Give us a kiss. I love you, Ruthie. Bugger *me.*'

There was a moment's silence.

'Cor,' Freddy said, 'he's *smashing*.'

Ruth looked at them. They were gazing at the parrot, their eyes shining. She forgot that they were boys from one of the roughest streets in Portsmouth and were now living at the poorer end of the village, that they had probably been bullying Sammy, that their fathers were petty crooks and their families lived in poverty, and saw them simply as little boys, little boys who had been taken away from their homes just like Sammy, and probably missed them as much as anyone else did, and who could be pleased by a talking bird.

'You can come and see him whenever you like,' she said, 'so long as you behave yourselves and so long as Sammy says you can. And you can bring some of the other boys too,' she added to Sammy. 'Two at a time though, mind, no more. And now, who wants another rock cake?'

Chapter Twenty-one

Once Silver had started to pick up things from Sammy there was no stopping either of them and Ruth began to get used to the sound of Sammy's voice about the cottage when he wasn't there.

'I've got sixpence,' the parrot proclaimed, managing to get a hint of the tune even if he didn't get all the words right. 'Jolly little sixpence. I've got sixpence to last me all my wife.' He paused, as if for effect, then went on, 'Tuppence to spend and tuppence to lend, and tuppence to take home to my life.'

Ruth laughed. 'He always gets those two words mixed up. Did your mother used to sing that to you?'

'Dad did,' he said, surprising her. 'It was his favourite song. Only he said he'd be lucky if he *did* have sixpence.'

So the father had played with him sometimes, Ruth thought. She was still waiting for the promised visit, but Portsmouth was having such a dreadful time now that it seemed unlikely he would be able to come. Sammy had told her that he worked for a shipbuilding firm and often went to sea, and when he was at home he acted as a fire watcher. Even the best father wouldn't find it easy to come out to the country in those circumstances.

'Poor little chap,' Lizzie said, coming round to her aunt with a few eggs one day. 'Look, Mum thought you'd be able to use these, they're only pullets' eggs so they're a bit small but they're really nice. We aren't going to be allowed to sell them any more, only to the official shops, but we can put a few by for family.'

'Oh, they're lovely,' Ruth said, putting them in a bowl. 'Sammy can have one for his tea for a special treat. They're just the right size.'

Lizzie sat down at the kitchen table. 'So his dad hasn't been out to see him, then?'

'No – well, I suppose you can understand it. He doesn't get much spare time, by all accounts, and it's so awful in Portsmouth just now . . .' The kettle came to the boil and Ruth made tea. 'It seems a shame, though. I mean, the kiddy's lost his mother, poor little soul, and then his brother was taken away, and now here he is, brought out to a strange place with people he never knew. It doesn't seem right.'

'Well, he doesn't seem to be worrying about that too much.' Lizzie glanced round the cosy room. 'He's fallen on his feet here, all right.'

'I do my best,' Ruth said. 'And I can't deny I've got fond of him.'

She poured two cups of tea and passed one to Lizzie. They drank in silence for a moment or two, then Lizzie said, 'These blitzes are awful. Everywhere seems to be getting them now, it's as if we can't do a thing to stop them.'

'Well, I think we're giving as good as we get,' Ruth said. 'Our boys are going over there night after night too. Not that that's much comfort to the poor souls here that have been bombed out,' she added sadly.

'Well, whether it is or not, there's hundreds of people dead, Auntie Ruth, and hundreds more injured . . . I've decided I've got to do something about it.' She looked at her aunt. 'I've volunteered to be a nurse.'

'A nurse? Oh Lizzie, I am pleased! Where will you be going?'

'Southampton, to start with. After that, I don't know. I'm going to be a – what do they call it? – a VAD, but if I do well I can train to be a registered nurse, like you. That's what I'd really like to do.'

'What does Alec think of it?'

Lizzie shrugged. 'It doesn't really make much difference to him, does it? He hardly ever gets home now and he knows I've got to do something, anyway. I can't just stop at home. It's either nursing or one of the women's Services.'

'Well, I think you'll make a lovely nurse,' Ruth declared. 'And what I say is, it's something you can always turn your hand to if you need a job. Like me, when Jack died – only, of course, we hope you won't need it in the same way,' she added hastily.

Lizzie gave her a wry look. 'It's all right, Auntie. I know what the chances are of being made a widow. I try not to think about it too much, but I know Alec could be killed at any moment. He might be dead now, for all I know.' She drew in a deep, wavering breath. 'It makes me all the more determined to *do* something. I just *can't* stop at home and let him and other people face all the danger. I've got to be in it too.'

'I think you're right,' Ruth agreed. 'We all have to do what we can and nursing's a fine thing to do, even if nurses aren't valued as they ought to be. The patients appreciate them and that's the main thing.'

The back door opened and closed, and Sammy scampered in. He looked so much better these days, Ruth thought, gazing at him fondly. He'd filled out a bit, his cheeks were rosy and his legs sturdy instead of being stick-thin as they'd been when he arrived. His blue eyes sparkled as he looked at her and Lizzie, and he was hopping with excitement.

'What is it, Sammy? Whatever's happened?' Perhaps his dad was coming, she thought with a sudden lurch of the heart, and half rose to look out of the window.

'It's Mrs Greenberry,' he said, his words falling over each other in their rush to be spoken. 'Where Tim and

Keith's sister used to be. Her cat's had *kittens* and she says I can have one, if you and Silver don't mind. *Can* I have one, *can* I? I'd look after it. I used to have a cat till – till it got run over. Or Dad drowned it,' he added with a quiver in his voice. 'Please can I have one?'

'Oh, Sammy, I don't know . . .' Ruth glanced at Lizzie. She'd always said she couldn't have a cat, not with Silver. It was one of the reasons she'd given for not marrying Albert Newton when he asked her – not that she'd wanted to anyway. But she knew that Sammy had had a cat of his own, a cat he'd thought the world of, and she thought it was more than likely that his father had drowned it. Nor could you blame him when the poor man was hardly ever at home and the government was actually telling people to have their pets destroyed . . . But letting Sammy have a cat here would bring its own problems.

'I really don't think Silver would like it,' she said. 'Think about when the kitten starts climbing; suppose it climbed up on his stand. He might bite its head off. It wouldn't be fair to the kitten, would it?'

Sammy's shoulders sagged a little. 'Wouldn't it?'

'Well, you wouldn't want it to be hurt, would you? Not a kitten.' She pulled the little boy close and held him to her. 'I'm sorry, Sammy, I just don't think it would be a good idea.'

'I could keep it in my bedroom,' he offered, but she shook her head.

'You can't keep a kitten in one room. It would have to come down here as well. No, I really don't think it would do. You just make do with Silver. Nobody else in the village has got a parrot, after all.'

Sammy went over to Silver's stand and gave him a sunflower seed. The parrot ducked his head to take it and Sammy scratched his crest.

'You wouldn't mind if we had a kitten, would you, Silver?' he asked, and Ruth and Lizzie looked at one another, hardly knowing whether to laugh or cry. 'You like cats really. Pussy's down the well?' he said coaxingly.

Silver turned his head sideways and looked at him narrowly. He cracked his sunflower seed and ruffled his feathers.

'Pussy down the well,' he said suspiciously. 'Who pushed him in? Sod the little bugger.'

Lizzie burst into laughter. 'See? That's what he thinks about cats, Sammy!' She smiled at his woeful face. 'Auntie Ruth's right, you know. It wouldn't work. Now, why don't you walk up to the farm with me? We've got a baby lamb in the kitchen, it's lost its mother and we're feeding it with a bottle. You can give it a name if you like.'

'A lamb?' He looked at Ruth, the kitten forgotten. 'Can I, Auntie Ruth? Can I go with Lizzie?'

'Of course you can. I'll come too. I want to put some fresh flowers on Dad's grave, so we'll walk through the churchyard. I picked some snowdrops just now, specially.'

The gardens were full of snowdrops and you could even see the noses of a few bulbs poking through the remains of the snow. Well wrapped up, for it was still cold, the three of them walked up the lane to the church and through the graveyard to Joe's resting place. The holly leaves Ruth had put there were wilting now and she took them over to the rubbish heap and filled the little jar with fresh water from a bottle before placing the snowdrops by the headstone.

'There,' she said, looking down at them. 'Dad'd like those. He was always fond of snowdrops.'

Dan Hodges too was thinking of graves and flowers. Nora lay in the little churchyard at the top of Deniston Road, where she'd been to church once or twice when they had first come to April Grove. He would have liked to take her back to Old Portsmouth, where she belonged, but the graveyard there had been bombed and they weren't taking any more burials. He hadn't known what to do until the undertaker had offered to talk to the vicar for him.

'St Lucy's isn't the actual parish church, it's what they call a daughter church, and there's not much room in the graveyard, but if your wife attended services there he'll probably accept her. Otherwise it's the municipal cemetery.'

Dan had shaken his head. 'She'd want to be in church ground. I never went much meself, but Nora always liked to go, and she took the boys too and sent them to Sunday School. Gordon's like me, lost interest, but Sam used to go regular. If you think she could go there . . . It'd be easier for me to go there, too. To see the grave,' he added in case the undertaker thought there might be more business coming his way.

So Nora lay in a corner of the tiny churchyard and Dan did his best to visit the grave whenever he could. Mostly, he went on his way home from work and it had never occurred to him to take Sammy. In any case, he had only managed to visit the grave a few times before Sammy was evacuated. He was away at sea for days at a time and scarcely ever at home in daylight. You couldn't go blundering about in a graveyard in the blackout and after the Blitzes started it was almost impossible.

He thought about it sometimes, wishing miserably that he could take her a few flowers, but there just wasn't a chance and there were no flowers about at this time of year anyway. Perhaps when spring came and the evenings were light, if the Jerries gave them a bit of peace for once. Perhaps he could get a few primroses or violets, or a bunch of daffs. She'd always liked the spring flowers best.

But when the light evenings came he found himself reluctant to go. Too much had happened. Portsmouth had been almost bombed to pieces: the January Blitz followed by another in March that was almost as bad. Once again the streets were blocked with the debris of fallen buildings, the water and gas mains were fractured and the electricity supply disrupted. Once again, Dan had found himself fighting fires, or digging through the rubble in a desperate attempt to find people who had been buried. Once again, he was plagued by memories of the Great War, when it seemed that he had lived all his life in a trench of mud, with shells whistling overhead and men screaming and dying all around him. I can't go on with this, he thought, I can't. It's too much to bear in one lifetime. And once he sat on a heap of broken bricks and put his head in his hands and wept.

'Come on, mate.' A fireman was beside him, laying a hand on his arm. 'Time you had a bit of a rest. You haven't let up all night.'

'Nor's anyone else,' Dan said wearily, lifting his face and wiping the dust and the tears into a slime with the back of his hand. He got up, swaying a little. 'I'm all right.'

The man regarded him. 'You oughter go home for a bit. Let your wife get you a cuppa, give you a bit of grub.'

But Dan shook his head. Home was where Nora ought to be, Nora and the boys, and home was an empty shell without them.

It seemed as if the bombing would never end. The second Blitz was followed by numerous raids all through the month and into April. The tally now, Frank Budd told Dan when they bumped into each other on their way home from work one evening, was forty-six. 'We had high-explosive bombs dropped in the dockyard a couple of nights ago, but luckily they fell in a part that nobody's in just now, so nobody was hurt, thank the Lord.'

'They'll get you next time, though,' Dan said morosely. 'Now they know where to aim.'

'Go on, they've known that all along,' Frank said. 'Stands to reason they've got maps, got them before the war ever started. It's not as if they were kept secret.' He glanced at Dan. 'How're you doing, anyway? How are those boys of yours?'

Dan shrugged. 'They're all right. Better off where they are. Gordon's getting a bit of discipline and Sammy's living the life of Riley out Bridge End. Writes me letters. He says he's got a parrot.'

'A *parrot*? Where'd he get that from, then?'

'Oh, it's not really his,' Dan said. 'It's the old woman's he lives with. Widow woman. He reckons it talks.'

Frank looked at him. 'Haven't you been out to see him, then?'

'When've I had the chance?' Dan said with a bitter laugh. 'What with all the overtime and the bombing . . . Anyway, I reckon he's better off without me. I never did him no good when he was home. He was always Nora's boy.'

'All the same . . .' Frank said. He'd managed to get out to see his boys, cycling the twenty-mile journey before the winter set in and the roads were covered in snow and ice, and saving up for the train fare so that he and Jess could both go out there at Easter, taking Rose and baby Maureen with them. 'I dare say he'd be glad to see his dad.'

Dan looked sceptical and Frank decided to say no more. It wasn't his business, and there was no doubt the nipper was better off out at Bridge End. Jess knew Ruth Purslow and said she was a good-hearted little body who would look after the boy. A nurse, he thought she was.

'Things don't look good in Greece,' he remarked. 'I saw in the paper they're talking about getting the men out. With Yugoslavia giving in, it gives the Germans a real hold. They'll be all over the Med soon.'

Dan grunted. Now that the evenings were lighter, he'd noticed a few flowers coming out in the back garden. They were ones Nora had planted when they first came to April Grove. He thought he might pick some and take them up to her grave.

It seemed a hundred years ago that Nora had died. It was like looking back down a tunnel, a long, dark burrow of misery that he'd have to crawl through to reach her again.

But I *can't* reach her again, he thought in sudden panic, I can't *ever* get to her again. She's gone. She's gone for ever.

To his dismay, he felt the pricking of tears in his eyes. Frank was still talking about Greece. It was said that Mr Churchill had agreed to withdraw from the mainland, but was insisting on holding Crete, where there were Australian and New Zealand troops as well as British. 'Now that Yugoslavia's gone, it puts those boys in a bad spot. To my mind, he hasn't got no choice, he'll have to get them out. It'll be like Dunkirk all over again—'

'Sorry, Frank,' Dan said, turning abruptly aside. 'I've got to go down this way. Something I've got to do—'

He marched off down a side road, leaving Frank Budd looking after him in some surprise. And no wonder, Dan thought, as he realised he'd turned into a cul-de-sac. Well, it didn't matter. He'd just needed a bit of time to himself, to recover from the shock of feeling tears in his eyes, the pain of remembering.

When she'd first died it had happened twenty times a day. Each morning, when he woke in an empty bed, and thought she must have gone down to the lav before the truth flooded back. The silence of the house, without her or Gordon, with only Sammy creeping about like a shadow and getting on his nerves. Getting his own breakfast – a cup of tea, a slice of bread and marge – and sorting out his own dinner. Nora had always made up a box for him, till those last few weeks when she'd been too poorly, but now he couldn't seem to manage it. He got himself a pie and chips from the stall outside the dock gates instead, and left Sammy a few pennies to get his own. And then there was the moment he came home again, letting himself into the cold, dark house. No fire – no lights – no Nora. It was then that the despair overwhelmed him, and it was that moment he feared most and postponed for as long as he could.

It wasn't quite so bad going home on a lighter evening, but as a rule overtime went on until dark anyway. Tonight was an exception. Tonight the sun was still in the sky, the house would be light and there were flowers in the garden. Tonight he'd go and see his Nora, and take her some.

There had been no raids on Pompey for three nights now. Plymouth had been the main target, and by all accounts it had been almost flattened. There had been pictures in today's paper of a huge area of devastation, barely a thing left standing, the whole of the city centre smashed to pieces. Thirty thousand people made homeless, it said. Thirty *thousand*! It was impossible to imagine, all those families trudging through the streets with their few remaining possessions piled into prams or wheelbarrows, or just lugged in battered suitcases or shopping bags. Your whole home reduced to the size of a shopping bag. Dan thought of the house in April Grove, poor and shabby as it was. They'd never had much, him and Nora, but even so it was more than would go in one shopping bag. It didn't bear thinking about.

He walked round the back way, past Tommy Vickers' garden with the Anderson shelter and the neat rows of vegetables that Tommy had just planted, and down the alley. His own garden looked a mess, he hadn't done any of the 'digging for victory' they kept on about – when had he had the time? – but the flowers Nora had planted were struggling bravely through the weeds. He didn't know what they were all called but they were pretty enough – bright little things, like coloured daisies, and those others were tulips, he knew that – and they'd look all right, tied in a bunch and stuck in a jam jar of water. He'd take them up straight after he'd had a bit of tea.

Shopping was another problem for Dan. He left for work at a quarter past six every morning and never got home before the shops shut. There was one place on the way home that stopped open late but you had to be registered at one shop now to get your proper rations, so he could only buy a few bits and pieces there. He worked on Saturday mornings too, so the afternoon was the only chance he had. Just about the worst time of the week, he thought bitterly, looking at the butcher's empty slab and the few scrubby vegetables left at the greengrocer's.

'Couldn't you keep something back for me once in a while?' he'd asked Mr Hines a week or two ago. 'A bit of stewing steak or a few sausages? You know I always come in on Saturday afternoon, and you got practically nothing left then.'

'Wouldn't be fair to me other customers,' Mr Hines said reprovingly. 'Queue up for hours, they do. I can't keep stuff under the counter for you, now can I?'

'Don't see why not,' Dan muttered, looking sullenly at the scrag end of mutton the butcher was weighing out. 'I work hard enough, don't I, getting ships out to fight this bloody war? I should've thought I was entitled to a decent bit of meat now and then.'

The butcher shrugged. 'You could always get registered somewhere else.' But Dan couldn't and they both knew it. And even if he could, the new butcher wouldn't be any more helpful.

'You want to get one of your neighbours to do your shopping for you,' Alf Hines suggested. He didn't really want to be unhelpful, even though he didn't like Dan Hodges all that much. It was just the way things were. He felt a bit sorry for the man, if truth were told, losing his wife the way he had. Mrs Hodges had been a nice little body and you could see she'd had a hard time of it, especially with that older boy of theirs getting into trouble. 'Wouldn't Mrs Vickers help out a bit?'

Dan shrugged. Freda Vickers probably would, if he asked her, but he wasn't going to. She and Tommy had done enough already, coming in to help Nora in those last weeks and then looking out for young Sam. The trouble was that when you let people help you they took over your life, stuck their noses in where they weren't wanted. He wasn't at all sure it hadn't been their doing that Captain Whiting had come nosing round and arranged for Sammy to be taken away. No, he wasn't going to ask the Vickerses, nor anyone else, to help him out.

And then, last Saturday, when Dan went in there were a few sausages and a bit of liver put by. Alf had produced them as if they were leftovers that no one else wanted, and his look had almost dared Dan to thank him. Maybe he wasn't such a bad bloke after all, Dan thought, as he picked some of the flowers, ready to take them to Nora's grave. The liver and sausages had been really tasty. He'd fried them together and there'd been enough for two good feeds with some mashed potato and a bit of cabbage. There was still a bit left for tonight. He'd have it with a tin of baked beans.

Thinking about all this had kept his mind off Nora. He went indoors and put the flowers into a jam jar. They made a bright spot of colour in the dingy room and he realised suddenly just how grubby it was. The spring sunshine seemed to show it all up, and it was made worse by the state of the windows. It all needed cleaning, he could see it, but how was he to get that done?

Dan made himself a cup of tea and warmed up his supper. Then he had a wash at the kitchen sink and brushed his hair. Time he went to the barber, he thought, looking in the cracked bit of mirror above the sink. Nora used to cut his hair, to save money, but when he'd tried he couldn't seem to get a proper cut with the scissors and it had looked more as if it had been chewed.

He stared at it with dissatisfaction. He'd wanted to smarten himself up a bit for his visit to Nora. Perhaps a shave would help. He took his cut-throat razor out of the drawer and started to sharpen it on the strop that hung behind the kitchen door. He mixed up the shaving foam and then hesitated, staring at his bristly face in the mirror.

He glanced through the scullery door and saw the

flowers Nora had planted and would never see, their colours bright and clear in the grubby jam jar. The silence of the house seemed to press down on him, like a weight that was too heavy to bear.

The sense of despair swept over him again, sudden and unexpected, and he lifted the razor to his throat.

Chapter Twenty-two

The third Blitz over Portsmouth began that same night.

Scarcely had the wail of the sirens died away and people rushed into their shelters than the bombs and the mines began to fall. They came by parachute, floating down like deadly mushrooms, or they came direct, whistling with ferocious intent. The Royal Hospital was hit, the town railway station, the main post office, the prison. The big McIlroys store was burnt out. One way and another, more than half the city was affected, and once again there were fires to fight, railway lines blocked, water and gas mains broken and electricity out of action. It seemed that the hell of it all would never end.

Tommy Vickers met Dan in the pub next evening. Both men had been out firefighting all night and both had gone to work that morning just the same. They were red-eyed with exhaustion.

Tommy brought his pint over to the small table where Dan was sitting, staring at nothing. He sat down and they looked at each other.

'Bloody mess,' Dan said. 'It's all a bloody mess.'

'I know, mate.' Tommy hesitated, then said, 'Did you hear about young Graham Philpotts?'

'Philpotts?' Dan shook his head. 'Never heard of him.'

'Well, you'll have seen him around. Used to knock about with young Betty Chapman. Joined the Navy at the beginning of the war – matelot, red hair, you must have seen him. Family used to live round this way before they went off to Gosport.'

Dan nodded without much interest. 'Yeah, I think I know who you mean. Not lately, though. That's the girl that went to be a Land Girl, isn't it? What about him?'

'Killed,' Tommy said briefly. 'He was helping young Gladys Shaw from number 13 – I dare say you know she drives an ambulance – and they were just taking someone into the Royal when it got hit. Mine fell on the entrance.' He was silent for a moment. 'He was a good kid, young Graham. Cheeky, you know, but not a bit of harm in him. I brought him in here once, sat at this very table we did, and give him a bit of advice. He reminded me of myself when I joined the Andrew as a young sprog. And now he's dead. Blown to bits, just because he was doing someone a good turn.' He shook his head. 'It don't seem right. It just don't seem right.'

'It's what's happening, though,' Dan said. 'All over the place. People getting killed, dying. And yet if you don't care – if you'd as soon be dead as alive – well, it seems you go through the lot without a scratch.' He stared into his beer. 'It all seems upside down to me. Don't make no sense, none of it.'

Tommy looked at him. 'You're not saying *you* don't care, Dan.'

'Ain't I?' Dan gave a bitter laugh. 'Why not? What've I got to look forward to, eh? What use am I to anyone?'

'Well, you got your boys.' Tommy was alarmed. There was something in Dan Hodges' eyes that gave him the shivers. A sort of blankness. It looked as if he really didn't care. 'You got them to look after.'

'Look after? Me? Come off it, Tommy, you know I've never done nothing for either of them boys. Nothing good, anyway. There's Gordon in an approved school, getting the discipline he oughter've got from his father, and Sam out in the country forgetting all about me – and I don't blame him, neither. I'm no good to neither of them, Tom, and that's the top and bottom of it. They're better off without me.'

Tommy was silent. He couldn't help agreeing with Dan, to some extent, anyway – and yet his heart told him this wasn't right. The man was their father. Boys needed a father and Dan wasn't such a bad sort when you thought about it. He'd had a rotten time in the Great War, Frank Budd had told him that, he'd been shell-shocked and you never properly got over that. And he worked all the hours God sent, and still did his bit of firefighting, same as the rest of them. He'd just never had much luck. That was his trouble.

'It'll be better after the war,' he said. 'When they both come home and things get back to normal – and they'll be that much older then, won't need so much looking after.'

'Older!' Dan said bitterly. 'They'll be bloody grown-up. And things aren't ever going to be normal, not in our house, Tommy, you know that.' He drained his glass and got up. 'I'm having another one. What about you?'

'No, thanks, Dan. I'll just finish this one and then I'll have to go. I promised Freda I wouldn't be late.' Tommy watched as the other man lurched over to the bar. Dan didn't ought to be drinking too much either, he thought, he was dog-tired already and if they had another raid . . . And you're not helping, Tommy Vickers, he berated himself. Talking about things getting back to normal, when the poor bugger's still not got over losing his wife.

Dan came back and set down another full pint. He slumped into his chair and looked at Tommy.

'I went up the churchyard last night, before the bombs started.'

Tommy glanced at him a little warily and took a sip of his beer. 'Oh yes?'

'I took Nora a few flowers out of the garden,' Dan said. 'Tulips and them others, I dunno what they're called. She liked them. I wanted to put them on her grave.'

'That's good,' Tommy said cautiously. 'She'd be pleased you done that.'

'There was already some flowers there,' Dan said. 'They didn't look as if they'd been there long.' He paused. 'You've got some flowers like that in your garden.'

'Yeah, well,' Tommy said uncomfortably, 'that's because Freda give your Nora the plants, see. Took cuttings and give them her last year. She'll be pleased to know they've come up and you took them to the grave.'

'It was your Freda took them others, wasn't it?' Dan said. 'I dare say she's been going up there regular.'

'Well – now and then, like . . . It's not meant to be anything against you,' Tommy said hastily. 'Only we know how you've been placed, and Free was fond of your Nora, specially in the last few weeks . . . She didn't mean nothing by it, Dan.'

'No, I suppose not. But see, what I felt when I got there and see them flowers there, I thought – I'm not even any use to her now, I can't even take her a few flowers. I was never any good to her when she was alive and I'm no bloody good now. I don't blame your missus, Tommy. I'm glad someone's been keeping an eye on Nora. But it oughter bin *me*,' he said, banging his fist down on the table so that their tankards rattled. '*I* oughter bin taking her flowers all these months. And I never did. I never even went near it. I just – left her there.' His voice ended on a bleak note and he repeated the words in a whisper. 'I just *left* her there.'

Tommy stared at him. 'But that weren't your fault, mate. What time have you had? You've been working all hours. And there's been the blackout. You couldn't go ferreting about in the churchyard in the blackout. I dunno when you think you *could've* taken flowers, not that there's even been any flowers to *take* till the past few weeks. That's why my Freda took it on. She knew you couldn't manage it.'

That wasn't strictly true. What Freda had actually said

was that she was surprised Dan Hodges couldn't find a minute or two to visit his wife's grave, and if he couldn't be bothered, well then, she would. But Tommy saw no reason to tell Dan that.

'Yeah, well, I'm glad she did,' Dan said, surprising him. 'It oughter bin me – and it *will* be me, from now on – but I'm glad someone took an interest. At least she knows someone cares a bit.'

'She knows you care too,' Tommy said quietly. 'If she knows anything, Dan, she knows that. And she's proud of you.'

Dan snorted. 'There ain't nothing to be proud of about me. It was a bad day for Nora when she took up with me, Tom, a bad day. I was never no good to her and I'm no good to the boys now. I'm just bloody useless.' He stared into his tankard. 'Bloody useless.'

There was a short silence. Then Tommy said carefully, 'I reckon it's time you went out to see that boy of yours, Dan. Young Sammy, out at Bridge End. He must wonder why you don't go out. The other dads do, when they gets the chance. Frank Budd goes on his bike.'

'Sammy! He won't hardly know me.'

'No,' Tommy said, suddenly losing patience, 'he won't, not if you leave it much longer. But he won't forget he's *got* a dad, Dan. He won't forget you exist. And he'll want to see you, it stands to reason. Boys *want* their dads. They *need* 'em. Look how those two nippers of Frank Budd's follow him round when they're home, look how he's taught them to box and all. And one day this war's going to be over and Sammy'll have to come home. You don't want him thinking you're a stranger, do you? You don't want him not knowing who you are then.'

Dan stared at him. Then he got up, so suddenly that his chair scraped backwards along the floor and almost toppled over into the sawdust. He lifted his glass and drank the last few drops, then banged it back down on the table.

'I'll be seeing you, Tommy Vickers,' he said gruffly and turned towards the door. He dragged it open and blundered through, almost knocking over two customers who were just coming in. They protested, but he ignored them and thrust his way past. Tommy half rose to his feet but then sank back.

Well, I suppose it had to be said, he thought, swishing around the last half-inch of beer in his glass. But I dunno why it was me had to say it and I dunno if it'll do any good. By the look on Dan Hodges' face it won't. It'll just make things worse.

He sighed deeply. He'd been slowly feeling more and more sorry for Dan over the past few months. But you couldn't deny it, the man was his own worst enemy. He didn't help himself at all.

As the weather improved, Sammy took to wandering off, sometimes by himself, sometimes with one of his friends or in a group. He had quite a collection of friends now – partly, she knew, because of Silver and partly because Terry's boxing lessons had given him the ability to look after himself against bullies. Ruth still couldn't help laughing when she thought of the day Dotty Dewar had come to the house to complain that Sammy had given her Ernie a black eye.

'Well, I dare say he deserved it,' Ruth had said. 'Your Ernie's always been a bully. Serves him right to get a taste of his own medicine.'

Dotty Dewar drew in a deep breath of indignation. Her hennaed hair looked as if it could do with a wash, and her loose, floppy bosoms threatened to spill out of her grubby blouse. She came a step closer, her face reddening. 'My Ern never hurt no one. He wouldn't hurt a *fly*. It's that evacuee of yours, always causing trouble, he is. He's known for it.'

'And he's known for bullying boys like your Ern too, I suppose,' Ruth said. 'I'd have thought a big boy like that would be able to look after himself. Have you actually *seen* my Sammy, Dotty?'

'I don't need to see him. Ern's told me what happened and that's good enough for me. Bleeding like a stuck pig, he was, when he came home. And his eye, well, I've never seen an eye come up like his done, I wouldn't be surprised if it's not damaged permanent.'

'Well, let's hope it teaches him a lesson, then,' Ruth said. 'He's been tormenting the little ones for too long. It's time someone stood up to him.'

The woman stared at her. 'Is that all you got to say? Aren't you going to do nothing about it?'

'What do you want me to do? Ask the butcher for a nice steak to put on it? Look, Dotty, if I was your Ern I'd be ashamed to go running home to mummy saying that a little boy like my Sammy had bashed him. Why, he's twice Sammy's size!'

'He's not. He can't be. My Ern says—'

'Well, here he comes,' Ruth said, hearing Sammy's footsteps running down the lane. 'You can see him for yourself, and then maybe you'll go home and tell Ern to stop bullying boys smaller than him, for one thing, and not to go crying to you when one of them turns round and gives him what for.'

Dotty turned and followed her gaze. A second later Sammy came round the corner. He stopped when he saw them and Ruth felt a grin break out over her face.

Sammy was wearing grey flannel shorts and a grey shirt, both clean on that morning. His fair curls were glinting in the sun and his blue eyes shone with innocence. He was carrying a bunch of primroses.

'I got these for you, Auntie,' he said as he saw her. 'There were lots down the railway cutting.' He glanced uncertainly at Dotty Dewar and hesitated.

'This is Ern's mum, Sammy,' Ruth said pleasantly. 'You've been fighting with him, she says.'

Sammy looked indignant. 'He was hitting Muriel Simmons. Terry told me boys ought to look after girls so I told him to stop, but he wouldn't. And then he said he'd hit me.'

'But he didn't, did he?' Dotty Dewar said belligerently. She had looked taken aback by the sight of Sammy, who was indeed only half the size of her big, burly Ernie, but now she stepped forward, raising her arms threateningly. You can see who Ern takes after, Ruth thought. 'You hit him first.'

'Only because I ducked, so he missed me.' Sammy looked at his right hand and Ruth saw that the knuckles were faintly bruised. 'I only hit him once. He fell over then, so I just took Muriel back to the vicarage and he run off.'

Ruth looked at Dotty and smiled. 'I think you'd better go home, don't you?' she said. 'Tell your boy to stop hitting girls. Tell him to pick on someone his own size.' She looked at Sammy again and couldn't help laughing. 'Mind you, I don't expect he will – not when even a little chap like my Sammy can knock him down!'

Dotty gave her a furious glare and turned on her heel. She stalked off down the garden path and out into the lane. Then she wheeled round and shouted at them both.

'You'll hear more about this, see if you don't! I'll go and tell the teacher. I'll tell the policeman. That evacuee of yours is a devil, for all he looks so pretty and innocent with his yellow curls and his big blue eyes. A *devil*, that's what he is!'

Ruth waved at her and the woman snorted and strode away out of sight. Ruth and Sammy looked at each other.

'Well,' Ruth said, 'so you've been standing up for little Muriel Simmons, have you?'

'He was hitting her,' Sammy said. 'He was trying to get her sweets off her. Anyway, me and her's friends. I said she could come and see Silver.'

'And so she can,' Ruth said. 'You bring her whenever

you like, and bring her sister as well. They lost their mother a little while ago, just like you, so they need someone to look after them and cheer them up.' She gave him a little hug. 'Come on indoors now, Sammy, and let's put those flowers in water. And then we'll take some of them to the churchyard, shall we? I'd like to put some on my dad's grave.'

Sammy spent a good deal of time at the vicarage, with Tim and Keith Budd and the two little Simmons girls. Stella was older and inclined to be bossy, but since the incident with Ernie Dewar, Muriel seemed to look up to Sammy as her protector. He had never had anyone look up to him before and it was a heady feeling.

'We're going for a picnic,' Muriel informed him one afternoon. 'Mrs Mudge is making two sorts of sandwiches. One lot will have Marmite in, and the others will have condensed milk, only she says we've got to eat the Marmite ones first or they'll taste horrible.'

'But Marmite already does taste horrible,' Sammy said. Ruth had tried several times to get him to eat this delicacy but he couldn't. It seemed to burn his tongue and he didn't like the colour either. It was black. You couldn't put black stuff on your bread.

'The condensed milk makes it taste horrible,' Muriel explained. 'It's too sweet, see. Are you coming on the picnic too?'

'I don't know. I haven't been invited.' Ruth had explained to him that you had to be invited to people's parties or picnics. You couldn't just go along. Sammy, who had never been to parties or picnics anyway, invited or not, had resigned himself never to being asked to either event, and his reply was no more than a simple statement of fact.

'Well, I'm inviting you,' Muriel said, as if it ought to have been obvious. 'And you could bring Silver too,' she added.

'Bring Silver?'

'Yes. He'd like it. He could fly about in the trees.'

'But what if he flies away?' Sammy asked doubtfully.

'He comes when you call him. I've seen him.'

This was true. Sammy had only to click his fingers and whistle when Silver was flying free in the room, and Silver would fly straight to him.

'I don't think Auntie Ruth—'

'She wouldn't mind,' said Muriel, who had met Ruth just three times. 'Anyway, she's at work and he's lonely when he's on his own. You said so.' She gazed at Sammy. 'You want to come on the picnic, don't you?'

Sammy couldn't tell her how much he longed to go on the picnic. Even the thought of Marmite sandwiches couldn't put him off. All the same, he had a niggling feeling that Ruth would not want him to take Silver and he still wasn't quite sure that Silver wouldn't fly away once he got out into the open air. But Muriel was right, he did always come when Sammy clicked his fingers. And if he took along plenty of sunflower seeds . . .

'All right,' he said. 'I'll bring him.'

'Go and get him, then.' Muriel was not going to let him off the hook. 'Go and get him now. You'll have to hurry because Stella's helping make the sandwiches and we're going as soon as they're ready.'

'But Auntie Ruth's at work – I won't be able to ask her.'

'That won't matter,' Muriel said. 'She'd say yes, so it'll be all right.' The words '*she wouldn't be able to say no*' hung in the air between them.

Sammy gave her a hunted look and bit his lip. 'I ought to ask . . .'

Muriel turned away. 'I'm going in to see if the sandwiches are ready and then we're going. We're going down your lane,' she added. 'We'll meet you at the gate. If you're not there we'll go on.'

Without you. She might as well have said it, loud and

clear. Sammy looked after her for a moment, wishing he could be as certain that Auntie Ruth wouldn't mind him taking Silver. But he could take the stand as well – Tim would help him carry it – and Silver would be tethered to it all the time. He wouldn't be able to get away. And Sammy was sure he'd enjoy being out in the open air, all among the trees.

He turned and ran back to the cottage as fast as he could. He couldn't risk being left behind. This might be the only picnic he would ever be invited to.

'Sammy hasn't heard from his dad in the last couple of days, has he?' Joyce asked when Ruth called in after work. 'There's been some terrible news from April Grove. Mrs Budd wrote and told the vicar, and Mrs Mudge passed it on to me in the post office. Some of the boys that were still there had been making a den or something in a bombed-out house. From what I can make out, they were collecting shrapnel and things, the way boys do, and picked up a live bomb as well. It went off, and one of them lost a leg and one was killed.'

Ruth stared at her. 'Oh, that's awful! Actually in April Grove, was it?'

'No, in another street somewhere, but one of the boys came from there, I don't know which one, and they all lived close by.'

'How dreadful!' Ruth exclaimed. 'Their *poor* mothers! It doesn't bear thinking of . . . April Grove. If my Sammy hadn't been evacuated he could have been one of those boys.' She shuddered. 'I'm so thankful he's out here with me. I just hope that father of his has the sense to leave him here – though he doesn't seem to show much interest, so I can't imagine him wanting the poor kiddy back.' She glanced out of the window, to the boys playing in the garden. 'Where is he?'

'Oh, he said little Muriel Simmons asked him to go for a

picnic with them – her and her sister and the two Budd boys. I said it would be all right. You don't mind, do you?'

'Mind? Of course I don't! I'm pleased to see him making friends. You know he gave young Ernie Dewar a nosebleed for teasing Muriel, don't you? Proper little knight in shining armour. She follows him everywhere now. I don't suppose Sammy's ever had anyone looking up to him like that.'

'Well, I don't think they're going very far. Just down to the woods, he said. I dare say they'll be back by six, wanting their tea just the same as usual. Picnics always seem to make youngsters hungry, no matter how many sandwiches they take with them.'

Since Sammy wasn't going to be home till later, Ruth thought she would pop up to the farm to see Jane. Terry had survived Africa and the taking of Tobruk, and was now somewhere in Greece. The situation there seemed bad and once again they were talking about evacuation. It's Dunkirk all over again, every time, she thought. Wherever we go the Germans are too strong for us and we get chased out, and they're raiding us every night, bombing all our biggest cities ... What hope have we got, really?

Jane was of the same mind. 'It's just bad news wherever you turn. I don't think the government knows what to do, for all Churchill's fine words. They're scared stiff we're going to be invaded, you know. There's barbed wire going up all round the coast, nobody's allowed on the beaches ... I've heard they've got the Home Guard standing by in East Anglia, they think it's *imminent*.'

'They're tearing the life out of the country,' Ruth said. 'But we still mustn't lose heart, Jane. Once we do that they really will have won – they can just walk in and take over, and nobody'll stop them. As long as we won't give in they can't beat us.'

'They said that in Norway,' Jane said bitterly, 'and look what happened. They walked in anyway. The Norwegians never gave in, but they never stopped them either and the Germans are in charge just as much as if they *had* given in. I can't see the point of it.'

'I suppose it saved a lot of people being killed,' Ruth said.

'And then there's France, half the country occupied by Germans. And it'll be Greece next. We'll be having to get them out of there, same as at Dunkirk, and my Terry's there, and I can't *sleep* for thinking about him. And then there's Lizzie, in Southampton. Every time there's a raid I'm thinking about her, wondering if the hospital's been hit . . . You don't know what it's like, Ruth – never having had any children of your own, you just can't *imagine* what it's like.'

'I can,' Ruth said, feeling hurt. 'Of course I can. Why, if it was Sammy—'

'*Sammy*!' Jane cried. 'That's all you think about – Sammy! *He's* not your child. He's just an evacuee. You've only had him five minutes and he'll be going back to his father one day and he'll forget all about you. I'm talking about my own *child*, Ruth, my *son* that I carried for nine months and gave birth to, and fed with my own milk. It's not a *bit* the same. You haven't got any idea.'

Ruth was silent for a moment. Then she said, 'Maybe you're right, Jane. Maybe I *can't* imagine what it's like to have a son in the war or a daughter training to be a nurse. I just wish I did. I wish I *had* had children – even if it did mean breaking my heart over them.'

The two sisters stared at each other. They'd always been friends, always able to confide in each other and share their troubles. Now, suddenly, they seemed to be on opposite sides of a high fence.

'I'd better go,' Ruth said, getting up. 'Before one of us says something we might regret . . . I'm sorry about Terry, Jane, I really am, and I hope you get good news soon. I hope we all do. But don't tell me I can't imagine what it's like to be a mother – please. I think I *can* imagine – and in any case, imagination's all I've got. Apart from an evacuee boy and a parrot, of course,' she added bitterly.

She turned and walked out of the kitchen, leaving Jane at the table with her half-finished tea in front of her. Ruth's heart was thudding. Hurt seemed to be making a hard, painful lump in the middle of her chest, so that she could only take shallow breaths. The lump was in her throat too, aching, and she knew she was in danger of crying. She held her head high, determined not to break down in the village street where someone might see her, and marched swiftly down the lane, wanting only to get indoors, into her own little cottage, where Silver waited for her with his silly remarks and the crooning voice so much like Jack's, and where Sammy had brought light into her life.

But when she got there and opened the front door, the cottage was strangely silent. She stood for a moment listening. Sammy was at the picnic, of course, enjoying himself in the woods with the two Budd boys and the Simmons girls. But why was Silver so quiet?

Slowly, dreading what she might find, Ruth opened the door to the living room. If anything had happened to Silver . . . He was still a relatively young parrot, but you never knew . . . I don't know what I'd do if I lost him, she thought, and peeped in, nerving herself for what she might see.

Silver was not there. His cage was empty, the door open, and his stand with its perch had disappeared.

Chapter Twenty-three

'See?' Muriel said. 'He *does* like being at the picnic.'

Silver was perched on his stand under a large oak tree. The leaves of the tree were just beginning to uncurl, like little brown fists, and the thick, spreading branches gave a light, stripy shade. The picnic had been spread out beside its solid trunk, on a carpet of dry, crackling leaves. There was a brown-paper bag containing Marmite sandwiches and another with the promised condensed milk. Mrs Mudge had provided a bottle of orange squash as well, and another bag full of rock cakes.

Sammy had brought some sunflower seeds. He gave one to Silver, who cracked it. The stand wobbled a bit on the uneven ground.

'Don't let him fall over,' Stella said bossily. 'You'd better keep hold of the stand.'

Sammy and Tim had carried it between them. It had been heavy and awkward, with Silver clinging to the perch on top and flapping his wings from time to time. All the way down the lane Sammy had been nervous, expecting someone to see them and call out to know what they were up to. It would have been worse still if Auntie Ruth had seen them. 'We've got to get him home before she comes back from work,' he said anxiously.

'But we've got to have the picnic first,' Muriel said. 'You can't go home before we have the picnic.'

'And we've got to have games too,' Stella declared. 'You can't have a picnic without games. I read that in my Enid Blyton book.'

At the mention of games, Keith looked round. He had been feeding Silver another sunflower seed. 'What games are we going to play? I've brought my ball.'

'We'll play hide and seek,' Stella said. 'You can be seeker first, Tim.'

'I don't want to be. I want to hide.'

'Anyway,' Muriel said, 'we ought to dip for it.'

'All right. We'll dip.' They all stood round in a circle and Stella pointed to each one in turn. 'Dip, dip, dip. My little ship. Sails on the water. Like a cup and saucer. Dip, dip, dip. *You* are *It*.' Her finger pointed at Tim.

He pushed out his lips. 'That's not fair. You made it be me.'

'No, I didn't. Anyway, you can't argue, it was a dip.' She skipped away. 'Come on, you've got to give us fifty.'

'Twenty,' Tim said. 'I'll give you twenty.' He turned away, put his hands over his face and began to count in a loud voice. 'One, two, three . . .'

'Mother caught a flea,' Silver joined in helpfully. 'Time for tea. I'm a little teapot, short and stout. Sammy, Sammy, shine a light, ain't you playing—'

'Shut up, Silver,' Tim said between giggles. 'I'm up to sixteen now. Seventeen, eighteen, nineteen, *twenty*. Coming, ready or not!'

He set off into the trees. The others had disappeared. Silver was left alone, standing on his perch in the middle of the wood. He flapped his wings and the stand wobbled and swayed.

'Ruthie?' he said, a little uncertainly. 'I love you, Ruthie. Let me be your sweetheart. I'm a little teapot, short and stout.' He paused. There was a clattering sound in the trees and a magpie flew to a nearby branch and stared at him. Silver backed away along his perch and the stand swayed again. Another magpie joined the first and they leant forward from their branch, peering at the intruder.

'Five and twenty blackbirds, baked in a pie,' Silver said.

He ducked his head sideways and eyed them. 'Sod the little buggers.'

The magpies launched themselves from their branch, circling round the little clearing. Silver gave a squawk of dismay and fluttered his wings frantically, lifting himself from his perch. The chain round his ankle tautened and jerked him back, and he grabbed the perch with one foot, missing with the other. He toppled sideways and hung there, screeching and flapping furiously, and the magpies flew towards him, stretching their necks to peck at him as they passed. The stand fell over.

'Silver! *Silver!*'

Ruth, running through the woods to look for Sammy, burst into the clearing and the magpies disappeared. She rushed over to Silver, who was now thrashing among the crackling leaves, and caught him in her hands, stroking him gently. 'Oh, Silver, Silver, my poor boy, what have they done to you? It's all right, it's Ruthie, Ruthie's got you. Oh, my sweetheart, my poor, poor sweetheart . . .'

The leaves crackled again and she looked up to see Sammy emerge from the undergrowth. His fair hair was tangled with scraps of leaf and twigs, and his face was white. He stared at her and she saw the others appear behind him – Tim and Keith, looking anxious and guilty, Muriel looking frightened, Stella mutinous. There was a moment of silence as they all stared at each other.

Silver was quiet in her hands. She looked down at him and parted his feathers gently, looking for signs of injury. To her relief there appeared to be none, although you didn't know what might have happened to his insides . . . Slowly she stood up, lifting the perch, and Tim ran forward to help her get it upright. She placed Silver on top and after a moment of uncertainty he clasped his claws round it and stood up.

Ruth looked at the children again. Sammy had crept

closer. His eyes had filled with tears but for the first time since she had known him Ruth felt no compassion.

'You naughty, *naughty* boy,' she said in a trembling voice. 'You *naughty* little boy. Taking Silver out of the house like that. Leaving him all on his own in the woods. He could have been *killed* by those horrible magpies. Don't you realise that? Whatever got into you? And the rest of you,' she added, turning her furious glance on the other children. 'You're just as bad. You all know I never take Silver outside, except into my own garden on nice summer days. I'd never bring him all this way. And it's too early for him to be out, he could have caught cold and died. Maybe he *has* caught cold.' Her voice shook again and she turned away. 'I'm taking him straight home and you're coming with me, Sammy. And when we get there you're to go straight to your bedroom and stay there until I tell you to come out. I'm very, very angry with you.'

She marched off to the edge of the wood and along the lane, with Silver now perched on her wrist and Sammy holding the stand and half running to keep up with her. The others looked at each other.

Tim looked down and scraped a hole in the carpet of leaves with one toe.

'I knew it was a daft idea, bringing Silver. Now she'll never let us go and see him again.'

'Well, you needn't look at me,' Stella flashed. 'It wasn't *my* idea.'

'It wasn't mine either,' Keith said, guiltily aware that he'd thought it was a smashing idea.

Muriel was close to tears. 'D'you think Mrs Purslow will tell the policeman?'

'Tell the *policeman*?' Stella echoed, rounding on her. There was a note of panic in her voice. 'Why should she do that? We didn't *steal* Silver.'

'Well, she might say we did. We never asked, did we?'

They looked at each other uncertainly. Then Tim bent down and picked up the bag of Marmite sandwiches.

'I s'pose we'd better take these back. We can't have the picnic now. It's all spoilt.'

Nobody argued with him. In silence they gathered up the uneaten sandwiches and rock cakes. Keith picked up the bottle of orange squash. Miserably, they trailed out of the wood and back along the lane.

They didn't look up as they passed Ruth Purslow's cottage. They kept their heads down, staring at the loose stones of the lane. None of them wanted to see her looking out of the window. None of them wanted to catch her eye.

'. . . and you're a very naughty boy,' Ruth said for the twentieth time. 'You know very *well* I don't take Silver outside. You *knew* I wouldn't have let you take him on a picnic. Didn't you? *Didn't* you?'

Silver was back in his cage in the living room. He was huddled on his perch, looking miserable, but he didn't seem to be hurt. He was suffering from reaction, Ruth thought, what they'd call shock if he was a human being, and she could only hope he'd get over it. She'd heard of parrots not talking any more if they'd been upset, and although her main concern was that he should recover and be healthy, she knew that she would miss his hoarse voice dreadfully if he stopped talking. More than that, she'd miss Jack's voice.

The thought brought a wave of misery and she looked at Sammy again. He'd gone to his room when they'd got home, but she couldn't keep him there for ever and once she was sure there was nothing more she could do for Silver she'd called him down for his tea. She gave him bread and milk in a pudding basin, and he sat with it in front of him on the kitchen table, stirring it half-heartedly.

'Well, didn't you?' Ruth persisted and he nodded miserably. He tried to swallow his sobs and hiccuped.

Tears were pouring down his cheeks. He stared up at Ruth and felt a cold despair grip his insides. She didn't love him any more. She didn't even like him. She wouldn't want him in her house any more, she'd get the billeting people to take him away. He'd have to go home, to the cold empty house where Mum no longer lived, where Dad went out for days at a time, where there wasn't enough food and no nice chairs to sit in, no warm fire. Or he'd be sent to the proved school, like Gordon. He'd be sent to proved school for stealing. For stealing *Silver*.

'So why did you take him? Why?'

He found his voice. 'Muriel told me to.'

'*Muriel* told you to? But you don't have to do what Muriel tells you.'

'I wanted to go on the picnic,' he said.

'Well, that didn't mean you had to take Silver with you.' She looked at his face and saw that it did. Taking Silver had been Muriel's condition for asking him to the picnic.

Children! she thought with a wave of exasperation. They just didn't live by the same rules as grown-ups. That was why you had to teach them, of course, that was why you had to discipline them and guide them and show them the difference between right and wrong. And you couldn't blame Muriel, not when you knew what a terrible time she and Stella had had. Perhaps she shouldn't blame Sammy either. But he should have known better. He *lived* with her and with Silver. He *ought* to have known.

'Well, you're a very naughty boy,' she said again. 'I'm very cross with you. You must never, ever, take Silver out of the house, do you understand? You must never even *touch* him again without asking me first. I'm sorry, Sammy, but I don't trust you any more. I didn't think you *could* be so naughty. Or so silly,' she added.

Sammy stared at her. He'd been crying ever since they left the woods. He'd cried all the way home and she'd heard him sobbing when he was upstairs in his bedroom. He'd come downstairs still shuddering with sobs, the tears only half dried on his face, and they'd been rolling down his cheeks as he sat miserably stirring his bread and milk. I've told him off enough, she thought. He knows he's done wrong. I'm just taking out my own upset on him and that's not fair. Yet she knew that there was even more to it than that. She'd already been upset by Jane's words about children when she'd come home and the moment when she had discovered Silver missing had been much worse than just losing a pet, however precious. It had been like losing Jack all over again – Jack and all the chance she'd ever have of having her own children.

Fresh tears brimmed out of Sammy's swollen eyes. He laid down his spoon and pushed away his bowl of bread and milk. He folded his arms on the table and rested his head on them, and began to cry again, even more loudly than before.

Ruth took a step towards him, but before she could lay her hand on his shoulder there was a sudden harsh knock on the door. She jumped and Sammy quivered. They both looked through the open door of the kitchen along the passage towards the front door. There was another loud knock.

Sammy's eyes dilated with fear.

'What's the matter, Sammy? Who is it?'

'It's the policeman,' he said in a trembling voice. 'He's come to take me away for stealing Silver. I'll have to go to proved school.'

'Of course it's not a policeman! You're not going away.' She went quickly along the passage, wondering what on earth could have happened now. Anyone from the village would have come round the back . . . She opened the door and stared at the man who confronted her.

He was big and dark, with black eyebrows. He was wearing rough working clothes and there was a cap on his rough black hair. He was nearly a foot taller than Ruth, and she had to tilt her head back to look up into his face. He glowered down at her and she stepped back hastily.

'Who are you? What do you want?'

'I'm looking for a Mrs Purslow,' he said in a deep voice. 'Someone told me she lived here.'

'I'm Mrs Purslow.' Ruth stared at him, feeling frightened. 'Who are—'

'You?' The black eyebrows drew together in a frown and she stepped back. 'But I was told you were a widow woman. I thought – I thought you'd be old.'

Ruth bit her lip. Then she said, 'You still haven't told me who you are or what you want.'

'Well, I'm Dan Hodges of course! Sam's father. I've come to see my boy. I suppose there's no objection to that, is there?' He sounded belligerent, on edge, as if he were either angry or nervous.

'You're Mr Hodges?' Ruth's heart sank. With her and Sammy both already upset, this was just about the worst time he could have come.

'That's what I said.' He looked past her and his face changed a little. 'Sam? Is that you?'

Ruth turned and saw Sammy standing in the kitchen doorway. She realised that the man probably couldn't see clearly in the dimness of the passage. She hesitated. 'Your dad's come to see you, Sammy.' For a moment she half hoped that Sammy would deny that this was his father. He was so big, so intimidating. But Sammy came slowly forward along the passage, his eyes fixed on the big man, and she knew that it was true.

'You'd better come in,' she said, standing back a little. 'We – we were just having some supper. Would you like a cup of tea?'

'I wouldn't say no. It's a long ride from Pompey.' He glanced behind him. 'Will the bike be all right out there? No one'll half-inch it?'

'It'll be all right,' she said stiffly. 'We don't have thieves at Bridge End.'

Sammy was still standing just behind her. He hadn't rushed forward into his father's arms and Dan Hodges didn't seem to expect him to. Ruth glanced uncertainly from one to the other and went past Sammy to the kitchen. She moved the kettle over on to the range and went to the sink to empty the teapot. Behind her she heard their footsteps as they came along the short passage, then Dan Hodges was standing in the doorway, with Sammy still hesitating behind him.

'Sit down,' Ruth said, indicating the table with its four chairs round it. Hers and Sammy's were still pulled out, where they had left them when they went to the door. Dan glanced at them, dragged out one of the others and sat down heavily. He looked tired, she thought, tired and miserable beneath his sweaty face and dark stubble. It *was* a long ride out from Portsmouth – at least twenty or twenty-five miles – and he'd probably done a day's work first. And he still had to ride back. Unless he thinks I'm going to put him up here, she thought, but if he does, he's got another think coming.

Sammy edged in through the door and slid round the table to his own place. He pulled his pudding basin towards him and looked at the contents. The milk had cooled and the bread swollen into a soggy, unappetising mass.

Ruth, feeling embarrassed, reached down and took the basin away.

'You don't need to eat that now, Sammy,' she said. 'I've got some oat biscuits in the tin. I expect your dad will like one as well.'

The tea made, she poured a cup for Dan Hodges and one for herself. Then she stood there, feeling ill at ease. Probably the man wanted to talk to his son on his own. Perhaps she ought to leave them to it. She picked up her cup and saucer.

'I'll go in the other room. Unless there's anything you want to ask me, Mr Hodges? How Sammy's been getting on out here, that sort of thing? I can tell you, he's been a good boy, no trouble at all—' She stopped, remembering what she'd been saying to Sammy when his father knocked on the door. A naughty, naughty boy. No longer trusted. And she hadn't been keeping her voice down, either. Had Mr Hodges heard her?

She looked at him again. She had to admit he was a good-looking man, in a rough sort of way – big and dark, with straight brows when he wasn't scowling, and firm lips. He was only wearing working clothes, of course, but in a good coat and trousers, with a clean shirt and a tie, he'd look really well set-up. The sort of man you'd notice, walking down the street.

Sammy was nothing like him, not a bit, he must take after his mother.

'I just wanted to see how he's getting on,' Dan Hodges said. 'I thought I ought to.'

Only *ought* to? Ruth thought, glancing at Sammy. He was nibbling an oat biscuit, taking tiny bites all round the edge. He always ate biscuits like that, nibbling all the way round and making them smaller and smaller until they disappeared. He was gazing at his father, but when Dan turned his dark gaze on him Sammy's eyes dropped and he stared instead at the table.

'Well?' Dan said to his son, 'ha'n't you got nothing to say for yourself? Cat got your tongue?'

Ruth stared at him, shocked. 'I expect he's feeling shy . . .' she began and faltered into silence when the dark eyes turned in her direction. 'I mean – it's none of my business, I know, but I have been looking after Sammy all these months and he does seem to be rather a shy little boy. And he hasn't seen you for quite a long time.'

'There's a war on,' Dan said curtly. 'I ain't had time to come traipsing out here to see him. I knew he was safe, or meant to be. He said he liked it all right, when he wrote. Anyway, I've come now.'

'Yes,' Ruth said faintly. 'Yes, I didn't mean—'

'Is our Gordon home from the proved school yet?' Sammy broke in suddenly. He had nibbled the biscuit into a perfect circle, about half its original size. He stared at his father.

'No, he's not. He won't be home for another year or more. You know that. I suppose he's told you about my older boy,' Dan said to Ruth. 'Told you about the trouble he got into.'

'Well, not much, no.' Ruth took a breath and looked at Sammy. 'He – why don't you go in the other room and see if Silver's all right, Sammy?' She gave him an encouraging smile.

'But you said I wasn't to go near Silver again. You said I was a naughty, naughty boy, and you said you'd never trust me again.'

Ruth closed her eyes for a moment. 'Yes, but I was cross with you then. I'm not cross any more and I know you'd never hurt him. Run along, now.' She watched as Sammy left the kitchen, then turned back to Dan Hodges. 'I don't think we ought to talk about it in front of him, but he's said hardly anything about his home – about you or his brother. In fact, I didn't know for a long time that his mother had died.' She met his eyes. 'I ought to have been told that, Mr Hodges. It would have helped us both if I'd known about his mother.'

'Why would it?' He looked puzzled. 'All you got to do is look after him. See he gets his dinner and cleans his teeth and goes to school. What difference does it make what you know about the rest of us?'

Ruth sighed. 'It makes all the difference in the world, Mr Hodges. It makes the difference between a miserable, lonely child and one who's happy – or as happy as possible in Sammy's situation. I'm not just here to see that he's safe and warm and fed, even though all that's important. He's a little boy, he's growing up, and I've got to be like a mother and a father to him. I've got to *help* him grow up.' She sat down and leaned across the table towards him. 'This war might go on for years, Sammy might be here for years. He can't just be left to grow up on his own, as if all that didn't matter.'

Dan stared at her and shook his head slowly. He looked tired to death, Ruth thought, as if he hadn't slept properly for weeks, and she wondered what had happened to him during the raids. There had been a really bad one only a few nights ago. And what about those boys Joyce had told her about, being killed or injured by a bomb they'd picked up? Sammy must have known them, so must Dan Hodges. Maybe that was what had made Mr Hodges want to come and see his own son.

'I dunno,' Dan said. 'I dunno about all that . . . Seems to me if a kid's got somewhere to live and enough to eat, that's all anyone can expect these days. It's more'n I ever had. I was lucky to get one decent meal a day in me belly, I can tell you.'

He picked up his cup, fitting his big fingers into the handle with difficulty, and drank. Ruth stared at him. She couldn't quite make him out. He looked and sounded rough, but there was still that other look about him, the impression that in different clothes, with a shave and a haircut, he'd look – well, quite imposing. And younger, too. At first sight, she'd put him at about fifty, but now she thought he couldn't be more than forty, if that – not much older than she was herself. And she'd been wrong when she thought that there was nothing of him in Sammy. There *was* something – a fleeting expression, a touch of something vulnerable in his eyes and the set of his mouth.

'Why don't you go in the other room and talk to Sammy for a bit?' she said more gently. 'I'll get you something to eat before you go back. You won't want to be too long if you're on your bike, because of the blackout.' It would take him a good couple of hours to ride back to Portsmouth, she reckoned.

'All right,' he said, standing up. 'All right. But I dunno what we'll have to say to each other. We never did have much. He was his mother's boy, Sam was, ever since he was first born. It was Gordon took after me.'

He went out of the kitchen and into the other room. Ruth tried to remember if Sammy had ever told him about Silver in his brief letters home. Well, it would be something for them to talk about. And with any luck, Silver would have recovered by now and make most of the conversation himself.

She set about frying some mashed potato left over from dinner, with some onions and a bit of bacon. There was an egg too, that she'd been saving for Sammy's tea and then not given him because she was cross. She put them in the frying pan and let them sizzle, listening all the while for Silver's raucous tones.

But there was no sound from the other room. And when she went in to tell Mr Hodges that his meal was ready she found him slumped in her armchair, fast asleep, with Sammy curled at his feet and Silver, evidently exhausted by his own afternoon's adventures, slumbering peacefully in his cage.

Chapter Twenty-four

Ruth had to fry the potato all over again when Dan Hodges woke, and the egg was like leather. He ate it all the same, wolfing it down as if he hadn't seen food for a week, then wiping his mouth with the back of his hand. He looked at her and she saw the awkwardness in his eyes.

'Sorry. Nora tried to teach me manners, but when you're hungry . . . I don't get much home-cooked grub these days, and I come straight from work.'

She stared at him, trying to picture the house he must go back to after work. The cold fireplace, the empty larder. When did he have time to do his shopping, clean the house, wash his sheets? She tried to imagine this big man standing at the kitchen sink, scrubbing at clothes on the washboard, or putting sheets through a mangle in the backyard, but she couldn't.

'Haven't you got anyone to help you? A relative, or one of the neighbours?'

He snorted. 'All me relations are down Old Portsmouth, where I ought to be. We never oughter gone to April Grove, only we were desperate for somewhere to live and a mate of mine told me there was a place for rent . . . It's five bloody miles from one end to the other, Portsea Island is.' He saw her blank look. 'I s'pose you do know Pompey's on an island. There's just a bridge, that's all, and April Grove's right up that end, Copnor way. *Old* Portsmouth, where me and Nora come from, that's down the other end, towards the harbour and Clarence Pier – 'cept there's not much left of *that*, since it was bombed.'

'But there must be someone who could help,' Ruth persisted, trying to keep to the thread of the argument. 'Your neighbours ... Doesn't Mrs Budd live in April Grove? She was out here for a while, we all liked her.'

'Down the other end,' he said. 'And she's got her own man to think of, and that girl of hers and the baby. Freda Vickers that lives next door used to give an eye to Sammy, but I don't want people poking round the house when I'm out. I'd rather shift for meself.'

'Mrs Vickers is a nice lady,' Sammy said. He was sitting at the table too, eating a fresh helping of bread and milk, and drinking cocoa. He wiped a moustache of cocoa from his lips in exact imitation of his father. 'She used to give me dinners.'

'Yeah, well, that's as maybe,' Dan said shortly. 'She's all right and Tom's a good mate but that still don't mean I want them round the house. A bloke's got to have a bit of privacy in his own home.'

He glanced up at the kitchen clock. 'I'll have to go. It'll be dark before I gets home and likely as not there'll be another raid. I'm a fire watcher, got to be on duty.' He looked at Sammy and hesitated, as if he didn't know what to say. 'So you're all right here, are you?'

Sammy glanced at Ruth and nodded a little uncertainly. 'So long as Auntie Ruth's not cross with me.'

'Cross with you?' Dan shot a dark look at Ruth. 'She is treating you right, ain't she?'

'Of course I am,' Ruth said firmly. 'And I'm not often cross with Sammy. It's just that this afternoon—'

'If you been a bad boy—' Dan began and Sammy shrank away from him.

'I didn't mean to be. But I wanted to go on the picnic, and Muriel said—'

'Muriel? Who's Muriel?'

'It's just a silly bit of mischief,' Ruth cut in. 'There's no harm done and Sammy won't do it again, I'm sure. He

311

really hasn't been any problem, Mr Hodges, and I'm sure he's happy here. He's welcome to stay as long as he likes.'

Dan looked at her. 'As long as he likes? And what about if it's years, like you said? Are you really willing to have my boy here with you for years? Till he's fourteen – fifteen – going out to work?'

Ruth took a breath. 'Sammy could stay here for the rest of his life, if he wanted to. He's like a son to me. You don't have to worry about him, Mr Hodges, you really don't.'

Dan stared at her. His brows came together in the frown that was already becoming familiar to her. He seemed about to speak; then he shook his head and got up from the table.

'It seems like everything's being took away these days. But I can't stop here talking about it. I got to get back to Pompey . . .' He looked down at his son. 'I'll come out again, soon as I can. You be a good boy now. Do what Mrs Purslow tells you, see, and no more mischief.'

'No, Dad,' Sammy whispered. His blue eyes were enormous as he looked up at his father. They stared at each other for a moment, the big man and the small boy, one so dark, the other so fair, and despite the differences between them Ruth felt a little catch at her heart at the likeness – that hint of sadness, of vulnerability, a reaching out from one to the other. Neither of them could make the first move, she thought, neither of them could break the glass barrier that seemed to stand between them. If only . . .

Then Dan Hodges moved abruptly and the moment was gone. He put his hand briefly on Sammy's shoulder and turned away.

'I s'pose I should say thanks for looking after the boy,' he said gruffly to Ruth and held out his hand.

She took it, feeling the warmth and the size of it, and looked up into his dark face. 'There's no need to thank me. I'm glad to do whatever I can for Sammy. I told you that.'

He nodded, then moved towards the door. 'Yeah. I

know. Well, I'd better get on. Don't want to be riding too far in the blackout. I'll come out again, some time.'

Ruth nodded in turn and watched him go down the garden path. He lifted his bike away from the hedge and glanced back to give a wave. She lifted her hand and turned to make sure that Sammy waved his own farewell. Then Dan Hodges cycled away and disappeared round the corner of the lane.

Ruth and Sammy looked at each other and went indoors.

'Well,' Ruth said brightly, 'that was nice, wasn't it? What a lovely surprise, seeing your dad like that. I expect you were really pleased, weren't you?'

Sammy looked up at her.

'Was it true, what you said? Can I really stop here for years and years, and be your boy?' He went into the living room and stared at Silver, who was waking up in his cage and stretching out his claws. 'Can I be here with you and Silver for ever and ever?'

'I tell you,' Dan said, lifting his tankard, 'I dunno properly what to make of it. The nipper was upset, anyone with half an eye could see that. He'd been crying his eyes out. And he was sat at the table with nothing but a bowl of bread and water in front of him, what looked as if it had been made for hours. And then she had the cheek to give me a lecture on what kids need. Said she'd got to be a mother and father to him – I mean, what sort of talk's that? Put some decent grub into his belly and make sure he goes to school, that's all she got to do. And it's not as if she didn't have any food in the place. Give me an *egg*, she did, and fried spuds and onions and all. My Sam wasn't getting any of that, though. Bread and water, that's all he was getting – though she did put some milk on the second lot, and give him a cup of cocoa, but I reckon she was just trying to put it on a bit, get round me, like.'

'But what was the idea?' Tommy Vickers asked. He'd

taken to dropping into the pub with Dan once or twice a week, whenever Hitler would let them. Dan wasn't such a bad bloke after all, once you got talking to him, he'd told Freda, and he seemed to need someone to chew the fat with. And now he'd been to Nora's grave, and cycled out to see Sammy, he seemed to be more human, somehow. 'Why should she want to get round you?'

'Well, she wouldn't want me complaining to the authorities about her, would she? Like that other widow woman what treated the Baker kiddy so bad, and those two sisters that had the Atkinsons. I mean, for all Jess Budd says about how well her boys have got on out at Bridge End, they ain't all saints in the country. I don't want my Sam treated bad.'

Tommy looked at him. It would be difficult, he thought, for Sammy to be treated much worse than he'd been at home, although that had been mostly neglect because Nora had been so ill and poor old Dan just didn't know how to manage without her.

'Well,' he said, 'however he's being treated, he's better off out there than back in Pompey, with all the raids we're getting. I mean, I know it's a week or so between them now, but we still don't know when they're coming. And it's not just the dockyard they're after, it's right in our own backyards too. They nearly got Hilsea gasworks the other night, and the railway line, that was blocked for hours till they cleared them unexploded bombs, and there was all them houses smashed. You can't feel safe. I wouldn't advise you to bring young Sammy home again, not with things as they are. It's not a fit place for youngsters. Look at what happened to that Cyril Nash, and young Jimmy Cross.' He didn't add what he'd said to Freda, that if Micky Baxter had been sent away when Gordon was, none of that would have happened. Cyril Nash would still be alive and Jimmy Cross would still have both his legs.

Dan was silent for a moment. Then he said, 'It's not just

that, Tom. I get the feeling that if I don't get him back here I'm going to lose him for ever. She wants to keep him. She as good as said so. Told me he could stay as long as he liked. Told me she looked on him as her own son.' He stared at Tommy across the little beer-streaked table. 'What I think is, this war's going to go on for a few more years yet. It's got to. There's too much of it, all over the world, to stop it any sooner. And by the time it's all over my Sam'll be a grown lad, out at work. He'll probably get farm work or something like that. He'll be a country boy, Tom. He won't want to come back to Pompey, and he won't want to leave that Ruth Purslow and come back to me.' He looked down again at the table. 'We won't have nothing in common any more. He'll have forgot all about me.'

Tommy looked at him. Everything Dan said made sense. Even if the boy wasn't being treated right, he wouldn't want to come back home – he'd never been treated right there, either, especially since his mother had died. And he would be used to the country, to country ways. He would have grown up with them.

'Well, I dunno,' he said at last. 'I know it seems a bit queer, Dan, but would it be so bad if he did? Not forget you, I don't mean that, but – well, make his life out in the country? If it's what he's used to by then? So long as he has a good life – isn't that what's important? And you'll still have your Gordon, when he comes home again.'

Dan raised his head and his eyes met Tommy's. They were dark, half-hooded by the black brows drawn tight across them. But deep within them Tommy caught a brief glimpse of the loneliness of Dan Hodges' heart and soul.

'What's important to me,' he said, 'is that Sam's all I got left of my Nora. Gordon – well, he's like me. He's tough. He'll make his own way and he'll always come back, when it suits him. But Sam's different. He's his mother all over again and I never realised it properly, not till I saw him out

315

there.' He drew in his breath. 'I can't let him go – not as well as her. I just can't.'

For a few days after Dan's visit Sammy was subdued and quiet. He seemed almost to have gone back into the shell he'd been in when he first arrived, Ruth thought, and wondered what had upset him most – the business over Silver, or his father's arrival. The way the two of them had been together was certainly a bit queer – not at all like a father and son who hadn't seen each other for a few months. They'd been more like strangers.

Silver, however, had recovered completely from his adventure and was even more vociferous than usual. His gravelly voice filled the cottage, declaiming every nursery rhyme, sea shanty, swear word and comment that he'd ever learned. He was quiet only when Ruth put on the wireless and she suspected that this was only because he was busy learning new words.

'It's *Workers' Playtime*!' he shouted, in the exact tones of Bill Gates, the announcer, after only the second time the programme had been broadcast. It was put on at dinner time, coming each time from a 'factory somewhere in England'. You never knew in advance where it would be, or who would be on it, and even the factory workers themselves weren't told until the day. It must be lovely to go to work and find that you'd be entertained in your canteen by someone like Arthur Askey or Max Wall, Ruth thought. The sort of people you'd never expect to see, unless you went to a proper theatre.

She and Sammy were listening to it as they had their dinner a week or so after Dan Hodges had been to Bridge End, when the back door opened and Jane came in. She put a paper bag on the table and looked at Ruth. 'I thought you might like a few eggs. The hens are laying well, we had some to spare.'

'Oh, thank you, Jane. That's nice of you.' The two

316

sisters looked at each other uncertainly. They hadn't spoken since the day of the picnic. Ruth knew that she ought to have gone to the farm to patch things up, but the hurt of being told she couldn't imagine what it must be like to be a mother had bitten deep and she just couldn't bring herself to do it. I will tomorrow, she'd kept telling herself. We can't be bad friends, me and Jane. But tomorrow had never come and now Jane was here.

'Look, Ruth, I'm sorry about what I said,' Jane said, all in a rush. 'I wasn't thinking – I was so upset over Terry, and our Lizzie being in Southampton, and even Ben having to register for war work. But I'd no call to take it out on you.'

'Oh, *Jane*.' Ruth got up and put her arms round her sister. 'You don't have to be sorry. It was me, taking offence where none was intended. I know you didn't mean anything by it.'

'It's just such a *worry*.' Jane sat down at the kitchen table, while Ruth took two cups and saucers from the dresser and moved the kettle to the hot part of the range. 'I mean, the news is so awful. It's spreading everywhere. Those terrible raids still carrying on – they say there's been thousands killed in Liverpool and London, all over again – I mean, there'll be nothing left, *nothing*. And I've just heard that the Germans have started to bomb Crete, and I *know* that's where Terry is. They've got all the men out of Greece itself now, so he must be. That's where they've taken most of them. And then I heard on the news that two transport ships had been sunk. Suppose he was on one of them? I just can't stop thinking about it, Ruth, I can't stop thinking about my Terry, drifting about at sea miles from anywhere . . . I can't *bear* to think about it, but I just can't *stop*.' She buried her head in her hands.

'Oh, *Jane*.' Ruth bent over her again, cradling her sister's head against her breast. 'I don't know what to say. I've been so selfish . . . Look, I'm sure he must be all right, they'd have let you know if he wasn't. And if he's gone to Crete he'll be safe, they wouldn't have taken them there else. They'll bring them back again soon, they're bound to. Our Terry'll be all right.'

The kettle began to whistle and she moved away to make the tea, while Jane found her hanky and sniffed into it. 'I'm sorry, Ruth. I never meant to break down like that. It's just that I've been keeping it bottled up inside of me, and when I started to talk about it . . .'

'I know.' Ruth poured boiling water into the teapot. 'One spoon per person and *none* for the pot,' she said ruefully. 'It'll be a bit weak, but we'll just have to get used to it . . .' She turned and caught Sammy's expression. He was gazing round-eyed at Jane, his face white. 'It's all right, Sammy, there's nothing for you to worry about. It's time you were off to school. Go along now and be a good boy.' She bent to give him a kiss and he scurried out of the door. 'They're on afternoons this week and so am I, so I'll have to be going soon . . . Oh Jane, it *is* good to see you again and I'm really sorry you're so worried over Terry.'

Jane was still dabbing her eyes. 'Thanks, Ruth. Let's talk about something else . . . I heard you've had Sammy's dad here?'

'That's right. Turned up all of a sudden. I think he'd decided to come on the spur of the moment, straight after work.'

'What's he like, then?'

'I don't really know,' Ruth said thoughtfully. 'He's a big man, like Reg Corner only a bit older, of course, and as dark as a gipsy – nothing like Sammy. And yet – well, there was something about him, a sort of look in his eyes, as if he was just a little boy inside, a little boy like Sammy who just needed to be loved . . .'

She stopped and Jane gave her a sharp glance. Ruth hesitated, coloured a little and went on, 'I can't say I took to him. Not the sort of man you'd want to cross. Mind you, I did tell him a few home truths, said little boys needed to be loved and looked after properly, not just fed and washed and sent to school. Trouble is, I think he thought I meant I wanted to take Sammy away from him. I was half afraid he was going to tell Sammy to pack his bags – not that he's got any to pack – and go with him.'

'D'you think he'd do that? Take Sammy back to Portsmouth?'

'Well, he didn't then, did he, and I dare say it'll be another six months before he shows up again, so I don't think we've got too much to worry about . . . It's not as if he seemed all that fond of the boy. They were like two strangers, didn't know what to say to each other.' She poured the tea and put the two cups on the table.

Jane sipped thoughtfully. 'It's a funny situation all round. The mother dying, and the brother being – where is he? Borstal? – and the father hardly wanting to be bothered. It sounds to me as if you've got Sammy for the duration.'

'That's what I think. And I'm not worried about that at all. It's what happens afterwards – when the war's over. Whenever *that's* going to be – some people seem to think it's going to go on for years and years. And there's others that think we're going to be invaded any minute, and have to live under the Germans, like all those poor souls in Poland. What'll happen to Sammy then, Jane? What'll happen to *any* of us?'

'I don't know, Ruth. But what I think is that we've just got to carry on as normal, as best we can. It's no use worrying how long the war's going to take, or whether we're going to be invaded. There's nothing we can do about those things and we've got enough to worry about anyway. What we've got to do is look after our own bit of the country. Keep life going at home. It's what our boys are fighting for, after all.'

They sat quietly for a moment, drinking their tea and

staring into an unimaginable future. Then Ruth stretched out a hand to her sister.

'You're right, Jane. And we've got to stop having silly squabbles. That makes us just as bad as them, in a way. I'm sorry I took offence.'

'And I'm sorry I gave it.' Jane squeezed her hand. 'I know it's been a sadness to you, not having children, and it was unkind of me to say what I did.' She touched the paper bag on the table. 'You'd better put these eggs in a bowl in the larder. I want the bag back for George's sandwiches tomorrow, he's going to be working right up the far fields and won't get home for his dinner.'

'And I've got to get off to the hospital. We're full right up at the moment with some of the poor souls that were bombed in Southampton. They've patched them up and sent them out here to be looked after.'

Ruth got up and found a bowl for the eggs. The two sisters went out of the door and along the lane together, parting at the corner. They paused for a moment.

'You'll let me know the minute you hear any news from Terry, won't you?' Ruth said quietly. 'And if you need me any time, just let me know. You know I'll do anything I can to help.'

Jane nodded. Her eyes were full of fear again and her lips trembled a little. With an obvious effort she bit back her tears and gave a shaky smile.

'I will, Ruthie. And you look after yourself too – you and that little boy. He's a fine little chap – you've done wonders with him since he came.'

He's done wonders for me, too, Ruth thought as she hurried across the green to the Cottage Hospital. I just hope his father doesn't decide to take him back to Portsmouth. I don't know what Silver and me would do without him now and that's the truth.

Chapter Twenty-five

As May drew on the news grew worse and worse. Liverpool had been virtually cut off by a Blitz that lasted for seven days. London, which might have thought itself to have suffered the worst of all during the terrible nights just after Christmas when St Paul's had stood alone in a sea of flames, endured worse still when over five hundred bombers came in one night, leaving the city in a strange, wintry darkness beneath a pall of sullen smoke. Westminster Abbey, the House of Commons, the Tower of London, the British Museum – the list of places hit read almost like a visitors' guidebook. And, as always, there were the thousands of homeless, the misery of people who had emerged from their shelters to find that they had lost everything.

Lizzie, now training in the hospital in Southampton, was almost frantic over Alec. The Atlantic convoys had been suffering heavy casualties, harassed by German U-boats, and she lived in terror of receiving the dreaded telegram that would tell her she was a widow. It was useless for her friends to tell her that there were still plenty of ships that had not been sunk; like her mother, she was sick with fear, both for her husband and her brother. When news came of the sinking of HMS *Hood*, the world's biggest battlecruiser, she was convinced that nobody could be safe, and even the retaliatory sinking of the German *Bismarck* a few days later failed to comfort her.

'Only three men survived, out of nearly fifteen hundred,' she wept when she came home for her half-day and sat in the farm kitchen with her mother hovering anxiously over her. '*Three*. It's so *cruel*. And a great big ship like that – what chance has my Alec got, in his little cargo boat?'

Jane tried to comfort her, but she was full of her own fear for Terry. News had come that the Germans were bombing Crete and, following hard on that, of the invasion by thousands of paratroopers. The RAF had left the island and the soldiers who had already been hurried out of Greece had few weapons left. It looked like another defeat.

'They say the Navy will get them out,' she said to Lizzie. 'I just hope they're in time. And I hope to God our Terry's one that gets away – that's if he's still alive at all.'

They sat together in silence for a few minutes, their arms round each other, clinging to the fear they shared and the hope they strove for. The same thought was in both their minds. So many men were being killed. So many men would never come home. How could they dare to believe – what right did they have even to *hope* – that their own two men, so dearly loved, would be among the lucky ones?

'I know it seems selfish,' Jane said at last, 'but we've got to hope all the same. It's the only way we can carry on.'

Lizzie nodded. 'I know. Keep the home fires burning and all that. But – oh, Mum – it's so hard. It's so horribly, *horribly* hard.'

At the beginning of June, exactly a year after the evacuation of Dunkirk, nearly twenty thousand men were rescued from the beaches of Crete. It was another harsh defeat, made worse by the fact that a further twelve hundred were left behind to be taken prisoner. To the relief of everyone at Bridge End, however, Terry was among the rescued.

He arrived home towards the end of the month, trudging along the lane with his kitbag over his shoulder one sunny afternoon, weary and shaken by his experiences. Sammy, walking home from school with Tim and Keith Budd, was the first to see him and ran shouting with excitement to spread the news.

'It's our Terry!' he yelled, bursting through the kitchen door. 'It's our Terry, he's back, he's home, he's coming down the lane *now*! Auntie Ruth, where are you? Terry's back. *Terry's* back!'

Ruth was upstairs, changing out of her nurse's uniform. She came running down the stairs, still pulling her pink blouse over her head.

'Terry? Are you sure?'

'Yes, it's Terry, it's Terry, we played football, he showed me how to box.' Sammy was hopping from foot to foot in his impatience. 'Come on, Auntie Ruth, or he'll have gone past. Tim and Keith are keeping him for me.'

'You make him sound like half a pound of sausages,' Ruth said, half laughing as she ran out of the door. She paused for a moment, staring at the tall young soldier standing at the gate, talking to the two Budd boys. 'Oh, you're right, it *is* Terry. Oh, it's so good to see you.' She ran forward and flung her arms around him. 'Oh, *Terry* – we didn't think – we weren't sure – your poor mother's been *frantic*.'

'Hello, Auntie Ruth.' He hugged her for a moment, oblivious of the disgusted stares of the Budd brothers. 'I know – we couldn't let anyone know – but we're here now. *I'm* here now. And they've given us all a couple of weeks' leave before we go back to camp, how about that? Not that they've got a camp for us to go back to at the moment, if you want the truth of it,' he added with the wicked grin she remembered so well. 'There's quite a crowd of us.'

'Well, I'm more pleased than I can say to see you back safe and sound,' Ruth declared. 'But you'd better get on home and see your mother straight away. If she hears you've wasted time standing here chewing the rag with me . . .' She turned to Tim and Keith. 'And you two had better get back to the vicarage. Tell Mr Beckett the news. Come along, Sammy.'

'Where?' Sammy asked. He had hold of Terry's hand and didn't look as if he meant to let go. 'Where are we going, Auntie Ruth?'

'Why up to the farm, of course, with Terry. You don't suppose I'm going to go back tamely indoors, not with the best thing that's happened to us since – since . . .' She cast about in her mind for a comparison and her eye fell on Sammy once again. 'The best thing that's happened since you came,' she ended softly. 'That's what this is. So come on, Sammy – I want to see our Jane's face when she sees her wandering boy come home again. It's going to be a picture, I reckon – a real picture.'

Jane's face was, indeed, a picture and Ruth wished she'd had a camera to record it. As she watched the incredulous joy break out she felt a pang of sadness, remembering how she had felt when Jack came home from his trips, and how she would have felt if he had come home that last time, instead of dying thousands of miles from home.

'Well, I'll be getting back home, then,' she said abruptly, overwhelmed by the sudden pain. 'You'll want to be on your own.'

'Don't be so silly!' Jane put out a hand and caught her sleeve. 'You're not going anywhere. We're going to have a celebration, that's what! I'll tell George to kill a chicken – there's one of the old hens hasn't laid for a month, she'll be a bit tough but I'll simmer her nice and slow – and there's plenty of veg in the garden, and I've got some nice bottled fruit for afters. And while we're getting it ready Terry can tell us all about Crete. I knew you were there, you know,' she told her son. 'I knew you must be in Crete, from the news. I just didn't know whether you'd got away or not—' Her mouth began to work suddenly and her voice shook, then broke with tears. 'Oh, Terry – Terry –'

'There, there,' he said, taking her in his arms again. 'It's all right, Mum. Don't cry now. I'm home, large as life and twice as ugly. And I'll tell you what – by this time tomorrow you'll be going on at me to tidy my room, just as if I'd never been away!'

'I won't.' She wept against his khaki serge chest. 'I'll never go on at you again, I'm so glad to have you back. I just wish you didn't have to go away again.'

'Well, we needn't think about that now,' he said, detaching himself. 'Though if I don't get a cup of tea pretty soon, I might think about turning right round this minute. They looked after us properly in camp, you know, cups of tea in bed of a morning and whenever we wanted them during the day. What does a chap have to do to get one around here, that's what I want to know!'

'Oh, you are a fool!' Jane hurried over to the sink and began pumping up water. 'Go and find your father, he should be getting the cows in, and tell him I want that hen. Maybe we'd better have it tomorrow,' she added as Terry went out into the yard. 'It'll take half the evening to cook. But I *would* like to have something special.'

'I've got a tin of ham,' Ruth said suddenly. 'I've had it by me ever since Christmas. We can have that with a bit of lettuce and some of my early tomatoes from the green-house, and a cucumber. And there are a few strawberries coming ripe too.' She got up briskly. 'Sammy and me'll go and get them straight away.'

'And I'll dig up some new potatoes,' Jane nodded. 'A nice salad, that's what we'll have. I'll boil a few eggs as well.' She looked out of the window. George had come out of the milking shed at Terry's call and stood in the doorway, staring unbelievingly before breaking into a shout of joy and running to greet his son. 'I'd begun to think this day would never come,' she said softly. 'I'd almost lost hope, Ruth.'

'It just shows we've never got to lose hope,' Ruth said

staunchly, and drew Sammy close against her side. I know he isn't really my son, she thought, but I'd feel the same way if I thought I'd lost him. I know I'd feel just the same way.

It wasn't quite so bad, Dan Hodges found, to be coming home to an empty house in the summer. With double summertime it was light until gone eleven at night, so however late he worked he still managed to get home in daylight. He could ride his bike to work, which saved on bus fares, and he liked riding home through the streets, trying not to think about the bomb-sites but noticing the gardens people had dug up to plant vegetables 'for victory'. He even began to think of planting a few veg in his own back garden.

Dan had never thought about the garden before. Nora had liked pottering about out there, growing a few flowers, and he'd dug it over for her when she asked him, but she'd barely had time to see her plants grow up. Tommy Vickers had neat rows of lettuces and beans in his garden next door, and a few tomatoes strung between sticks, and Frank Budd had an allotment and could be seen every evening setting off with his fork and spade over his shoulder, but Dan hadn't ever been interested. It was only since he'd been out to Bridge End that he'd started to think about it.

Dan had never cycled out of the city before. His bike had been purely a means of getting about, and he'd never been one for the country. In fact, he couldn't remember ever going beyond Denmead and had only been up on Portsdown Hill with Nora in their courting days. After that there'd never been the time.

The road through Porchester and along the top of the harbour had been busy enough, but once through Fareham the traffic had dwindled and only a few lorries and carts passed him. There were hardly any private cars on the roads anyway – those rich enough to own one couldn't get the petrol, and most of them had been stood up on bricks in garages 'for the duration'. He'd found himself cycling almost alone through leafy lanes, passing through small villages – Catisfield, Park Gate, Swanwick – with plenty of time to look about him.

Trees, he thought. I've never really noticed trees before. The ones in Pompey all looked a bit dusty and their branches had been chopped about, so that in winter they looked like gnarled fists being shaken at the sky. These trees were big and free, reaching up with a thousand twiggy fingers, and they were full of birds. He could hear them singing, almost deafening him as he rode along the quiet roads. Occasionally he spotted a rabbit scuttering into the hedge in front of him, and once an animal he was sure was a fox. Like a dog, but a rich, ginger brown with a thick, furry tail. And only a few minutes after that a squirrel darted across the road and up a tree, where it sat on a branch and chattered at him like a monkey. It was even redder than the fox, and its tail curled up behind it like a fancy dress. He nearly fell off his bike watching it.

Coming back, the dusk had been drawing in and he'd been riding faster, anxious to get home before it was properly dark. The trees had cast a deeper shadow and the birdsong had softened, as if they too were getting settled in their nests for the night. There were still animals to be seen, though – he'd been scared almost out of his life by a deer suddenly breaking cover from the woods and flitting across the road, its hooves barely seeming to touch the ground, and he'd been nearly as startled by an owl drifting past his head as silent as a ghost.

The streets of Portsmouth had seemed dingy and defeated when he arrived back, passing the derelict bomb-sites and the gutted buildings already beginning to grow over with weeds. Out in the country it had all seemed fresh and peaceful, with the cottage gardens full of flowers and vegetables, and the fields green with crops and grass. Out there the air had been full of the music of birds; back in Pompey, all you could hear was sparrows and starlings, squabbling incessantly. For a few minutes, as he drew up at last outside his own house and wheeled his bike up the back garden path, he felt a sudden yearning to be back there, among the trees and the fields with his son. Then he shook himself and sneered.

'Trees!' he'd muttered that evening, bending to unfasten his cycle clips. 'Fields! Pretty flowers! You're going soft, you are, Dan Hodges. Soft in the head. *Pompey*'s where you belong – and Pompey's where you'll stay. And young Sam's coming back too, one of these fine days. See if he isn't!'

All the same, the feeling that he'd experienced as he cycled through the woods and fields that day had stayed with him and he'd found himself noticing those sorts of things more – even in Pompey. In the front gardens he passed on his way to and from work he could see that people were growing little patches of lawn, shrubs and trees – some of them covered in blossom – and flowers of all sorts. Some of them had dug up their lawns and flowerbeds and were growing vegetables instead, as exhorted by all those posters of a boot shoving a spade into the earth. Dig for Victory. It looked nice, he thought.

There were plenty of bombed houses too, derelict sites where roofs had been smashed in and walls lay in a tumble of bricks. In those places the gardens were a wreck too and weeds had already begun to take over.

The allotments, where Frank Budd grew all the vegetables and soft fruit his family could eat, stretched away behind the house, almost like a bit of countryside in themselves. Dan stood at the window in the back bedroom, where the boys had slept, and looked out at them. It gave him a strange, pleasant sort of feeling to look at all that green, those neat, tidy rows of vegetables, those bushes.

You'd get that feeling all the time if you lived in the country, he thought.

There weren't so many raids now, but there were still enough to keep you on your toes. The RAOC camp in Copnor Road was hit in June and some of the military personnel killed. Nobody knew how many – that sort of news wasn't given out. A couple of days later a huge bomb fell in Torrington Road but didn't go off and a big crowd gathered to watch the bomb disposal engineers make it safe. After that it was another twelve days before the next raid, with the city showered by thousands of incendiary bombs and even some parachute mines. For some reason the Germans seemed to be concentrating on Portsdown Hill this time, and the gorse caught fire so that the city seemed to be ringed by a vast barrier of flame.

It was early in July, and Dan had been to the pub, but he hadn't had more than a couple of pints. He hadn't had the heart for more, somehow. He'd kept thinking about Sammy, out there among all those trees, and how Nora would have liked it there as well, and wondering what would have happened if she'd agreed to let him go out there earlier, if she'd been evacuated with him. Would she still have been so ill and died? Surely the country air would have made her better. Doctors didn't know everything, he thought, and if being among trees and fields made a rough bloke like him feel better, what wouldn't it have done for someone like his Nora?

He trudged slowly down March Street. Frank Budd was coming out of the allotment gate and turning towards the alley that led along the back of the houses in April Grove. He stopped and waited.

'Hullo, mate. All right?'

Dan shrugged and nodded. 'Can't grumble, I s'pose. Not more'n anyone else these days, anyway.'

Frank eyed him thoughtfully. 'You all right, on your

own? I know I didn't like it much when Jess was out in the country.'

'Well, it's the way it is, isn't it,' Dan said gruffly. 'We all got to do our bit. I gets a hot dinner down the canteen, and there's fish and chips or the British Restaurant for other times. You don't get a bad feed for tenpence.'

Frank nodded. It sounded a bit bleak to him, but he was lucky enough to have Jess, who had a good hot meal on the table for him when he got home and gave him a plate to heat up at work as well.

'I reckon Hitler's given up on the idea of invading us,' he said. 'He's more interested in Russia now. Going in from all directions, he is, got Stalin by the short hairs. Stupid fool wouldn't listen to Churchill when he told him the Germans were getting ready to invade and now the Red Army's going down like ninepins.'

Dan nodded. 'And it was on the news the other day, Japan's getting ready to join in too. I mean, why? What have they got against us? What are the Jerries to them? I don't understand it.'

'They're just taking the chance,' Frank said. 'While we're all looking the other way they'll nip in – here, that's good, *nip* in – and snatch everything away, like kids. And that means we'll have to fight *them*. Send blokes out there – just as if we hadn't got enough to contend with here.' He sighed and shook his head. 'It's a bad business, Dan, and I don't see where it's ever going to end.'

He shook his head again, shifted his tools on his shoulder and said he'd better get home, Jess would be wondering where he was. He trudged away down the alley, and Dan walked up his garden path and let himself in through the back door. Maybe I'll do a bit of digging at the weekend, he thought. Get in a few spuds or whatever it is you can plant at this time of year. I'll ask Frank about that next time I see him.

He went into the little scullery and shrugged off his

jacket, hanging it on the hook on the back of the staircase door. The house was silent, and even on this July evening it felt cold and unwelcoming. There were dirty dishes piled by the sink – cups he'd used for tea, plates he'd used over and over again for the meals he'd cooked himself, mostly fry-ups of sausages and whatever meat he could get from Alf Hines' butcher's shop, and the frying pan itself, thick with grease. There was a smell of yesterday's fish and chips; he'd dropped some of the newspaper they'd been wrapped in and forgotten to pick it up. A cloud of bluebottles rose from a few bits of batter and burnt chips still scattered among it, and he swore and picked it up to take it to the dustbin.

That too was full and stinking. He'd forgotten for two weeks running to put it down at the bottom of the garden for the dustmen to collect. He took it down there now. If it was by the gate, at least they'd see it next time they came.

As he trod slowly up the garden path, the twilight of the late evening gathering around him, he heard the distant drone of planes and then, rising all around him, the familiar and hated shriek of the air-raid siren. He stopped for a moment, feeling as if the rise and fall of the wail was coming from his own body, that he was screaming himself somewhere deep inside, that the misery of it all was gripping him in a harsh, unrelenting vice.

Why should we have to go through it all over again? he thought bitterly. Why?

It isn't fair. It isn't bloody *fair*.

Chapter Twenty-six

The raid that night was to be the last one over Portsmouth for over a year. It was a pathetic attempt, after the savage destruction of the Blitz, with bombs being dropped mostly in the sea and a shower of thousands of propaganda leaflets falling like confetti over the northern part of the city. Tommy Vickers found one in his garden and showed it to Freda, laughing all over his face.

'*The battle of the Atlantic is being lost* . . . Who do they think they're kidding? Looks to me like they've given up any idea of invading us, anyway. Got more to think about in Russia now. Going for the bigger plums.'

Freda looked at it sadly. 'Pity they didn't give up a bit sooner. Our Molly and Ron might still be alive.'

Tommy put his arm round her. Neither of them had yet got over the death of Tommy's sister and her husband in the January Blitz. It was six months now, but they still missed the couple who had been so close, spending Christmas and Easter with them, and going for days out in the summer. Freda and Molly had been best friends right from their first day in infants' school – in fact, that was how Tommy had come to meet Freda, when she'd come round to their house to play. It left a big gap when you lost someone as close as that.

Still, they'd done their best by young Clifford, offering him a home straight away when the Fratton house had been bombed. They'd got a bed-settee for the front room and it was his to use whenever he was on leave from the Army.

He didn't use it much, being away a lot now, but it was there when he did want it.

Eunice wasn't home much now, either. After the raid when she and Sheila had been at the cinema, both girls had decided to volunteer and now Eunice was in the ATS, in Army uniform just like Clifford – well, maybe not quite like Clifford, Tommy said with an attempt at his old humour, seeing as she wore a skirt – and only able to come home for short leaves. The house felt very empty without her.

'Well,' Tommy said now, 'I think this is a good sign, Free. Dropping these leaflets, I mean, instead of bombs. Either they've given up the idea of an invasion – which means we've *won*, when you come to look at it – or they've just got bigger fish to fry. And one of these days they're going to try a fish that's just a bit too big for them. A *shark*!'

'Like America, you mean,' Freda said. 'But they're never going to come into the war, Tommy. They've as good as said so. Give us all the help we need, but think they're better staying outside it all.'

'When what we really need is soldiers and sailors and airmen.' Tommy nodded. 'Well, we'll see. I don't reckon they'll be able to stay out much longer. What with Japan and China at each other's throats, and Russia getting dragged in – it's turning into a proper world war, Free, and a big country like America won't be *able* to stay out of it. You mark my words.'

Out in the country, it seemed as if there had been some respite. The news overseas was bad, of course, but at home as the long, hot summer drew on, things seemed a bit easier. Coal had been rationed, so the winter wasn't going to be easy, but winter was a few months off yet and you could get logs stacked up in the shed. The hens were laying well and there was good fresh milk from the cows, enough to keep the kiddies rosy-cheeked while the rest went off to the bottling plant for the townspeople. There was still some bacon from the pigs killed last winter and a new lot of piglets fattening up nicely. Even the fact that clothes had been rationed didn't bother the countrywomen as much as those in the towns. They went on wearing their old clothes for every day and saving their best frocks and costumes for Sundays, and didn't worry about fashion.

'I never was one for frills and pleats anyway,' Ruth observed on seeing that these were to be actually against the law, to save on material. 'My Jack always liked me best in more simple things.'

Sammy's closest friend was Muriel, who had the face of a cherub and the disposition of an imp. Sammy, who ought to have known better after the incident with Silver on the picnic, followed her lead in whatever she suggested and was always the one who ended up in trouble. They went fishing for sticklebacks, and he was the one who fell in the stream. They went bird-nesting and he was the one who tumbled out of the tree. They walked over the farmer's fields and it was Sammy who was chased by the bull.

'I don't know if it's him gets Muriel into trouble or the other way about,' Ruth said to Mrs Mudge when she went to the vicarage to apologise for Muriel's frock, torn when they'd got lost in the woods. 'They both look like little angels, with their fair hair and blue eyes – in fact, you could take them for brother and sister – but I don't think there's a child in the village gets into more scrapes than those two.'

'Well, it's all innocence,' Mrs Mudge said comfortably. She was sewing up the frock now, among a pile of other mending. With kiddies in the house there was always a bit of sewing to be done. 'I mean, they never do anything malicious or deliberately naughty. They just don't understand the country yet, that's all.'

'I suppose so. Mind you, my Sammy's turning into a real little country boy all the same. I didn't realise how his voice had changed till I heard Silver trying to sing that song he's taught him – you know, "I've Got Sixpence" – and I realised he talks just like all the other kiddies now. He's almost lost that Portsmouth accent.'

'Has his dad been out to see him again?'

'Two or three times,' Ruth said. 'He's a funny sort of man, Mrs Mudge. I mean, he can be quite nice for a while and then suddenly it's as if a shutter comes down and he looks like thunder. I can't make him out at all. I start off feeling sorry for him, then I think I rather like him and I end up almost frightened!' She hesitated. 'He's talked to me a bit, though. When Sammy's gone to bed. With these long light evenings he's been able to stop quite late before setting off home, and he sits in my front room and has a cup of tea or cocoa. Then he just starts to talk.'

'What about?'

'Oh, everything, really. His wife – seems she died of some blood disease, or so Sammy says. They used to live in a pub that her parents ran, in a really poor part of Portsmouth. Then the father and mother died and the brewery put someone else in, wouldn't let Dan and Nora stay. They were more or less thrown out on to the streets, and them with two little boys too. They found this place to rent in April Grove and D— Mr Hodges has to go five miles to work now, where he used to be able to just walk down the street. Then Mrs Hodges started to get ill and the older boy got into trouble and was sent off to approved school, and eventually the authorities decided Sammy should be evacuated. And a good thing too! Heaven knows what sort of a state he'd be in by now if they'd left him at home with his dad.'

'He sounds a rough sort of man,' Mrs Mudge said, biting off a new length of cotton.

'Well, he is and he isn't. I mean, you can tell he's never known any decent sort of life – I mean, men like him, working in the shipyards don't get paid much – and he

came from a bad area, but there's still something about him
. . . He's quite good-looking, really.'

'Well, Sammy's a nice-looking little boy.'

'Oh, he's not a bit like Sammy. He's as dark as Sammy's
fair. But sometimes – when he sits there and talks about his
Nora – well, he doesn't seem a lot older than Sammy. He
seems just like a little boy, missing his mother.'

Mrs Mudge glanced at her but said nothing. She sewed
for a while in silence, then pushed the basket away. 'There,
that's that lot done – till those boys come in with holes in
their socks and rips in their shirts all over again. Now, how
about a cup of tea?'

'Well, if you're making one,' Ruth said. 'I don't want to
use up your rations. I don't take sugar, anyway.'

Mrs Mudge laughed. 'It wouldn't matter if you did! Do
you know what the vicar's done? He's persuaded those
children to sell him theirs! Halfpenny a spoonful, he gives
them. That man's never properly grown up himself, if you
ask me.'

The two women laughed together. Perhaps men never
did properly grow up. And Dan Hodges, too, Ruth thought
as she walked slowly home a little later – somewhere,
hidden deep behind the dark, unhappy eyes and the wary,
suspicious face, and far below the dark anger that quivered
so unnervingly on the surface, there was a little boy who
had never properly grown up. A little boy who had endured
a poverty-stricken and even, perhaps, a brutal childhood; a
boy who had been sent too early to war and seen sights no
grown man, let alone a youth, should ever see. A boy still
missing his mother, buried in the heart of a man still
missing his wife. A boy, a man, who needed love.

But that's what we all need, isn't it, she thought. We all
need to feel special to someone else. We need to know we're
the most important person in someone else's life.

Dan Hodges is missing his Nora. Sammy's missing his

mum. Lizzie's missing her Alec. And I'm still missing my Jack, in just the same way.

A squirrel ran over the road ahead of her and scampered up a tree. Ruth stopped and put her hand on the rough, sun-warmed trunk and looked up into the thick canopy of leaves. They rustled softly above her and she caught a glimpse of the squirrel, russet-red, as it fled along a branch.

At least we're out in the country, she thought. Sammy and me and all the other little evacuees. At least we can give them a taste of what life can be, some good fresh food and good fresh air, and the trees and fields and the animals to comfort us.

She thought again of Dan Hodges, alone among the dereliction of the blitzed city, and felt tears come to her eyes.

Dan did start to dig his garden over a bit, but the hard, baked earth and the tangle of weeds defeated him. He stood with his old spade in his hand, looking down at the few clods he'd managed to turn over, and felt despondency wash over him.

Tommy Vickers came out into the garden next door and saw him. 'You want to wait till we've had a drop of rain,' he advised, leaning on the wooden fence. 'The ground's like iron now. Going to grow a few veg?'

'Well, I thought about it,' Dan said, 'but I dunno as it's worth it, just for me. I mean, when am I going to cook them? Don't seem much point, really.'

'Still, we all got to do our bit,' Tommy said. 'There's plenty of people haven't got gardens, that would like the chance to grow a few nice fresh spuds and carrots.'

'Well, they'd better come and grow them here, then.' Dan thrust the spade hard against the solid earth and it broke. He swore bitterly and threw the handle away from him. 'Well, that's bloody it! I ain't spending money on a new spade.'

'Come up the pub for a half,' Tommy suggested.

Dan shook his head. 'I'm fed up with the pub. It don't do no good, just sitting there drinking, and I only has a thick head next morning. Tell you the truth, Tom, I'm fed up with everything. When I'm outside I just want to be indoors and when I'm indoors I can't seem to stick that either. I can't stop still. The place is like the municipal dump and I can't seem to make it any better. There's stuff needs washing but the water's never hot. The milk goes sour overnight so I can't have a decent cup of tea in the morning, and if I buys a bit of meat it's always the scrag end because I can't get to the shop at the right time, and it goes bad anyway. It's just not *worth* it. *Nothing's* worth it.'

Dan's voice was close to breaking. Tommy stared at him.

'I could ask Freda to get your meat along with hers,' he suggested. 'I don't suppose she'd mind that. She couldn't take on all the rest of your shopping, mind,' he added quickly.

Dan shook his head. 'I told you, it'll only go off before I has a chance to cook it. Nothing keeps in this heat.' He rubbed a dirty hand across his face and sighed. 'Don't take no notice of me, Tom. I'm just feeling a bit down. I went up to see our Gordon last weekend.'

'Did you? How is he?' Tommy tried to remember how long Gordon had been sent away for. 'When's he coming home?'

'Not for another year at least. He's not so bad. They got a bit of a garden there; the boys look after it themselves. Growing their own veg, that sort of thing. He's been digging spuds. They sell any extra ones round the houses. It's all right, I suppose, but it ain't going to help him get his old job back down the boatyard, is it.'

'Maybe he'll get a different sort of job,' Tommy said. 'The main thing is, will it stop him getting into trouble again?'

Dan snorted. 'Who knows? Our Gordon'll go his own

way. If he can't get a job, he'll make a living some other way. He was talking about it last weekend. Says there's a mint to be made out of the black market, getting stuff cheap and selling it on. I don't reckon this approved school business does the boys any good at all, it just gets them together with bad lots and gives them all ideas.'

Tommy thought Gordon would always find a bad lot to get together with, but he didn't say so. He'd never trusted the older Hodges boy, with his sly eyes and sullen mouth. Had all his father's worst points and none of the good ones, that's what Tommy thought.

'Anyway,' Dan went on, 'if this war goes on much longer he'll be called up. He's nearly sixteen now. He'll come out of that place and go straight into the Army, that's what'll happen to him.'

To Tommy's mind that wouldn't be such a bad thing. Gordon would get proper discipline in the Army and do his bit for his country as well. He didn't wish any harm on the boy, wouldn't like to hear he'd got killed or anything, but being a soldier could be the making of him.

Dan was turning away. 'I'm going in now. Got an early start tomorrow.' He left the broken spade lying where it was. 'I dare say there'll be a warning the minute we gets our heads on the pillow, anyway.'

Tommy watched him go and turned to look at his own garden. The neat rows of vegetables and salads were a sharp contrast to the tangled mess in Dan's. You can understand the poor bloke feeling low, he thought. You've got to keep a garden under control right from the start. Same as the house. Same as kids. Same as everything, really.

Dan Hodges had left it too late. He'd left everything too late.

Chapter Twenty-seven

It seemed scarcely possible that the raids could be over but, as the months wore on through summer, autumn and into winter without the sirens sounding their banshee wail, it began to seem that Hitler really had given up his plan to invade Britain. It didn't mean that you could relax – the war was still being fought as hard as ever overseas – but people did begin to feel a bit better in themselves. The broken nights, the lack of sleep, the hours spent listening to the thunder of bombs or fighting the terrible fires seemed to be over and just being able to stay in bed all night was luxury.

Once again, people began to talk about bringing their children back from the country. This time, however, the authorities were cautious and refused to bring back some of the schools, so that if you wanted your children to get a proper education you had to leave them where they were. A few schools did reopen and Rose Budd, who had been going to classes in people's homes, found herself back in the classroom. She grumbled a bit and talked about leaving now that she was fourteen, but Frank insisted and said that since the school had a room full of typewriters she could learn both typing and shorthand, ready for work. She might even be able to get something in the civil service. That was a good job for a young girl.

Her brothers stayed at Bridge End. Frank wasn't convinced the danger was over – there was talk of Hitler producing a new secret weapon, worse than anything he'd sent over so far. They were both in the primary school, anyway, although Tim should have been going up to the 'big school' now. Unfortunately, some sort of mistake had been made over his age back in January and he'd been left out of the scholarship exams and had to wait another year.

'It's not like it used to be in Portsmouth anyway,' Rose told him when the boys came home for Christmas. 'There's barbed wire all round the beach and they say there's mines under the shingle, to stop an invasion. And they must think Hitler's going to start bombing again, because they're building lots of tunnels under Portsdown Hill for people to go in. You can get a ticket, and have your own bunk and everything. It's like caves and there's room for thousands of people.'

'Coo,' Tim said. 'I wouldn't mind sleeping in a cave.' He kicked disconsolately at the pavement. 'I was hoping there'd be a raid when we were home. I want to get some shrapnel.'

The raids might have lessened, but in all other ways the war had escalated. After the attack on Pearl Harbour early in December the Americans had at last come into active fighting – and with all guns blazing. It truly was a world war now, with no segment of the globe untouched. Almost every day brought news of new countries joining in. Apart from Japan, Britain declared war on three more in one week – Finland (which only two years before she had vowed to protect), Romania and Hungary. China, too, entered the fray, declaring war on Japan, Germany and Italy. The Far East, with its British colonies, was thrust into immediate danger and Hong Kong evacuated after only a few days of fighting. Australia itself was now at risk. In the Mediterranean the British naval fleet was so badly hit that the Admiralty was reported to be considering a complete withdrawal.

The news from Russia was heart-rending. As the Germans laid siege to both Moscow and Leningrad, there were reports of whole cities starving to death and thousands of civilians being butchered by the Nazi forces. That's what it would be like here, Jess Budd thought, and wondered if a few rolls of barbed wire along the beach would really be enough to keep out such a vicious invading force.

The young women of April Grove were joining up as well. Jess' niece Olive Harker, whose husband Derek was in the Army, had gone into the ATS. Her sister Betty was in the Land Army and friendly with a chap who was rumoured to be a pacifist – a 'conchie'. Gladys Shaw, next door to the Budds, had volunteered for the Wrens and young Diane was talking about the WAAFS.

Micky Baxter had been in trouble again. This time he'd broken into Ethel Glaister's house on the other side of the Budds and made a mess of the front room – turned the furniture upside down and all sorts of daft things. He'd been caught pinching things in the cinema too and once again he finished up in court, where he was sentenced to six strokes of the birch and put on probation. Worst of all, he had to go to Sunday School. Micky Baxter hadn't been to Sunday School since he was four and he'd caused so much trouble they'd had to ask Nancy not to send him any more. Having to go now was as much a punishment for the teachers, in their neat Sunday clothes, as it was for him.

Micky was furious. He decided to set up a secret army and found a new den where he and Jimmy Cross, together with some of the other children who were now at home met to collect war souvenirs and discuss how to beat the Germans.

Sammy who, like most of the children at Bridge End, didn't bother too much about the frightening news from other parts of the world, was looking forward to Christmas. He remembered the last one, when he'd hardly known what Christmas could be like, and hugged himself with excitement. There'd be carol singing by starlight, and a tree decorated with coloured glass balls and those special baubles Auntie Ruth had, shaped like trumpets and spears, and a stocking hung on the end of his bed on Christmas Eve. When he woke on Christmas morning it would be full – there'd be one of those puzzles with tiny round balls you had to get into little dents and a rolled-up paper tube you could blow so that it would stick out and squeak at the same time, and maybe a book and a new ball, and in the toe there'd be a handful of nuts and perhaps even an orange. After breakfast they'd go to church and all the rest of the village would be there, and then they'd go up to Auntie Jane's for dinner with all the family.

Only Silver wouldn't be able to go. Auntie Ruth said it was too cold for him to go outside, and he'd have to stay at home by himself all day and miss Christmas. It didn't seem fair.

'He doesn't know it's Christmas,' Ruth said sternly, remembering the last time Sammy had taken Silver outside. 'Parrots don't even know what day of the week it is, let alone anything about Christmas.'

'He does know. He sings "Jingle Bells".'

'Only because I taught him to. He doesn't understand what it means.'

Sammy wasn't convinced. He sat beside the parrot's stand and talked to him about Christmas. Silver listened, his head cocked to one side, and piped up whenever he heard a word he recognised.

'And we'll go out and sing carols and all the stars will shine. It'll be starshine at night, like in Auntie Ruth's poem. And there'll be a chicken for dinner, and a pudding with sixpences in and—'

'I've got sixpence,' Silver butted in. 'Jolly little sixpence. I've got sixpence, to last me all my wife—'

'*Life*,' Sammy corrected him. 'The wife bit comes afterwards. It's "Tuppence to lend, and tuppence to spend, and tuppence to take home to my wife". Anyway, after dinner there'll be washing up and then tea, and then we'll all play games. We'll play jelly race and family coach and land, sea and air, and we'll have a sing-song.'

'Sing a song of sixpence, pocket full of rye.'

'Yes, and then we'll have nuts and apples and things, and then we'll be tired and come home to bed.' Sammy gazed at the parrot, his eyes full of tears. 'And you'll miss it all. It's not fair.'

'So long at the fair,' the parrot agreed mournfully and rubbed his head against Sammy's sleeve.

'*Couldn't* we take him?' Sammy begged. 'If we put him in a box and wrapped it up in blankets? I wouldn't mind carrying him.'

'*No*,' Ruth said, beginning to feel exasperated. 'It's not just the cold, Sammy – the house will be full of people and it's a strange place for Silver; he really wouldn't enjoy it. He's much better off here.' She saw Sammy's woebegone expression and sighed. 'Look, I'll tell you what, you can come back just before tea and see him. You can give him some extra sunflower seeds as a special treat. How will that do?'

It wasn't as good as being able to take Silver with them, but Sammy could see there was no point in any further argument, and he nodded reluctantly. 'I'll come straight after dinner,' he told the parrot, who was now busy cracking open a walnut off Joyce Moore's tree. 'And we'll have a proper sing-song, all to ourselves.'

'Is Sammy's dad coming out to see him at all over Christmas?' Jane asked as she and Ruth rolled pastry for mince pies. The government had allowed extra rations of dried fruit for cakes and puddings, and Jane had made a couple of pots of mincemeat as well, with plenty of chopped apple to bulk it out. You couldn't have Christmas without mince pies.

'I don't know.' Ruth stamped out a dozen rounds with a teacup. 'He sent Sammy a postal order for five shillings, so that's something. And he put in a note, said he might manage to get over on his bike, but he never said anything definite. It's a shame, really, because I think the kiddy would like to see him. It's not that they're all that close or anything, but he's his *dad*, isn't he, and a boy likes to feel his dad thinks something of him.'

'I wonder how they'll get on when the war's over and Sammy goes home,' Jane observed, brushing milk over the tops of the little pies before bending to slide them into the oven. 'It'll be proper strange for Sammy to be back in Portsmouth after all this time. He's settled down so well out here now.'

Ruth didn't speak for a moment. Then she said, 'I hope he doesn't ever go back, Jane. I'd like him to stop out here. In fact, if it could be arranged, I'd like to adopt him.'

Jane straightened up and stared at her. 'Adopt him?'

'Yes. Why not? I haven't got any kiddies of my own, nor ever likely to. I'm getting on for forty, Jane, and I've never seen another man to match up to my Jack.' She hesitated for a moment, then went on quickly, 'Anyway, I don't know that I'd ever want to get married again. But a kiddy – a little boy – well, that's different. And I feel as if Sammy *is* mine. I'm proper fond of him, and to tell you the truth, if he went away now I think it'd break my heart!'

They stared at each other for a moment. Ruth's voice had broken on the last words and she wiped her eyes with the corner of her pinafore.

Jane moved towards her. 'Oh, Ruth. *Ruth*. I knew you were fond of Sammy, but I didn't really realise . . . Look, don't you think you ought to try *not* to be so fond of him? I mean, he's bound to go back eventually, isn't he? His dad'll *want* him back – he'll take it for granted. And the authorities – I mean, how could it be arranged? I don't know anything about how you adopt children.'

'Nor do I,' Ruth said with a little sniff. 'But I can find out – when the time comes. Anyway, at the rate this war's going on it'll be years yet. Mr Hodges isn't going to want

Sammy back before it's all over, it stands to reason. Sammy'll be here for a good while yet and by the time it's all over he'll be able to make up his own mind.'

Jane looked doubtful, but she went back to her pastry and said no more. Perhaps Ruth was right, she thought. It could be years before the problem ever arose, and a lot could happen before that.

Especially in wartime.

While Sammy was looking forward to carol singing by starlight and hanging up his stocking, Dan Hodges was sitting in the pub, trying to enjoy a Christmas drink with a few mates. The landlord had put up a few paper chains, a bit like the ones Sammy and Nora had made a couple of years back, and as Dan stared at them he felt the tears gather thick in his throat and stumbled to his feet.

'Not going already, Dan, are you?' one of his workmates said. 'You haven't stood your round yet.'

'Bugger my round.' Dan felt in his pocket and dragged out a few coins. He threw them on the bar. 'Here, get it out of that. I've had enough.'

The other stared at him. 'Dan Hodges had enough? Never thought I'd live to see the day!' There was a roar of laughter, but Dan wasn't listening. He was halfway out of the door, blundering past the heavy blackout curtain into the cold night air. With the thick, smoky atmosphere behind him, his head cleared a little and he stood for a moment gazing up at the stars.

He'd found a Christmas card from Sammy on the doormat when he got home from work the night before. It was another picture Sammy had drawn himself, of shep-herds sitting on a hillside surrounded by woolly sheep, under a black sky studded with white blotches that were presumably meant to be stars. In one corner was the huge white globe of the moon and there appeared to be a creature half-bird, half-man hanging from it. The angel Gabriel,

Dan supposed. Still, it was a cheerful sight and looked all right on the mantelpiece. It was the only sign in the room that Christmas was happening at all.

Christmas. Nora had always tried to make something of it, for the boys' sake. Decorated the place up a bit, got a tree from the market in Charlotte Street, got a few presents together. She'd knitted them all gloves, or jumpers, things they needed. Dan was still wearing the socks she'd made him, good thick socks they were too, just what he wanted for these bitter winters.

She'd bought them things as well, when she had the money: that red ball she'd given Sammy the last Christmas she was here; a toy gun she'd got for Gordon once, real as you like. He'd played cowboys and Indians for months with that gun, always the cowboy, of course. Nobody could say you had to be an Indian if you had a gun like that.

There'd been nothing like that this Christmas. All he'd managed to do was send both the boys a five-bob postal order. He'd thought about having them home – there'd been a chance Gordon could have been let home for two or three days – but the daft young fool had got in a fight a week or so ago and done a bit of damage, and that had put a stop to any hope of time off. And what sort of a Christmas could he give young Sam, all on his own, with not even a paper chain to cheer the place up?

Dan walked slowly down March Street. In almost every house people were getting ready for Christmas. Nippers were being brought home from the countryside to be with their families again, just for a few days. Because of the blackout, he couldn't see into the lighted rooms, but he knew they'd be hanging up paper chains and putting coloured lights on trees – even if you didn't turn them on because of the electricity, they'd still look pretty – and stringing Christmas cards over the mantelpiece. And the women would be making puddings and mince pies – Freda Vickers had told him there was an extra allowance of dried fruit and asked if he'd like her to make him a cake or a pudding along with her own. He'd shrugged, but said yes, she might as well, even though he knew he'd be eating it on his own, and a couple of days ago she'd brought him in a nice fruit cake – not iced, of course, but he wasn't bothered about that. He'd had a slice already. There didn't seem to be much point in keeping it for Christmas.

Dan went up the back garden path, past the Anderson shelter and the abandoned tumble of cold, half-dug earth, and the tangle of dead vegetation. He opened the back door and went into the scullery. It seemed even colder inside than out. He struck a match to light the gas and then went on into the living room to do the same there. The yellow light flickered and steadied, dulled by the film of grime on the glass shades. There was no need to worry about the blackout – Dan went to work before it was light and came home after dark, and only took down the shades at weekends, if then.

He looked around the room, at the two grubby, sagging armchairs, the scratched and battered table with its four wooden chairs. Once, there'd been a family of four sitting round it for meals; now, only one place was used and the plates Dan had been eating from for the past four days were still there, greasy and unappetising. The room was icy, the fireplace still full of ashes from the fire he'd lit last Sunday.

'Blimey,' he said, staring at it all. 'It's a bloody slum, that's what it is. A bloody slum.'

He dropped into one of the chairs. The place didn't look as if it had been touched for years. Dan and Nora had certainly never done any redecorating, and the wallpaper was dull and yellowed, with smoke stains where the gaslight had guttered and blotches where food had got spattered or someone had leant against the wall, by the door. There'd been a dog here too once, a biggish one – you could tell by the marks about two feet above the floor.

It hadn't been much better when they'd moved in, but

Nora had at least tried to keep it clean, until she got too poorly to do it. Even then, she'd got the boys to do a bit. Gordon hadn't been much help, but young Sam had tried, little as he was. He'd always tried to please his mother.

Dan leant forward and rested his head in his hands. The house had never seemed so empty, so cold. It wanted someone in it. It wanted a family again, a Christmas, with decorations and a bit of a tree and some presents. It wanted Sammy.

'I'm going to get him,' he said aloud. 'Buggered if I'm not. I'm going to clean this place up a bit, and get those paper chains out what he and Nora made a couple of years back, and get Alf Hines to put by a chicken for me, and I'm going to get him. He's going to spend Christmas here with me. He's coming back to April Grove where he belongs.'

Chapter Twenty-eight

Christmas Eve came in a flurry of snow showers. No real snow had fallen yet, although it was very cold, and as the afternoon light began to fade the clouds drifted away, leaving a bright, clear sky. There would be a moon later, so the carols this year would be by the light of the moon rather than that of the stars.

'When will it be time to go carol singing?' Sammy asked for about the twentieth time as he and Ruth put up the last of the paper chains.

'When it's dark, after tea. You know that, Sammy, from last year.'

'It seems a long time to wait.' He sighed, looking out of the window.

'It'll soon come.' She looked down at him as she pinned up the last paper chain. He was nine now and beginning to grow, but he still had an endearing 'little boy' roundness to his face, and his fair curls and blue eyes had won a good many hearts around the village. They also, she knew, won him a few taunts of 'cissy' and 'baby-face' from some of the other children, but Terry's boxing lessons had been effective and Sammy was now well able to defend himself. He had Tim Budd on his side as well and Tim was a match for any boy in the village, even Brian Collins.

Ruth got down from the kitchen chair she'd been standing on. She had already filled Sammy's stocking – the twin to the one he'd be hanging up empty that night – and wrapped up her present to him. It was a game of 'Sorry' that she'd found in the cupboard where she kept Jack's things – a cupboard she went to increasingly these days, looking for bits and pieces to give Sammy – and a new book, *Swallows and Amazons*. Jane had told her that Ben had read it when he was nine or ten and said he was sure Sammy would enjoy it too.

'Well,' she said, glancing at the clock, 'I think we could have a cup of tea now, don't you? I've just got a jelly to make, ready to take to Auntie Jane's for tea tomorrow, and then I think we're almost ready—'

Her words were drowned by a sudden heavy knocking on the back door. Ruth jumped, startled, and looked at Sammy. 'Whoever can that be? I hope it's not bad news about Terry. Or Alec – or Ben . . .'

After the evacuation from Crete, Terry had gone back to Africa, where he was in the desert fighting against Rommel's troops. Alec was at sea yet again, after getting home only twice during the entire summer, and Ben had been called up. He'd gone into the Air Force and, to everyone's surprise, become a pilot. He was stationed somewhere in Sussex and, like the others, couldn't get home for Christmas. The gathering would be smaller than ever this year, Ruth thought, with George the only man in the family left.

She hurried to open the door, her heart in her mouth, fully expecting to see a telegram boy in his dark-blue uniform, a brown envelope in his hand and his red bike propped against the fence. Instead, she found herself tilting her head to stare into the dark eyes of Dan Hodges.

Ruth's heart leapt. They stared at each other for a moment, then Dan's brows drew together and the swift uprush of unexpected emotion sank away, leaving her dismayed and apprehensive. She lifted one hand to her mouth.

'*Dad!*' Sammy was behind her, his voice high with excitement. Still bemused, she stood back as he pushed past her and clasped his father's arm. Dan looked down and she saw the expressions chase across his face. Surprise – uncertainty – and, finally, a faint softening of the hard features, a glimmer of emotion in the dark-brown eyes.

'Dad, have you come to spend Christmas? We're going carol singing as soon as it's dark. There'll be mince pies and *everything*. I've got a stocking to hang up. I'm going to get *presents*.'

Dan looked down at his son but said nothing. He laid his gloved hand on the boy's head and spoke to Ruth.

'I come to take him home.'

Ruth stared at him. 'Take him *home*? But – but it's *Christmas*!'

'Well, I know that, don't I? That's why I come. Place for a nipper at Christmas is in his own home, with his own dad. I rode me bike out –' he indicated the battered black cycle leaning on the fence '– and we're going back on the train. There's one in forty minutes, so the bloke at the station told me. I can put me bike in the guard's van.'

'But –' Ruth could find nothing to say. Sammy had dropped back a little and was staring from one to the other, his eyes wide and a little frightened. She gestured helplessly. 'You'd better come in. You must be frozen after that ride. I – I was just making a cup of tea.'

'I don't want to take advantage,' he said harshly, following her in. 'If you'll just put the boy's bits and bobs together – I wouldn't say no to a cuppa, all the same,' he conceded, dropping his gloves and scarf on the table. 'It's freezing brass monkeys out there, if you'll pardon the expression. I'm shrammed.'

Ruth slid the kettle over on the range and took some cups down from the dresser. She was glad of the occupation, to give her time to get over the shock of Dan's sudden appearance. Did he really mean to take Sammy back to Portsmouth now – tonight? On Christmas Eve, when the child had been looking forward so much to the carol singing and the party? Didn't he realise how much a part of the family Sammy had become? She looked at Silver, sitting on his perch in the corner, as if for help, but the parrot was quiet for once and merely stared back at her.

The kettle began to whistle. Ruth spooned tea into the pot, adding one extra in spite of Lord Woolton's advice, and went to the larder to get the milk. It looked fresh and rich as she poured it into the cups, not like that thin stuff she'd heard they got in the towns. It was milk like that, and butter, and eggs straight from the hens, that Sammy needed. Look how it had built him up. Why he was twice the kiddy he'd been when he first arrived.

'You don't really mean to take Sammy home now, do you?' she asked, putting the cups of tea on the table. 'Would you like something to eat? I've made some bread, fresh, and there's some blackberry and apple jam, you'd be welcome to a slice.'

Dan hesitated. 'I don't want to take your rations.'

'It's all right,' Ruth said quietly. 'You've had a long ride. Here.' She set the loaf, freshly baked that morning, on the table, and put the dish of farm butter and the pot of jam beside it. 'Sammy picked the blackberries,' she added. 'Didn't you, Sammy?'

'Yes,' he said. He sounded subdued after his first excited welcome – the most exuberant Ruth had ever seen – and sat at the table beside his father, watching as Dan spread the bread Ruth had given him. 'In September. They grow wild on the hedges. They're free.'

'So are the apples,' Ruth added. 'They come from my sister's orchard. It's just the sugar that's a problem, but the government did let us have extra for making jam, so we all made as much as we could.'

He's not interested in all that, she told herself. He's hungry and thirsty, and glad of what he can get, but he hasn't come all this way to hear about jam-making. He's come for Sammy. He's taking Sammy away for Christmas.

He's taking Sammy away from *me*.

'You don't really want to take Sammy back to Portsmouth, do you?' she asked again, after a moment, during which Dan ate as if he were famished. 'We'd got things all planned. We're going carol singing this evening and to dinner with my sister tomorrow. There's church as well, and games – he enjoyed it so much last year,' she added pleadingly, seeing no change in Dan's dark face. 'And this year – why, he's almost like one of the family. In fact, I was going to ask you—' She broke off abruptly, but not before Dan, raising his eyes suddenly, had caught her expression. Their eyes met and she caught her breath. He knows what I was going to say, she thought. He knows I want to keep Sammy here – not just for Christmas, but for always.

There was a long silence. Dan chewed his bread and kept his eyes fixed on her face. He swallowed and drank some tea. Then he got to his feet. 'Come on, Sam. Pack up what you got to take with you. We got a train to catch.'

Ruth was on her feet too. 'Mr Hodges – *Dan* – please! He's been looking forward to it so much. We've been making plans for weeks. Look at all these decorations.' She waved her hand about the room, bright with paper chains and firelight. 'Sammy made all these himself. He's been so happy—'

'Well, he can be happy with me. We got decorations too, ones he made with his mother. I've put 'em up, all ready for him. I'm his father, Mrs Purslow, and I've still got a home for him to come to. Where else should a boy be at Christmas but in his own home, eh? Tell me that. And I want him there. I missed enough, this past year, what with my other boy being away and their mother passing on. I don't want to miss no more. I wants my boy with me for Christmas, and that's it and all about it.' He turned again to Sammy. 'Go on. Go and get your stuff together.'

Sammy looked from one to the other. 'Auntie Ruth . . .'

'Go on, Sammy,' she said quietly. 'Go and do as your

father says. If he wants you to go home for Christmas you must go. It's for him to say.'

'But – the carol singing—'

Dan turned on him. 'Bugger the carol singing! You can sing carols in the train. You're coming with me, d'you hear? Now go and do as you're told, or you'll feel the flat of my hand!'

Sammy turned and scurried up the stairs. Ruth, horrified, stood by the table, one hand held out as if to stop Dan Hodges in his tracks. 'Mr Hodges! You can't—'

'I can and you know I can.' He paused, steadying himself, and looked at her. 'Look, I'm not saying you ain't been good to him, Mrs Purslow, and I'm not saying he ain't had a good billet here with you. But he's *my* boy, when all's said and done, and I got me rights.'

'Of course you have.' Ruth put a hand to her forehead. 'Of *course* you have. It's just that – if only you'd let me know sooner. If only *Sammy* had known . . . You will bring him back, won't you?' she asked, filled with sudden dread. 'Once Christmas is over – you will let him come back?'

There was a silence. Then Dan shrugged.

'Have, to, I suppose, won't I? The war don't look too good and we're busy in the yard. Bloody ships being sunk, left, right and centre. All the same, it looks like the bombing's over and that's the reason he's here.' He lifted his cup again and drained it. 'Ta for the tea, Mrs Purslow, and I'm sorry about this but Sammy *is* my boy and it's only right we should be together at Christmas.'

'I know.' She stood miserably by the table, not knowing what to say next. Then a thought struck her. 'His presents! His *stocking*! Look, you can take them with you, can't you? I'll put them in a bag. Only don't let him see them, will you? Look, there's this one empty, for him to hang up tonight, and this one full, for him to find in the morning. And here's his present – a game and a book. And – and –' she cast about wildly for something else to make Sammy's

355

Christmas a happy one '– here, take the rest of this loaf, and the butter and jam – and there's some cakes in this tin, you can have those – and this packet of jelly, good job I hadn't already made it.' She was thrusting the things into a shopping bag as she spoke. She grabbed some fruit from the bowl on the dresser, a few Cox's pippins, a couple of pears, an orange she'd been saving for Boxing Day. As she pushed them into the bag, Sammy came down the stairs, not clattering as he usually did, but quietly, as if even his boots were reluctant to leave. He dragged a couple of brown-paper bags behind him, bulging with his few clothes, hastily rolled into untidy balls.

He stood and looked at her. 'Auntie Ruth . . .'

'It's all right,' she said, bending quickly to kiss him. 'It's all right, Sammy, my love. You go with your dad and have a nice time, and we'll have another party when you come home. I – I'll think of you, when we're singing carols.' She straightened and looked at him, her eyes full of tears. 'Oh, *Sammy*!'

'Auntie Ruth!' He flung his arms round her waist, burying his head against her. 'Auntie Ruth, I don't want to go to Portsmouth! I want to stay here with you. Tell him I don't have to go! Tell him I don't!'

Ruth bit her lips hard. She looked up in dismay and saw Dan's expression tighten. She unravelled Sammy's fingers from her pinafore and clasped his hands, looking intently into his tearful face.

'I'm sorry, Sammy, but he's your dad and if he says you must go, you have to do it. You'll be back here in a few days, I promise. Now, you go with him, and be a good boy and have a happy Christmas.'

He looked at her as if he had been struck. Then, turning away, he trailed slowly towards the back door and out into the garden.

Dan gave her a curt nod. His face was shuttered. He wound his scarf round his neck again and picked up his gloves. 'I'll say goodbye, then. I'm sorry if this comes a bit sudden, Mrs Purslow. It ain't been easy . . .' He followed Sammy out into the gathering dusk, collecting his bike from the fence as he went.

Ruth stood in the doorway and watched them go, the big man and the small, hunched boy. The wind seemed colder than ever and there was cloud appearing again in the sky. Perhaps there wouldn't be a moon after all.

The carol singing had lost its appeal. She would go, but she wouldn't feel the same joy in it. She wouldn't see Sammy's picture of shepherds, washing their flocks by night, or hear his clear little voice singing 'Once in Royal David's City'. She wouldn't tuck him up in his bed, or see him hang up his stocking, or kiss him goodnight. She wouldn't hear his excited cries in the morning as he woke to the lumpiness of a filled stocking, or see his eyes grow huge as he discovered a silver threepenny bit in his helping of Christmas pudding.

The two figures had disappeared. She went back into the cottage and closed the door. It was cold inside, from the air she had let in, and colder still because Sammy was no longer there.

Would he really come back? She'd talked to him as if he would, as if they'd have another party for him to make up for the Christmas he'd missed. But there had been something in Dan's eyes, in his voice, that filled her with foreboding.

The man was lonely, she thought. He'd lost his wife and both his boys, and he was desperately lonely. He wanted someone back in his home, in his life, and Sammy was the only one. Once he'd got him there, he wouldn't let him go.

Poor Dan, she thought sadly. Poor, poor Dan.

'Oh, Silver,' she said in a voice full of tears, 'do you think we're ever going to see our Sammy again?'

Silver stood on one leg on his perch and scratched his head with the other. For once, he seemed lost for words and his beak remained closed as she scratched his head. She sighed and went to the cupboard to fetch her coat.

Silver didn't speak until she was just going out of the front door. She heard his voice as she stood for a moment letting her eyes get used to the darkness.

'Sod the little bugger,' she heard, and then, in Sammy's own voice, half Portsmouth, half country, 'Sam, Sam, shine a light. Ain't you playing out tonight?'

Chapter Twenty-nine

It seemed a long, exhausting journey back to Portsmouth.

Sammy, still bewildered by the sudden change in events, trotted beside his father along the lane to the little station. There was only one more train until after Christmas and the only other person waiting was an old man who lived some way out of the village. Sammy had seen him once or twice but never spoken to him.

'You one of the 'vacuees?'

Sammy glanced at his father, who nodded. 'My boy is. I'm taking him home for Christmas.'

The old man nodded. He had a small cardboard suitcase, its corners fraying and broken, and he was wearing a long mackintosh and had a scarf wound several times round his thin neck. Bushy eyebrows showed under his flat cap and there was hair sprouting from his nostrils. He stared down at Sammy and Sammy backed away a little.

'Right thing too. Nippers oughter be in their own places at Christmas. Us Bridge Enders don't want 'em under our feet then. Don't want 'em at all, tell the truth. Glad to see the back of 'em.'

'The widow woman Sammy was with seemed all right,' Dan said doubtfully. 'She didn't want him to come away.'

'Ah, uses 'em like slaves, some of 'em does,' the old man stated. He peered at Sammy. 'Bet she made yer work, eh? Gave yer lots of jobs to do about the place?'

'Yes, but—'

'There you are, see,' the old man said to Dan. 'Like slaves.'

359

There was a silence. Sammy wanted to say that the jobs Auntie Ruth gave him to do weren't nasty ones, they were just little jobs like his own mother would have given him. Brushing out the fireplace, making his own bed, sweeping snow off the path during the winter – that kind of thing. And cleaning out Silver's cage, which he'd actually *asked* to do. He wasn't a slave.

He didn't say these things because he knew that nobody would listen to him. The old man would talk him down, contradicting all he said, even if it contradicted what he himself had said a minute before. And Dad didn't really want to hear. He just wanted to get home.

And suppose the old man was right. Suppose Auntie Ruth *didn't* really want him . . .

The train chuffed along the track and they all got on. It was full of people going home for Christmas and by the time Dan had got his bike into the guard's van it was impossible to find a seat. They propped themselves in the corridor and watched the countryside pass by. It was dark by now, and the train was lit by only a few very dim, pale blue lights. It didn't seem Christmassy at all, apart from some of the other passengers being drunk.

Sammy stared hopelessly out of the window and felt a huge well of tears form inside him. By now, he should have been setting out with Auntie Ruth for the carol singing. Lizzie would be there, and Auntie Jane and Uncle George, and all the other people he'd grown to know and feel at home with. They would have gone round all the houses, singing about shepherds and kings and little babies, and he would have felt a warm glow spreading from his middle and all over him, right down to his fingers and toes. He'd been feeling it for weeks, in anticipation, and tonight it would have been the real thing.

And then there would have been the stocking. He'd been looking forward to the moment when he could hang it at the end of his bed. He knew he was a bit old for a stocking, because he didn't really believe in Father Christmas any more – he was nine, after all – but he liked having it and Auntie Ruth seemed to like it too. And there was no doubt that it did make Christmas day specially exciting, to wake up and find the stocking all lumpy and full at the end of his bed.

Best of all would be the party at Auntie Jane's. It would go on all day, starting with dinner after church, and not finish until nearly bedtime, after all the games and the sing-song. He and Auntie Ruth would walk sleepily home, warm with contentment, and the only fly in the ointment would be that Silver hadn't been there to share it all. Sammy still didn't think that was fair.

Now he would be even worse off than Silver, because he wasn't going to be there at all. He was going to be in the cold, empty little house in April Grove, with no one there but his father. Not Gordon. Not his mother. No decorations, no stocking, no Christmas dinner, no games. He bit his lip hard to stop the tears filling his eyes.

Dan was already wishing he hadn't come. The nipper didn't want to come home, that was obvious. He'd been looking forward to Christmas with that Ruth Purslow. And you couldn't really blame him. She was a really nice woman, he knew that, the sort of woman anyone would be glad to come home to. It was a home you'd be pleased to come to, as well – warm and comfortable, all cleaned up and bright with all those paper chains and that little tree in the corner. And the stocking she'd pushed into the bag he was carrying, along with the present wrapped up in brown paper – that showed she thought a lot of the boy and meant to give him a good time. Despite the old man's words, Dan knew she didn't treat Sammy like a slave – more like her own kid.

But that was just the point, wasn't it? She was treating him like her own kid – and he wasn't. He was *Dan*'s kid. His place was with his dad, not with strangers. Like it or not, he was a Pompey boy and nothing was ever going to change that.

It was time he came home for a bit, Dan thought. Time he remembered who he was and where he'd come from – where he was going to have to go back to, once all this was over. Nice and kind as Ruth Purslow might be, she wasn't his family and Bridge End wasn't his place. Pompey was his place, same as it was Dan's, and that was it and all about it.

Dan looked out of the window at the silvery darkness of the woods and fields, and sighed. Cold though it was, he'd liked riding out through the countryside, and it had been warm and welcoming in the little cottage. He could have settled down there for the evening easy as a wink – for the whole Christmas. And that Ruth Purslow, she was the sort of woman who'd make you feel at home, who'd look after you and make life seem – well, a bit more worth living. Like his Nora had, when she was young and well.

I'm fed up with Pompey, he thought suddenly. Fed up with the shipyard, and the streets, and the bombs, and the fires, and the sheer bloody *misery* of it all. I'm fed up with being on my own. I'm fed up with feeling so bloody *hopeless*.

He looked at Sammy again. Maybe I didn't ought to have brought him away, he thought, but he's all I got. Gordon's never coming home again. He'll go in the Forces straight from that approved school and God knows what he'll do then, but he'll never come home again, not to live. Sam's all I got left now, all I got to remind me of my Nora. I got to keep a hold on him. I *got* to.

The train steamed slowly through the countryside, stopping at all the small stations along the way. People got off, shouting eagerly to those who had come to meet them. A few people got on. The atmosphere was cheerful and excited, as all the passengers looked forward to being with their families for Christmas.

When the train arrived at Hilsea, Dan gathered his bags

together and told Sammy to stand by them on the platform while he went to get his bike out of the guard's van. It took him a few minutes to extract it from the other bikes and luggage that had been piled on top of it and the guard, who was anxious to get to his own home, barked at him to hurry up, for Gawd's sake. Dan, feeling all his misery and frustration well up inside like a ball of smouldering fire, turned on him.

'Don't you bloody tell me to hurry up! It's not my bleeding fault there's all this luggage, is it? It wouldn't do you any harm to lend a flaming hand, if you're in all that much of a hurry to get rid of us.'

The guard flushed with anger. He jerked at the handlebars of Dan's bike. There was a crashing sound, and half the luggage in the van fell over and tumbled together in a tangled heap. The guard swore.

'And a happy Christmas to you too, mate!' Dan snarled, wrenching his bike free and hurling it out on to the platform. 'Come on, Sam!' he shouted to the small, lonely figure standing at the far end. 'Get a move on. We're going home!'

It wasn't far from Hilsea halt to April Grove, but it was made more difficult by the damage that had been done to Dan's bike by its fight with the other luggage in the guard's van. It was too dark by now to see what was wrong, but there was obviously some obstruction somewhere that made it hard to push.

'You'd better carry these bags while I push the bike,' Dan said, handing Sammy the brown-paper carrier bags he had packed. There was still the shopping bag Ruth had given him, containing the stocking and present, and he hung this on the handlebars. It made the bike all the harder to control and that made his temper all the worse.

Together they trailed through the dark streets to September Street and down October Street to April Grove.

Every house was securely blacked out. Even Granny Kinch's house, which stood right in the middle of the terrace and looked directly up October Street, was dark, the door where she stood all day watching what went on firmly shut. Sammy wondered if Micky Baxter was inside or if he was roaming the streets, getting into trouble, even on Christmas Eve. He looked towards the cul-de-sac end where the Budds lived. Tim and Keith had come home too and would be in there with their mum and dad and sisters Rose and little Maureen. He bet they'd be having a good time.

Next door to number 2 the Vickers would be settling down to the celebrations as well. Sammy had heard that Clifford's mum and dad had both been killed in the Blitz, not long after Cliff had gone off to join the Army. He wondered if Clifford was there, or if he was fighting somewhere – in Africa, perhaps, like Terry, or in Italy.

He followed his father into the alley and up the garden path. Dan pushed his bike into the coalshed and went straight into the lavatory, not even stopping to open the back door so that Sammy could go inside. Sammy, who wanted the lavatory too, waited anxiously for his father to come out.

At last they were in the scullery. Dan lit the gas and Sammy looked around.

He hadn't been home for nearly eighteen months. When he left it had been a mess of clutter, old newspapers, dirty plates on the table, dirty clothes piled in one corner, the light dim from the dirty gas lamp. The cold linoleum floor had been greasy and smeared with dirt tramped in from outside, and the fireplace had been full of stale ash.

He had somehow expected it to be the same now but, to his surprise, it looked a bit better. Dan had obviously made some attempt to tidy it up and even done a bit of cleaning. The clutter had mostly been removed, the floor had been washed over, although there were still a few smeary patches, and the fire was laid, ready to be lit. The table had been spread with fresh newspaper to act as a tablecloth and the only unwashed dishes were a cup and plate from Dan's meal that morning.

He had even made an effort to decorate the place for Christmas. He'd found the old paper chains that Sammy and Nora had made together and hung them round the walls in a single string. He'd put a couple of brown-paper parcels, tied with string, on the shelf, and in the middle of the table there was a cake, with a plaster Father Christmas on it that Nora had bought years ago. The plaster was chipped now, making the red coat look a bit ragged, but you could still see who it was meant to be.

Sammy stood in the doorway and gazed around. There was no tree, and he knew there would be no carol singing and no big party. He felt again the bitter disappointment of all he was missing, but he could see that his father had really tried and knew that he mustn't see the tears that were so close. He bit his lip hard and gave Dan a wobbly grin.

'Happy Christmas, Dad,' he said in a small, shaky voice, and put the carrier bags on the table. 'Happy Christmas.'

'It just doesn't seem like Christmas now, without Sammy,' Jane said sadly. 'It's so queer, because we're missing all the others too – Terry, Ben and Alec – and yet it's Sammy we seem to be missing most. It's because he's the only kiddy, I suppose. Christmas just isn't Christmas without kiddies.'

'It's because we knew the others were going to be away,' Lizzie said. 'I can't say I'm missing Sammy more than Alec, because I'm not – not more than Ben or Terry, either. I miss them all. It's just awful not having them here, and worrying about what's happening to them . . . But we were expecting to have Sammy, to keep us bright, and now he's not here it seems hardly worth having Christmas at all.'

Ruth said nothing. They were at the table, having finished their Christmas dinner. It was just the four of them

– George and Jane, Ruth and Lizzie. It didn't seem like a Christmas dinner at all, not when you remembered all the past Christmases, with the table crammed with people, all talking and laughing at once. The jokes, the silly remarks, the laughter. The games afterwards, the songs, the stories round the fire . . . How could you do all that with only four people? Now, it seemed to have lost all its colour.

They listened to the King's speech. His hesitant voice sounded as if he too was having difficulty in finding something to be cheerful about. Of course, it was good that America was now coming into the war, but so many other countries had joined in as well that it was hard to know if there'd be any real advantage. There was fighting everywhere and the Yanks were bound to look after their own interests first. With the Japs to go after, would they even bother coming to Europe?

The King didn't say all that, but it was there, somehow, in the doubtful tones of his voice. It wasn't like the other year, when he'd talked about standing at the gate of the year and putting his hand into the hand of God. That had been poetic, and encouraging too. Now, it seemed that all they had to look forward to was more and more fighting. Years and years of it, and how could it ever come to a proper end, with nearly every country in the world at each other's throats?

'Let's clear up and have a game of something,' Jane said at last. 'We'll get one of the board games out – Ludo, or Monopoly. We've got to do *something*.'

'I might go back early,' Ruth said. 'I promised Sammy I'd go and see to Silver around teatime anyway. He was worried stiff the bird would be lonely, being left by himself on Christmas Day.'

'Oh, you can't do that,' Jane protested. 'You'll be all on your own Christmas evening. Pop over and give him his tea or whatever he has, and then come back here again. We can at least have the evening together. We'll play a few records.'

'I'll walk down with you,' Lizzie said. 'We'll have a chat to Silver and then come back. I'm not spending my day off sitting here with just Mum and Dad!'

'Thanks very much,' Jane said tartly, but she gave her daughter an affectionate nudge. 'Yes, you go down with your auntie. Nobody ought to be on their own on Christmas Day.'

'Your mum's right,' Ruth said sadly as they walked down the lane. 'People shouldn't be on their own today. And it's right that Sammy should be with his own dad. But I can't help missing him all the same.' She drew in a shaky sigh. 'If only I could be sure he's having a good time . . .'

'Surely his dad wouldn't have come all this way on his bike to fetch him if he hadn't meant to give him a good time,' Lizzie said. 'He's not a bad sort of chap, is he?'

'Well, I don't think he is, really. He just gives the impression – and being so big, he's a bit – well, intimidating. But you know he's been here a time or two now, and he's had a meal with me and Sammy once or twice, and when he settles in a bit you can see quite a different sort of man. I think he's had a hard life and it's made him seem hard too. And it's different being in Portsmouth now, with all the bombing. Everyone's a bit different these days.'

The cottage seemed strangely empty, with no one in it but the parrot. Even though the range was still warm and the room bright with colour, the fact that it was Christmas Day and there was no family sitting around, no noise and laughter made it seem unreal. Silver too seemed subdued, as if he knew there was something wrong, and he only mustered the energy to swear once all the time Ruth and Lizzie were with him.

'I tell you what I ought to have done,' Ruth said as they walked back. 'I ought to have asked Dan Hodges to stop with us instead of taking Sammy back to Portsmouth. Then they could both have had a good Christmas and Sammy would still have been here.'

'Yes, but he wouldn't necessarily have stopped here. I expect he'd already made arrangements at home.' Lizzie glanced at her aunt. 'You're not frightened he won't bring Sammy back, are you?'

'No, of course not!' Ruth exclaimed quickly, a sharp edge to her voice. Then she hesitated and said more quietly, 'Well, perhaps I am, a bit. It was so funny, the way he came out without letting me know beforehand. And the way he said Sammy's *his* boy . . . As if he was frightened I was trying to take the boy away from his father.'

There was a little silence. Darkness was closing in and there was a dry, chilly wind in the air. Ruth pulled her scarf more closely round her neck.

'I suppose he's right, in a way,' she said quietly. 'I haven't made any secret of the fact that I'm fond of the kiddy. And I've been thinking about adopting him, if I could. I don't want him to go back, Lizzie, and that's the truth of it. And that's wrong, isn't it, because he *isn't* mine, and I don't honestly think he ever will be.' She stopped in the middle of the lane and looked at her niece with eyes that were filled with tears. 'He's never going to be mine, Lizzie. I'm going to have to let him go back one day. But not yet, surely. Not for a long time yet.'

Chapter Thirty

Dan Hodges had done his best to give Sammy a good Christmas.

He'd got a small chicken from Alf Hines and a pudding in a tin from the grocer's shop. He'd made the jelly Ruth had given him, the cake Freda had made had been as good a Christmas cake as he'd ever had apart from the lack of icing, and he'd got the sort of sweets Sammy liked with his ration. Sammy had even found the stocking on his bed on Christmas morning, and there had been a present from his father as well, a Dinky toy car, not new because you couldn't get toys like that any more, but not very scratched.

Sammy knew that his father had done all he could, but it wasn't the same as being in the cottage. It wasn't even the same as being at home used to be, with his mother and Gordon. He'd never had a Christmas alone with his father and neither of them knew quite how to do it.

Dinner was a bit late. Dan wasn't sure exactly how long to give everything and they all seemed to finish cooking at different times, but eventually he got it all on the table. The chicken was a bit overcooked and the roast potatoes hard, but there were some quite good bits in the middle, and Sammy and his father both enjoyed the baked beans they'd done after the carrots had burnt to the saucepan. The pudding was all right, although the custard Dan had tried to make wouldn't come out right, it stayed thin and tasted powdery instead of 'turning' thick and creamy. Still, it had been a good try and Sammy, seeing his father wrapped in one of Nora's old pinafores and standing over the gas stove, stirring the pan, felt suddenly more like hugging him than complaining.

He was astonished by the feeling. He'd never wanted to hug his father before, not that he could remember. He stood in the door to the scullery, staring at him. He looked different today, somehow. More like a dad, instead of someone who was always tired, always worried, always a bit bad-tempered.

Dan turned his head and saw him. He grinned, and that was another surprise.

'We'll play that game Mrs Purslow give you, when we've had our dinner. What's it called, again?'

'"Sorry",' Sammy said. 'It's a bit like Ludo.'

'That's all right then. I used to like Ludo.'

Sammy couldn't ever remember his father playing Ludo. But after dinner, when they sat down by the fire and started to play Sorry a faint memory stirred in his mind. Perhaps they had done this sort of thing once, long ago, when Sammy was almost too small to understand the game. Perhaps he and Gordon and his father and mother had once sat round like this, shaking the dice and moving counters round a coloured board.

They had tea. The jelly hadn't set very well, but it tasted sweet and fruity, and the cake was good. There were fish-paste sandwiches and some Spam and beetroot, and although Sammy knew it wasn't like the tea they'd be having at Bridge End he enjoyed it just the same. Afterwards they did an old jigsaw puzzle that Dan had found in a cupboard, and then it was time to go to bed.

On Boxing Day Sammy woke to broad daylight and lay there for a while, puzzled by the silence in the house and thinking about Bridge End. He wondered if the carol singing had been as good as last year and if they'd had mince pies at the farm. He wondered if Auntie Ruth had found the present he'd made for her and forgotten to give her, in the haste to leave. It was a picture of Silver, painted with the paint box she'd given him for his birthday, and he'd made the frame himself from bits of wood given him by Uncle George. He wondered how Silver was getting along without him and he pushed his face into his pillow to soak up his tears.

After a while he rolled on to his back. There was no sound from his father. Sammy knew that there had been some bottles of beer in the cupboard under the stairs; he'd seen them when he went to see if his old toy box was still there. It had been pushed to the back but his old toys were still there – a few tin soldiers, their uniforms rubbed and scratched almost away, a tennis ball with a crack in it, some bits of Meccano and a tin money box which was, of course, empty. He'd played with them for a while, then pushed them back again, behind the bottles.

Perhaps Dad had had some of the beer after Sammy had gone to bed.

Sammy got up and went downstairs. The fire had died out and the room was cold and unwelcoming. He thought of the kitchen at Ruth's cottage, warmed with the glow of the range, and stirred the ashes a bit with the poker. There was no sign of any heat. He went outside, found the ash bucket and cleared the fireplace. There was a bundle of wood in the shed and he laid the fire as Ruth had taught him, putting a few lumps of coal on top.

He went out to the scullery to find something to eat. There wasn't much – the leftover chicken would be wanted for dinner and the cake must be saved for tea. There was half a loaf of bread, and he sawed off a thick slice and spread it with margarine, remembering the time he'd done that at Bridge End and cut his hand. When he'd eaten that he stood wondering what to do for a few minutes, then let himself out of the back door.

Tommy Vickers was in his garden, collecting a few vegetables. He looked round in surprise.

'Blimey, my Freda was right, then, when she said your

dad had been out to fetch you home. Here, let's have a look at you.' They approached the fence and stood one each side of it, studying each other. 'Well, you've grown, I'll say that! Twice the boy you were when you went away.' He raised his voice, calling towards the house, 'Here, Free, come and see what the cat's dragged home!'

Freda Vickers came out, drying her hands on a teacloth. 'Well, if it isn't young Sammy! How are you, my love?' She leant over the fence and put both hands on his head, drawing him close so that she could give him a smacking kiss. Sammy felt his cheeks burn with embarrassment and glanced past her down the row of gardens, hoping that no one had seen, but he was pleased all the same. 'Home for Christmas, then? Have you been having a nice time?'

They all looked at each other. Sammy was sure they must know he hadn't been having a nice time. Well, not as nice as at Bridge End, anyway. He looked down and scuffled the path with his toe.

'How d'you like being out in the country?' Tommy asked, covering up the awkward pause. 'Learnt to milk a cow yet?'

Everyone asked the evacuees that, as if every house in the countryside had its own cow. Only a few children were actually on farms. But Sammy nodded. He'd helped Uncle George with the milking quite a few times.

'It's easy,' he said proudly. 'All you do is squeeze its titties.'

Freda looked startled and Tommy grinned. Cheered by this, Sammy went on, 'I've seen lambs being born too. They come out of sheep's bottoms. Uncle George told me all animals come out of their mothers' bottoms.' He stopped, suddenly embarrassed again, and averted his eyes from Freda's motherly figure.

'So how long are you stopping home, then?' Tommy asked. 'Or have you come back for good?'

Sammy shook his head. 'Oh no, I'm going back

tomorrow. Auntie Ruth's expecting me. They're going to have another party, because I missed yesterday. I don't suppose there'll be any more carol singing though,' he added sadly. 'Not till next year.'

'Well, I dare say we'll see you again before you go back,' Tommy said. 'Knock on the door to say cheerio, OK? Don't go without, mind.'

Sammy nodded and watched them go. He stood by the fence, wishing he could go indoors with them, and just before their back door closed he heard Tommy's voice, talking to Freda.

'I dunno. It ain't what Dan said to me the other day. What he told me was he had a good mind to bring Sammy home for good. He didn't say for definite, I know, but when I saw the nipper out in the garden just now I thought—'

The door slammed. Sammy felt the sound throb through his body. He stood very still.

For good. For *good*. That meant *always*. It meant he wasn't going back to Bridge End. It meant he would never see Auntie Ruth, or Uncle George and Auntie Jane, or Lizzie or Terry or Ben again, *ever*. It meant he wouldn't see Silver.

He turned and went slowly into the house. He stared at the table where they'd played Sorry and done the jigsaw puzzle. He looked at the fire he'd laid so carefully, and the plate with the crumbs from his bread and marge. Then he dropped into his mother's armchair and curled himself into a tight ball.

Dan found him there when he finally stumbled down the stairs, thick-headed from his lonely drinking after Sammy had gone to bed the night before, miserably uncertain of himself and whether he'd given the boy the Christmas he ought to have. He stood for a moment at the scullery door, looking at the huddled figure, then swore to himself and stamped out of the back door to the lavatory.

It's no good, he thought, standing in the tiny outhouse.

I'm no good as a father. I was no good as a husband and I'm no good as a dad. And this bloody war's just making everything worse. It's taking everything away and poor bloody sods like me just don't have a chance.

Dan Hodges went back to work the day after Boxing Day, leaving Sammy alone in the house. Although it was a Saturday there was no weekend off for the shipyard or the docks. Two days had been lost for Christmas and the time had to be made up. 'I might have to go to sea again,' he said to Sammy. 'It'll only be for two or three days. There's a bit of grub left over and there's a few bob on the mantelpiece with the ration books, so you can go up the shop and get a few bits in. I'll be back by Tuesday for certain.'

Tuesday seemed a very long way away. Sammy had been used to being left at home on his own, before going to Bridge End, but Ruth had never left him for more than an hour or two. The days stretched ahead of him, bleak and empty.

'But when can I go back to Bridge End?' he asked. 'Auntie Ruth's expecting me.' He had spent all day yesterday persuading himself that he'd been mistaken in what he had heard. Mr Vickers must have got it wrong. Dad couldn't be meaning to keep him in Portsmouth, he just couldn't. Now, he began to wonder again, and to panic.

Dan rubbed his hand across his face. He felt tired and bewildered. All Christmas Day he'd thought he and Sammy were getting on OK. He'd thought it could work out, keeping the nipper at home so that they could be like a proper father and son, talk to each other about what they'd been doing during the day, even do things together once the war was over and there was time for these things. A bit of fishing in Langstone Harbour – watching the football down at Fratton Park. That sort of thing. Him and Sammy, and Gordon too, once he was home again. A proper family.

But finding him all huddled up in the chair in the

morning had spoilt all that. He'd suggested more games of Sorry, he'd found another jigsaw, but nothing seemed to work. Sammy seemed to have retreated from him, become a stranger again. They couldn't talk to each other any more.

It's that Ruth Purslow, he thought. He's more fond of her now than he is of his own dad. And to tell the truth, Dan couldn't really blame him. Ruth was a real nice woman, the sort of woman any boy would like for a mother, the sort of woman any man would like for a wife, if it came down to it, with that warm smile and that coppery hair and those green eyes. But Sammy was *his* boy just the same. It wasn't right that he should get too attached to strangers.

He looked at Sammy's anxious face. 'We'll see about that when I get back. There ain't no hurry, is there? School don't start till the week after next.'

'No, but—'

'We ain't had a bad time, have we?' Dan said, looking at him. 'I've given you a good Christmas. Best I could manage, anyway.'

'Yes, Dad.' Sammy knew that his father really had done his best and it was wrong not to be grateful. He knew that Auntie Ruth would tell him that he mustn't grumble, not when people did their best. Mum would have said the same.

'Well, then,' Dan said. 'You spend a bit of time at home with your dad, all right? Won't hurt you.'

'No, Dad,' Sammy said. 'Can I go out to play?'

'Well, I suppose so. Can't stop in on your tod all day. Don't get going off anywhere with that Micky Baxter, mind, he's been in trouble again. Never out of it, that boy, and why they never sent him away like our Gordon's beyond me . . . The Budd nippers are home, you can play with them if you like. Frank Budd's all right.'

He went off on his bike to cycle the length of Portsea Island, from Copnor down to Old Portsmouth. Sammy stood in the cold room, wondering what to do. It was only six in the morning, still pitch dark and far too early to go outside. It would be hours before any other children emerged on to the streets. He couldn't light the fire, there was barely enough coal to have it alight just in the evenings, and the shops wouldn't be open until nine.

There was some tea in the pot, still quite hot, and a drop of milk left in the bottle. He poured himself a cup and took it back to bed, like his mother used to do. He climbed in and sat with the blankets wrapped around him, drinking his tea and letting the tears roll unchecked down his face.

I want Auntie Ruth and Silver, he thought, and then, suddenly missing his cat desperately, I haven't even got Tibby. I don't even know what happened to her, not really.

He finished his tea and put the cup on the floor. Then he lay down and rolled himself tightly in his blankets.

I want to go back to Bridge End, he thought desolately. I want to go back *now*.

The Budd boys were going back to Bridge End on Monday. Tim told him when Sammy met them in the street outside, kicking a ball against goal posts chalked on the black wall of the end house of March Street. Keith, whose ball it was, was practising keeping it in the air with one foot while he hopped on the other.

'Stella and Muriel came for Christmas in our house too,' Tim said. 'Their dad's still away, at sea. We're all going back on Monday. Our dad says we can go on the train by ourselves now. When are you going back?'

'I don't know. My dad's gone to work. He might not be back till Tuesday.'

'Tuesday!' The boys stared at him. 'Who's looking after you, then?'

Sammy shrugged. 'Nobody. I'll be all right.'

'But you'll be on your own *all night*,' Keith said, his eyes round at the thought. 'Tim and me haven't ever been on our own all night.'

'Wish we could be,' Tim said. 'It'd be smashing. Go to bed when we like – why, we needn't go to bed at all if we didn't want to. We could stop up all night and play games.' He gazed enviously at Sammy. 'You could even go out if you wanted. Go and see all the bomb-sites.'

'In the dark?' Sammy said. 'There's a blackout, in case you haven't noticed.'

'There's a moon too. You'd be able to see all you wanted. Coo, wish I could do it, wish I could go out all night.'

Sammy played football with them for a while, but when they had to go in for dinner he was left on his own again. He wandered about for a bit, but there were no other children out to play and eventually he went back indoors and looked for something to eat. There was some bread and a tin of Spam and another of sardines, and there were some potatoes that could be baked in the oven. There were a few tins of vegetables – carrots, peas, butter beans – and two eggs. There was also a tin of Bournville cocoa in the cupboard and half a pot of blackcurrant jam. On the mantelpiece were his and his father's ration books, and three shillings so that he could go and buy food.

Sammy wondered what would happen if his father didn't come home at all. Suppose the ship got blown up? Would anyone bother to come and tell Sammy? Did anyone even know he existed? Even if they did, they probably thought he was out at Bridge End. He wondered if they had Auntie Ruth's address. After all, the lady who had taken him there in the first place hadn't even got his name right.

Mrs Budd came up the street to see him late in the afternoon, just as it was beginning to get dark. He was sitting in the cold house, trying to play all four positions of Sorry by himself, and came to the door with wide, scared eyes when she knocked. He looked up at her and saw the concern in her face, the motherliness, and wanted to cry.

'Sammy, what's this I hear about your dad not coming

home till Tuesday? Tim and Keith told me. They've got it wrong, surely.'

Sammy shook his head. 'I don't know, Mrs Budd. He just said he might have to go to sea for a few days. He has to see that the engines are working right.'

Jess Budd shook her head and tutted in exasperation. 'I know that, Sammy, but didn't he have any idea about whether he would have to go or not? Don't you really know when he'll be back?'

Sammy shook his head miserably, feeling that somehow this must be his fault. He gazed up at her and Jess Budd's expression softened.

'There, there, Sammy, I'm not cross with you. I'm just worried about you, here all on your own.'

'I'm all right, Mrs Budd. I've got some Spam and some bread, and the milkman came this morning, and I've got a bar of chocolate Dad gave me for Christmas that I've only had one square of, and I'm allowed to turn on the wireless.' The wireless was one Dan had built himself a few years ago, when everyone was doing the same. It crackled for about five minutes as it warmed up, and the voices faded frequently, usually just when you most wanted to hear them, but it was company and Dan said he'd had the accumulator charged only last week so it should be all right for a while.

'Well, you'd better come down to us for tea,' Jess said. 'Tim and Keith and the girls are going back tomorrow, so we're having a special tea for their last night. That's unless your dad comes back,' she added. 'He'll be wanting you to stop with him then.'

'Can I come now?' Sammy asked, not wanting to be left alone again. 'I could leave him a note so he knows where I've gone.'

Jess agreed to this, and Sammy found an old envelope and scribbled his note on it, then put on the coat Ruth had given him and followed her down the street. He felt cheered at the prospect of tea in the Budds' house, where he had never been before, and an evening of games with children he knew well and often played with at Bridge End. It was even better that one of them was his best friend of all, Muriel Simmons.

Tomorrow they would be gone, back to the village. Sammy would be left alone again. But just for now he pushed the thought away.

Jess was not at all happy about allowing Sammy to go back to number 2 to spend the night alone, but as Frank said, you never knew if Dan Hodges might come back late and expect to find the boy there.

'I know you've left a note, but it's interfering just the same,' he said. 'Sammy's his boy and it's for him to say. If you ask me, it'll be all the worse for him, stopping here when I take the nippers back to Bridge End.'

Jess had to agree. Still uneasy, she took Sammy back at nine o'clock and saw him into the empty house. With no fire lit it was icy inside and she was glad she'd brought one of their stone hot water bottles with her. She went upstairs and pushed it into Sammy's bed.

'Now, promise me that if the siren goes you'll come straight down to us. You can come in our shelter. I don't want you here by yourself.' She looked around at the bleak little bedroom and sighed, thinking of her own boys snug in their bunk beds, with pictures of aeroplanes and ships cut from comics pinned up on their walls. The sooner this little chap's back with Ruth Purslow the better, she thought. 'Are you sure you'll be all right, Sammy?'

He nodded and she saw him into bed, then went back to her own house. At the door she had a sudden thought and went back again, knocking at the door of the Vickers' house instead.

'Would you mind keeping an ear out for young Sammy, next door? He's in there all on his own, doesn't know when his dad'll be back. I've had him down with us all evening but he's determined he's got be home now in case Mr Hodges does come home. I don't like leaving him on his own, but what can I do?'

Tommy looked at her in concern and called to his wife. Freda came out to the step, pulling the inner door shut behind her so that no light would escape. 'Don't you worry, Jess, we'll listen out for him. And if the siren goes we'll take him down to our shelter. You'll be crowded enough in yours, with eight of you.'

'Well, I won't say I wouldn't be grateful.' Jess looked at them unhappily. 'You don't think Dan Hodges means to keep Sammy at home, do you? Frank could have taken him back with our lot tomorrow, but Sammy doesn't seem to think he'd want that.'

'It's a crying shame, the way that kiddy's been treated,' Freda said with sudden force. 'You've seen what it's like in that house, Jess. I'm not saying Dan Hodges doesn't do his best, but he just doesn't have the time to look after the place. And a man can't make a home like a woman does. I tell you what, it'll be a crime if he keeps that little boy at home now, after he's been out in the country and had a good home.'

'Well,' Tommy said, 'there's nothing we can do about it if he does. He's got a father's rights. I know we stuck our oar in before and got Sammy moved out to the country, but that was because of the bombing. I don't know that the authorities would be so bothered now. We haven't had a proper raid for months.' He looked at Jess. 'Anyway, don't you worry, Jess. We'll keep an ear out and make sure he's OK.'

Jess went back to number 14, feeling a little comforted. Tommy and Freda were a nice couple, she thought, and Sammy would be all right with them close by. Not that it was right, him being on his own in the house, but Tommy was right, he was Dan Hodges' boy and Dan had his rights. You could only interfere up to a point.

It was a shame Sammy couldn't be going back tomorrow with her own boys and the Simmons girls, though. After all, what was the point of keeping him here when his father wasn't even at home in the evenings?

I expect Dan will take him back next week, she thought. Perhaps he'll get next Saturday off, or take him on Sunday. I expect that's what he means to do.

Sammy lay in his narrow bed, his arms wrapped round the stone hot water bottle Jess had given him. She had rolled an old pullover with it and it felt comforting against him, but he was still lonely for Ruth and Silver and Tibby, his cat. The house, small as it was, seemed big and empty around him and it was cold despite the stone bottle.

He wondered when his father would come back and felt again the fear that the ship might be sunk and Dan Hodges never return. What would he do then? Would he be able to go back to Bridge End, or would he have to stay at number 2 for ever, to look after it if his father had gone? How did you pay for a house? He'd heard his father grumble about the rent often enough, but where did you get the money from? Would he have to go out to work? Could a boy his age earn enough to pay for rent and food and coal and everything? Would he even be allowed to stay here, on his own?

Freda Vickers gave him some dinner on Sunday and Mrs Budd came to see him into bed again that night. He could see that she didn't like leaving him, but he assured her he wouldn't be lonely and eventually she left, making sure the front door was firmly locked behind her. Sammy fell asleep at last and woke on Monday, sure that Dad would come home today.

But what if he didn't? He went outside and saw Tim and Keith and the two little Simmons girls set off up October

Street. Jess Budd, Rose and Maureen went with them to wave them off on the train. Sammy stood at the bottom of the road, watching them go and wishing he could go with them.

Granny Kinch, Micky Baxter's grandmother, was standing in her doorway as usual, her brown tweed coat buttoned up to the chin and a black crochet beret pulled over her steel hair curlers. She nodded at Sammy.

'See *they're* goin' back, then. What about you, ain't you going back to the country?'

'I don't know,' Sammy said a little forlornly, then frowned and added with more determination, 'Yes, I'm going as soon as Dad can get time off to take me. He rode his bike out to get me,' he added.

'Hm.' It was difficult to tell whether she approved of this or not. 'Our Micky's never bin sent. My Nancy wouldn't have it, her boy going away from her. She thinks families oughter stick together.'

Sammy said nothing. Like most of the children in April Grove, he was half afraid of Granny Kinch and half fascinated by her. She could be very sharp if she felt like it, yet at other times she'd send Micky up to the shops to buy a bag of toffees and she'd get all the children crowded round the door and toss the sweets among them for them to scramble for. At least, she used to do that before the war. Now there were neither so many children nor so many sweets.

She still stood at her doorway, though, watching all that went on. Nothing much happened in either April Grove or October Street without Granny Kinch knowing about it.

'Well,' she said finally, 'I suppose if you really wants to go back, there's nothing to stop you. What with your dad working long hours and nobody else at home, there ain't much for you here. I can see that. Here.' She felt in the pocket of her coat and dragged out a couple of pear drops, half melted and stuck together. 'Here's something to suck.

Always cheers you up, something to suck, that's what I say.'

Sammy took the sweets and drifted back to number 2. They were fluffy from Granny Kinch's pocket and although he would have had no hesitation in eating them from his own pocket, he didn't somehow fancy them. Auntie Ruth would have made him throw them away, he thought, and regretfully did so, tossing them into the fireplace where they immediately became balls of cold ash. He sat and stared at them for a bit, thinking about Bridge End and wondering if the Budds were on the train yet and how long it would take them to get there. They'd probably arrive in time for dinner. His mouth watered at the thought of a thick stew, full of vegetables, with dumplings floating on the top. Or a lentil soup, made with a knuckle of bacon and some onions.

He looked in the cupboard. The tin of Spam was still there. He quite liked Spam, but he didn't fancy it today. He wanted stew.

He went back into the living room and looked at the mantelpiece where the ration books lay, with the three shillings left for if Dad didn't come home till Tuesday evening. Even though today was Monday, Tuesday night seemed like years away. He stared around the small, cold room, at the sagging armchairs with their stained upholstery, at the bare linoleum floor with its threadbare mat, at the scratched table and the wooden chairs, and suddenly he could bear it no longer.

He ran upstairs and pushed his few belongings into the brown-paper carrier bags Auntie Ruth had given him. He came down again, picked up the three shillings and his own ration book, and ran out of the house, slamming the door behind him.

He might be just in time to catch the same train as Tim and Keith and the girls. And if not, there'd be another one along soon. There was bound to be.

Chapter Thirty-one

Dan Hodges arrived home on Tuesday evening. The minesweeper he'd been working on had developed a fault in its engine and he'd had to go to sea with it. Then it had been deployed to deal with several suspected mines off the Isle of Wight, with no time for Dan to be put ashore. He'd been half expecting it, but that didn't make his temper any better and by the time he arrived home he was tired and irritable. The only bright spot in the dreary, never-ending round of toil was that Sammy would be there waiting for him.

He walked up the back garden path, noting with approval that there was no light showing. The nipper had had the sense to put up the blackout then, unless he'd never actually taken it down. Dan hoped he hadn't been sitting in the dark all this time and for the first time he wondered how Sammy had managed without him. Well, he ought to have been all right. There'd been food in the house and money for some more, and it wasn't the first time the kid had had to fend for himself. Dan himself had had to manage when he was the same age.

He pushed open the back door. It was cold in the scullery, but then it always was. He pulled the door shut and struck a match to light the gas.

The door to the back room was open. There was no light on in there and it was just as cold as the scullery. Slowly, Dan moved into the room and lit the gas there as well. He looked around the room.

It had a cold, empty look about it, as if no one had been

there for days. The table was bare, except for an empty milk bottle and a cup. The paper chains drooped forlornly from their strings. The game of Sorry had gone, and the jigsaw puzzle was back in its box.

Dan moved over to the fireplace. The fire had been laid but not lit. On the mantelpiece he found his own ration book, lying by itself. There was no sign either of Sammy's book or the three shillings he had left to buy food.

Dan stared at the dusty shelf. He felt behind the black marble clock that had belonged to Nora's parents, but found only a gas bill. He looked at the candlesticks, one at each end, as if they could tell him something. He turned and stared around the room again as if he expected to see Sammy hiding behind a chair, ready to jump out with a laugh on his face.

The room was still empty. In fact, it felt even emptier and much, much colder.

'He's gone,' Dan said slowly. 'He's gone and left me. He's took his ration book and the money and his Christmas presents and everything, and just buggered off. And I know where to, as well. And I'm bloody sure I know who took him!'

He turned on his heel and stamped out through the door leading to the passage. He went out through the front, leaving the door swinging open, not caring about whether light might be showing or not, and stormed down April Grove to hammer loudly on the door of number 14.

'Come out here, Frank Budd!' he yelled. 'Come out here, and tell me what you done with my boy. He was all right – we were *both* all right. We had a good Christmas. He was going to stop with me, with his dad, where he belongs. You come out here and tell me just what right you had to take my boy away from me, and come out quick before I breaks this bloody door right down!'

The door opened slowly and Frank Budd stood there. The two men glared at each other. They were both big men and a fight between them could have been a nasty affair. But Frank Budd was no fighter, for all he'd taught his boys to box, and he simply stood there, unmoving, staring at Dan until finally Dan quietened down.

'What in the name of God's all this shouting about?' he demanded sternly. 'What do you mean, what have I done with your boy? I haven't done nothing with him. I haven't even seen him since Saturday afternoon, when he come down here and had his tea with us. If you ask me, Dan Hodges, it's what *you* done with him that we all ought to be asking. He's your boy and it don't seem to us that you've been looking after him at all. So whatever's happened, it's *your* fault – not mine.'

Dan stared at him. 'You haven't seen him since Saturday?'

'That's what I said.'

'But – but it's *Tuesday* now.'

'I know,' Frank said. 'And it seems to me that what you're saying is that you've left that nipper on his own for nearly four days. That's neglect, that is. You could go to court for that.'

'Never mind that,' Dan said, a note of panic creeping into his voice. 'The point is, where is he? And how long's he been gone? I thought he must have gone back to Bridge End with you.'

Frank shook his head. 'I told you, we ain't seen him. At least, I haven't. I dunno about Jess.' He called over his shoulder and Jess came to the door and stood beside him. Her eyes widened when she heard that Dan didn't know where Sammy was and she looked at her husband in dismay.

'But I went up there on Sunday evening to see him into bed and then I went again yesterday. When I saw he wasn't there, I thought he must be in with the Vickerses. Freda said she'd keep an eye on him and I reckoned she must have decided he ought to be in the house with them.' She put her hand to her mouth. 'I meant to go in again this morning, but our Annie came down and told me Mum was poorly with flu and I've been up and down to them ever since. Oh dear, whatever's happened to him? That poor little boy . . .'

'Now, don't start getting in a state,' Frank said quickly. 'The chances are he's taken himself off back to Bridge End. I dare say he's there now, sitting beside Mrs Purslow's fire and having a hot cup of cocoa before he goes to bed. She probably thinks you sent him back, Dan.'

'Well, how can I find out?' Dan asked desperately. 'It's too late to send a telegram now.'

'Ring up the vicar,' Jess said with sudden inspiration. 'He's got a telephone. You can ring from the box at the top of the street – I do it sometimes, to talk to the boys. He'll be able to tell you if Sammy's back with Mrs Purslow.'

She ran back indoors to scribble down the number and Dan marched swiftly to the telephone box at the top of October Street. He asked the operator to connect him and pushed his money into the box.

'Well, I haven't heard that Sammy's come back,' the vicar said doubtfully when at last they were connected. 'But he might have done. I'll go along and find out. Can you telephone me again in about half an hour?'

Half an hour. Dan stood uncertainly outside the telephone box. He might as well go home, make a cup of tea. He was hungry too – he'd been hoping that Sammy would have thought to put a couple of spuds in the oven for their supper. After a moment he went into the fish and chip shop and bought a pennyworth of chips and a piece of cod. He could eat that straight out of the newspaper and then come back up to the phone box again.

The half-hour seemed more like three days. He ate the fish and chips quickly and drank a cup of tea while standing at the table. Then he set off again for the phone box, waiting impatiently outside for a young woman to finish a call to her boyfriend. She came out at last and he pushed his way past her.

He'd had time during the past half-hour to think of any amount of things that might have happened to Sammy. Suppose he hadn't gone back to Bridge End at all. Suppose someone had got into the house and kidnapped him, taking his ration book and the money as well. Suppose he'd been run over – got lost – fallen into the sea . . .

'Is that you, Mr Hodges?' The vicar's voice sounded sharp and anxious in his ear and Dan felt his heart lurch.

'Yes. Yes, it's me. I couldn't get in before, there was some silly girl . . . Is he there, Mr Beckett? Is he back with Mrs Purslow? Is he all right, is my boy all right?'

There was a pause. It seemed to Dan that the vicar was never going to reply. Then the voice came again, heavy with the tone of one who doesn't want to deliver bad news.

'I'm sorry, Mr Hodges, he's not. Ruth Purslow hasn't seen or heard of him since you took him home on Christmas Eve. Nobody in the village has.' There was another pause and then a deep sigh. 'Wherever Sammy is, Mr Hodges, he hasn't come back to Bridge End.'

Jane and George were just settling down to listen to the nine o'clock news. Like everyone else, they were desperately anxious about what was happening in the Far East. Since Pearl Harbour a whole new war seemed to have been unleashed, with British possessions as well as American in peril. Hong Kong had fallen on Christmas Day itself, the Philippines were under threat and the Japanese seemed to be marching through the whole of Malaya, right down to Singapore itself. Everyone was aware that the threat was not just against the Far East, terrible though that would be. Australia itself, one of Britain's favourite colonies, whose men were already far from their own homes, fighting on Britain's behalf, would be next in line for Japanese invasion.

Nor was that all. The north Atlantic convoy, including

Alec's ship, was being attacked daily by U-boats, which seemed to come from nowhere. The great city of Leningrad was still under siege, with thousands dying in the streets every day. And it was the same everywhere – in Africa, Norway, Burma, Siam, a war was being fought so cruel that there had never been its like in all history, and so bitter that nobody could see its end.

'It's just awful,' Jane said when the news came to an end at last and the warm, north-country tones of J. B. Priestley took over with his 'Notes'. 'You just can't imagine it, can you, all the world fighting like that? How did it happen, George? How did we get into this? I mean, all we wanted to do was stop Hitler marching into Poland. I just can't understand how it's spread like this.'

George took his pipe from his mouth. 'I know, love. But the way I see it, war's like a car that's got a starting-handle but no brakes. And it's running downhill. There's nothing anyone can do to stop it till it gets to the bottom.'

'And then it'll crash,' Jane said quietly. 'And what sort of a world is going to be left after that?'

George shook his head as if he had no answer. But before he could speak there was a loud hammering on the kitchen door and Ruth burst in, her eyes wild, her coat dragged on anyhow and her hair flying. She came to a stop, staring at them both, and leant one hand heavily on the table, pressing the other against her side.

'Ruth!' Jane was on her feet. 'Heavens above, whatever is it?'

George dropped his pipe. He too lumbered to his feet. 'Sit down, girl. You look as if you've seen a ghost. What's happened?'

Breathless from the run from her cottage all the way to the farm, Ruth stared at them. She shook her head, almost gulping for breath, then blurted out, 'It's Sammy – Jane, Sammy's missing! Nobody knows where he is.'

'Sammy? Here, sit down.' Jane pressed her sister down

into a chair. 'Now, get your breath back and then tell us. George, push the kettle over, will you? Now, love, what's all this about? Sammy's in Portsmouth with his dad, surely. How can he be missing?'

Ruth shook her head. She felt up the sleeve of her cardigan for a hanky and rubbed it across her wet face. 'He's not. That's just it. He's not in Portsmouth and his dad doesn't know where he is. Nobody's seen him since Monday morning.' She raised frantic eyes to her sister. 'He could have been missing for nearly two whole days, and nobody even knew he'd gone.'

Jane and George looked at each other, nonplussed. Jane gave Ruth's arm a squeeze and went to make the tea. She looked back over her shoulder. 'I don't understand. How could his dad not know he's been missing? And how have you come to hear about it?'

'Well, they thought he'd come out to Bridge End. I mean, where else would he go? And so Dan – Mr Hodges – he rang up the vicar to see if he knew anything. And Mr Beckett came down to me himself and told me the poor little boy had gone, left the house while his dad was at sea. Took his ration book and some money, and his bits and pieces – the presents I put in his stocking and the game of Sorry and all – and just went. And they thought he must be trying to get out here, but he hasn't arrived, Jane. And there's no more trains tonight, so where is he? *Where is he?*' Her voice rose in a wail and she covered her face with her hands, sobbing as if her heart would break.

Jane gave George another swift glance.

'I still don't understand why they don't know how long he's been gone,' she said when Ruth's sobs diminished a little and she was able to sip the tea Jane put in front of her. 'I mean, surely he was there this morning when his dad went to work—'

'That's just it. I don't know all the ins and outs of it, Jane, but it seems Mr Hodges went to work on Saturday morning and never came back till today. He works on ships, you see, small ones like minesweepers and things, and he often has to go out with them for a day or two to see that the engines are working right. Well, he went off on Saturday, and Tim Budd says Sammy went down to tea with them that afternoon, and apparently the woman next door said she'd keep an eye on him if there was a raid, and he was there Monday morning all right because Tim and Keith have told Mr Beckett they saw him when they were on their way to the station and gave him a wave – but nobody's seen him since. The woman next door said she thought Dan had changed his mind and sent him off with the others, and Mr Budd got home late that evening and went off to work early next morning and he's been working overtime today, only got home about eight o'clock. So until Dan came home tonight, nobody knew Sammy was missing.' She stared at Jane, her eyes wide with fear. 'He could have been gone ever since yesterday morning. Oh Jane, where is he? Wherever is he?'

Jane stared at her helplessly. 'Oh, Ruth. That's dreadful.' She looked at her husband. 'What should we do, George? We can't just sit here and do nothing.'

'Well, we can't go out looking for him neither. Not at this time of night, with the blackout and all. We don't even know where to start.' He lifted his hands helplessly. 'Seems to me the best thing we can do is go and see the vicar and see what he thinks. Maybe those other children will know something. Then we'll have some idea what to do tomorrow. I suppose it'll have to be reported to the authorities – the billeting people, maybe even the police.'

'The *police*!' Ruth echoed, horrified.

'Well, he's missing, isn't he? The police will have to be told. Not that it's our business, not strictly,' he added heavily. 'It's Dan Hodges ought to be doing any reporting there is to be done. I don't know that we've got any right to do anything at all.'

'But he was my evacuee!' Ruth cried. 'I'm his foster-mother.'

'Yes, but he wasn't with you when he went missing,' George pointed out. 'He was in his dad's care then.'

'His dad was at *work*! He was gone for four days – you can't call that *care*.'

'To all intents and purposes,' George said firmly, 'Sammy was in his care. It's his responsibility what's happened to the boy. But that don't mean we can just stand by,' he added more gently. 'I don't mean that, Ruth. I just say we can't go to the authorities.'

'We can go and see Mr Beckett,' Jane said. 'Like you said, we can talk to him. He'll know what to do.' She went to the back door and took down her coat. 'Come on, George.'

'What – now? It's getting on for ten o'clock.'

'Well, of course. You don't expect us to wait till tomorrow, do you? And you'll be milking in the morning, you won't have time then. No, we must go now, before it gets any later. Mr Beckett won't mind. He's probably expecting us.' She had her own coat on by now and held out George's. 'Come on, George.'

Ruth stood up and waited miserably while they got ready. She looked at the table and bit her lip. The tears had begun to creep down her face again.

'I just can't bear to think of him,' she said shakily. 'Out there somewhere, in the cold and the dark, all by himself. Oh Jane, where is he? What's happened to him?'

Jane took her arm and drew her gently towards the door. 'We'll find him, Ruth. Don't worry. I'm sure he's all right, wherever he is. We'll find him for you.'

As Jane had said, Mr Beckett wasn't at all surprised to find them on his doorstep ten minutes later. He held the door open and ushered them into the kitchen, where Mrs Mudge was sitting in a wooden rocking chair by the Aga, knitting.

There were two mugs of cocoa on the scrubbed wooden table and an open book beside the other armchair. On the dresser there was a pile of comics, and children's drawings were pinned round the walls.

'Come in, come in. Take off your coats.' He pulled out chairs around the table and they unwound their scarves and sat down, perching on the edges of the chairs. 'No, Mrs Purslow, you have my chair here by the stove . . . This is a sad situation. It seems as if the little boy could have been missing for some days.'

'Have Tim and Keith said any more?' Ruth asked anxiously. 'Have they got any idea where he might have gone?'

The vicar shook his head. He sat down on one of the kitchen chairs and leant his long thin arms on the table. His mild blue eyes reflected Ruth's anxiety.

'I'm afraid not. I asked them of course, and the girls too, but none of them had any idea. Keith was of the opinion that he might have run away to sea, but I think we can discount that . . .' He smiled very slightly. 'I think myself that he must have been trying to come back here. Where else would he go? This was home to him.' He turned his glance on Ruth. 'I'm sure he knew he would be welcome.'

'Of course he would!' she cried. 'Why, he was like a son to me! I *wanted* him to come back – I thought it was understood he *would* come back. I don't see why he had to run away at all, not unless his father was cruel to him. And – and –' she hesitated, biting her lip, then went on quickly '– I don't believe he is a cruel man – not really. He's had a hard life and he doesn't know how to look after a boy, but he's not cruel.'

'Not cruel!' Jane exclaimed. 'Going off and leaving a little boy like that for four whole days! If that's not cruel I don't know what is!'

'Well, be that as it may,' Mr Beckett said, 'the important thing now is to decide what we must do to find him. The police will have to be notified, of course –' Jane gave her husband a swift glance '– but to tell you the truth, I think that's really Mr Hodges' responsibility. However, we can perhaps go to the railway station and see if the guards know anything, if we can find those who were on any trains he might have used.' He rubbed his hand over his face. 'Of course, we don't actually know which day it was. But he surely can't have been wandering about all this time—'

A loud hammering on the door interrupted him. The women gasped and Ruth put her hand to her mouth. George gave them a quick look and got to his feet. 'I'll answer it if you like, Vicar. It might be the police already.'

Ruth had both hands at her mouth now, the palms together as if she were praying. 'If anything's happened to that little boy . . .'

Jane got up too and went to stand beside her sister, her hand squeezing Ruth's shoulder. Mrs Mudge's knitting had fallen to her lap and her fingers were twisted together. Mr Beckett untangled his long body and followed George to the door.

'Don't let any light show—' he began, but George was already stepping back as the new arrival pushed his way inside and stood blinking for a moment or two in the light, staring around at them.

It was Dan Hodges.

'I've been down to your cottage,' he said to Ruth, who was staring at him in disbelief. 'You weren't there so I come on up here. I come all the way on me bike, in the pitch dark. I couldn't wait about till tomorrow.' He turned his eyes, red-rimmed from the cold, from one person to the other and, as if his legs would support him no longer, sank on to one of the kitchen chairs. His face was grey with exhaustion, all the truculence wiped away, leaving only the drawn lines of fear. 'Where's my Sammy, eh? Where's my boy?'

There was a long silence as they all gazed at one another.

Then Ruth got up. She went to the bowed figure at the table and laid her hand on his shoulder. Her expression, though none of the anxiety had diminished, had softened.

'We don't know, Dan,' she said quietly. 'We don't know. But we're going to find him. Now that we know he's missing, we're all going to do our best to find him.'

Chapter Thirty-two

Dan had been to the police station as soon as it was realised that Sammy was missing and they had promised to start asking questions around the neighbourhood first thing in the morning. There wasn't really anything else they could do, the station sergeant told him, not at the moment. They had to find out when he was last seen – who had seen him – if he'd actually got on a train or a bus, or was just wandering around Portsmouth still. They couldn't begin to do that in the middle of the night.

He'd had a few questions of his own to ask Dan, too. How was it the nipper had been left alone in the house for four whole days? Didn't Dan realise when he went off on Saturday that this might happen? And if he had, why hadn't he asked a neighbour to look after the boy? Why, most of all, hadn't he let him go back to Bridge End like the other kiddies?

When Dan had finally left the station he felt as if he'd been put through a mangle. I know I didn't oughter've left him like that, he thought, but I just couldn't face letting him go off again. I couldn't face the place being empty every night when I come back from work. And I was frightened I'd lose him for good. He liked it too much out at Bridge End. He was getting too fond of that Ruth Purslow and she was getting too fond of him. That was what it was.

He'd cycled home through the darkness, but when he got there he couldn't settle. The house was too bleak, too unwelcoming. I don't blame the kid not wanting to stay, he thought, looking around. It's no home at all, not like he had out there. He *was* better off at Bridge End. He's fallen on his feet there. Ruth Purslow was a nice woman, a good woman, and Dan could have trusted her to look after his boy properly. He *should* have trusted her.

Ruth Purslow would make a good mother for any boy. She'd make a good wife too. If things could just have been different . . .

He had started to take his coat off as he came in. Now, unable to rest, he shrugged it back on again. The evening seemed to have been going on for ever, but it was still only eight o'clock. If he got on his bike now, he could get out to Bridge End before ten, even in the dark.

Bridge End was where Sammy was heading and that was where Dan was going to be.

Catching the train to Bridge End was, Sammy had found, not quite as easy as he'd supposed.

He was too late to catch up with Frank Budd and the other children as they made their way to Hilsea halt, but the man in the little hut told him there would be another train along soon and he bought his ticket. It left him with some money to spare and he jingled the coins in his pocket, feeling suddenly rich. 'I've got sixpence, jolly little six-pence . . .'

Of course, it was Dad's money really, but it had been meant to last Sammy till Tuesday, so it wasn't really stealing. Although he supposed that once he was back at Bridge End he'd have to send it back, or keep it till the next time he saw his father. Dad wouldn't let him keep it. He couldn't afford to give Sammy three shillings, just like that.

He was feeling cold by the time the train steamed along from the town station, and scrambled aboard, glad to be out of the wind. The sky was lowering, with yellowish-grey clouds pressing down on top of Portsdown Hill. He found a seat and sat down, squashed up between two soldiers.

The train was a slow one. It chuffed along, breathing heavily as if it were really too tired to make the journey and stopping at every opportunity, even between stations. Sammy stared out of the window. Apart from the journey home in the dark on Christmas Eve, he had only been on a train once in his life, when he was first evacuated, and he had no idea what he should be seeing. They'd go along the top of the harbour, he thought, so there ought to be sea and boats . . . When he saw these he relaxed, and settled back to enjoy the journey and the feeling that he was grown-up enough to make it all on his own.

The soldiers started to light cigarettes and the compartment was soon filled with thick smoke. Sammy felt his eyes begin to smart. He closed them and listened to the rhythmic clackety-clack of the pistons as they drove the engine along, and the answering rattle of the wheels on the track. *Do-do-dee-do, do-do-dee-do, do-do-dee-do, do-do-dee-do* . . . The sound set up an answering rhythm in his brain, a rhythm that, together with the stuffy atmosphere in the smoke-filled compartment, lulled him first into a doze and then into a heavy sleep.

He woke with a start to find the soldiers all standing up, getting their kitbags off the racks overhead and pushing their way out through the narrow door into the corridor.

Sammy struggled to wake. 'Are we here? Are we at Bridge End?'

The nearest man turned and glanced down at him. 'Bridge End? Never heard of it, son. This is Brighton.'

'Brighton?' Sammy stared out of the window. He'd heard of Brighton – Tim Budd had told him they'd been there once – but surely it was further from Portsmouth than Bridge End. Had he gone past the stop?

'What am I going to do? I wanted to go to Bridge End.'

The soldier was halfway out of the compartment. He paused, his kitbag wedging in the doorway, and looked back. 'You'd better get off, kid. Ask the stationmaster. He'll put you right.'

He went on quickly to join his mates and Sammy stared after him. Then he heard the whistle blow and, panic-stricken, snatched up his own bags and scurried after the soldiers, tumbling out on to the platform just as a porter was coming along to slam the door shut.

'Here, what are you up to? You could get killed, playing the fool like that.' He stared at Sammy with suspicion. 'You ain't travelling without a ticket, I hope?'

'No! I've got a ticket – I bought it at Hilsea.' Sammy scrabbled in his pocket to find the scrap of cardboard and handed it over. 'Only I think I've gone too far. I wanted to go to Bridge End.'

'Bridge End? Where's that when it's at home?'

Sammy stared at him. 'It's a station. It's where I'm evacuated.'

'Well, it ain't on this line,' the porter said. 'You'd better come along with me.'

He put his hand on Sammy's shoulder and marched him along the platform. Sammy scuttled along beside him, his heart thumping with fear. What was the man going to do with him? Would he take him to the stationmaster? To the police? He was sure it must be a crime to go too far for a ticket. Would they take him to prison, or to the proved school, like Gordon? Would they tell his dad, or Auntie Ruth, what had happened?

The porter led him through a green door and into a small office, with a cluttered desk and two telephones. Behind the desk there was a man in railway uniform, with a large white moustache. A fire burned bright and warm in the fireplace and Sammy realised just how cold he was.

The stationmaster picked up a cap that was lying on his desk and fitted it on to his head. There was a smart badge on the front and, with his bristling moustache, it made him look very important. Sammy gazed up at him, quaking.

'Hallo, Jenkins.' The stationmaster's voice was stern. 'What have you got there? Travelling without a ticket, was he?'

'No, sir, he's got a ticket, but it's not for Brighton. It's not for anywhere on this line that I can see.' The porter held it out. 'It's for a place called Bridge End.'

'Bridge End, eh?' The older man took the ticket and stared critically at it. 'Hm. It's today's ticket all right.' He fixed Sammy with a piercing look. 'If you were supposed to be going to Bridge End, what were you doing on the Brighton train?'

'Please, sir, I didn't know it was the Brighton train. I don't know where Brighton is.'

He heard the porter draw in his breath. 'Don't know where *Brighton* is? Blimey, what do they teach 'em at school these days?'

'Not much, I should think.' The stationmaster sighed and looked at Sammy again. His voice had lost a little of its sternness. 'Do you know where Bridge End is?'

'It's where I'm evacuated,' Sammy said again.

'Well, do you know where it's near? Any big towns or cities?'

Sammy thought for a minute. 'Yes. It's near Southampton. We went there once and Lizzie said she'd take me to see the docks where the liners used to go.'

'Southampton!' The stationmaster nodded. 'So it's *that* Bridge End. There's another in Wales,' he added to the porter, 'and probably half a dozen more, if we only knew it. Well, that's easy enough,' he said, addressing Sammy again. 'You've got on the wrong train, haven't you? This is in the opposite direction from where you want to be. What you've got to do now is get a train going back to Southampton and that'll take you back to Bridge End, see? It's quite simple.'

Sammy looked at him. 'But I don't know if I've got enough money.'

'It's all right. You haven't gone off the station, so the

ticket you've got will be all right. As long as you don't try to go any further, mind,' he added, sounding stern again. 'You've got to get off at Bridge End, or you'll be in trouble.' He nodded at the porter. 'Take him over to platform five and see he gets on the Southampton train, Jenkins. There's one due in twenty minutes.'

The porter nodded and led Sammy out of the office again. Sammy looked up at him. He wasn't all that old after all, he thought. Probably about the same age as Terry and not nearly as frightening as Sammy had first thought.

'Here you are,' the porter said, stopping by a bench. 'You can wait here. The train'll be along in twenty minutes, like Mr Hopkinson said. You can get on it by yourself all right, can't you?'

Sammy nodded. He glanced past the porter at a stall which was selling cups of tea and penny buns. 'Will I have time to get a bun?'

'Don't see why not. Got enough money?'

Sammy felt in his pocket and nodded. The porter went off along the platform, whistling, to start sorting out some sacks of mail that had been dumped off the last train, and Sammy left his bags on the seat and went along to buy himself a drink and a bun. They were good buns too, he thought, and bought two more to take with him.

That left two pennies to jingle together in his pocket. The fare and the food had cost him more than he'd expected. He wouldn't be able to send the money back to Dad after all, but it had been left for his food so it didn't matter that he'd nearly spent it all. He wouldn't need any more, now that he was definitely going to be on the right train for Bridge End.

'I've got sixpence,' he sang to himself again. 'Jolly little sixpence. I've got sixpence, to last me all my life. I've got *tuppence* to lend and *tuppence* to spend, and *tuppence* to take home to my wife.'

There was a shrill whistle from down the track and a

train came steaming along from the other direction. Sammy ran to collect his bags and waited until it stopped. Then he scrambled aboard and found himself a corner seat where he could see out of the window. He was determined not to miss the little halt at Bridge End when they arrived.

It wasn't until the train had rushed through several stations and halts without stopping that he began to feel afraid that it wasn't going to stop at Bridge End at all. The signs had all been taken down in case of invasion, so it was impossible to tell just where they were. They went over a river, with a lot of small sailing dinghies and yachts moored in it and muddy banks that told him it must be close to the sea, and then plunged once again into woods and fields. He couldn't remember ever having seen the river before, nor could he remember the great wide expanse of sea that was visible now, with bigger ships moving along it. He stared out in panic. Where was he?

Where was Bridge End? Where was the church, with its square tower and the vicarage standing close beside it? Where were the fields and woods he expected to see, the places that had become so familiar to him over the past months, the places he had come to think of as home?

They were leaving the countryside behind now and running beside another river. In a few minutes they crossed it, and rows and rows of houses flashed past the window. They were in a town, a big one, perhaps even a city. Where could it be?

With a great fuss of steaming and whistling, the train came into a large station. It slowed down at last and drew up beside a long, busy platform. Sammy peered out and looked in both directions before climbing cautiously down, and above all the clatter and noise he heard the announcer's voice.

'Southampton. This is Southampton.'

Southampton. He had gone too far. And he remembered the words of the stationmaster at Brighton. 'Don't try to go any further. You've got to get off at Bridge End, or you'll be in trouble.'

I *couldn't* get off at Bridge End, Sammy thought miserably. The train didn't stop. All the same, he dared not try to go through the barrier. This time he was sure he'd be taken to the police and from there almost certainly to the proved school. They wouldn't give him a second chance.

Frightened, lonely and in desperate need of a lavatory, Sammy looked up and down the platform, then made his way along to the very far end, away from the sign that said Way Out.

There must be another way of getting out of the station and once he was out, he would have to think what to do next.

Dan was given a bed for the night at the vicarage. There was plenty of room, Mr Beckett said, and although Dan said he would sleep anywhere, he wasn't bothered about a bed, the kitchen floor would do, Mrs Mudge took him up to the last remaining spare room, where there was a folding camp bed among the boxes and suitcases that had been stored there for years. She shook out the old mattress and checked it for damp, then spread some blankets over it and gave him a couple of pillows. 'You'll be all right here. It's no worse than an air-raid shelter, after all.'

'It's a blooming sight better than most of 'em,' Dan said. Mrs Mudge had been kind enough and obviously wanted him to be comfortable, but her manner was a bit short, as if she were angry with him. And no doubt she was, he thought ruefully, no doubt they all were, for treating Sammy the way he had. Taking him away from Ruth at Christmas and then leaving him all on his own . . . I don't think much of meself, come to that, he thought. I dunno what I was thinking of to do it. I'm a pretty poor sort of a father.

'Thanks for the supper,' he said awkwardly. Once they'd

decided what to do, the housekeeper had got out the frying pan and cooked him up a real nice bite to eat, with bubble and squeak made from leftover potato and cabbage and stuff, and even a bit of bacon chopped up with it to make it tasty. Bacon! Dan hadn't seen a rasher for months.

'That's all right. The bathroom's along the corridor there.' Mrs Mudge gave him a sharp nod and went away, leaving Dan on his own in the cluttered room. It wasn't cluttered like number 2 April Grove was cluttered, though. This was *decent* clutter – stuff that could still be used. And it was looked after, too, you could tell that. There was hardly any dust and no cobwebs at all.

Dan had never stayed before in a house he didn't actually live in. He'd never even been inside a house as big as this one, with five or six bedrooms and several rooms downstairs – and a proper bathroom, where he went to wash, with a huge bath on its own legs and a lavatory next door. He crept along the corridor, feeling intimidated by the size of the place, and was thankful to shut the door at last and lie down on the camp bed.

He didn't sleep, though, or not for a long time. He drew the curtain back once the light was off and lay awake, staring through the window at the stars and wondering where Sammy was. His boy, Nora's boy, somewhere out there on his own – lost for days, wandering by himself. Why? Why had he run off like that? Why couldn't he have waited until Dan came home again?

He knew I wanted to keep him there, that's why, Dan told himself. He knew and he didn't want to stay. He wanted to be back here, with these people he's got fond of, where he feels safe and where he's properly looked after.

But if that was what he wanted, why had he never arrived? What had happened to him after he left April Grove and where was he now?

The questions circled endlessly in Dan's brain, gradually turning into a procession of nightmare pictures – Sammy, trying to walk to Bridge End, lost and helpless in strange fields or woods. Sammy, hurt and alone, starving in a ditch. Sammy, kidnapped and held captive. You did hear of such things, and Sammy was a nice-looking nipper with that fair hair and those big blue eyes. Dan didn't want to think of what might happen to him . . . But as his mind slipped into uneasy slumber it forced him to think of it. He saw the pictures and he couldn't get rid of them.

Bloody fine father I've turned out to be, he thought, jerking awake for the twentieth time. *Bloody* fine.

Chapter Thirty-three

Sammy had found his way out of the station. If you went right down the platform to the far end, where the goods wagons were being unloaded, you could slip through to a yard that was crowded with lorries and out into the road. He scurried between the vehicles, keeping his eyes sharply open to avoid running into any of the men working there, and he was almost out of the yard when he heard a shout go up. By then it was too late for him to be caught. He was out through the open gates and away up the road, scampering like a rabbit. It was only when he turned a corner and stopped to catch his breath that he realised he'd lost his carrier bags.

I must have left them on the train, he thought, the tears coming to his eyes. My Sorry game. My jigsaw puzzle. The jumper Auntie Jane knitted me for Christmas. The car Dad gave me. And my pyjamas and new pants and vest, and my woolly gloves.

He was swept by an overwhelming grief for all he had lost. Everything he had ever loved, it seemed, was taken away from him. His granny and grandad at the pub. His home, when they'd moved to April Grove. His mother. Even his brother Gordon, who had teased and bullied him and stolen his chocolate, but was still his brother. And now his carrier bags, holding all he possessed.

He stopped for a moment and felt in his pocket. There were five coins left in it, and he drew them out and stared at them. A King George penny, with Britannia on the tail side. A halfpenny, with Queen Victoria's head and a sailing ship. Two farthings, both with perky little wrens on their tail sides.

Tuppence. That was all he had left. Tuppence.

Tuppence to spend . . .

Somehow, it didn't sound so jolly any more.

I can't even get back to Auntie Ruth and Silver, he thought desolately, walking unseeingly along the narrow streets, tears pouring down his face. I haven't got enough for the fare and I don't know which way it is to walk, or how far it is. I can't ever get back.

The day was almost over. Darkness was creeping through the streets, bringing with it a deeper cold. Sammy began to wonder where he could spend the night. Soon, he wouldn't be able to see where he was going, and although he knew he was somewhere near the docks he had no idea exactly where he was. He'd only been to Southampton once, with Lizzie, and they hadn't come to this part, with these mean streets.

The streets came to an end and he found himself trudging beside a long, high wall. There were arches in the walls, making alcoves like those he had seen in the church at Bridge End, where the vicar kept statues of saints. There were no saints in these arches, however; only bundles of rags that, when he peered closer in the hope of finding something to wrap round his shivering body, turned into snarling human beings, their faces ravaged with disease and starvation. He jumped back, terrified, and ran away, pursued by shouts. It was worse than Old Portsmouth, he thought. But perhaps, after the bombing, Old Portsmouth was like this now, too. Perhaps there were people there living on the streets, bombed out of their houses with nowhere to go and no money for food.

Will I be like that soon? he wondered. Will I have to sleep against walls, under wet, smelly arches, with nothing to eat and nowhere to go?

He came to a bomb-site, where a whole row of houses

had been destroyed in one of the raids. Some of them were still half standing and he crept about until he found a door hanging open. There was even a bit of furniture in the room he went into – a broken chair, a couple of sagging, stained cushions. He moved carefully, afraid that this place too might be occupied, but to his relief there was no one there.

He pulled the cushions into a corner and curled himself up on top. He was suddenly desperately tired and, hungry, thirsty and unhappy though he was, he fell into a deep, heavy sleep.

They scarcely knew where to start next morning.

'I think you should tell the local police too,' Mr Beckett said to Dan as they ate breakfast in the big kitchen. 'I know you've been to the ones in Portsmouth, but we don't know how far Sammy might have got. We'll go and see Constable Percy as soon as we've finished.'

Dan pushed his porridge into a heap in the middle of the bowl. 'It's not him that'll have to look, surely. It's the Pompey coppers. I'll have to go back.'

'Well, we don't really know who should be looking, or where, do we?' the vicar said. 'It seems most likely that Sammy would have tried to come back here. The question is, why didn't he arrive?'

Dan shoved his bowl aside and leant his elbows on the table. He put his face in his hands. 'I been asking myself that all night. I don't know. I don't bleeding *know*.' He heard Mrs Mudge's sharp, disapproving gasp, but Mr Beckett didn't seem at all concerned about his language. 'I wish I'd never gone to work on Saturday. I wish I'd brought him back here. I wish I'd never taken him away.'

Mr Beckett looked at him compassionately. He had worked in other parishes before coming to Bridge End, some of them in city slums, and he knew that men like Dan Hodges had hard lives, working long hours at unpleasant jobs for little pay. Their homes were poor because they had no money and no opportunity to improve them. They lived from hand to mouth and when they lost their jobs, as so many had done during the difficult years before the war, they came close to starving.

'You did what you thought was best,' he said gently to the bowed head. 'You wanted to have your son with you for Christmas and why not? But it's no use reproaching yourself now. What we have to do now is find Sammy. You've been to the Portsmouth police, and what we need to do now is see Constable Percy and get things moving from this end. It's possible the Portsmouth men have already contacted him and it will save him the trouble of coming here.'

'Let's go now, then,' Dan said, getting up. 'I can't eat any more – begging your pardon, Mrs Mudge, but I don't seem to have no appetite.'

As they were pulling on their coats, the kitchen door opened and Ruth Purslow came in. Her face was white, her eyes shadowed as if she too had been awake all night. She looked at the two men and crossed to Dan's side, gazing up at his face.

'I had to come. I can't just stand by and do nothing.'

'Of course not, Ruth.' The vicar gave her arm a comforting pat. 'We're just going to see Constable Percy. He may have some news.'

To their surprise the local policeman did indeed have news. He had written it down as it came to him over the telephone and he read it out to them in a slow, careful voice.

'The Portsmouth police have already been to check up at the local railway stations and it seems that a lad answering Sammy's description bought a ticket on Monday morning. He'd missed the train but he was told another one would be along in twenty minutes. However, when the train arrived he was no longer on the platform.' Constable Percy lowered the sheet of paper and looked at them. 'It seems he either changed his mind or got on the wrong train.'

Ruth stared at him in dismay. 'The wrong train! But where would he have gone?'

'Well.' Constable Percy consulted his paper again. 'It seems that before the Bridge End train came in – that's the slow, stopping train of course – there was one to Brighton. And another one to Waterloo. He could have got on either of those.'

'Waterloo? But that's in *London*!' Ruth whispered, appalled. 'Oh, poor little Sammy! All by himself in London. He'll be frightened out of his wits.'

'We don't know that he went there,' the vicar pointed out. 'He could have got on the Brighton train.'

'But even if he did – what would he do once he got there? How would he manage?'

'Well, he's a sensible boy,' Mr Beckett said. 'He'd ask a policeman, wouldn't he? We always tell the village children that if they're lost or in any sort of trouble they should go to the nearest police station.'

Dan shook his head. 'My Sammy wouldn't do that. He's scared of coppers. Ever since our Gordon was sent away . . .' He sighed. 'It's my fault. I never give a thought to bringing them boys up proper – left it to their mother and what could she do, sick as she was? I tell you what, I been a dead loss all round. No bloody use to nobody.'

Ruth glanced at him quickly. He looked utterly worn down, she thought, defeated. He looked as if he'd lost every shred of belief in himself. She moved and put a hand on his arm.

'It isn't all your fault, Dan. You did your best. You went to work and earned a living for your family, and you've been doing good war work too, going out on those ships and risking your life . . . Sammy's told me. He's told me all about it.'

'Sammy's a good boy,' he said, his voice shaking. 'But

you don't want to believe everything he says. I've been a bad father and I know it.'

'Well,' Mr Beckett said after a short pause, 'be that as it may – and only you know the truth, Mr Hodges – the important thing now is to find him. We know he may have got on a train to either London or Brighton.' He looked at the policeman. 'Is there any way of finding that out?'

'They're asking the guards now. They know which ones were on those trains, so if either of them saw Sammy they may remember him. He'd have had the wrong ticket, see.'

'And what would they have done?' Ruth asked.

Constable Percy looked embarrassed. 'Well, as to that . . . It's an offence, see, Mrs Purslow, to travel on a train without a ticket. Or the wrong ticket, adds up to the same thing. He could have been charged at a police station. Or they might have just put him off at the next stop, or even let him go back and start again. As long as he hadn't left the station—'

'So Sammy may have gone to – to Brighton, or London, and then turned round and gone back to Portsmouth? But if he did that, why hasn't he turned up at Bridge End? It's two nights now.' Ruth's voice rose a little and she began to cry. 'Something awful's happened to him – I know it has. Oh Sammy, *Sammy*—'

Without even thinking about it she turned and buried her head against Dan's chest. Automatically, he put his arms round her and held her close. They stood very still for a moment, then he began to stroke her hair.

'Don't cry, Ruth. Don't cry now. We'll find him. We'll find our boy . . .'

There was a silence. Ruth lifted her head away and they looked into each other's eyes for a long moment. Then Constable Percy cleared his throat and Mr Beckett spoke quietly.

'I think I know what could have happened.'

They all turned and stared at him. Ruth stepped away from Dan and he let his arms fall. The vicar went on.

'Suppose he was put off at the next station, or maybe at Brighton or even Waterloo, and told to get the train back to Portsmouth. Suppose he was told which train to get on to reach Bridge End. And then, suppose for some reason he missed the station. It's easily done. All the signboards have been taken down, people are missing their stations all the time. Sammy wouldn't have any idea when he was supposed to get off – especially if he'd already been frightened once by being on the wrong train.'

'So where would he have got off?' Dan asked. 'Don't tell me he went to somewhere like Plymouth next! Blimey, we'll never know where to look. He could be anywhere.'

'Well, he might have got off at Southampton. He'd know by then he'd gone too far.' Mr Beckett turned to Ruth. 'Has he ever been to Southampton?'

'Yes, once. Lizzie took him to see where the liners used to dock. He was fascinated by the ships.' Ruth's voice shook. 'I used to tell him some of my Jack's stories. And Lizzie used to give him Alec's news as well. You don't suppose . . .'

'He'd never get aboard a ship,' the vicar said firmly. 'But he might well find himself in Southampton. And isn't Lizzie there now, working in the big hospital? He might have gone to her.'

'But she'd let us know straight away.' Ruth put her hand to her mouth. 'Unless he got to the hospital but couldn't find her – it's a huge place, not like our little Cottage Hospital here. Oh, I'm sure you're right, Mr Beckett, that's what he'll have done.' She turned to Dan. 'We'd better go to Southampton. We'll go to the hospital and find Lizzie, and if he turns up there she'll be ready for him. Oh, Mr Beckett!'

'We don't *know* that that's what's happened,' the vicar

warned her. 'It's mere supposition. Sammy might not have gone to Southampton at all. It's no more than an idea.'

'But it's a chance!' She pulled at Dan's sleeve. 'Let's go at once! There's a bus – or we can catch the train. We've got to try, at least.'

He stared at her. 'I can't – I got to get back, I got to go to work in the morning. Oh, my God!' He put his hand to his head. 'What am I going to do? If I don't go back I'll lose me job, I'll lose everything, and it's not just me, it's the war, I've *got* to do me job – but I can't go off without knowing where my boy is, I *can't*.'

Ruth felt a great welling up of pity for the bewildered man, so big yet so helpless. Poor chap, she thought, he's never really realised what Sammy meant to him till this moment. He just doesn't know what to do . . . She moved closer, laying her hand on his shoulder, wishing she could give him some comfort. But her own anxiety was too great. She needed comfort too. Even though Sammy wasn't her child, she needed the comfort needed by any bereft mother.

Mr Beckett looked at them. 'Tell me where you work,' he said to Dan. 'I'll telephone and explain. I'm sure it will be all right . . .' Hoping it was true, he glanced at the policeman. 'It's worth a try. And you could try the station too,' he added to Ruth and Dan. 'There are any number of places you could look.' It would at least give them something to do, he thought, better than torturing themselves by waiting here at Bridge End. 'But you must keep in touch. Telephone Constable Percy here whenever you get the chance, just in case there's any news.'

'We will.' Ruth was almost dragging Dan out of the door. 'There's a train in five minutes. We'll be just in time—' They were gone, leaving the vicar and policeman together, looking at each other.

'Well,' Mr Beckett said a little doubtfully, 'I suppose they may be lucky. But it really was no more than an idea.

There are any number of things that could have happened to Sammy.'

'There are,' the policeman agreed heavily. 'And there are any number of people who go missing these days, kiddies among 'em. If he's fallen into a dock – or got took away by someone – we might never know anything about it. We might never see that nipper again and that's the truth of it.'

The same thought was in Ruth's mind as she sat with Dan Hodges on the train to Southampton.

'Suppose we don't find him?' she said, staring out of the window. 'Suppose we never find out what's happened to him? You hear such awful things . . .' She turned to Dan, staring at him with huge green eyes. 'I'm sorry, Dan, I know he's your son, not mine, but – but I'm as fond of him as if he was my own. I don't think I could bear it if anything's happened to him.'

Dan stared back at her. She saw him bite his lips, saw him blink very quickly as if trying to force back tears. He's as upset as I am, she thought. He's not a hard man at all, not really. He's just had a hard life. He's as good a man as any other underneath it all. He could be kind and gentle, if only he'd let himself. He could be loving . . .

She remembered how he'd held her, in the front room of the police house. The feel of his big hands as he'd stroked her hair, the comfort of his arms, the gentleness in his voice.

'I couldn't bear it either,' he said in a shaky voice. 'I'd never be able to forgive myself if anything's happened to that boy. It's all my fault. I was supposed to look after him and look what I've done. I've let him go. And God knows what's happened to him now.'

'It's not all your fault,' she said. 'You wanted to see him for Christmas. He's your boy, after all. And you've got a job to do – you didn't know you were going to have to go to sea.'

'I knew there was a chance of it.' He paused for a moment and then said, 'If we find him – *when* we find him – I want him to come back to you. If you'll have him, I mean.'

'If I'll have him? Whatever makes you say that? Of course I'll have him!'

'Well, after all this trouble I've caused you might say you don't want no more to do with either of us.'

'I won't ever say that,' Ruth said positively. 'I won't ever say that, Dan. Not about you – and certainly not about Sammy. You must see how fond of him I am.'

'I do,' he said. 'I knew it already. And Sammy's fond of you too, and I don't mind telling you I didn't altogether like it when I first saw it. I suppose if you come down to it, I was jealous. I'm not proud of that, but there it is. But – well, now I think that it's what Sammy needs that matters most and he needs a good home, like you've give him, with someone that cares about him. So I'd like him to stop with you for the rest of the war – if you'll have him.'

'And what happens after the war?' Ruth asked quietly.

Dan paused for a long moment before answering. Then he said, 'That ain't going to be for a long time yet, Ruth. The way the world's going, it's going to take years to sort out this mess. Our Sammy's going to be a few years older by then and I reckon he'll have got used to the country. I don't think he'll want to come back to Pompey, not the way it'll be then.' He stopped speaking for a moment, then went on, 'And I dunno as I'll want to stop in Pompey myself, when it's all over. It's not the same there any more. All the bombing, it's wrecked the place and I've lost heart with it. And since I been coming out to Bridge End . . .'

'What?' Ruth asked, as his voice died away and he stared out of the window. 'What do you mean, Dan?'

'I've never been out in the country much,' he said. 'The first time I rode out on me bike, through all the fields and the trees – well, it was different from what I'd thought. It made me feel different about myself – sort of quiet. Peaceful. I've never felt like that before. Never.' He was silent again. 'I been wondering if me and Sammy couldn't sort of start again, somewhere like Bridge End. I wouldn't mind getting a job in the country, if there's anything going. I can turn my hand to most things and I'd be ready to learn. Trees,' he said thoughtfully. 'I wouldn't mind learning about trees . . . I haven't *decided* nothing, mind,' he added quickly. 'I've just been wondering.'

Ruth looked at him for a moment. She thought of Sammy, staying with her until the war was over. She thought of Dan moving out to be with him, perhaps renting a cottage nearby. She thought, for a moment or two, of Jack.

The train was running into the town now, between narrow streets and crowded little houses. Ruth looked out of the window and thought of Sammy, perhaps wandering through those very streets, bewildered and lost. Sammy, the little boy they both loved.

Dan seemed to be thinking the same thing. He shook himself a little and said with sudden roughness, 'I dunno why I'm talking like this now. I ought to be thinking about finding him. That's the first thing we've got to do. Oh, Ruth –' he turned to her in sudden anguish '– Ruth, what am I going to do if we don't find him?' He bunched his hand into a fist and thumped it on his knee. 'What in God's name am I going to *do*?'

Ruth gave a sudden sob. She moved a little closer and put out her hand. She laid it over his and rested her head against his shoulder.

'We'll find him,' she whispered, praying that it might be true. 'We'll find him, Dan, together.'

Chapter Thirty-four

Sammy had woken on Tuesday morning, stiff and cold. He lay for a moment staring around him at the unfamiliar walls, filthy with smoke, soot and dust. For a few minutes, he could not think where he was.

Then a bitter wave of memory swept over him. He was lost, somewhere in Southampton. He had spent the night in a bombed building. He didn't know where he was, or how to get out of the town. He didn't know how to get back to Bridge End and he didn't have enough money anyway. It was bitterly cold and he'd lost all his possessions, his toys, his book, his gloves and his woolly jumper. He was hungry and thirsty, and he had only just enough to buy himself a penny bun and something to drink.

He had tuppence. That was all. Tuppence.

Sammy sat up. He drew his knees up to his chin and wrapped his arms round his shins. He leant forward, rested his head on his knees and began to cry.

After a while his sobs died away a little and he lifted his head again, sniffing and rubbing his nose with his sleeve. Auntie Ruth had told him not to do that, but he'd lost his hanky as well, and Auntie Ruth wasn't here. He wished she were. He wanted to see her again. He wanted to see Silver and hear his raucous voice. He wanted to see Lizzie, and Uncle George and Auntie Jane, and Tim and Keith Budd, and Stella and Muriel and all the others.

He wanted to see Dad.

I shouldn't never have run away, he thought miserably. It was bad of me to take Dad's money and go off like that.

This is my punishment for being bad. Mr Beckett said in church that if you were bad you'd be punished and it's true. I wish I hadn't done it.

I wish I could see Mr Beckett again.

It was cold, sitting in the ruined building, and he got up and stretched. The cushions had been damp and his clothes clung to him, cold and wet. He flapped his arms against his sides in an effort to warm himself up, then crept out of the broken walls, looking cautiously about in case someone saw him. It was probably against the law to hide in bombed houses, and he didn't want to get into trouble with the police and end up in a proved school, where nobody would ever be able to find him.

There was nobody about as he walked slowly along the road. It was a narrow street, lined on both sides with small terraced houses, much the same as the ones in April Grove. Two rooms downstairs, with a scullery tacked on the back and an outside lavatory beyond that, and two small bedrooms upstairs. Room for a family like his, with two boys or girls, or even for a bigger family like the Budds, with two of each. The sort of house that Sammy thought almost everybody in the world must live in, unless they were rich and had three bedrooms and a real bathroom, and a garden in the front.

He wondered what time it was. It was lightish, although the heavy clouds threw a dark shadow over everything, and it must be going to work time for a lot of people, as the streets were full of walkers or cyclists and the trams and buses were crammed. There was an occasional car and a few delivery vans, most of them dragged by weary horses. He thought it was probably about eight o'clock.

He wondered if Dad would be coming home tonight and what he'd do when he found Sammy had gone. He'd be angry at first, but he probably wouldn't mind all that much. He'd just think Sammy had gone back to Bridge End, and swear a bit because the money had gone and then go up the pub. And Auntie Ruth wouldn't be worried because she would think Sammy was still in April Grove. In fact, he thought, nobody would worry about him. They'd all think he was somewhere else and after a while they'd forget about him.

Bleak, cold fear touched him for an instant as he looked into a future of wandering the streets of Southampton, cold and starving, until eventually he fell down and died. And nobody would know. It might be weeks, months, perhaps even years, before anyone realised he wasn't where he was meant to be and by then it would be too late.

If only I could get back to Bridge End, he thought. If only I knew the way . . .

He didn't know how long he walked before he arrived at the docks. He knew he was there because of the noise, a familiar noise to him from the docks at Camber in Old Portsmouth, and because of the increased bustle. He could see the funnels of the ships too, above the long wall, and hear the occasional hoot. There would be stalls somewhere near, he thought, places to buy buns and something to drink. He walked on beside the wall.

When he came to the big gateway he paused and peered inside, and caught his breath.

There were ships there, moored at the jetties, not liners but big cargo ships. But between the gateway and the jetties was a wide expanse of roadway and in the middle of the roadway there was a train.

It wasn't a real station, he could see that. The train was on tracks that just seemed to run along the road, like a tram. But it was pulling wagons behind it, and as Sammy watched it came to a halt and a man began to unload boxes and stack them at the side of the road.

Maybe the train will go to Bridge End, he thought with a leap of his heart. Even if it doesn't, it'll go to the station and I could get off it there and get on the train to Bridge End without having to buy a ticket. And when I get off, I can just tell the man that Auntie Ruth will give him the fare. He knows me and I know she'd do that. I *know* she would.

Without another thought he ran through the gate towards the train. He ignored the shouts of the man who was in charge of the gate and scampered as fast as he could across the wide expanse of roadway. His heart thudding, his one objective to reach the train and somehow get aboard before it moved away, he did not even notice the second set of tracks until he was running over them. He tried to avoid them, but caught his foot and fell headlong, his arms flung out in front of him. As he fell he heard more shouts, loud shouts, filled with panic and dismay. And he heard too the mournful whistle of another train and felt the rumble of its coming in the steel tracks beneath his cheek.

With a screech of brakes and a shudder of pistons the train drew into the station and jerked to a halt. Ruth and Dan looked out of the window at the busy, bustling platforms, the mass of people scrambling to get on and off.

The same thought was in both their minds. If Sammy, too, had come to this station, what on earth would he have done? Wherever could he have gone?

It's hopeless, Ruth thought, climbing down and staring helplessly around. It's like looking for a needle in a haystack.

But even haystacks could be taken to pieces and even needles would turn up, eventually. You just had to keep on looking until you found them.

'We'll go to the hospital first,' she said. 'We'll see Lizzie. She might have some ideas where we could go, if nothing else.'

Lizzie was at Southampton General Hospital. Ruth had been there several times, had even worked there once for a while, before she got her job at the Bridge End Cottage Hospital. But now the streets all looked so different, with the bomb damage and the attempts at shoring up and rebuilding, that she found it difficult to remember the way.

'It was down this way, I'm sure,' she said, but after three wrong turnings decided she'd have to ask the way. Even then, the first person they asked sent them off in entirely the wrong direction and they walked a good mile before realising the mistake.

Dan swore and then apologised. 'I know I ought to mind me manners. Nora used to try to keep me up to scratch, but since she went – well, everything's gone to pot, me included.'

Ruth smiled wryly. 'You're all right, Dan. You've just had a bad time.'

He grunted. 'You keep making excuses for me, I dunno why.'

'Well,' she said, 'we all need someone to make excuses for us. Oh, thank goodness, there's the Bargate – that big stone wall and gateway across the road. We won't have much further to go now. I just hope Lizzie's on duty, or we'll have to walk all the way round to Alec's parents' house.' She glanced at Dan. 'You must be getting hungry.'

'It doesn't matter about that,' he said brusquely. 'All I want is to get my boy back safe and sound. I'll think about eating then.'

They trudged on a bit further. The clouds were pressing right down now and there was an icy wind, which seemed to blow right through to their bones. Ruth shivered and bent her head against it, then gave a little cry of relief as they came at last within sight of the hospital buildings. In another moment they were inside its big doors and a nurse was listening as Ruth began to ask about Lizzie.

'Nurse Warren? Yes, I know her. She's on men's surgical. It's up those stairs and along the corridor – but I don't know if she's on duty now—'

Her last words went unheeded as Dan and Ruth ran up the marble stairs. Almost as if they expected to find Sammy himself waiting for them, they hurried along the big, empty corridor. The ward doors were open and Ruth gave a little exclamation as she saw Lizzie, sitting at a small table just inside the door.

'Lizzie!'

Lizzie turned and came swiftly to her feet. 'Auntie Ruth!' Her eyes went past Ruth to Dan. 'Mr Hodges! Oh, thank heavens you're here. But –' her brows came together in a bewildered frown '– how did you get here so quickly? I've only just sent the telegram.'

Ruth stared at her. 'What telegram? We haven't had any telegram.'

'No, that's what I mean. I only sent it half an hour ago – you wouldn't have had time—'

'Lizzie,' Ruth said, taking a deep breath and forcing herself to speak slowly, 'what was the telegram about? Is it Alec? Or his mother, or father?'

'No, of course not,' Lizzie said. She looked from Ruth to Dan and back to Ruth again. 'It's Sammy, of course. I sent you a telegram about Sammy.'

'*Sammy*! You mean – you know where he is?' Ruth grabbed her niece's arm and shook it. 'Where? Where is he? He – he's not hurt, is he? He's – he's not—'

Lizzie caught both Ruth's hands in hers and pressed her gently into her own chair. She bent slightly so that she could look into her aunt's eyes and spoke very clearly.

'Auntie Ruth, Sammy was brought into hospital yesterday. He was down in the docks. He – he fell in front of a train and—'

'Oh, *no*!' Ruth's hands flew to her face. She stared at Lizzie, then at Dan, and he moved quickly to her side and put his hand on her shoulder. Lizzie met his eyes.

'How is he?' he asked in a shaking voice. 'How badly is he hurt? I want to see him.'

'Yes, of course. I'll just ask Sister if I can take you to him. He's in the children's ward – he's had an operation.'

She looked at Dan and her eyes were full of tears. 'When he came in, nobody knew who he was. I would never have known he was here if I hadn't been sent down to the ward this morning with a message. I saw him lying there – so pale – he was unconscious, but of course I knew him at once. I told the sister and she let me send the telegram straight away.' They were hurrying along the corridor, back towards the stairs. 'It's down here ... What I don't understand is what had happened. Why was he down in the docks at all? And why did you come here, if you hadn't had the telegram?'

'Never mind all that,' Dan said roughly. 'Just let's see him. And tell us what's the matter with him. How bad is it? Is – is he going to be all right?'

Lizzie paused. They were at the doors to the children's ward now. She glanced through the small glass window and turned to face Dan and Ruth. Her face was grave. 'They won't know for certain until he comes round from the operation,' she said quietly. 'He – he was hit on the head, you see. They won't know how successful the operation's been until he comes round again.'

She did not say the words that were in all their minds. She did not say: *if he ever does come round.*

Sammy opened his eyes to find the faces of the two people he loved most in all the world beside his bed watching over him. He blinked for a moment, then smiled sleepily and tried to hold out his hands.

'*Ow*. It won't move.'

'You've got a broken collarbone, Sammy,' Ruth said, tears in her eyes. 'You broke it when you fell in front of the train. And you had a nasty bang on your head too.' She paused, remembering what the doctor had told them and added anxiously, 'Do you know who we are?'

Sammy stared at her. 'Course I know who you are. You're Auntie Ruth.'

Dan cleared his throat. 'And me, Sammy? You know who I am?'

'You're my dad.' He stared from one to the other, memory slowly returning. 'I was in the dockyard,' he said slowly. 'There was a train – I wanted to get back to Bridge End. I've been a bad boy,' he added regretfully and looked at his father. 'I'm sorry I took the money, Dad.'

'That doesn't matter. What matters is that we've found you and you're all right – well, you will be when your collarbone's mended and that bump on your head's gone down. You're safe, that's what matters.'

Sammy looked from one to the other. Ruth could see that he was tiring and needed to sleep. He said anxiously, 'What'll happen now? Will I have to go to proved school for taking the money?'

'No, of course not! You'll come back to Bridge End with me. And your dad will come out to see you as often as he can.' Ruth hesitated, glanced at Dan and added quietly, 'You're coming home.'

'Home,' he whispered. 'Do I live with you now, Auntie Ruth? Properly? For ever?'

'For as long as you like,' she said, her eyes full of tears, and once again glanced at Dan.

'But what about Dad? If he's still in Portsmouth . . .'

'We'll talk about that later,' Dan said firmly. He reached out and took Ruth's hand and she gripped it, folding her lips hard together. 'We'll talk about it when the war's over and done with.'

Sammy looked at them again. What he saw seemed to satisfy him, and he lay back with a little sigh and closed his eyes.

'I'll be able to teach Silver lots of new things,' he said dreamily. 'I'll be able to teach him anything I like.'

His breathing steadied and they knew he was asleep. They sat there for a little longer, Ruth holding Sammy's hand and Dan holding hers. Then they got up to creep away.

'We'll be able to take him home pretty soon,' Ruth said. 'Now we know his head's all right, we'll be able to take him as soon as he's had a good sleep and the doctor's had a look at him.' She looked down at the small figure, barely making a hump in the bed, at the fair hair and the shaved patch where the lump had been inspected. 'Poor little fellow. We must make sure he's really settled now.'

'We will,' Dan said. 'I won't take him back to Pompey again. All I want is to know he's safe and happy. So long as I can come out and see him whenever I can. To – to see you both,' he added with a touch of anxiety.

'Come whenever you like,' Ruth said and smiled at him, thinking how different he was from her first impression of him. He's like a man who's always been locked away, she thought, and for a long time only Nora had the key. Now, after the terrors of the past few days, Dan had unlocked his heart again and she felt as if the key had been handed to her. What she would do with it she didn't quite know. As he had told Sammy, they would talk about it after the war.

'Is that what's left of your money?' she asked, glancing at the locker beside Sammy's bed, and Dan followed her glance and nodded.

'I suppose it must be. Look at it. A penny, a halfpenny and two farthings. That's all he had, poor little tyke.'

A penny, a halfpenny and two farthings.

Tuppence to spend.

If you have enjoyed
Tuppence to Spend, don't miss

A Promise to Keep

Lilian Harry's latest novel in
Orion hardback

ISBN: 0 75285 126 8
Price: £9.99

Chapter One

'Thursday!'

Thursday Tilford, enveloped in a mass family embrace, laughed and cried and kissed all at once, and finally begged for mercy.

'You're suffocating me! I can't breathe!' They stepped back and she found herself with just her mother's arms still around her. Tears brimming from her eyes, Thursday held her close for a moment.

'Oh, love,' Mary said at last, pulling a hanky from her sleeve and wiping her wet cheeks, 'it's *so* good to have you home again.'

'It's good to be here. But it's not for long, mind,' Thursday warned her. 'I've only got a few days' leave and then it's back to Haslar. The war's not over yet by a long chalk.'

'No, but it could be soon,' Jenny piped up. She had gone back to her favourite position on the hearthrug where she had been playing with little Leslie. 'They say there's something really big going on all along the south coast – tanks and all sorts heading for the beaches, and—'

'And you didn't ought to be talking about it!' her father said sharply. 'For goodness sake, our Jenny, the war's been going on for nearly five years; you ought to know by now about walls having ears and all that. I hope you're not opening your mouth like this when you're working down at the hospital.'

'Course I'm not,' Jenny said in an injured tone. 'It's just in the family. Anyway, Thursday'll be there to see for herself soon. I bet Portsmouth's one of the main places the invasion's going from—'

'Jenny! That's *enough*.' Walter gave her an angry glance. 'Family or not, we didn't ought to discuss it. It's too easy to let something slip when we shouldn't – not that *we* know any secrets,' he admitted, 'but you just don't know who might be listening or what they might pick up on. Least said, soonest mended.' He opened his tobacco pouch and stuffed his pipe, pressing the baccy down hard with his thumb. Jenny folded her lips wryly and shot Thursday a comical look. Thursday felt her lips twitch. Not much had changed at home, she thought. They might all be two years older than when she had last seen them, and Jenny training as a nurse at the Royal Infirmary, but Dad was still doing his best to rule the roost and Jenny still cheeking him and getting away with it.

'Never mind all that,' Mary said, giving Thursday's arm a little shake. 'Come and sit down, love, and I'll make a cup of tea. We're all pleased to see you back safe and sound, and that's the main thing. I can't tell you how worried I was, all the time you were at sea.'

'We're all waiting to hear about Egypt,' Jenny added. 'Aren't we, Dizzy?'

Denise nodded. She had pulled Leslie back on to her own lap and he leaned into her and slid his thumb into his mouth. Thursday knelt beside her cousin and gazed at her little godson, marvelling at his soft cheeks and long lashes. 'I've missed two whole years of him,' she mourned. 'He was still a baby when I went away – he's a real little boy now.'

'Three years old,' Denise said proudly. Her face clouded a little. 'His daddy hasn't seen him since he really was a baby.' She looked at Thursday. 'How was Vic when you saw him? He's hardly told me anything.'

Thursday hesitated. She'd still not decided how much to tell Denise about the injuries her young husband had received in Africa. 'I'll come round and have a chat tomorrow,' she said quietly. 'We can't talk properly in this scrum. But he's all right, Dizzy, and he talked about you and Leslie the whole time. You don't have to worry about that.'

Her Uncle Percy cleared his throat. 'The main thing is, he's safe, or as safe as anyone can be these days. And Denise knows she's always got me and her mother to turn to.'

'That's right,' Flo agreed. 'It's just as well she stopped at home with us when Vic was called up. She can carry on with her job and I can look after the baby. Not that he's any trouble at all, the dear little soul,' she added, chucking her grandson under the chin so that he giggled and curled himself more deeply in his mother's lap.

Thursday smiled and turned to take a cup of tea from her mother. 'How about our Steve, have you heard from him lately?'

'Oh yes, he writes regular. He doesn't say a lot, mind you, they're not allowed much paper for a start, but he seems to be going on all right and I don't think they treat them too badly either in prison camp. They have football matches and get up concerts and that sort of thing, and we're allowed to send parcels, when there's anything to send, which isn't all that often. I don't think the food's very good but at least he's alive and more or less safe.' She shook her head. 'I don't like thinking of him treated like a criminal, but I don't mind admitting I'd rather that than have him fighting.'

Thursday nodded. The Tilfords were lucky that Steve was a POW. She thought sadly of her cousins Mike and Leslie – Mike posted missing, believed killed, at Dunkirk and Leslie shot down in his Spitfire. No wonder poor Auntie Flo thought the world of her grandson, named after them. He and Denise were all she had left now.

It was obvious that Leslie was the apple of everyone's

eye. It seemed almost impossible to believe that Uncle Percy had refused to look at him when he was born. He and Flo had been horrified when Denise, at only fifteen, had admitted that she was pregnant, and furious with Vic even though he'd believed her to be eighteen. The fact that Denise had lied to him didn't excuse him taking advantage, Percy had raged. They weren't married, not even engaged, nor likely to be if Percy had anything to do with it. He'd wanted the girl sent away somewhere quiet to have her baby and get it adopted, but at this Flo had put her foot down. Out of wedlock or not, she told Percy, this was their grandchild, and it could be the only grandchild they'd ever have. They couldn't, they just *couldn't*, let the baby go to strangers.

Walter and Mary had been just as dismayed. Girls who had babies without being decently married were ostracised, and the whole family tainted. Flo's stance had surprised them – she'd always been one to worry about what the neighbours would say – but she'd been so determined that everyone had had to accept it, and with Denise flatly refusing to give up the baby, Percy had been forced to agree to their marrying as soon as Denise turned sixteen. And, as Mary had observed, babies brought their love with them. Even if they hadn't been wanted, they all seemed to make themselves a place in the family, and little Leslie Michael Stephen – named after his two uncles and Thursday's brother Steve – had been barely a fortnight old when he'd won his grandfather round. Even Vic, who had got his call-up soon after his son's birth, had been accepted, especially by Flo who had never forgotten the way he had comforted her when she'd got the news about Leslie. 'As good as a son to me,' she'd said, and refused to let Percy say another word against him.

As Mary handed round the tea and a plate of biscuits, Thursday sat in her mother's armchair, trying to get used to the feeling of being at home again after two years in

Egypt. She looked round at the familiar room and the faces she'd missed so much. There'd been changes while she'd been away. The saddest was that her little dog, Patch, had died. Mary had written to tell her he was ill with distemper, and Thursday had known at once what the next letter would say. When it arrived, she'd left it unopened for a whole day, waiting till nightfall to read the bad news. Oh Patchie, she'd thought, the tears dripping on to the sheet of paper, oh Patchie. And she'd remembered how he'd come to her as a puppy on her twelfth birthday, struggling out of the cardboard box in which her father had brought him home and licking her face as she lifted him into her arms. He'd been with her during all her growing-up years, her special friend, rushing to meet her when she came home from school or work, sleeping on her bed whenever he could sneak up the stairs, keeping so close to her that Steve had once said he was glued to her leg. And now he was dead. Patchie. Her Patchie.

Thinking about him brought the tears to her eyes again. Now she was home, it was as if he'd only just died, and the sorrow of knowing he would never rush to her again came as fresh as on the day she'd received her mother's letter. Then, catching Mary's eye, she blinked back the tears and smiled. I've cried for him once, she thought. I'm not going to spoil this homecoming by doing it all over again.

'Is Auntie Maudie coming over? I want to see her before I go back.'

'She's on duty a lot this week. I thought we'd pop over to Ledbury on the train one afternoon. Day after tomorrow, if that's all right with you.'

'I'll come too,' Jenny suggested. 'We can talk about operations and things.'

Mary frowned. 'You know I don't like—'

'It's all right, Mum, I'm only teasing. But you can't expect three nurses to get together and not talk about their job! I always have a natter with Auntie Maudie when I go over, and she's sure to be interested in what Thursday's been doing.'

'Of course she will,' Thursday said. 'And I want to thank her again for the little nurse's watch she lent me. Uncle Bill gave it to her in the First World War, and I've worn it all the time. It's been a godsend on the wards.'

'Well, so long as you don't start talking about blood,' Mary said, and everyone laughed. 'Now look, we didn't know just what time you'd be getting home today so I haven't done anything special, just a few Spam sandwiches, but we're all here again for Sunday dinner. Your father's going to kill one of the hens—'

'Not Aggie!' Thursday broke in, and her mother gave her an exasperated look.

'No, not Aggie, I daresay she'll outlive us all if you've got anything to do with it. It's one of the others, that you don't know so well. And don't go down the garden giving them all names – you know once they've got names nobody likes to eat them. There's plenty of veg from the allotment, and some soft fruit for pudding, so it'll be a real old-fashioned Sunday dinner. When d'you have to go away again?'

'I knew you'd ask that,' Thursday said. 'I'm just surprised you've waited so long – usually you ask the minute I walk through the door. "Hello, Thursday, nice to see you, when are you going again?" Can't wait to get rid of me, as usual.'

'You know I didn't mean that!' Mary's face was pink as everyone laughed again. 'Oh, you're awful, the lot of you. I can't say a word without getting picked up on it . . . I only want to know so that I can make arrangements. And so I don't wake up one morning to find you've gone.'

Thursday gave her mother's arm a squeeze. 'You know I wouldn't do that. And I'm only teasing, you know that too. I've got a week – so that's next Wednesday, thirty-first of

May.' She stretched her arms, nearly knocking her cup off the arm of her chair. 'A whole week at home! Luxury.'

'Time to tell us all about Egypt,' Jenny said wistfully. 'I wish now that I'd volunteered as a VAD, instead of going for State Registration and getting stuck here in Worcester. Would have done, if I'd known you could go to places like that.'

'You're better off as you are if you want to be a real nurse. We're just dogsbodies most of the time, doing all the dirty work, though we do get to talk to the patients a bit more – the QARNNs just don't have the time. But we'll never be trained like you are.' Thursday took another ginger biscuit to show her appreciation, aware that her mother would have saved these specially for her return. 'Anyway, what I want to know now is what's been going on while I've been away. How about Mrs Hoskins – is she home or is she off with that fancy man of hers again? And that boy who got sent to approved school – is he back terrorising the neighbourhood? I've got a lot of catching up to do.'

Jenny giggled. 'You certainly have! Freddy Barnes went into the Army and he's won two medals already – his mum's like a dog with two tails. As for Mrs Hoskins, she's had so many fancy men even she's lost count, and—'

'Pipe down, Jenny!' Mary said sharply. 'You know what we think about that sort of gossip. I'm surprised at you for encouraging her,' she told Thursday. 'I'd have thought you'd have learned better, being with those other girls. They tell me a lot of the VADs are real upper-class.'

Thursday grinned. 'They are. But they like a good gossip as much as anyone else. It's just upper-class gossip, that's all. You should hear what they say about the lords and ladies they know and what goes on in big houses with all those bedrooms. Why, Louisa Wetherby once told me—'

'*Thursday*!' her mother expostulated, and the girls dissolved in giggles.

Thursday winked at her sister and cousin, and whispered, 'Tell you later,' and then said aloud, in a demure voice, 'Sorry, Mum. Let me get you another cup of tea, and then you can tell me all the things you want to tell me about, all right?' She got up and took her mother's cup, then bent suddenly and kissed her. 'D'you know what? It feels *much* more like being at home when you tell me off than when you treat me like an honoured guest. So just carry on that way, will you? Because that's what I've missed most.'

Mary shook her head at her. 'Stop it do, or you'll have me in tears again. As if I've ever told you off! Didn't tell you off enough, that's what your father always used to say.'

Thursday smiled and went out to the kitchen. She filled the kettle and put it on the stove, then stood leafing through the pile of cookery books and pamphlets her mother had collected. *Potato Pete's Recipe Book: Two Ways of Reconstituting Dried Eggs*, and *Try Cooking Cabbage This Way* . . . She turned to find her Cousin Denise standing beside her. The younger girl looked at her.

'You will tell me the truth about Vic, won't you – what happened to him and – and how he is now. I'm sure there's more than he's told me, and I've got to know.'

Thursday laid her hand on her cousin's arm and nodded. 'I will, I promise. But you mustn't worry, Dizzy. He's just the same as he ever was, really. And he misses you and Leslie all the time.'

Denise nodded and sniffed, brushing her hand across her eyes. 'I miss him too. I really do love him, Thurs, I always did. It wasn't just a – what did they call it? – infatuation. We really did love each other. That's why I lied to him about my age. I was so scared I'd lose him if he knew the truth.'

'Well, that's all over now.' Thursday warmed the teapot

436

with a drop of hot water from the kettle. 'You're married and you've got your little boy, and one day soon Vic'll come home and you'll be able to get a place of your own and settle down properly.' The kettle boiled and she made the tea. 'Go and get the cups, Dizzy. I'll come and see you tomorrow and tell you all about when I saw him in Egypt.'

She stood for a moment alone in the kitchen, listening to the chatter from next door. There would be a lot of talking to do in the next few days, a lot of stories to swap and a lot of reassurance to give. And then she would be going back to Haslar, the Naval hospital on the shore of Portsmouth Harbour where she had first become a VAD. Another kind of homecoming, in a way. I wonder how much will have changed there, she thought. And I wonder what's going to happen next. Something big, Jenny said – perhaps even an invasion. Can this really be the beginning of the end of the war, after all this time?

Denise came back with the cups and Thursday began to fill them with tea. Just for now, she'd forget all about it. Just for now, it was enough to be at home in Worcester with her family.

During those few days' leave, Thursday saw Denise only a couple of times. She was working long hours at the glove factory, making khaki gloves for soldiers, navy-blue ones for sailors, grey ones for airmen and leather ones for officers. 'Once this is all over I'm never going to look at a glove again,' she declared, coming in for a late supper after three hours' overtime when Thursday was round at her aunt's the next evening. 'I'd rather have chilblains!'

She lay back in her mother's armchair, her eyes closed. Thursday looked at her pale face and thought of Vic, lying in his hospital bed. They're just kids, the pair of them, she thought, and they're not the only ones either. This whole war's being fought by kids.

'I had a letter from Vic today,' Denise said, opening her

eyes suddenly. 'I told him you were coming home. He says you just about saved his life, Thurs.'

Thursday coloured. 'I didn't do much. I just sat beside him at night. I think it helped that I could talk about you and Leslie, that's all.'

'Well, whatever you did he thought a lot of it. And so do I.' Denise closed her eyes again. 'I'm glad you were there.'

Thursday bit her lip and nodded. 'I'm glad I was there too. It was strange having someone from the family out there in Alex. We hardly knew each other before – when you got married – but we got to know each other quite well in the hospital. He's a nice chap, Dizzy. You're lucky – you've got a good husband.'

'Well, I always knew that!' Denise said, with a flash of her old spirit. 'Knew that right from the start. But then you do, don't you – when it's the right one.' She closed her eyes again. 'That's if he still thinks I *am* the right one.'

'Oh, he does!' Thursday hesitated, then took a breath. 'Look, it's a long time since I saw him and I expect it's different now, but – well, he was wondering if you'd still fancy him. You see—'

'But of course I'll fancy him!' Denise exclaimed. 'I fancied him the minute I first saw him. Why on earth shouldn't I?'

'Because he doesn't look quite the same.' Thursday searched for the right words. She'd known for a long time that this moment must come, that she would have to prepare Denise for her first meeting with Vic. 'Dizzy, he was badly burned. His face was blistered all over – and parts of his body too. It's probably not so bad now as when I last saw him, but he's bound to be scarred.' She looked helplessly at her cousin. 'I'm sorry, but you ought to know – so that it isn't too much of a shock.'

There was a short silence. Then Denise said in a small voice, 'Is it very bad?'

'Quite bad,' Thursday said honestly. 'I'm really sorry, Diz.'

Denise bit her lip. She looked at Leslie, who was on the floor engrossed in a game with some old lead soldiers. Then she took in a deep breath and shrugged.

'I don't see that that's so awful – so long as he's not still hurting from it. He'll still be the same old Vic underneath, won't he?'

'Yes,' Thursday said with relief. 'He'll be the same old Vic. He was in Egypt, anyway. We got on really well.'

'That's all right then,' Denise said. She lifted her chin a little and looked Thursday in the eye. 'You know what Gran says – handsome is as handsome does, and I reckon my Vic will always be handsome to me, no matter what other people think. But thanks for telling me. I wouldn't want to look as if I was upset by it, the first time we see each other again.'

Thursday nodded, relief washing through her. It had been one of the things that had haunted her about coming home – the necessity of telling Denise about Vic. Even now, she wasn't sure that she'd really prepared her for the puckered, dead-looking skin that covered all one side of Vic's face now and stretched down his body. Perhaps later on she'd tell her more, but she'd learned that such shocks took time to absorb. Denise would ask for more information when she was ready.

'He really does love you, Dizzy,' she said quietly. 'He told me that. He just wants to get back to you and Leslie. Nothing else really seems to matter to him.'

'It doesn't matter to me either,' Denise said. 'Just to have us together again, a proper family – that's all we want.' She paused. 'All anyone wants, I suppose. Funny that it takes a war to bring it home to people what's really important about life.'

The brief leave over, Thursday set out on the familiar train journey to Portsmouth. And as she walked down the pontoon from the railway station and stepped aboard the waiting pinnace, she felt herself jerked back four years, to the moment in 1940 when she had first stared out over Portsmouth Harbour.

Four years! Four – no, *five* – years of war, years that had torn her and millions of other young men and women from their homes and families and thrown them into lives they could never have dreamed of. Thrown many of them to their deaths, she thought sadly, remembering the long lists of names in newspapers, the reports on the wireless, the soldiers and sailors she had herself nursed, both here in England and during her years abroad. And here she was, home again, and still it wasn't over.

'Come on, love,' urged the matelot waiting to cast off. 'You're not here on your holidays, you know. Mind you,' he added, glancing at her, 'you look as if you 'ave been. Look as if you've been in the South of France sunning yourself, you do. And what's that ribbon you're wearing? Been serving overseas?'

Thursday nodded a little self-consciously. She'd been proud to be presented with the medal that indicated her service abroad, but reluctant to display it until her father had told her, bluntly, that it was her patriotic duty to do so. 'That's an encouragement to others, that is,' he'd said, knocking his pipe out on the fender. 'It's good for people to know what girls like you have been doing to serve your country. It gives 'em summat to hold up their heads about, summat to hope for. You wear it, and be proud to.'

'So where you been, then?' the matelot asked now, still eyeing the ribbon. 'Africa?'

Thursday nodded. 'Egypt. I've been there two years. But I was at Haslar before that, and now they've sent me back. It feels queer, coming home again after all this time and the war still on. Somehow I always thought we wouldn't come back till it was over.'

'Maybe it won't be too long now,' the sailor said cryptically, looking out over the busy scene. Thursday followed his glance. The harbour was thronged with ships – some tied up at the main jetties in the dockyard, others moored out in the harbour, with smaller boats, ferries and tugs bustling between them. And as the Naval pinnace made the short crossing to the Gosport side she could see through the entrance that the Solent itself was just as crowded. Something was obviously going on – something big.

'What is it?' she asked curiously, but the sailor glanced at her sideways and tapped his nose.

'What we don't know can't hurt us. But you must've seen the roads, all jammed up with Army stuff. Been coming in for the past few weeks, so I've been told – lorries, tanks, DUKWs, you name it, it's there. American, too, a lot of it. Second Front, innit? And they say it's all being master-minded from just over Portsdown Hill.' He seemed to remember his first words and shut his mouth firmly. 'Shouldn't have said that.'

Thursday looked at him. There was nobody else in the boat, but everyone knew that you had to be careful what you said, especially about anything military. *Careless Talk Costs Lives* – the notices had been everywhere at the beginning of the war, and there had been cases of people put into prison for making casual remarks that could have been helpful to the enemy. A girl only had to be overheard in a teashop, telling a friend that her sweetheart's ship was sailing that night, and it could end in the ship's being torpedoed and sunk. Spies and Fifth Columnists, it seemed, were everywhere.

She turned her eyes again towards the crowded harbour. There was clearly a big 'flap' on, and from the look of the ships and the determined air of the smaller boats hurrying between them, it was obvious that the matelot was right – it was the long-awaited Second Front. Everyone was expecting it, had been for months – it was why she and the other VADs had been brought home. The theatre of war was moving back to Europe.

Jenny had been right too. It was the invasion. The invasion of Europe by Britain, and by her allies – America, Canada, Australia and the rest. This was what the country had been waiting for.

'I came by train,' she said, 'and it was packed with Navy types. But you're right, we did see a lot of Army vehicles on the roads, and all along the country lanes. You mean they're planning to take them all on ships? But how?'

He shook his head. 'We don't talk about it, not more'n we can help. There ain't no need. Everyone can see what's going on, and we all know the beaches have been closed for months. Gawd knows what they've been doing there, building bloody great concrete towers it looks like – not that you can see much past all the barbed wire. We might have our own ideas what they're for but we don't ask. And if you take my advice, you won't neither.'

Nothing's changed, Thursday thought, remembering how she and Patsy Martin – Patsy Greenaway now – had come to Portsmouth by train on that bitterly cold, snowy day in 1940, not daring to talk about where they were going or why, in case there was a spy in the carriage with them. It all seemed a very long time ago: the train getting stuck in huge snowdrifts so that the passengers – mostly soldiers – had climbed out to help dig a way through; their surprise at the harbour station with its wooden platform and glimpse of the sea surging beneath them; the massive icicles that had formed beneath the structure; the sloping pontoon to the Gosport ferry crowded by the workmen swarming out through the dockyard gates.

And the ships! It was like a different world, different from anything either she or Patsy had ever seen, except in pictures or at the cinema. The frigates, the destroyers, the enormous, towering bulk of the aircraft-carrier *Ark Royal* looming over them in their tiny pinnace. One of the greatest ships of the Royal Navy, she thought sadly, remembering the flight of aircraft it had taken to the besieged island of Malta, the battles it had fought, the pride everyone had felt in its name. And now it was gone, sunk by a U-boat off Gibraltar.

The sailor brought the pinnace alongside the Haslar jetty, and Thursday turned her head and looked up at the hospital where she had begun her days as a VAD. How ignorant we were, she thought. We knew nothing about the Navy, nothing about nursing. We had no idea of Haslar's history: nearly two hundred years old and one of the first real Naval hospitals. And we certainly had no idea of what we were going to face. The ships coming back from Dunkirk. The wounded sailors, some of them no more than boys. The men who would die before our eyes.

She thought of Tony West, who had kissed her before he went to sea and then come back with his face so badly damaged he would never kiss again. And Susie, the little girl whose leg had been amputated on the night of the big Blitz. And all the others who had passed through Haslar's wards – Stoker Davis, with his amazing tattoos, who had been a hero at sea yet made a fuss like a baby when he was given an enema; the young German, Heinz Schmidt; the sailor who had told her about the great queues of men standing in the water at Dunkirk, being shelled and machine-gunned as they waited for rescue, watching their comrades die around them. And that brought her back again to Tony, one of the first to arrive with his terrible injuries, his torn and broken face . . .

We didn't have a clue what war could be like when we first arrived, she thought, gazing along the paved way that led from the jetty straight through the entrance and under the arcade. We had no idea that these tramlines would be used for trolleys to bring men from the boats to the wards, just like they'd been used for the past two hundred years. We didn't know anything about the Navy or the way it worked, or the words it used; we didn't know what the matelot meant when he told us to 'turn starboard' – we didn't even know what a *matelot* was. Her lips twitched again, and she gave the sailor who had brought her over – a matelot himself, in his square rig uniform – a sudden grin.

'Well, thank Gawd for that,' he said, raising his eyebrows. 'Thought you'd been turned into stone. I was just about to pinch you to see.'

'You'd have found out pretty soon I wasn't,' she said, laughing. 'I can pack quite a punch when I'm pinched! Sorry, I was just taking it all in – thinking about the first time I came here. It seems so long ago.' She bent to hoist her kitbag on to her shoulder. 'Thanks for bringing me over. I'd better go and find out where I'm supposed to be. I wonder what changes there'll have been.'

'Not many. A place like this don't change much. Pity we can't say the same about the town.' He glanced past her at the buildings of Gosport across the creek, and Portsmouth on the far side of the harbour. 'Taken a fair battering round here – but you'd know about that, if you were here in forty-one.'

'Yes,' Thursday agreed, thinking again of the Blitz. 'Yes, I do.'

She climbed on to the jetty and walked slowly along the marble-smooth paved way that had been trodden by so many thousands of feet over the past two centuries. Haslar Hospital, so difficult to reach by land from Portsmouth, had been ideally situated for bringing wounded sailors from ships in the harbour and the Solent. Standing on the very edge of a low cliff, now retained by a steeply sloping sea wall, it looked straight out across the Solent to the Isle of Wight, yet here on the other side it was sheltered by the neck of the harbour and its own twisting, narrow creek. The phrase 'Up the creek without a paddle', she'd been told when she first came here, had actually originated in Haslar Lake, as it was called, and probably came from the days when sailors brought here had had only a small chance of surviving.

Treatment was better now, especially with the wonderful new drug, penicillin, which had just been brought in – but there had still been plenty of deaths. All the same, Thursday felt proud as she passed under the low, vaulted roof of the arcade and remembered how she and the other new VADs had stood here and cheered so loudly that Madam had come to see what all the noise was about, and reminded them that they were in a hospital. And even prouder when she recalled those dark days after Dunkirk when the wounded men had poured in, coming by boat and being trollied up the tramlines just as in the old days, and coming into this arcade to be sent to the wards . . .

So many memories, she thought, pausing at the other side of the arcade to gaze across the wide quadrangle at the avenue of trees leading to the little church, and at the gracious Georgian façades of the buildings that stood at each side. So many friends, so many patients. I wonder where they all are now. I wonder if there are any still here . . .

'Tilford!'

Thursday jumped. The voice was unmistakable and, when she turned, the woman striding towards her seemed to have stepped straight out of her thoughts. The tall, elegant figure emphasised by the belt clipped round its narrow waist, the thin, aristocratic face, the bright brown eyes and, most of all, that crisp, clear voice.

'Madam!'

'So you haven't quite forgotten us, then.' Miss Makepeace, the Red Cross Commandant at Haslar, who had been in charge of all VADs there since the war began, surveyed her just as she had done on that cold, snowy afternoon when Thursday and Patsy Martin had first arrived. It was a cool, assessing look, as if she were sizing you up and considering your fitness for the job, and once again Thursday found herself holding her breath and hoping she would not be found wanting. Then that familiar warm twinkle came into the bright eyes, the firm lips twitched into a smile, and the smooth brown head nodded as if some test had been passed. 'It's good to see you again, Tilford.'

'It's good to see you too, Madam.' Thursday glanced around the big open space. 'It's good to be back.'

Miss Makepeace gave another sharp nod, as if that were only to be expected. Where else would one want to be, but at Haslar? But Thursday felt a small twinge of guilt as she spoke, for her words weren't entirely true. It *was* good to be back, in a way, but the past two years had been filled with so many new sights and sounds and experiences, that coming back to where it had all begun seemed to be something of an anti-climax. There was nothing new to discover here in Haslar. She knew it all so well. And she was so much older now than when she had first arrived – so much more experienced, so much wiser, so much sadder . . .

Worst of all, Dr Connor Kirkpatrick wasn't here – and Haslar without Connor was an empty place.

Madam was watching her, those bright brown eyes as keen as ever, missing nothing. 'You won't have much time for nostalgia, Tilford. There's plenty of work on its way, as you may have guessed. You'll find some of your old friends here, I dare say, so there'll be lots of news to catch up on, but the first priority is to find out where you'll be working. Sister Tutor will decide that, but you can have a meal first and get settled in. You're in your old dormitory – I expect you can remember the way.' She turned, as if Thursday were already dismissed from her mind, then turned back and gave her that warm, well-remembered smile. 'I've had excellent reports of your work in Egypt. Of all my girls, in fact. Well done – I'm proud of you.'

Thursday blinked back the sudden tears. 'Thank you, Madam.' She hefted her kitbag on to her shoulder and began to climb the familiar stairs to the dormitory. Nothing had changed here either, she thought, treading the old brown linoleum between the brass strips on the edge of each step. She wondered who would be in the dorm with her. Old friends, Madam said, but the last she'd heard of Patsy, she was in Scotland. And Jeanie Brown had been posted abroad at the same time as Thursday, only two or three months after Patsy's wedding to Roy Greenaway in June 1941, and someone had told Thursday that they thought she'd been killed. And what about Helen Stanway, who had shown them all around the hospital on their first day, tall, bony Ellen Bridges from Dorset, Anne Davis from Kent, and Susan Morrison from near Guildford? Where were they all now? Would she find any of them waiting for her in the dormitory?

And of course, there was Vera Hapgood, she thought with a wry smile. The least popular girl at Haslar, sallow-faced and brooding, with a sarcastic and bitter tongue. What had happened to *her* in the past two years? Would she be back at Haslar?

The only ones Thursday knew about were her great friend Elsie Jackson, from Portsmouth, and Louisa Wetherby – Louisa who was 'posh' and had been to boarding school in Great Malvern, not far from Thursday's own home in Worcester. She, Elsie and Thursday had been together in Alexandria, working side by side in the same wards, and had become good friends despite the difference in their backgrounds. We've been through too much together not to be, Thursday thought. It doesn't make any difference when you're emptying bedpans together. And we've all learned a lot since we started here as VADs together, way back in 1940.

The sense of having stepped back into the past was even stronger as she came to the door of the dormitory. How many times had she climbed those stairs, worn out after a day on the wards or a night on the town? How many times had she run out, still fastening her cap, terrified of being late for duty? *'Navy time is five minutes early, nurse . . .'* She could hear Sister Burton's voice now, reproving any girl who was even a few seconds late, and she remembered the jokes about the ship sailing without you if you weren't on time. And Haslar *was* a ship, in Navy terms – a ship where every man, however badly wounded, was on active service, and every nurse's task was to get the patients fit to return to sea. In order to maintain the atmosphere and discipline of a real ship, the terminology was the same: 'deck' for floor, 'heads' for lavatories, 'quarterdeck' for the long, tree-lined avenue leading to the little church of St Luke.

The familiarity of it all flooded back and, as she pushed open the door, Thursday almost expected to see exactly what she had seen on that first January day and so often afterwards – the rows of beds with their neat counterpanes, each with a blue anchor embroidered on its centre, and the girls either sitting or lying on them or clustered around the stove in the middle of the long room, drinking cocoa. Elsie Jackson, half asleep as usual. Patsy, darning her stockings. Jeanie knitting a navy-blue balaclava or socks. Ellen Bridges reading *Woman's Own*, Louisa Wetherby writing a letter home, Vera Hapgood sitting apart from them all, as if she were better in some way. And Anne and Susan playing draughts or snakes and ladders, looking up to suggest a game of Ludo with some of the others . . . The picture was so clear in her mind that it came as a shock to see the beds replaced by two-tier iron bunks, and an even bigger shock to see the different faces turned towards her. The strange, unknown faces.

Thursday stopped abruptly, feeling almost as if she'd been thrown into a different world. The faces blurred before her, swam a little and then settled again into sharp focus. She was able to see their expressions – enquiring, friendly, smiling. And then, with a sense of joyful relief, to recognise one or two.

'Elsie, you bad penny! And *Patsy* – I didn't think you'd be here! Oh, and Ellen and Susan too – oh, it's lovely to see you all again.' She found herself enveloped in hugs, returning them with tears running down her cheeks. 'Look what you're doing, you're making me cry! Oh, it's so *good* to be with you, you horrors.'

'You're making us cry too,' Patsy said, grinning through her own tears. She'd hardly changed at all, Thursday thought, still as small and bright-faced, her dark curls as exuberant as ever. 'Just shows how awful it is to think we're all back here where we started.' She turned and held Thursday's hand high in the air, as if showing her off to the rest of the girls in the long room. 'This is Thursday Tilford. She was here with us in 1940 and 1941, all through the Blitz. Not a bad nurse, all things considered, and she makes a smashing cup of cocoa.'

The girls looked at her with varying expressions. Some of them must be quite new, Thursday decided, for they looked no older than twenty or twenty-one, the age at which VADs were taken on. Others were her own age or older, and clearly at least as experienced as she. Thursday wondered where they had been serving and what stories they could tell. She smiled around at them, and they grinned back and waved or lifted their cocoa mugs in salute. It's all right, she thought with relief. We'll be friends. And then, catching the dark, sardonic eye of Vera Hapgood – well, most of us will.

For the time being, however, it was her own old friends she was interested in. Patsy had saved her the bunk above her own – 'you being so much taller than me' – and Elsie's was next to it. The three of them sat down together and gazed at each other. Two years – it wasn't so very long, really. You wouldn't expect many changes in that time. And yet, even though Patsy seemed much the same, there *were* changes – a splay of tiny lines at the corners of her eyes, and around her lips, lines that made her look as if more than two years had passed. And when you studied her more closely you could see a haunted expression in her eyes. Thursday, staring at her, felt a sudden stab of fear.

'What's happened?' she asked. 'Where've you been these past two years? I seem to have lost touch. Is everything all right, Pats? Is – is Roy all right?'

Patsy nodded. 'He was, last time I heard. But there don't seem to be any letters getting through now, and you've seen what's happening – all the troops coming south, the ships crowding into the Channel. People say it's the Second Front – the invasion. And Roy's ship . . .' To Thursday's dismay, she saw tears gather in her friend's eyes. 'I don't know if I can take much more of all this worry,' she said defeatedly. 'He's been sunk twice – caught in an engine-room fire, nearly drowned. I mean, for God's sake, he's not a *cat*, with nine lives. He's just an ordinary sailor. How lucky can anyone be?'

'I don't know,' Thursday said. She thought of the day they'd met Roy Greenaway and the other two sick-berth attendants they'd gone around with – Doug Brighton and Tony West. Three breezy young sailors, looking forward to getting back to sea as soon as the VADs were sufficiently trained to replace them on the wards. Three cheeky, bantering young men who had cycled over Pneumonia Bridge into Gosport and taken them to tea at the Swiss Café or gone dancing at Lee and Grange. Three young men with their whole lives to look forward to – and now Tony was dead and the other two still facing peril. 'I just don't know, Pats. I can't say he'll be all right, because none of us knows what's going to happen. But we can think about him – pray, if you like. They say it helps.'

'Do they?' Patsy said tonelessly. 'It didn't help Tony, or all those other young chaps who got killed, did it? They're just as dead as if nobody'd given them a thought.'

They were silent for a moment, then Elsie spoke in her old, brisk, matter-of-fact tone. 'Come on, Pats. No use looking on the black side. We're here to do a job of work and we're not going to be much use if we sit about grizzling.'

Patsy looked at her and then grinned. She reached out and took Thursday's hand. 'It's all right, Thurs. I'm not the only one with a bloke out there. And at least we've had our share of happiness. And now we three are back here together, and there's a lot of hard work coming. It's the best thing, hard work – especially our sort.' She straightened her shoulders and went on determinedly, 'It's going to be good, us being here together again. It's going to be really good, Thursday.'

'Yes.' Thursday squeezed her hand and then got up and went to the window. She looked out over the hospital grounds, at the wall that ran alongside the top of the sloping sea wall. She could just see the green bulk of the Isle of Wight across the Solent. The sea was crowded with ships, some at anchor, some steaming for the harbour entrance. She gazed at them and thought of Patsy's words and of the sailor who had brought her across in the pinnace.

Something big was about to happen. And when something big happened in wartime, it always meant casualties.

There would be plenty of hard work to do in the coming weeks and, as she thought of what lay ahead, Thursday braced her shoulders and lifted her chin. Whatever had happened to them since they had last been here, she and the other VADs would be ready for it.

And I'm looking forward to it too, she thought. Not to the wounded men, but to helping them get better. And to working here with Elsie and Patsy, and whoever else is here too.

Patsy was right. It was going to be good.

All Orion/Phoenix titles are available at your local bookshop or from the following address:

> Mail Order Department
> Littlehampton Book Services
> FREEPOST BR535
> Worthing, West Sussex, BN13 3BR
> *telephone* 01903 828503, *facsimile* 01903 828802
> *e-mail* MailOrders@lbsltd.co.uk
> (Please ensure that you include full postal address details)

Payment can be made either by credit/debit card (Visa, Mastercard, Access and Switch accepted) or by sending a £ Sterling cheque or postal order made payable to *Littlehampton Book Services*.
DO NOT SEND CASH OR CURRENCY

Please add the following to cover postage and packing

UK and BFPO:
£1.50 for the first book, and 50p for each additional book to a maximum of £3.50

Overseas and Eire:
£2.50 for the first book plus £1.00 for the second book and 50p for each additional book ordered

---

BLOCK CAPITALS PLEASE

name of cardholder ....

.... *delivery address*

address of cardholder .... *(if different from cardholder)*

....

....

....

postcode ....   *postcode* ....

☐ I enclose my remittance for £ ....

☐ please debit my Mastercard/Visa/Access/Switch (delete as appropriate)

card number ☐☐☐☐☐☐☐☐☐☐☐☐☐☐☐☐

expiry date ☐☐☐☐   Switch issue no. ☐☐

signature ....

prices and availability are subject to change without notice